DISCARD

Has the World Ended Yet?

D1205971

HAS THE WORLD ENDED YET?

STORIES BY

Peter Darbyshire

A BUCKRIDER BOOK

Buckrider Books is an imprint of Wolsak and Wynn Publishers.

Cover image: Assembled using illustrations by Earle K. Bergey and H.V. Brown, scans from timetunnel.com
Interior images: Scans from timetunnel.com, except for page 282 from openculture.com
Cover and interior design: Michel Vrana
Author photograph: Arlen Redekop
Typeset in Adobe Caslon Pro, Futura BT, DCC Hardware and Sivellin.
Printed by Ball Media, Brantford, Canada

The publisher gratefully acknowledges the support of the Canada Council for the Arts, the Ontario Arts Council and the Government of Canada.

Buckrider Books
280 James Street North
Hamilton, ON
Canada L8R 2L3

Library and Archives Canada Cataloguing in Publication

Darbyshire, Peter, 1967-
[Short stories. Selections]
    Has the world ended yet? : stories / Peter Darbyshire.

ISBN 978-1-928088-44-8 (softcover)

    I. Title.

PS8557.A59346A6 2017   C813'.6   C2017-904868-6

Contents

Has the World ENDED YET?

Titan is the first person in the world to see the angels. He's drinking his morning coffee at the kitchen table and watching the house across the street when they start falling from the sky. The house across the street looks just like his house. Every house on the street looks just like his house. The only things that are different are the colours of the front doors. He got lost the first few times he drove home after moving here. He never got lost returning to the Hero Hall. He could still find the Hero Hall today if they called him back. He sometimes wonders if that will ever happen, even though he knows it won't.

Titan is watching the house across the street because he's looking for the woman who lives there. He doesn't know her name but he knows her. Sometimes she leaves the blinds open when she changes. He thinks maybe she does this on purpose. He thinks maybe this is some sort of sign language.

Inviselle sits at the kitchen table with him, fading in and out but never turning completely invisible like she used to. Not like when they met in the Hero Hall, when he had to use the special goggles designed by the Masterminds just to be able to see her. She hasn't been able to fully vanish in years. She can't see him watching for the neighbour because she has some sort of mask over her face. It's one of those organic paste things, made of passion fruit and the essence of bees' dreams or something like that. Zucchini slices cover her eyes. Titan married an invisible superhero but now he lives with a vegetable named Michelle.

Titan forgets all about Inviselle and the neighbour when the first angel falls from the sky and smashes a crater into the front yard. The house shakes with the impact, and car alarms go off all along the street. Titan sips his coffee and looks up at the sky. More angels fall from the clouds, dropping down all over the city, leaving burning trails of sparks in their wake. The clouds are a dark red colour he's never seen before.

Titan looks back at the angel in his yard as it climbs out of the crater, its skin smoking. It brushes dirt and grass from its wings, like it had just stumbled and fallen, nothing more than that. It's naked and has the body of a man. A perfect man. Iron pecs, cut abs, arms like cannons, a dick that belongs in the porn files hidden away on Titan's computer. The angel reminds Titan of himself, back before his skin softened from stone to mere flesh again and his strength faded to that of a normal man.

The angel looks at Titan, and there is none of the customary recognition in its eyes. It's like the angel has never seen the videos of Titan in his prime. Then it wanders around the side of the house, out of sight.

Inviselle takes the zucchinis from her eyes and looks at the falling angels. "Are they shooting a movie?" she asks. "Or are the clones invading again?"

"It's the end of the world," Titan says, looking up at the burning sky. "Thank God."

* * *

THE SKY darkens to a deep crimson while they fuck in the bedroom. It's the colour of all the blood they spilled in their golden age. Titan used to like fucking Inviselle when she was invisible. Then he could imagine she was anyone in the world. Now she can't quite fade away, so he always knows it's her. The blinds are open and he looks at the neighbour's house every now and then, but he doesn't see her in any of the windows. They watch the angels continue to fall from the sky.

"I thought it would be finished by now," Inviselle says.

Titan doesn't say anything. He rolls off her and closes his eyes. He tries to imagine what the supers are doing in the Hero Hall right now.

When Inviselle gets out of bed and goes into the shower, Titan wanders back to the kitchen without getting dressed. He toasts a bagel and eats it at the window. The angels are still coming. He takes a multivitamin with his orange juice. The bitter taste reminds him of the gas the molemen had pumped into the Hero Hall the last time they'd attacked.

Titan goes down into the basement. It's still unfinished, even though they've lived in the house for nearly five years now. When they first moved in, he had plans for it. He wanted to build a danger room. When he revealed that to Inviselle, though, she opened two bottles of wine at once and got him drunk while saying maybe it was time to think of other lines of work. He never brought it up again. Inviselle talked about maybe a home gym in the basement. A sauna. Another bedroom. But the only thing Titan had ever put in was the supers simulator. He'll never finish the basement now. That makes him feel better about the end of the world.

He turns on the simulator and the holograms fade in around him, the program starting up where he'd left off last time. He is in the middle of the ice caves, with frozen zombies all around him. He puts on the Titan simulator suit, which the game company gave him as a gift. He looks down at his body as the game begins. His skin is shiny metal again, no longer the dull concrete colour it took on when he hit middle age. His muscles bulge so much they threaten to rip the battle uniform he wears. He smashes through the zombies that swarm him, going deeper into the ice caves. He tries not to think about the fact that he has set the game to easy mode. He remembers when he fought his way through the ice caves in real life. He can't even keep up with his memories anymore. He destroys zombie after zombie, tearing them limb from limb, until the power goes out.

* * *

INVISELLE IS in the bedroom closet when Titan goes back upstairs. She's holding a black dress in one hand, combat pants and a sweatshirt in the other. Her uniform hangs untouched at the back of the closet.

"What are you supposed to wear to the end of the world?" she asks.

Titan ignores her and goes to his closet. He stares at his real uniform for a moment. He can't remember the last time he put it on. Then he dresses in one of his office suits, just like any other morning. It takes him three attempts to get his tie right, just like any other morning. He spent all his life hitting things, so he's never been very good with the small gestures. When he's done, he gives Inviselle a kiss on her cheek, just like any other morning.

"You're going to work?" she asks, finally noticing his suit. "During the apocalypse?"

"I remember when the apocalypse was our work," he says.

* * *

TITAN IS the last one to arrive at the office. His boss, Precog, is tacking up a new schedule on the bulletin board when he walks in. The schedule lists the appearances Titan and all the other retired supers are supposed to make over the next week. Titan doesn't even look at it. He knows what it will be: car dealership and furniture store openings, corporate cheerleading events, a few colour commentary spots on some super fan show or another, maybe a company dinner or two, where drunk executives will make him shout out the battle cry that was his motto as a hero.

"We're not going to live forever!"

It makes him wish he'd used his powers for villainy instead of good. Most of the villains he'd battled over the years were living comfortable lives in retirement thanks to all the money they'd stolen. There was a gated community in Palm Springs and another one being built in Antarctica. They didn't need to keep selling their old myths like Titan did just to pay the mortgage.

"You know something I don't know?" he asks Precog. His boss's power back in the day had been the ability to see anywhere from a few minutes to a few years into the future. It had been a bit random, but the big events usually came to him, so the heroes had enough time to prepare for their major battles.

"I know the world never ends if you don't let it," Precog says. It sounds more like a corporate cheer than a premonition, so Titan lets it go. He walks past Precog, to his desk.

Precog was the one that told Titan his super days were over. One day after Precog retired, he came to visit Titan in the Hero Hall. Titan was in the gym, bench-pressing a school bus. The other supers cleared out of the place when they saw Precog was there. They all knew the only reason Precog ever came back to the Hero Hall was to let a super know his days were over.

"You must have the superpower equivalent of dementia," Titan said when he put the bus back down on the vehicle rack. "I've never felt stronger."

"I saw your end three years ago, back when I still had my power," Precog told him. "I saw the end of all the supers back then. I recorded them all. I saw the company I would start, too. You'll be at your desk there two Mondays from now."

Titan didn't say anything. He lifted a skull of one of the Dragonborn. It was heavier and harder than anything else on Earth. Normals couldn't even lift it. He crushed it to powder in his hands as Precog watched.

"When one world ends, another always begins," Precog said. "You will remember that over the days to come." And with that he turned and left the gym.

The next Monday Titan and the other supers fought the Ageless, who hit him with a dozen curses. It was Titan's last day as a super. The following Monday he showed up at Precog's company to find his desk waiting. Sometimes Titan thinks Precog was to blame for his end as a super. Sometimes he thinks about crushing Precog's skull like he had crushed the skull of the Dragonborn.

Titan goes to the cubicle he shares with the Sandman. The Sandman is surfing porn on his computer. This is what the Sandman does every morning to start the day. Back when he was a super, he used to stop time to save people from car accidents and shootings. It was an open secret among the supers that the Sandman also used to stop time to wander through the showers at women's gyms and spy on other supers at their homes.

Titan once asked the Sandman why the tech department didn't put some sort of porn filter on his computer. The Sandman said the tech guys wouldn't be able to find half their porn without him.

Titan looks at the Sandman's screen. It shows a woman and a man in a gorilla suit. Titan turns away and opens the bottom drawer of his desk. This is where he keeps all his medals and keys to cities and framed letters of thanks he earned as a hero. At one time they meant something. Now they're just props. He puts them in a stationery box.

"This is no time to get reckless," the Sandman says.

"This is exactly the time to get reckless," Titan says.

The man in the gorilla costume is now fighting a man in a super costume while the woman looks on.

"Hot," the Sandman says.

Titan takes his box and leaves.

Precog is waiting for him at the front doors to the office. He stares at the box of awards and then holds out his hands to Titan. "Whatever's bothering you, we can fix it. I've already scheduled an appointment with an empath."

Titan puts his hand on Precog's head. He feels the skull beneath his fingers. He remembers how easily bone snaps. How it can be ground to powder. He thinks he'll at least try to crush Precog's skull if he says just one more word.

But Precog doesn't say anything else, so Titan drops his hand and walks back out into the end of the world.

* * *

TITAN STOPS at an exotic car dealership on the way home. He's driven past it every day for the last year, to and from work, in traffic jams each way. He's pictured himself in every car on the lot. They're a far cry from the Ethereal Flyer, but he'll never set foot in that again. Even so, most of the cars in the dealership are still out of his price range. All the Lamborghinis and Ferraris are gone, anyway, when he walks in the door. There's nothing but a couple of Porsches left in the showroom.

"We had people lined up outside the door this morning," the salesman tells him. "It was like they'd just got their welfare money."

Titan offers the salesman his box of trophies and medals and keys for one of the Porsche roadsters. The salesman looks through the box for a moment and then shrugs.

"What the hell," he says. "It's the end of the world, right? May as well do a good deed for once in my life." He takes some keys out of his pocket and tosses them to Titan. Titan gives him the keys to his old car.

"What am I supposed to do with that?" the salesman asks, looking out into the parking lot.

"Burn it," Titan says.

* * *

TITAN RETURNS home to find Inviselle in the black dress, preparing for a party. Bowls of chips and vegetables and dip sit on every table, and she's making sangria. She tells him she called everyone they know.

"Wouldn't it be nice if it happened with all of us here together?" she asks.

Titan goes across the street, to the other woman's house. She answers the door drinking red wine straight from the bottle. She doesn't say anything, and for a moment the two of them just stand there, looking at each other. Titan waits for some sign of recognition from her, showing she knows who he is. But she just stares at him like she's never seen him before in her life.

"I'm having an end of the world party," Titan says.

"What about her?" the woman asks. They both look at his house. Inviselle flickers in and out as she moves past a window. An angel drifts slowly overhead, watching them.

"It's the end of the world," Titan says.

The woman hugs herself.

"Do you have any drugs?" she asks.

* * *

TITAN DRIVES them to Buddha's place. He really wants to open up the Porsche, but the other drivers are all over the road so he keeps his distance and stays well under the speed limit. He's never been in such a nice vehicle. Back when he was a super, he travelled most places in the Ethereal Flyer or the Wisp just teleported them wherever they needed to go. Neither way was what he would call luxurious. Titan doesn't speak during the drive and neither does the woman. He thinks he should ask her name but he's let it go so long it may be awkward now.

Buddha lives on the top floor of a condo tower. He buzzes them up right away when Titan calls him from the lobby. For as long as Titan has known him, Buddha has always been home.

Buddha is sitting at the kitchen table when they walk in. He's organizing little plastic bags of drugs into various piles. The walls are covered in framed photos of supers. Buddha only sells to retired supers, and sometimes he takes photos for payment. What cop or prosecutor is going to mess with a drug dealer who has all the former heroes as customers?

On a monitor mounted on a wall, CNN shows a live feed from one of the space stations.

"Has the world ended yet?" an astronaut asks, staring into the camera. Behind him, another astronaut looks out a window at who knows what.

"We're here for drugs," Titan says.

"That's what I figured," Buddha says, popping a blue pill into his mouth like it's candy.

"I'm having a party," Titan says.

Buddha looks at Titan, then the woman and then goes back to sorting his drugs.

"It's an end of the world party," Titan adds.

"Who's going to be there?" Buddha asks.

"I have no idea." He hasn't invited anyone and he doesn't know who Inviselle invited.

"You should come," the woman says. "And bring all your drugs."

Titan and Buddha both look at her. Then Buddha shrugs. "No discounts, though," he says. "I don't care what sort of holiday it is."

"It's the end of the world and you're concerned about making money?" Titan says.

"This is no time to abandon my principles," Buddha says and starts gathering up his drugs.

* * *

OUTSIDE, BUDDHA shakes his head at the Porsche. "This is what you dream about?" he asks.

Titan doesn't say anything. He doesn't want anyone to know what he dreams about.

They drive back to the house to find another angel standing in the yard. It's looking in the front window. Its skin is streaked with mud and several feathers in its wings stick out at odd angles.

"Maybe it's come for us," Titan says. He honks the Porsche's horn but the angel only glances at them before turning its attention back to the window.

"It's like some sort of peeping Tom," Buddha says.

"Maybe God's a pervert," the woman says.

"I wonder what kind of drugs God would do," Buddha says.

Titan parks the Porsche in the driveway and they go inside. The house is crowded with people. Titan knows most of their faces but can only remember a few of their names. He hasn't talked to some of these people in months, if not years. He doesn't care. He says hello and shakes hands and laughs at their jokes about the apocalypse. It's just like doing another work event. He moves in the direction of the bedroom with the woman from across the street. When he finds the Sandman in the living room, though, he stops and asks him what he's doing there.

"Precog says you're serious about this quitting thing," the Sandman says. "I'm supposed to support you as a valued team member and provide friendship incentives for you to stay." He smiles at the woman from across the street. "Have we met?" he asks her, but she just looks at him and doesn't say anything.

"I'm done with the company," Titan tells the Sandman. "I'm done with everything."

"All right," the Sandman says, still smiling at the woman. "All right."

Buddha sits down on the couch and spreads his bags of drugs on the coffee table. On the monitor on the living room wall, CNN is now showing a riot in the streets of Jerusalem.

"I've never been there," Titan says. "I guess now I'll never get the chance."

"I wouldn't want to be there at this particular moment," the Sandman says.

"Maybe not right now," Titan agrees. "But maybe before."

"How is it any different now?" the Sandman asks.

Titan shakes his head. He turns to the woman from across the street, but she's not there anymore. He looks for her in the crowd, but he can't find her. He looks back at the monitor.

"It seems we may have been premature in one of our earlier reports," an anchor says. "It turns out Hawaii hasn't sunk into the sea. But stay tuned – it still may."

"If you don't come back to work, can I have your computer?" the Sandman asks.

Titan walks away from him without answering. He looks for the woman but can't see her anywhere. He goes into the kitchen, but she's not there either. He checks outside, thinking maybe she's gone home. Her house is dark, the street empty.

Titan looks up at the sky. There are rifts in the clouds now, with lights shining through the holes. Angels rise up to them from all over the city and pass through, out of sight. The angel in the yard is still looking in the window. Titan goes back inside.

He pushes his way through the crowd and remembers when crowds used to part before him. He opens the door to the guest room first, but it's empty. Then he opens the door to the bedroom he shares with Inviselle.

The woman from across the street is there, on the bed. She's wrapped in an embrace with Inviselle, who's strobing in and out of sight. They both stop and look at Titan.

"I've been watching her for months," Inviselle says.

Titan doesn't say anything.

"She undresses for me," Inviselle says.

Titan doesn't say anything.

"She's a mind reader," Inviselle says.

The woman from across the street smiles at Titan. "You can watch," she says.

"Hot," the Sandman says from behind Titan.

Titan goes back into the living room. CNN shows an angel walking across the lawn of the White House. Secret Service agents in black suits step out from behind trees and bushes, guns in their hands. But they just watch as the angel walks past them and into the White House. One of the agents says something into his lapel. Another agent sits down on the lawn and cries.

Titan goes down into the basement. The simulator is back on. The ice zombies feast on his fallen body on the floor of the cave. Titan ignores them and takes off his clothes. He puts on the simulator uniform. He wants one of his real uniforms from the closet, but he doesn't want to go back into the bedroom again. He goes upstairs in his simulated uniform, then outside and onto the lawn.

The angel turns away from the window, toward him. Titan punches it in the face. There was a time when his fists could shatter buildings. The angel just rocks back a bit. He punches it again, then again and again. There's blood on the angel's face now, and on his hand. He doesn't know which of them is bleeding. He keeps hitting it, even though it doesn't fight back, until he's out of breath and has to step away.

He bends down for a moment, resting his hands on his knees. The angel pants in unison with him. When Titan looks up, he sees people staring from all the windows. The Sandman toasts him with a drink. Inviselle and the woman from across the street stand in the doorway, wrapped together in a bedsheet. Inviselle covers her mouth with her hands. The woman from across the street nods like she knew this would happen. Titan can see the monitor in the living room through the window. The astronauts are screaming.

The angel doesn't take its eyes off Titan. It doesn't even blink.

Titan straightens up, even though he still hasn't caught his breath. He adjusts his uniform.

"All right," he says. "We're not going to live forever."

For a few seconds there are no sounds but their breathing. Then a distant siren begins somewhere.

"We're not going to live forever!" Titan cries, although he's not sure if his words are a challenge or a plea.

The angel's lips twist into something that could be a smile. Then it spreads its wings and lunges at him, and Titan rushes to meet it.

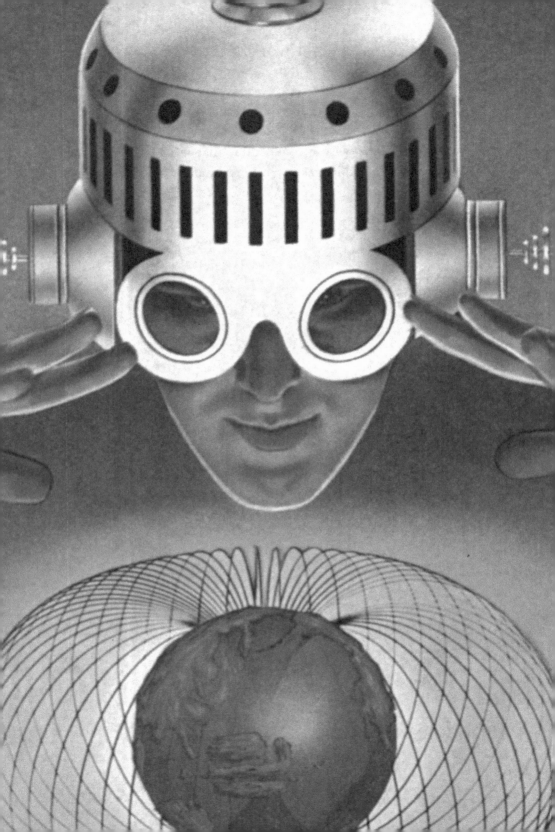

Casual MIRACLES

Most of the people who wanted miracles found Zane through Craigslist. He had an ad he never took down in the Casual Miracles section. There was no other miracles section, but Zane wasn't capable of other kinds anyway.

He'd been performing miracles for years, ever since the accident, so he was no longer surprised at what people wanted. The week before, a woman had called him to her house and asked him to change her locks. When Zane told her she needed a locksmith, she'd hugged herself and said it had to be done right now. The next day, a man messaged him a photo of rims he wanted for his truck. Zane messaged him back to let him know people only got one miracle. Was he sure that was what he wanted to spend it on? The man replied that the rims had been discontinued and he couldn't find them anywhere.

Zane always performed the miracles. He'd learned early on not to judge. He charged extra for people like the man who wanted rims, though. But not the woman who wanted her locks changed. He figured she had her reasons.

Then there were the people he wanted to help, even though sometimes he couldn't. The way the miracles ended for him was one of those situations.

It began like most of them did, with a text.

23

I'm looking for a miracle.

Who isn't? Zane texted back.

The next text was just a street address. If Zane had looked it up first, maybe he wouldn't have gone. But he didn't bother to check it. He just got in his Corolla, which still had the dent of the woman in the hood, and followed the directions his phone gave him until it said he had arrived. The address was a low, long brick building surrounded by a small park with paved walking trails. A woman sat on a wooden bench in the park beside a man in a wheelchair with a blanket wrapped around his body. Both of them stared at Zane as he drove by, looking at the sign over the front doors of the building. New Peace Hospice.

Zane could have kept on driving. Maybe he should have kept on driving. But he was here. He parked on the street so the Corolla's oil leak wouldn't stain the hospice's driveway or parking lot. He felt a place like this had to be respected. He checked the address again to make sure it was right and then went inside.

A woman stood in the lobby, watching him. She was pregnant and looked like she was going to give birth at any moment. She was running her hands over her belly when he walked in and she didn't stop.

"You're the angel," she said. It was half question, half statement.

"That's what I've been told," Zane said. He didn't like the name people used for miracle workers like him, but he understood why they used it. He'd long ago given up trying to get people to use some other word. He didn't really know what to call himself, after all.

"We need you this way," she said and turned to walk down a hall.

Zane looked around the lobby. A woman sat behind a reception counter, watching him. Past her was the entrance to a small cafeteria. A man sat alone at one of the tables, tethered to an oxygen tank. Classical music played somewhere, but Zane didn't recognize it. He followed the woman down the hall. Most of the doors on either side were open, but he didn't look inside them.

The woman led him to a room that looked like a hotel suite. There was a bed, a small table under the window, a dresser with a vase of dead flowers on it and a couple of chairs. A landscape of nowhere in particular hung over the bed. The bedside tables were covered in photos of young men, women and children. Pill bottles were scattered among the photos. An elderly woman lay in the bed, the blankets up to her chin. She took a long, shuddering breath every now and then. A middle-aged man in a suit sat in one of the chairs. He looked at Zane, then went back to looking at the woman in the bed.

The pregnant woman sat in the other chair while Zane stood at the foot of the bed. He looked down at the older woman, who took another ragged breath as he watched.

"I can't save her life," Zane said. "That's not the kind of miracle I can do."

He didn't think it was the kind of miracle anyone could do. He'd never heard of it happening, anyway.

"We know," the pregnant woman said. "The other angel told us the same thing."

"What other angel?" Zane asked.

"The one who helped me," she said and put her hands on her stomach.

The man in the chair looked at her, then back at the woman in the bed.

"Pregnancy is a life-and-death kind of thing," Zane said. "I didn't think that was possible." It wasn't supposed to be. That wasn't how the miracles worked. Not that Zane had ever heard of, anyway.

"I didn't think so, either," the woman said. "But I had to try. She said it wouldn't matter in the end."

Zane looked at the woman's swollen stomach. He wondered what it meant.

"Maybe you know her," the woman said. She took her purse from the table and rooted around in it for a few seconds, then pulled out a phone in a flip case. She opened the case to reveal a photo of another woman with her hands on the pregnant woman's stomach. It was taken before the pregnant woman was pregnant.

Zane stared at the photo. He recognized the angel in it.

"I keep her here to remind me of what's possible," the pregnant woman said. "I mean, it took a few years, so at first I thought it hadn't worked. But now look at me."

The man in the chair looked at her again and didn't look away this time.

"How did you find her?" Zane asked. He knew the other angel didn't have a Craigslist ad like him. He'd looked for one many times and never found anything.

"Our priest knows her," the pregnant woman said. "We told him about our troubles and one day she was just sitting there in the pews after Mass."

Zane turned his gaze back to the woman in the bed. It was all there in the room: birth, life, death. And the angel.

"What do you want from me?" he asked.

The pregnant woman stepped to the edge of the bed and took one of the other woman's hands in hers. It looked like she was lifting a stick.

"She's never seen the baby," she said. "She doesn't even know I'm pregnant. She's been asleep for months. I . . . we want her to wake up. Just long enough to see."

The man in the chair closed his eyes and let out a long sigh.

Zane nodded and put his hand on the woman's shape under the blanket. He kept it there until he heard the sound of the miracle. He didn't know how to describe it to people. It sounded like the buzz and squawk of the old modems they used back at the start of the computer days, only the electronic sounds were made by a chorus of human voices. The sound moved through him and then was gone. He pulled his hand back from the woman and nodded again.

"What do you want?" the pregnant woman asked, and Zane knew she meant payment. Nobody was ever really comfortable talking about it. Even Zane didn't like to talk about it sometimes.

"Just tell me how to find your priest," Zane said.

The pregnant woman tapped out something quickly on her phone and Zane felt his phone vibrate in his pocket when the message arrived. He didn't look at it.

When the woman in the bed opened her eyes, Zane turned and left without another word.

The man in the cafeteria was still sitting there when Zane went back out into the lobby. The woman at the reception desk watched him go. It took him three tries to start the car, which wasn't bad. He thought about driving home and pouring himself a drink, but he went to find the priest instead.

* * *

ZANE MET the angel Agnes Bath when she fell onto his car from an overpass.

He was driving his Corolla on the highway when the world suddenly split into pieces in front of him with a bang that he felt throughout his body. It took him a second to understand the world hadn't come apart, that it was just his windshield cracking in several places. It took him another second to realize the cracks had been caused by the woman who had smashed down into the hood, as if she had fallen from the sky, although he thought right after that she must have fallen from the overpass he had just driven under.

He pulled over to the side of the road immediately, and by some small miracle all the other cars on the highway managed to avoid him. It was only when he put the car into park that he started to shake.

"God!" he said. "Jesus!"

That was when the woman on his hood sat up and looked at him through his cracked windshield. For some reason, she smiled despite the fact she must have been broken on the inside. He thought maybe she was a homeless woman or a junkie who had been trying to commit suicide even though she was wearing what looked like work clothes: a suit and a blouse, which was torn, presumably from the impact.

Zane got out of the car and reached for her, then held back. He didn't know what he was supposed to do here. Would he injure her more if he moved her? He thought there was something about spinal cords or necks or something he had to be careful about. He wasn't sure what his insurance covered.

"What can I do to help you?" he asked her, because he couldn't think of what else to say.

"You already have," she said. She reached out and took his hand. And that was the first time he heard the choir inside him.

It wasn't like it was now. There wasn't the shriek of voices that accompanied the miracles. It was more like a low hum that suddenly filled his body. He looked around, wondering where the sound was coming from, but didn't see any other people. There was just passing cars.

"I'm Agnes," the woman said, shaking his hand. "Agnes Bath."

"I'm Zane," Zane said, looking behind him to try to see who or what was causing the hum.

"I'm sorry, Zane," Agnes said. "I want you to know that. I'm truly sorry."

"Sorry for what?" Zane asked. But Agnes had let go of his hand and was sliding off the hood of the car, leaving a dent behind in the shape of a body, arms outspread like sweeping wings. She walked away from him, along the shoulder of the highway. She lifted her hands up to the sky as she went and laughed.

"You're probably not all right," Zane called after her.

"I've never been better," she called back.

He looked at his damaged car. "Who's going to pay for this?" he asked, but there was no one to hear him.

The humming continued after he had driven home and poured himself a drink to stop the shaking. It was only in the silence of his apartment that he realized the sound was coming from inside of him.

He thought at first that it was just the stress from the accident, that it would fade with time like the shaking. But instead it kept growing. Then a low vibration joined the humming. He had a feeling like something was building inside of him wherever he went – the grocery store, the employment office, the community police office to report the incident with Agnes, where the cop he talked to nodded as he listened but didn't write anything down. It was as if there was something inside him he didn't understand that was trying to explode, in ways he didn't understand. He couldn't sleep at night, and he couldn't think of anything else but how to make it stop. It was like puberty all over again. He needed some sort of release but he had no idea how to achieve it.

He drove back to the scene of the accident to try to understand. He parked on the shoulder right before the overpass and looked up at it, then at the grey sky beyond. There was a lone red helium balloon floating high overhead, but he wasn't sure if it was a sign of anything or not. He got out of the Corolla and looked in the weeds growing at the side of the road, like there might be some clue there.

When Zane looked back at the road, a traffic jam had somehow formed in seconds. There were lines of cars ahead of him and behind him, filling the lanes. The cars stretched away in both directions as far as he could see. People sat in their cars and stared straight ahead or talked to themselves or shook their heads or swore or did the things you do when stuck in traffic.

Except for the man in the car beside Zane. He rolled down his window while still looking straight ahead.

"Do you know what's happening?" he asked.

Zane shook his head. "I don't," he said. "I really don't."

"I would give anything for a way through this," the man said, still not looking at Zane.

And that was when it happened.

The humming inside Zane suddenly swelled into the shrieking chorus of voices that he would learn to associate with the miracles. The pressure inside him suddenly broke, and he felt a great release, as if something he couldn't see was flowing out of him and into the road.

And then the cars in front of the other man suddenly parted to either side, the drivers pulling to the left and right to open up a lane down the middle. The man laughed and drove forward into the open space the other drivers had created for him.

That was when Zane realized he was an angel.

* * *

THE NEW address the pregnant woman gave him was for a church. Our Lady of Perpetual Suffering. Zane thought it was an apt name, given that it took him forty-five minutes to get there because of road construction. While he drove, he thought about the time a different man had asked him to part traffic, although for the whole day in that case. He told Zane he wanted to feel what it was like to be important. Zane had granted him the miracle and hadn't charged him anything.

The church was empty when Zane went inside, but it was lit up by candles everywhere. Zane sat in a pew and waited. He looked at the saints and angels in the stained glass windows that lined the walls and wondered if they had been people like him or if they had actually performed miracles that mattered.

After a time a man came through the sacristy door wearing black clerical clothing. He glanced around the church and looked surprised to see Zane sitting there. He nodded and then busied himself by bending down behind the pulpit to work on something. Zane got his attention by making all the candles in the church flare up for a few seconds, long enough that the priest straightened up at the pulpit and glanced around again to see what was happening. When the flames died back down, the priest looked at Zane.

"You could have just said hello or something," he said.

"I'm trying to find a woman," Zane said.

"This isn't really the place for that."

"Agnes Bath. She helped another woman get pregnant. I'm told you introduced them."

The priest studied him for a moment without saying anything. Then he walked out from behind the pulpit and down the aisle, to sit in the pew across from Zane.

"I should have known you weren't someone new looking for a little salvation," he said.

"I could have been," Zane said.

"You know, hardly anyone comes into the church these days." The priest gazed around at the empty pews. "Not since all you miracle workers showed up."

"Most people call us angels."

"Well, I don't," the priest said. He looked at the Christ in the stained glass window at the back of the church, crucified in a broken rainbow. "But that's the trouble, isn't it? We all prayed for the angels to come back, but we got you instead. And you don't make any difference at all."

"I don't tell people what miracles to ask for," Zane said.

"No, but you show them miracles can't really change anything. So why bother searching for God when he's not going to help you anyway?"

"If anyone knows the answer to that, it should be you."

The priest smiled a little but didn't look away from the people in the windows. "What exactly do you want with Agnes?" he asked.

"I just want to find her and talk to her," Zane said. "It's a long story."

"She's easy enough to find, but I think you'll have a hard time talking to her," the priest said. "She's in a cemetery now."

Zane absorbed that in silence for a moment. "What happened to her?" he finally asked.

"I think you know what happened," the priest said, looking back at him now.

"Which cemetery?"

"Eternal Garden. She said she wandered the grounds for a week and didn't recognize any of the names there."

Zane nodded and stood up. "What do you want?" he asked.

The priest laughed, a low, dry sound. "I want more people to come to church."

"There are some miracles even I can't manage," Zane said. But he looked at the Christ in the stained glass long enough to hear the sound of the miracle, then walked out as blood started to trickle from the Christ's wounds.

* * *

THE SKY had turned fiery with the setting sun by the time Zane reached the cemetery. There were no other cars in the parking lot, although there was a bouquet of flowers resting in one of the parking spaces. The gate to the cemetery grounds was locked for the evening, but that wasn't the sort of thing that could stop someone like him.

Zane wandered the cemetery alone, like he was the last man left alive, until he found the grave of Agnes Bath. He looked down at the grave marker for several minutes, until he began to grow cold. It looked like all the other grave markers. If he hadn't known better, he would have thought it the grave of just another person. But if he hadn't known better, he wouldn't have been here.

Zane knew he couldn't resurrect Agnes. That was far beyond the power of a casual miracle. But perhaps there was another way to talk to her.

He reached down and put his hand on the grave marker until he heard the sound of the miracle moving through him. He looked around but didn't see anything. He wondered if maybe his idea hadn't worked after all.

Then Zane heard the sound of swearing coming from the earth underfoot. He stepped back just in time to watch the ghost of Agnes pull herself from the ground, like she was digging her way out even though the grass remained undisturbed. She dragged herself out on hands and knees, then pushed herself to her feet and brushed imaginary dirt from her limbs. She was as ethereal as Zane had always imagined a ghost – he could see right through her to the grave markers stretching away in rows until they disappeared in the deepening gloom.

Agnes didn't look the way Zane remembered her, though. Her skin was drawn tight over the bones of her face and arms, and she looked more like a skeleton than a person. Zane realized his miracle had created a ghost of the Agnes that was in the grave, not the one who had been alive. Still, it was better than no miracle at all.

She looked at Zane and sighed. "What the hell do you want? I thought I was done with all this."

"What happened to you?" Zane asked.

"Isn't it obvious?" Agnes asked. "I died."

"I thought we couldn't die," Zane said. "I've tried."

"I know," Agnes said, nodding. Her twisted hair fell over her face and she didn't try to move it. "I tried for years after I got my powers. Once every few months at least. I just finally gave up. You can't die as long as you've got the miracles in you. But the thing is there's no 'we.' There was me with the power and then you with the power. Once I gave it to you, I could do anything I wanted. So here I am."

Zane lifted his hand and put it through one of her arms for a couple of seconds, to see if he could. He didn't feel anything, even though it was harder to see his hand on the other side of her. It was like looking through a thick fog.

"How did you give me the power?" he asked.

"I don't know," Agnes said. "I just did." She looked down at the ground. "Sorry about that."

"I've tried to give it away," Zane said. "With maybe dozens of people. I can't figure out the trick to do it."

"You have to find the right person."

"How do you find the right person?" Zane asked.

"You just know," Agnes said. "It's like when you're dating and you're not expecting anything and then you go out one night to a bar to meet friends and your entire life changes. Maybe it changes for the better, maybe for the worse, but it changes." She looked back up at him and brushed the hair from her eyes now. "Like when I saw you coming to save me. I knew you were the one."

"I was just driving down the road and you jumped onto my car," Zane said.

"It was like our eyes met across a crowded club."

Zane looked at the graves all around them. He wondered if there were any other angels in the cemetery. He wondered if maybe someday he would get to die and be buried and forgotten in a place like this.

"That's all you wanted to know?" Agnes asked. "You probably could have found everything I've told you on Google."

"Did you hear the modem sound when you did miracles?" Zane asked.

"What modem sound?"

"Like an old computer modem. Only it's made of human voices."

"All I heard was someone breathing. At first I thought maybe it was God. But then I realized it sounded a lot like my ex-boyfriend. So I tried not to think about it too much."

Zane didn't know what to say to that. He rubbed his face with his hands and stared up at the sky. This wasn't going like he had expected. He wasn't even sure what he wanted from her. His phone vibrated in his pocket but he ignored it.

"Is this all you raised me from the dead for?" Agnes asked. "It hardly seems worth it."

"How do you do a real miracle?" Zane asked, still gazing up at the sky.

"What do you mean, 'a real miracle'?"

"Something life or death, something that matters."

"If I had known how to do that, I'd probably still be alive and you'd be wandering around as just another person," she said. "I don't think anyone knows how to do a real miracle. Maybe not even God, if he exists."

"You made the baby," Zane said.

"What are you going on about now?" Agnes asked. "Are you all right? Maybe you should be talking to a therapist, not me."

"The woman who wanted to have a baby but couldn't. The priest sent you to her."

"Oh, her. That was nothing. No different than dyeing someone's hair or showing them a photo of the life they could have had with that past lover."

"You helped her to have a baby," Zane said. "You made a life. That's a real miracle, not fixing someone's car."

"Is that what you think?" Agnes asked.

Zane looked back at her. "I've never been able to do anything life or death like that."

"No, I mean you think the baby is actually going to live?" Agnes asked. She shook her head. "It's just another casual miracle. That woman's life won't be any different a year from now."

Zane stared at her as he finally understood. Agnes looked back at him with her dead eyes. The phone in his pocket buzzed again.

"Are you going to get that?" Agnes asked.

Zane took out the phone and looked at it. There was a series of text messages waiting. They all said the same thing. *HELP!* He scrolled through them until he saw the older message that told him who they were from. It was the pregnant woman.

"I guess you'll be going now," Agnes said. "I'd like to say it was nice to see you again, but . . ."

Zane stared at the messages for several seconds, not sure what he should do. Another one arrived as he stood there.

WE'RE AT THE HOSPITAL! HELP!

He turned and started back toward the car. He wasn't sure if the ghost of Agnes had been real or if he had just imagined her because it was what he wanted.

"You won't be able to do anything," Agnes said as she sank back into the grave. "None of us can do anything."

* * *

ZANE DROVE to the hospital and left the car in the parking lot without paying. There was no time. He went in through the ER entrance and walked past all the people staring at the television and floor and ceiling as they waited, and went up to the nurse behind the reception desk.

"You have a woman losing a baby here," he said.

"We have a lot of women who lose babies here," the nurse said, not looking away from her computer.

"I've come to help," Zane said.

"Are you family? Or a doctor?" the nurse asked. She glanced at him and then back at her computer. "You don't look like a doctor."

"I'm an angel."

"That baby is going to need more than your little miracles." The nurse hit the keys on her keyboard hard as she typed. "We all are."

"I'm the only hope the baby has," Zane said. "We both know the doctors can't save it."

The nurse looked at him again and this time didn't look away. There was blood in one of her eyes from who knew what.

"I can give you your own miracle," Zane said. "No charge."

The nurse didn't seem to move but a door opened beside the reception desk. The nurse nodded at the open doorway. "She's in the first private room after the trauma beds."

Zane went through the door and down the hallway beyond. The hall was lined with beds. A young boy wearing an oxygen mask sat on one with his mother, watching something on her phone. They both looked up at him hopefully as Zane walked past, and he looked away. He didn't meet the eyes of the elderly man with the shaking legs in the next bed, or the teen girl with the bloody arms in the bed after that. He didn't meet the eyes of the nurses or doctors or any of the other patients as he walked through the ER and to the row of private rooms on the other side. He opened the first door and stepped into the room, ignoring the nurse who called after him from somewhere amid the trauma beds.

The pregnant woman was alone in the room. She lay on a bed surrounded by machines. She was attached to the machines by wires stuck to her head and stomach. Her stomach was otherwise bare, except it was covered in some sort of gel. The machines were all sounding alarms. The woman was crying as she held her hands to her stomach.

"I'm sorry," she said when she saw Zane standing there. "I know you can't help. I know that's not how the miracles work. But I don't . . ." She turned her head to the wall for a few seconds, then looked back down at her stomach.

"They're going to bring him out," she said. "They say it's his only chance."

"They won't be able to save him," Zane said.

The woman nodded like she understood. "So that's why the other angel was able to help me," she said. "Because she knew. She knew this would happen. It wouldn't matter in the end."

Zane went over to stand at her side. He looked down at her stomach. He was hoping to see the baby move, to see some sign of life, but there was nothing. The machines kept up their alarms.

The woman looked up at him. "There's a rainbow around your head. Is that a halo?"

"That's the drugs they put you on," Zane said. He knew he had never done anything to deserve a halo.

"You can't do anything, can you?" the woman asked. "None of you can."

Zane didn't answer her. Instead, he put his hand on the woman's stomach. The gel was sticky and warm under his fingers. He could feel the woman's breathing, maybe even a heartbeat.

"What are you doing?" she asked.

"I don't know," he said.

But he did know. He knew this was the one. And then he felt something push against his hand from inside the woman's stomach. The baby. Maybe a hand or maybe a foot. The baby was reaching out to touch him.

"No one can die when they have the miracles inside them," he said.

"What are you talking about?" the woman asked. "What are you doing to my baby?" She tried to sit up, but she was tangled in the cords from all the machines.

The sound of the miracle rose inside of Zane, and this time the chorus of voices was the loudest it had ever been, like every person on earth was a part of it.

"It's all right," he said as he pushed back against the baby's hand or foot, whatever it was, even though he wasn't really sure whom he was talking to. "Everything is going to be all right."

First CONTACTS

The first we knew of the world's end was when the bodies fell burning from the sky. Signs of things to come, although we didn't realize what they meant at the time.

They smashed into our cities, into bank towers and shopping malls and car lots and apartment blocks. When we first saw them blazing down from the heavens, we thought maybe the aliens had finally answered our calls, for better or worse.

But they weren't aliens, or even alien weapons. They were mummified people in spacesuits. Our soldiers came and gathered up the scorched remains, and our scientists studied them in labs. The rest of us studied them in videos online.

And we recognized the suits.

They were the kind worn in the early days of the space race, back when we still dreamed about the future. The suits were charred and torn from their descents and impacts with the earth, but the flags survived on some of them. Flags for nations that existed in name only now.

CCCP.

Republic of China.

USA.

We didn't know what the bodies meant, so we tested their DNA. We found matches around the world.

A dead spaceman had the same DNA as a Wichita man who'd dreamed of becoming an astronaut but had become a cargo pilot instead.

A dead spacewoman's DNA matched that of a woman in Hong Kong who wrote poems about the stars.

A dead spaceman's DNA profile was identical to that of a man who owned a Moscow nightclub called Sputnik.

The dead who fell from the sky were ghosts. But they were ghosts of the living.

We wondered about time travel, about wormholes, about cosmic strings. The dead were a question, but we had no answer.

So we turned all our telescopes and looked past our moon, in the direction the bodies had come from. And saw more dead astronauts drifting our way through space. And beyond them, the fragment of another moon. But, like the dead, it also belonged to us.

We identified part of Mare Tranquillitatis on it, and we found the Apollo 11 landing site, the flag buried in dust. Just like on the moon that continued to orbit us.

But this ghost moon was different from our moon in other ways. It had water mines and solar farms. Buildings ruptured by meteors, with more bodies drifting through the tears in the structures. This other moon had been colonized, but now it just held colonies of the dead.

We searched for answers as the remains of the other moon came at us on a collision path.

We thought maybe the universe was infinite, which meant anything was possible – even another us.

We thought maybe we'd collided with an alternate universe.

We thought maybe space-time had become corrupted.

We thought maybe the universe's OS had crashed.

But we didn't know the cause. We knew only one thing.

They fared no better than us.

We All Go
INTO THE NIGHT ALONE

I found the ghost in the cemetery downtown, or what was left of downtown, anyway. He was just standing there at the foot of the grave, staring at the white chrysanthemum on the freshly turned earth. Or maybe he was staring at something else. It was hard to say what ghosts really saw.

There were white chrysanthemums on all the graves. I didn't know who was bothering to put them there. The cemetery staff were long gone judging by the weeds and the garbage scattered throughout the place. No one had bothered to move the little golf cart that had crashed into one of the trees near the gate months ago. I didn't think anyone was coming back here, not unless they were dead already.

The ghost, whose name was Michael Thane, didn't seem to notice all the burning buildings in the city's skyline. It didn't mean anything, though. Most of us had gotten used to the fires and wreckage since Judgment Day, or whatever you wanted to call it. There were fewer alarms and sirens now, but there were enough that they must have masked my approach. Thane didn't look up from the grave until I was nearly upon him.

He tried to run, because that's what ghosts always do when they see me. I don't wear a uniform or a badge or anything else like some of the others do, but the ghosts know I'm a ferryman before I even say anything. Maybe it's the way I carry myself. Or maybe it's the gun in my hand.

I looked at the grave marker as I went past and saw Thane's name inscribed on it in a simple script, and just the dates of his life. It wasn't exactly a premium stone, either. I'd been expecting more, maybe a statue or a line of poetry or two. His wife, Cassandra, was an artist but unlike most artists she wasn't short on money. Maybe she was a minimalist. Or maybe she thought there was no point in getting elaborate with a grave marker. Who was going to see it now, after all? Just Thane and me and whoever left the flowers.

I wasn't surprised to find Thane at his own grave. I was expecting it, in fact. The cemeteries are always the first place I look when I get a call about a ghost. The dead that come back, they can never really believe they're dead. Maybe that's why they return in the first place. They usually go to the cemeteries to check out their own graves, like that somehow makes it real. What would you do if you were a ghost?

I chased Thane through the rows of the dead, each of them with their single white flower. I wasn't sure what to expect from him, because every ghost is different once they come back. Sometimes they go right through the grave markers and the cemetery fences and whatever else they want. Sometimes they turn invisible and try to hide. Sometimes they try to put their hands into your chest and grab your heart. No two ghosts are alike. They're not even really like their living selves. They're just strange echoes of who they once were.

But Thane ran like a normal man, so I chased him down like a normal man. I tackled him among the graves and he was solid enough I could have believed he was alive if his file hadn't told me different. When he tried to throw a punch up at me from the ground, I hit him across the forehead with the barrel of the gun. He curled up and wept for a bit, and that was that. I stood and waited for him to finish. We were in no hurry, after all.

The sun was setting by the time he got back to his feet, and we stood there for a moment and watched the sky turn red. I held the gun at my side and didn't bother threatening him with it. I knew he wasn't going to run again and so did he. We walked back to his grave as the day faded into night and I saw the chrysanthemum had been kicked off by one of us. I nudged it back on with my foot. It was stained from the earth now. So it goes.

"You're not supposed to be here," I said.

"None of us are supposed to be here," he said. He looked at the burning buildings, which were like torches in the sky now. The lights of something flashed high overhead. A plane, maybe, or just a drone. Maybe something else. It was hard to say. "Or didn't you get the memo?"

"I didn't get mine yet," I said. "But I got yours."

"The ferryman come to take me to the land of the dead."

"Somebody has to do it." Because that was my job. Escorting the dead back to death, so they didn't run around loose in the world of the living and cause problems. More problems than we'd already caused, anyway. It wasn't a job for everyone, but I had a way with the dead.

"And what if you didn't take me back?" he asked.

"If I had a dollar for every time I'd heard that, I could retire and let someone else argue with the dead."

He came along to my car willingly, but I kept my gun ready, just in case. You never know how these things are going to play out, and the dead always have their own ideas about things.

I got in behind the wheel and Thane got in the passenger seat beside me. Most times the ghosts get in the back, but it doesn't really matter where they sit. It's like that old saying: it's the journey that matters.

We drove away from the cemetery and toward the shattered skyline. Darkness didn't exactly fall because all the fires lit up the night, but it was as close as we could get these days. I steered the car around some wrecked vehicles and a couple of bodies that hadn't been picked up by the cleaners yet. We passed a grocery truck going in the opposite direction. The driver lifted a hand off the wheel in greeting and I did the same. It was like driving through some idyllic place in the country instead of the ruins of the city. Thane looked out the window and shook his head.

"You may as well get comfortable," I said. "It'll probably take a while."

"What did you do before?" he asked, not looking any more relaxed. I couldn't blame him. How do you get relaxed about death? Even I didn't have the answer to that.

"Before what?" I said.

"Before Judgment Day."

"Does it matter?"

"I don't know," he said. "It must matter to someone."

"Maybe it does, but not to me."

We came across a semi on its side, halfway in a Starbucks. It blocked the way so I took us down a side street where there was a dead horse lying on the sidewalk, with a patio umbrella sticking out of its body. It wasn't the strangest thing I'd seen. It wasn't even close.

"Where are we going?" Thane asked. "Or are we even going anywhere?"

"We're just driving," I said.

"Just a couple of guys driving through the night," he said, looking back out his window, as we passed a row of cars that for some reason all had crushed roofs, as if something had fallen from the sky and onto them.

"For now. Eventually I'll look over and you won't be there anymore. Then it will just be me driving through the night."

"And where exactly will I be?"

"I don't know," I said, which was more or less the truth. "We all go into the night alone."

But if it had happened like that, I wouldn't be telling you this story now.

"What if I said it doesn't have to be like this?" Thane asked. "What if I actually gave you someplace to drive?"

"I'd say I've heard it all before," I said.

"I have money stashed away. A lot of it."

"How much is a lot?"

"If you have to ask," he said and laughed.

I kept driving nowhere and waited for him to tell me more.

"I just want to live a little while longer," he said.

"Why's that?" I asked. "It's not like the quality of life is better these days."

"I don't know what's waiting for me on the other side."

"Who does?"

"I like to think there's someone who knows. That might make all this bearable."

I had to slow down to drive through a roadblock in the financial district. Three cop cars sat empty in a line across the street, their doors open and the lights on their roofs flashing. The bank towers looming above us were burned out already. It was like we were in the ashes of some great blaze.

"You want to see Cassandra again," I said.

"You seem to know all about me." He looked up at the darkened buildings and shook his head. "What a waste."

"It's all in the file."

"Who gave you the file?" he asked.

"Someone who's good with files," I said. We'd all discovered all our special talents after Judgment Day. Some people had learned they were good at surviving. Others had discovered they had the files suddenly and mysteriously in their heads. Others realized they were ghosts. We were all little miracles in a world that didn't care. I'd found out I was a natural ferryman. No one really knows why you need a ferryman to escort the ghosts back to death. It's just one of those things that happened after Judgment Day. Like the universe had said *enough* and started making rules, even if those rules didn't make much sense.

"Is how I died in the file?" Thane asked.

Sometimes the dead honestly didn't know. A truck hit them from behind or an overpass collapsed on them or whatever. They came back not even knowing they were dead, let alone what had killed them. But Thane's death was memorable, and I knew he wouldn't be forgetting it anytime soon.

"Timothy Burn killed you," I said. "He shot you in the side with a handgun. And then did those other things. In your office just after Judgment Day. When everyone thought the world was actually going to end."

"But it didn't end," Thane said, still looking at the towers. "It never does."

"Security cameras caught the whole thing." I hadn't seen the video, but August had. She was the recorder I normally worked with. She'd described it to me in a Starbucks that was somehow still open.

"A guy in a blue uniform comes into Thane's office," she'd said, staring over my shoulder as we sat at the table, listening to the café's jazz. "Stains on the uniform from I don't know what. Timothy Burn, that's his name. Bald with a goatee. No family. Gun in his right hand. Doesn't look like Thane recognizes him. Thane starts reaching for the phone but Burn shoots him in the right side. Thane gets his hand on the phone but can't pick it up. Burn waits for him to bleed out enough that he's weak. Then he pulls him out of the chair and drags him over to the wall. He goes into the other room and comes back with a screw gun. He lifts up Thane and stretches his right arm out. He screws Thane's hand into the wall. Does the same with the left. Leaves Thane there crucified to the wall."

It wasn't necessarily the sort of death you expected, but it didn't come as any surprise in these days, either. Everyone had their own take on Judgment Day. I'd paid for the coffee and hadn't said anything else to August.

"Maybe there will be a trial someday, when everything gets cleaned up," I told Thane.

"And I'll still be dead," he said.

"Why did he kill you?" I asked. It wasn't in the file. Maybe it was in Burn's file, but that didn't matter to me because I didn't have it and he wasn't dead yet.

Thane shook his head. "I don't even know who he was. I guess he worked at the company, because he had the uniform. Maybe he wanted something he didn't have. A raise or better hours or a different parking space. Maybe he didn't like management. Maybe he was just mad because I didn't remember him. We didn't exactly talk about it beforehand."

Or maybe he'd wanted Cassandra. Although he didn't really strike me as her type. I figured she was more into the rich-and-dead set.

"I'm not going to help you get revenge on Burn," I told Thane. "That's not what I do. He'll be dead one day soon enough. The two of you can work it out then."

"It's all yours," Thane said, and I knew we were talking about the money again. "You just have to let me go."

"You can't stay a ghost forever. Someone else like me will track you down."

"It won't be your problem, though, will it?" Thane said, turning to me. "It will be theirs."

"How much money?" I asked again.

"All of it," he said.

I looked at the empty cop cars in the rear-view and thought about what I could do for Emily with that money.

"What's the address?"

* * *

THANE DIRECTED me to a condo tower along the new transit line. The tracks were buckled in places and a train sat frozen on a journey to nowhere, its windows all blown out. The tower looked like it had been untouched by Judgment Day, though. Maybe that was what money could buy you.

We left the car in the street and I didn't bother to lock it. We hadn't seen another living human being since the truck driver who had waved at me. Most of the survivors had fled into the country after Judgment Day. I doubted it was any better there, but I wasn't planning on visiting to find out. Not as long as I had Emily to look after.

The glass walls of the building's lobby were somehow still intact but the doors were locked. I stepped aside and let Thane punch in the code on the keypad. I wondered how long he would be able to keep physical form. It was different with every ghost. Some were fading even as they came back, but others stayed a long time if they had the motivation. Thane looked pretty physical. I wondered about his motivation.

We got in an elevator and Thane pushed the button for the penthouse. It scanned his finger and thought about it for a second, and then we rose up like the world hadn't ended.

"This place isn't in your file," I said as we went. Thane owned a half-dozen properties around the city, but there weren't any notes about this one.

"It's owned by a company," Thane said, looking at his reflection in the elevator wall. "And I own the company that owns the company."

I thought maybe it was a place he kept for sex with men or women, or maybe to take his drugs, until the elevator opened and we stepped into the penthouse. Everything was white – the walls, the furniture, the appliances, the rugs on the white tiles. Even the paintings that hung wherever there weren't windows were sculpted layers of white paint. There wasn't a bit of colour in the whole place beyond us.

"This is like a shrine or something," I said.

"It's where I come to think about what I've done," Thane said, looking around. "And what I need to do."

When I looked through the windows, I could see everywhere. It looked like the entire city was still on fire. So I tried not to look out the windows again.

"Cassandra make all these paintings?" I asked.

"In a manner of speaking," he said, looking around the room. "She works in many different mediums."

It wasn't exactly an answer, but I didn't push him on it because I thought it was all the answer I was probably going to get.

"Where's the money?" I asked.

Thane walked over to the nearest painting. "It's underneath the canvas. There's money inside all the paintings."

He reached out to take the painting from the wall, but I waved him away with the gun. "I'll do that part," I said, because I didn't know what was behind the canvas and he did.

He looked at me for a few seconds, his arms still outstretched toward the painting. Then he shrugged and stepped away.

"It's your life," he said.

I stepped past him and grabbed the painting by the top of the frame with my free hand. I pulled it from the wall and the world exploded in even more white and a sound I can't describe, which left me unable to hear. I tried to grab hold of Thane so he couldn't get away, but now I was lying on the floor near the entrance instead of standing by the wall, so all I could grab was air. The explosion had thrown me across the room.

I got up with all the ability of a small child and looked around in time to see Thane stepping through a glass door out onto the patio. He glanced back at me as I pointed the gun in his direction. I couldn't keep my hand steady enough to centre the sights on him, though.

Thane stepped up onto the railing and then walked off without even stopping. He didn't fall, though. Instead, he just kind of drifted down out of sight as I stumbled forward. By the time I managed to get out onto the patio and look over the railing, he was disappearing into some smoke that had drifted down the street from a car fire at the end of the block. He didn't look back at me and I didn't bother with the gun. We both knew I couldn't hit him from this distance.

I checked myself for injuries and found a messy red hole in my left side. Something had gone in there and not come back out. Blood oozed from the hole, but slow enough that I knew I had time left on this earth yet.

I went back inside the penthouse again and looked at the painting I had grabbed. There was a charred black hole in the centre of it, and I could see different-coloured wires and bits of red and blue plastic wrapping behind the canvas. The only colour in the place. The wall where it had hung was scorched black, too. The wall looked like an abstract painting now.

I had thought maybe Thane had been going for a weapon, but it had been some kind of trap. An art trap. There hadn't been any money or any guns. There had only been a bomb set to take out the person who moved the painting. If I'd been a little less lucky, maybe I would have been the one standing around a cemetery next, looking at my grave and wondering what had happened.

I looked at the other paintings and wondered if they were all bombs, too. I suspected the whole place was probably a trap. Thane had played it like he didn't have any special powers back in the cemetery, when he clearly could have escaped me there by floating away or through things. He'd brought me here just to try to get rid of me or at least leave me behind. He must have been planning for this moment when he was still alive. He knew a ferryman would come for him. And he'd planned all along to get rid of that ferryman so he could do whatever it was he'd returned to do.

I went back down to the car and I wasn't surprised to find the tires all flattened. That was all right. I had a few surprises of my own.

* * *

I TOOK THE stairs into the parking garage beneath the condo tower, because the elevator wouldn't recognize my fingers like it had Thane's. The garage was half-full of cars, so I checked them until I found one that wasn't locked, which didn't take as long as it should have. I got in and started it up, and it ran like it had been waiting for me all this time. I was worried about the garage door not working, but it opened for me as I approached, like I was going out into a normal world.

I drove my new car across the city, detouring around streets that were blocked off by abandoned vehicles or collapsed buildings. At one point I drove through a pack of lions that were lying in the middle of the street. I imagined they had escaped from a zoo somewhere, but I didn't rule out the possibility that I was hallucinating from blood loss. The lions scattered around the car, then gave chase for a moment. It was a half-hearted kind of pursuit, like they were following their instincts but didn't really know why. The street I was on at the time was more or less empty of cars, though, so I was able to lose them.

I stopped at the hospital along the way, because I had about an hour to kill before I had to be at my destination. I left the car in the half-empty lot. I figured some vehicles had just been abandoned there, judging by the dust on their windshields. I went in through the ER entrance because it was after hours and the main entrance was locked.

The waiting room was strangely empty, as if everyone who was left in the city had just given up on trying to fix themselves. The triage nurse looked at my bloody side and waved me to her desk, but I didn't sit down.

"I'm here to see a patient," I said and told her Emily's full name.

"You look like you should be a patient," she said.

"Maybe. But I had it coming."

"Visiting hours are over," she said.

"I may not have another chance," I said.

She looked me up and down some more and then buzzed me through the door without saying anything else.

I went down the hall and took the elevator up to Emily's ward. The nurse there knew me by sight and just waved at me. I nodded instead of waving back. I didn't want to lift my arm in case she saw my wound and gave me the same speech as the other nurse. I went into Emily's room and sat on the chair by her bed.

She looked the same as the last time I'd visited. She always looked the same. She was gaunt and pale, with tubes running into her nose and down her throat, and an IV in her arm. She looked like an old woman on her deathbed instead of a teen. The machines made the usual noises they made. I didn't say anything. I never did. It wasn't like she'd ever opened her eyes for me, anyway. That was just as well. I don't know what I'd say to her.

No one else came in when I was there. The nurses always left me alone with Emily. But the one outside smiled at me when I left the room again, after my hour was done.

"I'm still praying for her," she said.

"Maybe somebody will finally listen," I said.

I went back out to the car and continued on to Our Lady of Infinite Sorrow church. It was around eight o'clock when I arrived. I parked a few blocks away, in front of a gated playground with a forgotten stroller inside. The church was dark and closed for the night, even in these troubled times. But I knew from the file this was where I needed to be. I checked the mirrors for the lions every now and then, but I didn't see any signs of them. I didn't see any signs of Thane either. But I knew he'd be here. He hadn't set me up back in the condo just so he could aimlessly wander the ruins.

I checked the wound in my side because the pain wasn't going away. The blood had slowed but was still oozing out. I wasn't sure how much I could lose before it was too much. I put it out of my head along with the pain. There was only one way to find out.

I didn't have to wait too long before a car drove up from the other end of the street and parked in front of the church. It was a nice car, a brand I didn't recognize. Something European, maybe, or some limited edition from one of the tech companies. It was so quiet I couldn't even hear it. A woman got out and looked around, but she didn't appear to see me. I knew her from the file. Cassandra. Thane's wife.

She went up the stairs to the church and unlocked the doors with a key she took from her pocket. She looked around one more time and then went inside. I sat there for a moment longer in case she was cagey like Thane, and then I got out of the car and went down the street to the church. I went up the stairs myself and tried one of the doors. It was still unlocked, so I slipped inside. I thought about taking out my gun, but it didn't feel right to do that in a church.

Not that it looked like a church inside. I mean, it did and it didn't. There were the pews and the stained glass windows and the crucifixes and all that. Too many crucifixes, in fact. They lined the walls, in every size and form imaginable. There were wooden crucifixes with the classic depiction of Christ, or just empty. There was a crucifix made of plastic bags taped to one wall, and a crucifix wrapped in bar codes hanging on the opposite wall. A large crucifix hanging at the back of the church was made of video cameras. Their recording lights all burned red.

Cassandra sat in one of the front pews, her head bowed. There was no one else in the place, but she had lit candles that cast shadows everywhere, even into the stained glass windows.

I must have made some sound, because she turned and looked at me. I held up my hands to show her I meant no harm. That was when she stood up and pointed her own gun at me.

"That's a fine way to act in a church," I said.

"There's no better place to ask forgiveness if you have to shoot someone," she said.

"I'm not here for you," I said. "I'm looking for Thane."

"My husband is dead," she said, but she looked like she was thinking over my words anyway.

"You know it and I know it, but he doesn't know it."

"Oh my God. He came back." It was a statement, not a question.

"He did," I said. "And I think he's trying to find you."

"How did you know I was here?" she asked.

"You come here every night. I figure he knows your schedule as well as I do."

"You're a ferryman."

"I've been called worse," I said. "But yeah, that will do for now."

She looked past me, at the door I'd come through. "He'll be here any minute now then."

"I imagine so," I said. "And I don't think he'll need a key like you did."

"All the money I donated couldn't buy me salvation, but at least it bought me a key when everyone left," she said.

"Are you the one who turned this place into whatever it is?" I asked, nodding at the crucifixes.

"I've been waiting for someone to come along and make it better," she said. "Where else would you go?"

"I don't think the person who's coming is who you think it is," I said.

"Drop your gun," she said.

"I'm not holding a gun." I waved my empty hands a little.

"Put it on the pew in front of you and walk away from it. Or I'll make you a ghost right now."

So I took out the gun and placed it on the seat of the nearest pew and then backed up a few steps.

Cassandra kept an eye on me and didn't look at the gun. Which could have meant anything at all or nothing.

"What does he want?" she asked.

"What do the dead ever want? Maybe to say goodbye. Maybe to spend more time with you. Maybe to say sorry for all those things."

"Let me try again," she said. "Where is he?"

"If I knew the answer to that, I wouldn't be here, would I?"

"So you lost him?" She looked somehow disappointed.

"You're too good of a ferryman for that to happen," Thane's voice said. I looked around but I didn't see him until he stepped out of one of the stained glass windows on the wall. He was hiding in the body of some man in robes I didn't recognize. He drifted down to the floor as he looked at Cassandra.

She stared at him but kept the gun pointed at me.

"You're supposed to be dead," she said.

"And yet here I am," he said. "Even though you don't sound happy to see me." He walked along the pews until he reached the aisle, where he stopped.

"I should be, but . . ." Her voice trailed off. I couldn't blame her, given the circumstances.

"But what?" Thane asked.

"The video," she said. "I saw you die. Everyone saw you die."

He nodded at her like he understood. Who knows – maybe he did.

"I did die," he said. "But here I am anyway."

"A ghost," she said.

"If you like." He walked up to her and put his hand on the gun, gently lowering it. And then she collapsed into his arms and he caught her. I looked away because even ghosts who blow me up and women who point guns at me deserve their moment.

They went down the aisle and past me, to the front doors of the church. Cassandra held on to Thane's arm like a new bride.

"I've been praying for this to happen, but I never really thought it would," she said.

"It's not what I imagined, either," Thane said.

"We'll go to the house in the country," Cassandra said as they reached the entrance. She opened one of the doors onto the darkness outside. "We'll start all over and this time we'll live forever."

There was a flash of light outside, and a sharp crack a second later. It took me a few seconds to realize it was a gunshot, and by that time Thane was slumping to the floor of the church, his face already a mask of blood from the hole in his forehead.

I went for my gun because it seemed like the sort of moment I should have a gun in my hand. But Cassandra turned and fired several shots at me, and one of them was lucky enough to hit. A star of pain flared in my side, above where I'd been hurt earlier, and I cried out and curled around it, trying to contain the fire to that one spot. She could have finished me off then, but I guess she just wanted to keep me away from my gun, not kill me. She looked down at Thane and said, "I always knew you'd come back." She looked past me, and that's when I understood.

I glanced over my shoulder, at the cross made of cameras. The lights on them all telling me they were still recording. I thought again about what Thane had said, that Cassandra worked in different mediums.

"You're filming this," I said. "You were filming this all along because you knew we were coming."

"Even better," Cassandra said. "I'm livestreaming it. I was hoping to record the end of the world. I thought maybe the world could end with art."

"Like those paintings in his penthouse. They almost killed me."

"This is how the world ends," Cassandra said. "Not with a bang but with a video."

"If I'd known things would have gone like this, I'd have asked for a bigger cut." This was the man who walked out of the night and into the church. A bald man with a goatee. Even through the white haze that was my vision, I recognized him from the file. Burn.

The two of them looked at me and then down at Thane, who continued to leak ghost blood onto the floor. I wasn't sure, but this may have been the worst moment I'd had in a church yet.

"Money?" I managed to ask Burn. "You're doing this for money?" My mouth tasted like blood even though I didn't think I was bleeding there. Maybe something was going on in my mind because of getting shot.

"Would it make you feel better if it were about something else?" Cassandra asked. "Love, maybe?" She looked around at the crosses lining the walls of the church and laughed.

"It's always about the money," Burn said. "I mean, that's why you're here, right? Because I'm guessing he didn't convince you to take him to that secret condo of his because you wanted to check out his art collection. I'm doing it for the money as much as you are."

I could tell from the look he gave me that he knew about Emily. I wondered for a second what secrets he had in his life and then I put it out of my mind. There were enough secrets in this church already.

"How long have you been following us?" I asked. I pushed myself a little way along the floor, away from them. Toward my gun. They didn't seem to notice. I hoped no one watching on the livestream would message Cassandra or Burn if they noticed. If there was anyone watching.

"Since the cemetery," Burn said. He nudged Thane's body with his foot, but Thane didn't move. "I figured if he'd come back, that's where he'd go first. I talked to a ferryman about it. He was willing to share his tips of the trade for a bottle."

"A bottle of what?" I asked.

"Does it matter?" Burn said.

"I wish it didn't," I said.

"If wishes came true, maybe you'd still be back in that hospital with whoever you were visiting," Burn said. "You should have stayed there." And I knew I was never going to see Emily again if he had his way.

"So he's doing it for the money," I said, trying to buy some time. I needed a distraction and I had an idea what that distraction could be. "What about you?" I asked, looking at Cassandra. "Don't tell me you're doing it for the art."

"When we're gone, the art is all that we'll leave behind," she said. "There won't be any us. There'll just be what we've done. It took me most of my life to realize that."

"And all of Thane's," I said.

"It's not art if you're not sacrificing something." She pointed the gun at his head. "I don't think I want to see him come back again, though."

I pushed myself another foot or so up the aisle. The pew holding my gun was beside me now.

Burn looked at the cameras on the back wall and crossed himself. He was either asking for forgiveness for what he had done or what he was going to do.

"You can't kill him for good no matter what you do," I said. "Not now that he's a ghost. The only one who can get rid of him is a ferryman."

"That sounds rather convenient for you," Cassandra said.

"I don't think it has to be this ferryman in particular," Burn said, pointing his gun at me. "I think any ferryman will do. Like the one already on my payroll."

I grabbed the gun from the pew, and the movement ignited the star in my side again. My vision burned white, and I knew I couldn't shoot them both, if I even was lucky enough to hit one of them in my state. But I was pretty sure I knew something they didn't. So I threw the gun to Thane.

Who rose up and caught it in one motion. He still had the hole in his head and his face was still a mess of blood. But he was a ghost, and I knew ghosts didn't give up that easy. If they did, they wouldn't have come back in the first place.

"Art," he said and laughed.

Cassandra screamed and shot him. So did Burn, who'd spun to follow the gun I'd thrown and found himself facing Thane. I guess maybe they were hoping they could kill him a third time. But they hadn't even really killed him the second time.

"Oh no," Cassandra said, and she looked down at two blossoms of blood on her shirt, one over her heart and the other in her stomach. She touched the fingers of her free hand to the higher one and stared at the blood like she didn't understand what it was. She looked at Burn, but he was on his knees, looking at his own bloody hands. He'd been shot once, in the throat. The blood geysered out of him, onto the floor and the gun he'd dropped.

Thane stood between them, looking at the gun in his hand like he had fired the bullets. But he hadn't. I knew what he had done. He had turned insubstantial so their bullets had gone through him. He'd become a true ghost and they'd shot each other.

"You didn't come back for me," Cassandra said.

"I came back for both of you," Thane said.

Cassandra and Burn both fell the rest of the way to the floor then. Burn's hand reached out to Cassandra but didn't quite reach her. She stared at the cameras and didn't blink again. Thane looked down at both of them and shook his head.

"This is how it ends," he said. He sounded disappointed.

I still wasn't entirely sure what had happened between the three of them. Maybe Cassandra had paid Burn to kill Thane and that was all there was to it. Maybe there was more to it than that. Maybe it really was just about the money and the art. It didn't matter anymore. What mattered now was I was lying, shot, on the floor of a church with two people I'd gotten killed because I hadn't done my job. And the killer still had my gun.

Thane looked at me as if reading my thoughts. He tapped the gun against his leg a couple of times.

"Are you all right?" he asked.

"I don't think so, no," I said.

"Maybe you should go to the hospital and keep that girl company again," he said.

"Was everyone following me tonight?" I asked. I got to my knees and then I had to rest there for a moment or more.

"I figured Burn would be watching the cemetery like you were, so I followed you to see if I could find him."

"Why didn't you kill him at the hospital? It would have made things easier here."

"Because I had to know for sure. And I didn't know for sure until Cass led me straight into his bullet."

I got to my feet and even managed to step to the next pew. It really was a house of miracles. I held out my hand and he looked at me for several seconds. Then he came over and gave me back my gun.

"You're all done here," I said.

"Yeah," he said, looking back at Burn and Cassandra. "I guess I am now."

I looked at them, too. Their blood was mingling on the floor at this point.

"It's not your fault," Thane said. "I had backup plans for my backup plans if you hadn't taken me to the condo. This would have happened one way or another."

"It's always someone's fault," I said.

"Blame me if that makes you feel better."

"It doesn't." I looked at my side but didn't like what I saw, so I looked away again.

I went up the aisle to the cameras and turned them all off, one after the other. I looked into the last one for a second, at whoever was watching, if anyone was watching, but I didn't say anything. What was there to say?

When I was done, I went back down the aisle and we stepped over the bodies to go outside. Blood was running down the steps. We walked up the street to the car I'd taken from the parking garage. I got in behind the wheel and Thane sat in the passenger seat again. I started the car and we drove through the night. I turned on the headlights but only the one on the driver's side worked.

I didn't take us anywhere in particular. I just drove around the city. There was nowhere really left to go.

"Do you think they'll come back?" Thane asked at one point, and I knew he was talking about Cassandra and Burn.

"They'll be someone else's problem if they do," I said. But I knew their deaths were on me, no matter what Thane said. Just add them to the list.

We found our way back to the cemetery, which was accidental. I hadn't intended to drive there, but sometimes it works out that way. There were no cars parked outside, but there was a girl wandering through the graves. The headlight lit her up but she didn't seem to notice. She had a backpack and an armful of white chrysanthemums. She laid a single one on each grave she passed. When she ran out of them, she reached into the backpack and pulled out another armful. We watched her until she went out of sight behind a large stone crypt. So that was one mystery solved.

"Isn't that something," Thane said.

"It most definitely is something," I said.

We sat there for a time, watching the cemetery, but I didn't see the girl again. I checked my side once more and saw blood everywhere. I wasn't sure if I was going to make it through the night.

"Who is she?" Thane asked, and I shook my head.

"I've never seen her before," I said. "Maybe she's another ghost."

"I meant the girl in the hospital."

"She's just a girl."

"Daughter?" Thane asked. "Distant relative? The child of a friend?"

"No one I really know."

Thane looked over at me. "Then why visit her in the middle of the night? And obviously on a regular basis, if the nurses let you in like that?"

"She's someone I'm responsible for," I said.

"How are you responsible if you don't even know her?"

"Her parents were my first case. This was before I knew what I was. They came back to look after her. They waved me down in the street. I was just driving around after Judgment Day. I didn't know what to do. They told me about her when we drove. By the time we got to the hospital, they were gone. That's how I knew I was a ferryman. If it hadn't been for me, maybe they could have looked after her. So now I look after her for them."

He was silent for a time and I thought maybe he'd gone. When I looked over, though, he was still there.

"The money is in the picture in the bathroom," he said. He kept on watching the cemetery. "A little emergency fund. It's the only one, so leave the others alone."

"All right," I said. "I guess I should thank you."

"No, you shouldn't," he said.

I got out of the car and went and got a chrysanthemum from Thane's grave. I thought maybe Emily might like a flower in her room. When I got back in the car, Thane was gone. I had a feeling that he hadn't just snuck away, but that he was really gone this time.

I drove away from the cemetery and kept driving. I didn't know where I was going, which was fine as I didn't have anywhere to go. I passed another car driving in the other direction. The man driving lifted a few fingers off the wheel in a greeting, and I did the same. I wondered how many of the other lonely cars out there had people like me in them. How many of us were just passing the time until there was no time left for us?

One day I'll find out.

One day we'll all find out.

Déjà Yu
MAKES THE PAIN
GO AWAY

The Trailer

THE WORST thing about being dead is the pain. I felt like I was being crushed inside for months after the heart attack. Like I was forever frozen in that moment of death.

The kids tried to help ease it before Tyler, my wife – my ex-wife now, I guess – took them away with her. Samantha, my daughter, told me the pain meant my heart was broken. She said it would feel better if I came home again. Jesse, my son, said maybe being dead is like when you scrape your knee or elbow. You get a scab for a while but then the pain goes away.

Tyler wouldn't talk to me after I died. She wouldn't even see me. She changed the locks after she kicked me out. I tried to come back to visit the kids, but she wouldn't let me in. I had to talk to them through the door, or on the phone. Samantha said Tyler worried I'd give them whatever it was I had. But I didn't have anything.

My doctor said all the dead feel the pain. He said there are different theories about it. The people who think our condition is caused by all the preservatives or modifications in our food say it's a chemical by-product. The religious people think it's purgatory, that we'll be able

63

to die for good once we've suffered enough. The medical experts think it's the body's memory hanging on to the last seconds of life. My doctor said if I think feeling my heart attack all the time is bad, I should try to imagine what burn victims feel.

I just wanted it to stop.

The Willy Loman

THE SECOND-WORST thing about being dead is you have to keep working. I still had my share of the mortgage payments, even though I didn't live in the house anymore. And now I also had to pay rent for a new apartment. Gas and insurance for the car. Phone bills. I didn't have to eat anymore, but I kept the fridge and cupboards stocked with groceries in case Tyler ever let the kids come and stay with me. It was a waste of money but still.

All the bills meant I had to keep on with the life I had despite being dead. I got dressed in my work clothes in the morning and went into the office along with everyone else. That was actually easier to do thanks to the fact I didn't need to sleep anymore now that I was dead. I went to the food court with my co-workers for lunch and watched them order the same meals I used to order and eat. I looked at the images on the video menus, of the men in suits with hamburgers, the children with fish sticks and fries, the women with salads, but I couldn't make myself hungry. I went to the bar after work with my co-workers and ordered drinks I didn't drink. I did everything but play minigolf with them.

That's because I had my heart attack on the seventh hole of Maximum Mini Golf in the Evergreen Mall during a game with two of my co-workers, Dylan and Hakim. I was ahead for the first time ever against those two. I was leaning on my club, watching Hakim tap a putt into the Wheel of Vegas when suddenly I couldn't breathe. I knew he was aiming for the Free Massage at House of Pleasure, but he hit the Free Gym Pass at House of Pain instead. That's when everything froze inside me and I fell to the fake turf.

I have to give Dylan and Hakim credit – they did what they could for me. Dylan performed his best impression of the CPR he'd seen in movies, while Hakim called 911 before taking photos of the scene with his phone. One of those photos – me with my tongue sticking out and my shirt torn open as the paramedics worked on me – went around the office mail afterward. I forced a laugh and a shrug when I saw it on people's computers and tried not to think about what was happening to me in that photo. But I couldn't forget staring up at the monitor over the hole as I lay there, unable to move, unable to do anything but watch the different images it flashed: a flag waving in the wind, a set of Nike minigolf clubs and balls, a smiling woman who promised to make me a millionaire off my accident lawsuit. When the paramedics rolled me away on the stretcher, the monitor showed a beach on a tropical island somewhere, with the caption Your Ad Could Be Here.

The paramedics did their best to save me, too, but I was already gone by the time they arrived. That's what the driver told me later in the hospital after the emergency-room doctor pronounced me officially dead. "Tough break," the doctor said, putting away the paddles he'd been shocking me with and handing me a release form to sign.

"Are you sure?" I asked him. "Can I get a second opinion?"

He looked at the paramedics. The driver nodded and said, "Dead." The other one was playing a game on his phone and didn't even look up.

I signed the release – it took several attempts because I still wasn't used to the numbness that comes with being dead. But sometimes now I wonder what would have happened if I hadn't signed it – if I wasn't officially dead.

Anyway, the paramedics drove me home in their ambulance. I lay on the stretcher in the back. There was no room for me to sit anywhere. The driver said the living dead were turning into a real epidemic. He offered to take me to Maximum so I could finish the game with Hakim and Dylan but I said no, they were probably too far ahead of me now to catch up. Then he offered to tell my wife so I wouldn't have to, but I said no to that, too. I said there were some things a man had to do himself.

In all honesty, I was planning on keeping it from Tyler, but she knew from the moment I walked in the door. She looked up at me from her yoga mat in the living room, and then leaped to her feet and ran screaming for the bedroom, where she locked herself in.

I knocked and knocked on the door, but she wouldn't let me in. "Go away," she screamed. "I'm in mourning!"

I went back to the living room and watched a few minutes of a yoga show on her tablet. A man was twisted into an impossible position. "Just hold it," he said. "Keep holding it."

Tyler threw all my clothes out the bedroom window and then called me on my phone to tell me to get out. I was glad we'd sent the kids to urban survival camp for the week. But I didn't know then that I'd never see them again.

"I'll sleep on the couch for a while," I told Tyler. "Until you get used to the new me."

"Until death do us part," she said and disconnected.

I went out and picked up my clothes. My neighbours were having a barbecue and everyone stood there with drinks and hamburgers in hand, watching me gather my shirts and ties, but no one said anything.

I called a taxi and waited in the front driveway. All the houses on the street looked the same. When we'd first moved here, I'd gone home to the place across the street by accident and didn't realize it until I was at the front door. It was for sale now. I wondered if having a dead neighbour was bad for property value.

I took the taxi to my car in the Evergreen Mall's parking garage. I sat in the car for most of the night because I couldn't sleep. I thought at first it was because of the shock of being dead and what had happened with Tyler. And trying to figure out how to explain it to the kids when they got home. I didn't know back then that I'd never be able to sleep again. That's why you see so many people like me working the night shift at convenience stores.

Eventually a security guard driving around the garage stopped and shone his flashlight on me without getting out of his car. He told me I had to move on. There was a lineup of cars at the exit. Each one had a lone man inside. I drove to the office and got to work paying my bills. And that's been my life ever since.

The Hollywood

NOT LONG after I died, I got promoted.

In fact, I got promoted because I was dead. I was put in charge of the Déjà Yu beauty products account. The next-worst thing about being dead is people can tell we're dead. We have the tint to our skin, the smell, the stillness when we're thinking about what happened to us. The Déjà Yu beauty products are supposed to make us look alive again. Creams to put colour back in our skin. Aftershave and perfume to mask the smell. Balms to make our lips look warm. Eye drops to sting our eyes and remind us to blink. Shock pads for our chests to remind us to breathe.

Just like any other beauty product, they don't really work. My team's job was to make people think they do.

Before I died, I was junior member of the development team, which mainly meant I made runs to Starbucks for coffee and to Kinko's for the mock-ups of the ads. But the email the partners sent around the office a few weeks after my death said I was now in charge of the team because of my unique circumstances. I was the only dead person in the office, the email said. Congratulations, the email said.

My co-workers all sent me their own emails saying I looked good. They said they could barely notice the difference from when I was alive.

I could tell from the looks that Dylan and Hakim gave each other over the cubicle walls that they wished they'd tried harder to save me.

I didn't really want to be in charge of the Déjà Yu account. I didn't really know what I was doing.

The day of my promotion, I moved my monitor around in my cubicle so no one could see the screen. I opened one of the company's Screenplay for Success™ templates and studied its rules.

The Trailer: Set the scene.

The Willy Loman: Make the audience identify.

The Hollywood: Give the audience some drama to keep them entertained.

The Pitch: The product.

The Punchline: Leave the audience happy and willing to buy.

There were large spaces in between each rule where I was supposed to add my notes. I couldn't think of anything to fill the spaces. I closed the file and logged on to Facebook instead. I watched videos of Tyler and me and the kids at the local Disney Time. I wanted to cry at the shot of Jesse and Samantha holding hands with the Goofy in the army uniform, but my tear ducts didn't work anymore. I phoned my old number to talk to the kids again, but there was no answer. I tried to leave a message but the voice mail was full.

The day after I was promoted, Hakim wandered over and asked if we were going to have a meeting about the Déjà Yu account. He said everyone had run out of spam to read.

I told the office manager I had to hold a meeting and she put us in the Coke room, which is a sign of how seriously the partners took the Déjà Yu account. I'd only been allowed in the Pepsi room before. The Pepsi room is just a standard meeting space with Ikea chairs and a table, but the Coke room has Herman Miller chairs and a video screen.

My team consisted of three people: Hakim, Dylan and Phoenix, an intern from the university marketing program. I wasn't sure if Phoenix was her real name or not. When I sat beside her, she pushed her chair farther away from me.

We all stared at the blank video screen for a while. It took me a moment to realize they were waiting for me to say something.

"Does anyone have any ideas?" I asked.

No one said anything. They all looked from the screen to me. I looked back at the screen. The only thing I could think of was my family at the Disney Time.

"Home video," I said. "We're going to make a home video."

They kept looking at me.

"We'll show them want they want," I said. "Life like it used to be."

I put Dylan in charge of finding us a set, Hakim of putting together a film crew from our regulars. Phoenix said she could get actors for free from the university's drama program.

"We need older people," I told her. "People with kids."

"Half the people in university now are older than you," she said. "The place is full of people who've lost their jobs to zombies."

I said that would be fine and let's not use the word *zombie*. I went back to my cubicle and called home again. Still no answer. The voice mail was still full.

Dylan found us a house to shoot in a few days later. It was in a sub-division on the outer edge of the city. River Spring or River Canyon or River Valley or something like that. It was an area of scrubland, near an incineration plant. I didn't see a river anywhere.

The house had a mortgage foreclosure notice on the door, but there was still furniture inside. It was nicer than the furniture in my old house.

"Why didn't they take all this stuff?" I asked. "They could have got this out before the locks were changed."

"The bank guy told me they owed money on everything inside the house, too," Dylan said.

"I still would have taken it," I said.

The director and cameraman Hakim hired both wore T-shirts with the Soviet Union's hammer and sickle on them. They stood outside the house and talked about how many African families would fit inside it while they smoked hand-rolled cigarettes. When I went out to say hello to them, they just stared at me and didn't answer.

I went back inside and found Hakim. He was in the kitchen, going through the cupboards, inspecting the glasses and plates.

"Where did you find these guys?" I asked him.

"We couldn't go with the usual union guys," Hakim said. "On account of you."

"What's wrong with me?" I asked.

"Union crews can't work with zombies. They've got concerns about outsourcing and seniority."

"Can we not use that word?" I said.

Hakim shrugged and dropped some shot glasses into his shoulder bag.

I looked out the window at our film guys again. They were unloading their gear from their van now. "But communists are okay working with me?"

"I didn't say that," Hakim said and walked away.

But the real problem was the actors.

When Phoenix drove up with them, I could see they were dead. All of them – the man, the woman, even the little girl. They stood outside, a little apart from each other, and stared at the house without blinking.

I pulled Phoenix aside, around the corner of the house. "What is this?" I asked her. "I thought you were getting me students."

"They are students," she said. "They came back to school after they died and lost their jobs. Except the girl. She still has a job."

I looked around the corner of the house, at the girl. She was brushing the hair of a doll.

"She's been dead for decades," Phoenix told me. "She was one of the first, back before anyone knew it was happening. She's actually a drama prof at the university. Revelatory hiring practices."

I went back inside. Hakim was unpacking the kit of Déjà Yu samples for the actors. I took some of the cream from his kit and put it on my arms and face. Hakim watched me but didn't say anything.

The director came over and asked me what the plan was for the shoot. "Just make them look normal," I said.

"What do you mean, normal?" he asked.

"Make them look like a real family."

I went into the bathroom and studied myself in the mirror while the actors put on the Déjà Yu stuff. The cream made me look a little alive again, but I didn't feel any different.

The director decided to do a breakfast scene. I sat on the couch and watched them shoot it in the kitchen. The director told the little girl to ask her parents for a new phone. He told the woman to say she was getting plastic surgery done again. He added she should look like she was on antidepressants. He told the man to think about the money he was going to take from Third World countries when he went to work.

"So it's just like before I died," the man said.

"Exactly," the director said. "Act it like it's the morning of your death."

I closed my eyes while they shot the scene.

When they were done, I told the crew to come back the next day. I told the actors we wouldn't need them anymore.

"No offence," I said, "but the last thing dead people want to see in an ad is more dead people."

"I was thinking the same thing myself," the man said.

"Maybe plastic surgery is the way to go," the woman said.

The girl didn't say anything, just kept brushing the hair of her doll.

I pulled Phoenix into the bathroom and told her to come back the next day with living actors. She sighed but nodded. I went back to my apartment and tried to call home again. The voice mail was still full. I watched cop shows all night long. They were all the same: a man took his family hostage; the police surrounded the place and sent in the dead cops, maybe even some dead dogs. The cops got shot but it didn't matter. Sometimes they brought everyone out alive. Sometimes they killed the hostage-taker and brought him out screaming that he was going to sue them for the bullet holes in his chest or head or both.

In one show, the cops killed everyone in the house. It was a drug lab, and they shot the wrong bottle of something and the place blew up. The cops and the newly dead family all staggered out different doors, but then the man and his wife and son all found each other in the front yard and hugged, their skin still smoking from the fire.

And that's when I came up with the idea to get my family back.

The Pitch

THE NEXT day, Phoenix showed up with a real-life family. Not only were they alive, but they were actually a family. A man, a woman and their son. I could tell they were together by the way they sat on the couch, leaning against each other without saying anything while they waited for the cameraman and director to set up for the shot again. It was just like how I used to watch movies with Tyler and the kids.

"Where did you find them?" I asked Phoenix.

"They're mine," she said.

"You don't know how lucky you are," I said, but she just shook her head.

The director gave the same set of instructions to Phoenix's family as he had to the dead actors, even the comment about taking money from Third World countries.

"I thought communism was dead," I said.

"So are you," the director said, "and yet here you are."

Hakim didn't bother putting any of the Déjà Yu cream on the actors, seeing as they were already alive. I put some on my face and hands again while they tested the lights for the scene. I thought maybe it would work eventually if I just kept applying it. Hakim watched me but didn't say anything.

When they started shooting the scene, my skin began to burn. By the time they reached the part where the son asked for a new phone, I felt like I was on fire. I ran for the bathroom to wash off the cream, but the taps in the house didn't work anymore, so I rubbed the cream away with a towel instead.

When I looked in the mirror, my skin was pitted and eaten away where the cream had been. I went back out into the kitchen. Everyone stared at me. Hakim couldn't conceal a small smile. Phoenix and her family all put their hands to their mouths, even the boy.

I couldn't stand them seeing me like that, so I left.

I went home. My home where my family lived, not my apartment. I rang the doorbell and then knocked when no one answered. Then I kicked in the door. I waved at my neighbours, who watched from their windows, and went inside.

I was going to kill my family. I was going to do it as gently as I could, so they wouldn't hurt after. Maybe pillows over their faces or carbon monoxide in the garage. Then they would understand. Then they would be like me. Then everything would go back to the way it was.

But no one was home.

And no one would ever be home again.

The place was empty, all the furniture gone, everything gone. Just some outlines in the carpet upstairs where the beds and dressers had been. Not even a note left to say where they'd went.

My phone rang. It was the executive assistant for the partners. She said they wanted to know where I was.

"I don't know," I told her.

She said they'd heard about what happened. She said they wanted to know the status of the Déjà Yu account.

I went to the bathroom and looked at myself in the mirror while she talked. There were still spots of cream on my forehead and neck. My skin was still burning, and strips of it were peeling off now, hanging from my face. The skin underneath looked raw but was grey instead of red.

I understood everything then.

I was dead.

"Are you there?" the executive assistant asked me.

"Yes," I said and disconnected.

I went back to Maximum Mini Golf in Evergreen Mall. I bought a pass and took a club and a red ball from the clerk, a teen girl who had a phone in her hand the whole time.

"You were here the other week," she said. "You're that guy that died."

"I guess I am," I said.

"So what's that like?" she asked.

I didn't answer her. Instead, I went to the first hole and played through to the seventh. I waited my turn behind the other players and I recorded my score on my little scorecard like everyone else. When I reached the seventh hole, I lay down on the grass and looked up at the monitor overhead. It showed a hamburger patty sizzling over open flames and then the flag.

Two men had just finished the seventh hole and were recording their scores. When they saw me on the ground, they took a few steps toward me and then stopped.

"Are you . . . ?" one asked, while the other took out his phone.

The hamburger was replaced by an attack helicopter blowing up a car in a desert somewhere. Men in suits and ties stood in the desert and cheered.

I didn't hurt anymore. My skin didn't hurt from the cream, my chest didn't hurt from the heart attack.

I didn't feel a thing.

I am dead.

The Punchline

THE MONITOR shows the Your Ad Could Be Here tropical island again. I close my eyes and imagine the videos of Tyler and me and the kids at Disney Time once more.

I imagine a motto superimposed on the videos of my family. The videos of my life.

Déjà Yu Makes the Pain Go Away.

I imagine the ad playing on the phone of the man standing over me now. Playing on my computer at work. Playing before movies. Playing on monitors in restaurants and stores in malls everywhere.

I imagine the ad is so successful it gets me an actual office at the agency, with my name on the door. My name added to the partner list. My name on every business card and company email.

I imagine I'm lying on the floor of my empty house.

I imagine the rest of my life.

The Infinite
SHADES OF GRIEF

The Diver had gone deeper into the Drift than anyone else, but even he barely knew what secrets it contained until he met the nurse.

It happened when he went into the hospital to hide from the ghosts. It was at the start of his dive, when he'd only been in the Drift for a few minutes. He'd been walking down the sidewalk, making his way around the abandoned cars and not really paying close attention to the green haze of the Drift that shrouded the remains of the city. The ghosts weren't usually found in the shallow parts of the Drift, so he was relaxed and thinking about Lucas. That was when the white forms grew out of the Drift at the end of the block and the Diver stepped over to a school bus for cover.

Nobody knew who the ghosts were, although almost every diver had a theory. Government patrols trying to keep looters and mourners and others out of the Drift. Alien scouts on security patrols while the invasion force assembled. Maybe even organized bands of thieves or squatters trying to keep the divers away from their areas. The only ones who could say for certain were those who got too close to the ghosts. The Diver stumbled across their bodies every now and then while exploring the city.

The Diver went in through the open door of the bus and climbed up inside. He stepped over forgotten backpacks on the floor and crouched behind a seat halfway down. A phone sat on the seat he hid behind. The Diver didn't bother checking to see if it had any life left. No electronics worked in the Drift.

He looked through the cracked windshield and watched the ghosts come. They were spread across the street in a loose line. Men and women in full-body white hazmat suits, with assault rifles in their hands. The buildings around them hung tilted over their heads, as if they had stopped in mid-fall, and the street was frozen in mid-waves. The ghosts had to walk up and down the swells of pavement. The Drift was constantly moving, ebbing back and forth around the crash site, and the city moved with it, like it was caught in an unseen current that swayed buildings and shifted the streets around like ripples in the sand of a lake.

Or maybe it was more like a dream than an invisible current. The Diver had a feeling like he'd been trapped in a nightmare since the crash had happened. A nightmare that grew worse by the second as he watched the ghosts make their way around the vehicles that had been left in the street by those who had fled the city. The ghosts didn't look in any of the cars or vans. It was like they'd checked them already and hadn't found what they were looking for.

The Diver waited until they reached a transport truck jackknifed across the road and they had to go around it. They were out of sight for a few seconds. The Diver went out the back door of the school bus. He may have been safe in the bus if they weren't checking the vehicles, but he was worried the ghosts would be able to hear him breathing if they got any closer. He wore a scuba tank on his back and kept the regulator in his mouth the entire time he was in the Drift. Most divers did. That was how they'd earned the name divers. You could breathe normally most places in the Drift, but not everywhere. There were invisible pockets of strange air and deadly gases scattered throughout the Drift. The Diver had once found a man suffocated on the steps of a church even though he had an air tank on his back. His regulator was in his hand, just inches from his lips. Ever since then, the Diver always used his regulator from the moment he stepped past the barricades outside and walked into the shimmering, shifting light of the Drift.

The Diver dropped down onto the street behind the bus. He had to step around more backpacks and a couple of mismatched shoes lying on the ground. He ran for the hospital in the other direction from the ghosts. He kept the school bus in between him and the ghosts and crouched down to hide among more ripples in the pavement. It was only when he had almost reached the hospital that he realized it was the one where Lucas, his son, had been born. The doors to the ER were frozen half-open or maybe half-shut, from when the hospital had lost power along with the rest of the city after the crash. The Diver slipped through the doors as the ghosts came around the sides of the school bus.

The waiting room was dark but enough light came in from outside that he could see all the chairs were unoccupied except for a few jackets. The Drift had a bluish tinge in here. An empty baby stroller was jammed in the doorway to the treatment wards, stopping the door from closing. The Diver stepped around it, into the hallway beyond, and pulled the stroller after him. The door slowly swung shut, locking with a metallic click that was louder than he liked.

The Diver looked into the nurses' station to his right, but he didn't see anywhere to hide. There was only a window of glass between the station and the waiting room. He went deeper into the wards. It was almost pitch-black in the triage area, so he had to go slow. Even so, he bumped into a stretcher pushed up against the side of the hall. A blanket covered the form of a person on it. He lifted the blanket in case it was Lucas. He checked all the bodies he found to see if they were Lucas. His son had never come out of the Drift after the crash, so he still had to be in it. The body was an old woman, though, who stared sightlessly up at the dead lights overhead. She was as perfectly preserved as all the other bodies in the Drift. Another mystery that maybe someone would figure out someday. The Diver pulled the blanket back up over her face and went deeper into the ER.

He stopped in front of another nurses' station and looked around. He was surrounded by empty hospital beds and machines whose purposes he didn't understand. He was in a trauma ward. There were other hallways leading away, deeper into the hospital, but he didn't know where to go and he didn't want to become lost. A shadow moved under the door he had closed, catching his eye, and he looked back the way he had come. The door moved a little in its frame, as if someone was trying to pull it open. The shadow under the door shifted from side to side, then faded away. The Diver didn't hear a thing other than his breathing, but he stayed there for a moment longer, not moving.

"Are you here for the children?"

The woman's voice came from behind him, and the Diver spun around, reaching for the knife strapped to his leg. It wouldn't do any good if one of the ghosts were behind him, but he had to do something.

The woman wore nursing scrubs instead of a hazmat suit. She stood in the nurses' station and held a temperature monitor instead of an assault rifle. She looked at the knife, then back at him. She didn't say anything else, so the Diver took the regulator out of his mouth so he could speak.

"What children?" he asked.

"The babies," the nurse said. "I've been looking after them since whatever it was happened. I thought they would send an emergency response team." She looked past him, at the door. "Is it just you?"

"Maybe I can help," the Diver said.

The nurse took him down one of the other halls and up a flight of stairs to the next level of the hospital. The stairwell was so dark he couldn't see anything and had to hang on to the handrail and feel each step with his feet.

"What's your name?" the nurse asked him out of the darkness as they climbed, and he had to think how to answer that. No one had asked him that question for some time. He'd gone by many names in the past – Michael, Mr. Andre, CEO Andre, Dad. But none of those names fit him anymore. Now everyone just called him the same thing.

"The Diver," he said.

"The Diver," she said. "That's a curious name."

"This is a curious place," he said.

"You don't have any other names?" she asked. He knew she was doing her job, trying to gauge his state of mind and see if he was someone who was really here to help or if he needed to be checked into the hospital himself.

"Names don't really matter anymore," he said.

He walked into a wall before he realized they'd reached a landing. He turned in the darkness and followed the nurse's voice up more steps that climbed in the opposite direction. She could have led him to walk right off the steps and into the void and he wouldn't have known until it was too late.

"It must be bad, whatever it is that's happening," the nurse said. "I haven't seen anyone since the hospital was evacuated."

"Nobody knows what it is," the Diver said. "I mean, it was an alien crash. But we don't know what kind of alien."

"An alien?" the nurse asked. "Like refugees?"

"An alien spaceship," the Diver said. "It fell into downtown." Even as he said it, he realized how his words failed to capture what had really happened. There were no words that could capture it. "We're still not sure if anyone was on board or not, but it did all this. It made the Drift."

They reached the next floor and left the stairwell. There was enough light coming in the windows of the rooms that the Diver could see again. The nurse turned to look at him, and he couldn't help but notice the wisps of green drifting around her head.

"What's the Drift?" she asked.

The Diver looked around. He didn't see any signs of life, although there were some crayon drawings by children on one wall. He couldn't hear anything other than the sound of his own breathing.

"Where are the babies?" he asked.

The nurse took him down the hall and into a room with a half-dozen incubators. There were a half-dozen babies in the room, too, but they weren't in the incubators. Instead, they drifted in the air like stray balloons. They wore diapers and onesies, and one of them trailed a blanket off one foot. They were shrouded in colours the Diver had never seen before, each one a different shade. There was no end to the colours in the Drift. The babies didn't make a sound and the Diver knew they were all dead. He'd seen stranger things in the Drift but not many.

"My son was born in this hospital," the Diver said, watching the dead babies drift around. "He spent some time in this room, in one of these incubators." He remembered the sleepless nights spent sitting in a chair, holding him. Now he was sleepless for other reasons.

"Maybe I was the nurse that looked after him," the nurse said.

"It was a long time ago," the Diver said, shaking his head.

"I can't even remember how long I've been here."

The Diver couldn't remember how long it had been since he'd seen Lucas. He couldn't remember the number of days anymore, and that bothered him although he didn't know why it bothered him.

"Where is your son now?" the nurse asked.

The Diver stepped back out of the room and looked up and down the hallway again, but it was still empty.

"I'll tell someone on the other side. They'll send help. You're better off staying with the babies until then."

"Why are you here if not to help?" the nurse asked, following him out into the hall.

"I'm a diver," he said. "People hire me to look for things in The Drift."

"What kind of things?"

"Things that can't be replaced. Keepsakes they left behind in their apartments when they fled after the crash. Cremation urns. Jewelry. Maybe pets if their owners think they're somehow still alive. Sometimes they just want me to bring the bodies back."

"Do they ever hire you to find missing people?"

The Diver looked back at the floating babies in the nursery. He already knew the next question the nurse would ask.

"Can you find someone for me?" she said.

The Diver didn't say anything, so she went on. She looked back at the babies now, too. "I've been trying to reach my daughter. But she's not answering her phone."

"None of that stuff works in the Drift," the Diver said. "No one knows why."

"I want to know that she's all right." The nurse closed her eyes. "I just want to see her again."

The Diver didn't say anything for a moment but he knew he couldn't refuse her. He'd never refused anyone who'd asked him to find someone in the Drift.

"She's a nurse, too," the nurse said, like she knew what the Diver was thinking. "She worked downtown, in a walk-in clinic."

"Which one?" the Diver asked, but the nurse just shook her head.

"I've never been there," she said. "Why would I go to a clinic?"

The Diver nodded and turned back to the stairs. "I'll look for her but I never make any promises."

"What about you?" the nurse asked.

"What about me?"

"Who are you looking for?"

He left the nurse alone with the babies and went back down the stairs. By the time he found his way out onto the street again, the ghosts were gone.

The Diver had never told anyone he'd started diving the Drift because he was looking for Lucas. His son had disappeared in the crash, as well, although he'd been lost to the Diver for long before that. They'd fallen out over the Diver's previous life as an assets fund manager for a firm that broke apart distressed companies. Something that didn't mean anything at all now. It was a life the Diver could barely remember. Lucas had worked for a credit counselling firm in one of those office towers downtown, as if to atone for his father's sins. The Diver had gone to the office after the crash to look for Lucas, but it had been as empty of signs of life as Lucas's apartment. Broken windows and overturned desks and chairs, but no bodies. The Diver didn't know if Lucas was alive or dead. He thought maybe if he kept searching the Drift he would find some sign of his son. He would at least know.

The Drift had never given him any signs of Lucas, but it did give him a sign of something now. When he left the hospital, the mist of the Drift swirled past him, like a current heading in one direction. Down the street, toward the centre of the city. It was green and red and blue and a dozen other colours now.

The Diver noticed all the cars had been moved while he was in the hospital, too. Where before they had been scattered around the street facing in all directions, left where their panicked drivers had abandoned them after the crash, now they all pointed in the same direction the Drift flowed. The Diver wasn't sure what was happening, but he figured he may as well go along with the Drift, too.

The Drift was always moving, but never like this. It slowly shifted across several dozen blocks of the city around the crash site, moving this way and that way. Sometimes it left the streets at its edges uncovered, but it always came back, like a tide, and covered them up again. That was how it earned its name. That was why the barricades and caution tape never came down. It was a gradual process, though, and not something you could see happening. The Diver had never seen the Drift flow like this before.

He checked his oxygen level on the air tank and saw he had maybe an hour left. Enough to reach the city centre and explore for a few minutes and still get back. The longer he stayed downtown, the greater the chance he'd run out of air before he could make it out of the Drift. But he figured he'd have to chance it. There weren't many divers that went as deep into the Drift as he did. If he didn't look for the nurse's daughter, no one probably would.

He reached the next block and now all the cars on the street were filled with water, even though there was no water to be seen anywhere in the street itself. Dark shapes moved within the cars, pressing up against the glass as if to look at him. The Diver kept walking. He'd learned not to look closely at the strange things that happened in the Drift.

He couldn't ignore the sounds, though.

He was looking up at a billboard over the street at the next intersection when he heard the shots. The billboard showed white clouds in a blue sky with the words You Can't Put a Price On. The Diver didn't know what he couldn't put a price on because the rest of the sign was burned away. The shots were the jackhammer sound of automatic weapons fire. They went on for a couple of seconds and then stopped at the same time the Diver did. It sounded like they were a few blocks distant. The Diver didn't know what they meant. He wasn't sure if the sound meant the ghosts were ahead of him or if it was just another strange element of the Drift.

He waited for a minute but he didn't hear any other sounds, so he kept on walking. He came across the other diver a few minutes later, coming down the street toward him. The Drift parted around him like it was a river flowing around debris. They met in front of a clothing store that held a jumble of fallen mannequins in its broken window.

The man wore a tank and regulator like the Diver's. He was dressed in an urban camouflage uniform with a black backpack. He also wore goggles that looked like they were meant for skiing or some similar sport. He held an assault rifle in one hand but he didn't aim it at the Diver because he was leaning on it instead, using the weapon to keep himself standing. His stomach and legs were wet with blood.

"I think the ghosts are actually real ghosts," the other man said, like he knew the Diver. "Because they don't die when you shoot them. The bullets just go right through them." He didn't seem to notice that the Diver didn't have a gun or that there didn't seem to be anyone else around.

The Diver looked around for someplace for them to hide and saw the pharmacy across the street. The windows had shattered and fallen away but the shelves inside looked untouched.

"There might be something ..." he said, stepping over the broken glass and into the pharmacy. He didn't know how to finish because he wasn't a doctor. He wasn't sure what the other man needed.

"We need to get out of here," the man in the camouflage gear said but followed him inside anyway. He staggered down one of the aisles and sat in a chair by the pharmacists' station. He looked back outside and shook his head. "This is like a dream."

The Diver had thought that many times himself but didn't say anything. He grabbed a bottle of Advil off a shelf and tossed it to the other man. "Take some of these while I try to find something to stop the bleeding." He looked up at the signs hanging from the ceiling, but he wasn't sure which one applied to this situation. He finally decided on First Aid and headed for that aisle. "Are they following you?" he asked.

"We scattered in all directions when they attacked," the other man said around a mouthful of Advil. "They went after the others. But they'll come back for me."

The Diver collected all the boxes of bandages he could find. The regular ones for small cuts and scrapes, the long ones used to treat athletic injuries and the others. He went back to the other diver, who laughed and then winced at the pain it caused him.

"I've got better in my backpack," he said.

The Diver dropped the boxes of bandages on the floor and leaned over the man to open his backpack. There was a roll of garbage bags inside and a box of latex gloves on top of a bundle of dust masks. There was also a crowbar and hacksaw, and underneath those a roll of surgical tape.

"You don't usually see divers so deep in the Drift," the Diver said. He was trying to ask a question without asking any questions.

"We were trying to reach the ship," the other man said. "The alien ship." Like there were any other kinds.

The Diver gently pushed the man back so he could unzip his jacket. The man's white shirt underneath had turned nearly black with blood in its lower half. The holes in the shirt were small but the Diver knew by the amount of blood that the bullets had hit something significant. The Diver wiped his hand on his pant leg.

"We weren't going to do anything that mattered," the man said. "Not anymore. We were just trying to find things to sell."

The Diver wrapped the tape around the man's stomach even though he didn't think it would do any good. "Things to sell." He wound the tape around and around until he couldn't see any of the blood on the shirt anymore.

"Artifacts. People's valuables. Whatever," the man said.

"The crash wiped out the financial district and now everything is in ruins," the Diver said. "And you're looking for things to sell."

"None of us have worked since the crash," the man said, but his words were a whisper now. His eyelids fluttered several times as he tried to take in the blue cloud that was coalescing around his head.

"What is that?" he asked. "Am I seeing things?"

The Diver didn't say anything. He knew it was a sign the other man was dying. The cloud that was taking shape was the manifestation of grief, the grief of the people that loved and cared about the other diver. He'd seen it countless times before, sometimes around bodies, like the babies in the hospital, sometimes around things people had left behind in the Drift. Usually photos and pieces of clothing and that sort of thing. The grief was always a different colour. As if there were infinite shades of grief.

That was when the Diver heard the crunch of boots on broken glass outside the pharmacy. He moved fast, heading for the far end of the store. He didn't bother trying to save the other diver. He left the roll of surgical tape hanging from him. He knew the other diver couldn't be saved.

He hit the last aisle and turned up it. He walked as fast as he could past rows of greeting cards while still remaining silent. If it was the ghosts again and they had spread out, he was trapped. He wouldn't get out of the pharmacy alive. But he could hear the other man muttering where he'd left him in the chair, and he hoped that the sound would draw the ghosts.

The Diver paused at the end of the aisle and looked around the corner of the shelves. Rows of cash registers were in between him and the broken windows that led to the street beyond. The cash register nearest him had a box of condoms and some mouthwash on the conveyor belt, but the others were empty. The Diver didn't see ghosts in the front of the store or in the street outside. That could only mean they were in the store, most likely moving down the aisles toward the other diver.

The Diver walked past the cash register in front of him and toward the empty window. He had almost reached it when a burst of gunfire erupted behind him. He threw himself through the window, expecting to feel the shots hit him any second. But nobody was firing at him. He got to his feet outside, brushing pieces of broken glass from his shirt and pants, and looked back into the store. He still didn't see anyone. They must have been shooting the other diver.

The Diver knew he wouldn't be able to outrun the ghosts or whoever it was in the pharmacy. The street was too open to get very far. He had to hide and hope for the best. So he went over to the clothing store and stepped up into the window, careful not to cut himself on the shards of glass that remained in the window frame. He lay down on the floor of the display, which featured a mock miniature cityscape that had been largely crushed by the mannequins. He pulled a couple of the mannequins over him and waited like he was just another body, holding his breath so the regulator wouldn't make any sounds.

He lay there for less than a minute before he heard the boots crunching on glass again, this time outside the window of the clothing store. Something white moved at the edge of his vision. A ghost. He waited for the sounds to pause, for someone to start pulling the mannequins off of him, but none of that happened. The ghosts, for it sounded like there were several of them, kept walking. The sounds faded away and then the Diver couldn't hear anything at all, not even his own breathing.

He wanted to wait there longer, to make sure the ghosts had moved on, but he didn't have enough air left in his tank. He needed to get moving.

He pushed the mannequins off him and looked out into the street. It was empty again. He climbed out of the window and down onto the sidewalk. The glass underfoot was all broken into tiny shards now, as if countless people had walked upon it. The Drift swirled around him in a rainbow of colours as it kept flowing toward the city centre. He followed it once more.

He came across an ATM in the side of a building that was spitting out money. It didn't resemble any money the Diver had ever seen before. It was made of paper and plastic and what looked like glass. Some of the pieces were square while others were triangular. Like the Drift, it was all different colours, blue and green and red and everything else. Some of it fell to the ground while other pieces floated past the Diver.

He stopped at the ATM and stared at it because he remembered it. He'd stood here once before with Lucas, the last time he had seen him. Before the crash. They'd met for lunch at a restaurant down the block. The Diver looked that way and sure enough, there it was. He could see the tables through the window. They were set with plates and cutlery as if the dinner service was about to begin, even though the place was dark and empty.

After they had eaten, the Diver and Lucas had walked along the same sidewalk the Diver walked now, until they had reached the ATM. The Diver had taken out money, although he didn't remember how much. There had been a homeless man standing by the ATM. He had asked for money and the Diver had said no without really looking at him. The homeless man had walked out into the street cursing and held up his hands to stop the traffic. The Diver couldn't remember what he'd said. Maybe something about the homeless man needing a job. Or maybe he'd said something about how the homeless man should stop bothering those with jobs. But he remembered what Lucas had said.

"Maybe he had a job," his son had said, watching the homeless man sit down in the middle of the street. "Maybe he lost it when you took apart his company looking for loose change."

The Diver looked into the street now. It was clogged with abandoned cars, the doors on some of them hanging open like the owners had known they were never going to come back. He could see bags of groceries piled up in the back of a van, and an empty child seat in another car. There was an open space in the street where the Diver thought the homeless man may have sat. He wondered what had happened to him.

The Diver thought maybe the fact he had stumbled across the ATM was another sign, so he kept following the Drift.

It led him to the strangest scene he had witnessed yet, and he had witnessed many strange things in the Drift. He turned a corner at an intersection and saw all the cars on the new street were floating in the air, like the babies had been back at the hospital. They moved like garbage caught in the water, some spinning slowly end over end, while others bobbed in place. There was more debris among them: a couple of baby strollers, a woman's long black jacket, a half-opened umbrella, bits and pieces of food that looked as if they hadn't aged any in the Drift.

The Diver stopped and stared. He wasn't sure if he should walk this way or not. He didn't know what he would do if he lifted off the ground and started floating, too. It took him a moment to notice the walk-in clinic beside an Apple store in the ground floor of one of the buildings, a modern glass-and-metal tower that bent this way and that as it climbed through the air. He thought its odd shape had more to do with the architect than the Drift, though. The building across the street looked normal enough. It was older, raised in a time when they still adorned towers with gargoyles and style. The gargoyles were all facing different directions, but the head of one on the third floor was turned his way, as if it were looking at him. The Diver wished he had more than a knife. It wasn't the first time he'd wished that.

The Drift seemed to have stopped flowing now. The Diver figured if it had been a sign, this must have been the place it was leading him toward. He looked around the street and saw a Starbucks, a dry cleaner's, a convenience store and a sushi place. He went over to the walk-in clinic and looked through the window, because he couldn't see why the Drift would have led him to any of the other places.

An empty coffee cup and a magazine floated around the inside of the clinic, but there were no signs of life. The windows were still intact so he opened the door and went inside. The seats were all empty, not even a piece of clothing left behind. The Diver checked each of the examination rooms, but they were empty, too, other than an anatomy poster floating over the examination table in one.

It was only when he reached the nurses' station at the rear of the clinic that he saw why he had been drawn here. A bulletin board on the wall held a few charts and memos and several photos. Among them was a picture of two women in scrubs standing in front of the ER at the hospital. The Diver didn't recognize the younger woman in the picture, but he recognized the older woman who had her arm around the younger one. The nurse with the babies.

He took the photo from the bulletin board and studied it for a moment. Then he put it in his pocket and went back outside. He had only so much air.

Back on the street with its floating cars and everything else, he glanced up at the gargoyle that he thought had been looking at him. And saw that it was in fact looking at him. It had turned its head to gaze down at the clinic now, and it appeared to be staring right at him.

The Diver stopped in the doorway and stared back at the gargoyle as a wheelchair tumbled end over end past him. A blanket was caught on one handle of the wheelchair and waved like a flag in the air.

"You need to hide," the gargoyle said. "The ghosts are coming."

The Diver didn't see its lips move but he heard its words anyway. He decided there were only two possible options for what was happening.

The first was that he was going mad, if he wasn't mad already. The second was that the gargoyle was actually talking to him. If it was the first case, then there wasn't much he could do and playing along with his madness likely wouldn't hurt. If it was the second case, then he needed to hide immediately.

The Diver went across the street to the other building, ducking under a low-floating delivery van as he did so. Its bumper hit the pavement and the van bounced higher into the air, somehow threading its way between a bus and a car. The Diver wondered if it was just luck or if there was something guiding the vehicles as they moved through the Drift.

He went into the building through a revolving door on the ground floor. He was in a lobby with a tiled floor and art deco paintings of airships and skyscrapers on the walls. He found the stairs and made his way up to the fourth floor, where the gargoyle was. The doors were propped open at each landing, so there was enough light that he could see the stairs this time. He came out into a long hall lined with office doors and windows at either end. The carpet was worn and the walls were scuffed. One of the office doors said Mysterio Magic and another said Particularly Private Investigations. The Diver ignored them both and went to the window that overlooked the street he had been on. It had an old latch that allowed him to open the window and swivel it outward enough for him to climb onto the ledge. His air tank hit the window when he did so, but it didn't crack the glass. The Diver was relieved about that. He didn't want to add to the damage in the city.

He kept one hand on the wall and walked along the ledge, trying not to look down. The gargoyle was at the corner of the building. It watched him come but didn't say anything until he sat down beside it. He had to turn sideways to stay on the ledge because of the air tank, and he put a hand on the gargoyle to keep his balance. It didn't seem to mind.

"Tell me if I'm going crazy so I don't waste any more air talking to you," the Diver said to the gargoyle.

"*You should probably be quiet anyway,*" the gargoyle said and turned its head to look down the street, the way the Diver had come originally.

A half-dozen ghosts came along the street now, spread out in a loose line like before. They looked in all the cars they passed, and under them. They looked in the storefronts. They even looked in the garbage bins at the intersections of the streets, though the Diver didn't know how anyone would have managed to hide in one of them. The one place they didn't look was up, otherwise they would have seen the Diver sitting beside the gargoyle.

The ghosts went down the street and disappeared into the Drift. The buildings faded into dark shapes amid clouds of white and purple and orange and all the other colours that flowed into and through each other. They were silhouetted by a strange glow that came from farther beyond them, a glow that didn't make any sense to the Diver's mind. It was every colour imaginable at once and no colour at all. The Diver had seen the glow on many dives but had always stopped himself from getting too close. It was the alien ship and he wasn't sure he wanted to know what he would find at the crash site.

"*Those guys are assholes,*" the gargoyle said.

The Diver turned to look at the stone creature. "That's not exactly the sort of thing I would expect a gargoyle to say," he said.

"*I'm not a gargoyle,*" the gargoyle said. "*Not really.*"

"You look like a gargoyle."

"*I used to be a day trader. I worked in one of those offices over there.*" The gargoyle looked in the direction the ghosts had gone. "*I saw the ship come down. It was like a piece of the sky had broken and fallen off. It crashed right into a building I'd worked in a few years back, before I'd traded jobs. I thought I'd gotten lucky.*" The gargoyle made a sound like rocks knocking together. The Diver figured it to be a laugh, although he couldn't be certain.

"I take it you weren't a gargoyle back then."

"*I don't know, maybe some people said I was. But I was just another man, you know?*"

"So what happened?"

"*People went up to the ship to see if they could help. I watched the whole thing from my office window. The cops hadn't managed to quarantine the area yet. There were some military guys there but they were still getting out their white suits and stuff. Some people walked up to the ship and found a door. They opened it like the ship was just a car or something. The door wasn't even locked. Maybe it had broken in the crash. Maybe whatever was inside wanted them to open it. I guess it doesn't matter anymore.*"

"The ghosts are soldiers then?" the Diver asked.

"*They're not anybody,*" the gargoyle said. "*They're not soldiers any more than I'm a gargoyle.*"

The Diver took a deep breath from his air tank. He was worried he was maybe breathing too much of the air of the Drift and something in it was affecting his mind. He looked at the gauge on the tank and saw he was down to his last quarter of air. He wouldn't be able to make it back out of the Drift on the tank.

"*They opened the door on the alien ship and everything exploded. There was this flash of light. Or maybe lights. All the colours. It blew up the people who opened the door. It blew up everyone else that was even near it. The soldiers and the cops and everyone that had gone up to the ship to look at it. It blew up all of us in the office. It knocked me through all the walls and windows out of the office. It knocked me all the way into this gargoyle on this building.*"

The Diver looked at him for a long moment. It was a strange claim, but it wasn't any stranger than some of the things the Diver had seen in the Drift.

"So your body is inside there?" He put his hand on the gargoyle's shoulder. It felt like stone.

The gargoyle suddenly reared up, standing on its legs and spreading its wings wide. The Diver fell back and nearly went over the side of the ledge, but managed to hold himself up.

"*There is nothing inside me,*" the gargoyle said. "*My body is gone. This is all I am now. This is all we are now. We are all trapped in The Drift and we will never be ourselves again.*"

"Who opened the alien ship?" the Diver asked.

"*A man. A woman. All of us. Does it matter?*"

"Maybe. Maybe it matters to someone."

"*Tell it to the ghosts,*" the gargoyle said, looking past the Diver again.

The Diver turned and saw one of the ghosts walking back down the street out of the Drift. The ghost carried an assault rifle in its hands. The ghost was looking up this time, right at the Diver and the gargoyle.

"*Good thing I'm trapped in something that's made out of stone, but you'd better get out of here.*"

The Diver was already moving, pulling himself through the window before the ghost could shoot him. He ran for the stairs and went down them two at a time. Somehow he managed to not fall. He thought that if he had, he wouldn't have been able to reach the lobby before the ghost. But the ghost still wasn't at the building when the Diver ran out of the stairwell.

He went out into the street without stopping and lunged behind a cargo van that came tumbling down toward him. There was the sound of hammering on metal, and the Diver knew without looking that the ghost was shooting the van. The Diver kept moving, keeping the van between them as it drifted down the street. He ran to the dark Apple store. The door was closed but someone had broken all the glass out of it, so the Diver ducked and tucked his arms in and went through the door. His air tank clanged off the side of it, so he knew there'd be no hiding from the ghost now.

He ran deeper into the store, slipping off the air tank as he went. He laid it behind a table of iPhones on the right. He opened up the regulator to free flow, and the sound of hissing air filled the silent store. The Diver grabbed an iMac from the wall to the left and dropped behind a table full of iPads just as the van lifted back up into the air and the ghost came toward the store.

This time the Diver didn't hear broken glass crunching underfoot like he had when he'd hid under the mannequins. He didn't know where the ghost was until it appeared in between the tables and pointed its gun at the Diver's air tank on the floor.

The Diver rose up behind the ghost and lifted the iMac over his head. The ghost sensed the movement and spun about as the Diver brought the iMac crashing down, straight into the ghost's dark face visor. The edge of the iMac crashed through the thick lens and into the ghost's face beyond.

Only there was no face. The iMac didn't hit anything. Instead, it kept going without hitting resistance until it caught the back of the suit's head and pulled it down. The ghost lifted up off its feet, caught on the iMac, and fired a burst from the gun into the store's ceiling as the Diver stumbled forward, off balance, and then fell to the floor, upending the ghost.

He landed on the ghost and he felt all the air rush out of the suit under his weight, like he'd fallen on a blow-up doll and ruptured it. An explosion of white light burst from the broken visor of the ghost's suit, which still had the iMac embedded in it. The suit deflated and the ghost was still.

The white light drifted toward the door, shifting from a cloud into a humanoid shape as it went. It walked through the doorway and out into the street. The Diver picked himself up off the floor and looked down at the suit, which remained empty. When he looked back at the street, the light was gone.

The Diver wasn't sure what had happened. Maybe the ghosts were people that had been blown up like the gargoyle. Maybe they'd been blown into the suits and animated them in the same way. Maybe they were aliens from the crashed ship. Maybe they were something else entirely. The one thing he did know was he had to keep moving. The shots the ghost had fired were sure to draw other ghosts.

He strapped on the air tank again and cut off the free flow of the regulator. There was almost no air left now. He picked up the ghost's gun and slung it over his shoulder. He left the iMac and the ghost's empty suit lying together on the floor.

Then he went back out into the Drift.

He looked up at the gargoyle and it looked back down at him but didn't say anything this time.

He went back to the hospital the same way he had come. Away from the clinic and the vehicles drifting through the air. Past the ATM that still spat strange currency out into the world. Past the pharmacy, where he imagined the dead diver was still inside. Past the shop with the mannequins, where he had hidden from the ghosts. He breathed deep of the Drift now because he had no choice.

He didn't move with any stealth and didn't try to hide but he saw no ghosts. He didn't see anyone else until he saw his reflection in the doors to the emergency room. He looked at himself for a moment and then went inside. He took off the air tank and laid it on a stretcher in the waiting room, along with the assault rifle.

The nurse was in the nursery with the babies again. She sat in a chair holding one close to her and humming a lullaby while she watched the others drift around the room. She looked at the Diver when he entered but didn't say anything.

"I found your daughter," the Diver said.

The babies all spun around to look at him with their dead eyes. But the Diver only looked at the nurse.

The nurse looked at the Diver, then past him, as if she expected to see her daughter step out of the shadows behind the Diver.

"Outside," the Diver said, and he went back down the stairs and through the waiting room and out into the street again.

He stood there for a moment, watching the Drift swirl across and through the empty cars and abandoned strollers and forgotten purses on the sidewalk and everything else. He saw colours he had never seen before bloom and fade away in seconds. For the first time in the Drift, he realized he couldn't hear the sound of his breathing.

The nurse came out a minute later, the babies swirling around her. She'd let go of the one she'd been holding and her hands were free now. She looked around again, up and down the street, then back at the Diver.

"Your daughter is dead," the Diver told her. "And so are you."

The nurse kept staring at him and said nothing. The babies spun around them faster, stirring up the Drift.

"I don't know what happened to you," the Diver told her. "But they left you for dead along with the babies when they evacuated the hospital. Maybe they were going to come back for you, but the Drift . . ."

The Drift swirled around them in what seemed like every colour imaginable and many that weren't. It grew thicker by the second. The nurse's features were starting to blur now, and the babies were slipping in and out of the mist as they circled.

"I know what happened to her, though. She was close to the crash. There was an explosion. It made people into other things. It made the Drift."

Maybe it had been the nurse's daughter who had opened the door to the spaceship and caused the explosion, the Diver thought. She would have been the sort of person who tried to help. Maybe.

"She's dead," the nurse said, looking off in the direction of the crash.

"No more than you," the Diver said. "She was blown up. But not into nothing. She was blown into something else. She's the Drift. I think most of the people who went missing in the crash are the Drift."

His son. He knew now his son was part of the Drift. He didn't know how he knew that, but he knew it.

The nurse looked back at the Diver. "So the world has ended then?"

"Maybe," the Diver said. "For some of us, anyway."

"And what happens next?" the nurse asked.

"I don't know," the Diver said.

The babies drifted away, off into the Drift in all directions. The nurse let them go. Maybe she wasn't a nurse anymore. The Diver wasn't sure. He wasn't even sure if he was the Diver anymore.

The babies disappeared one after another, and then the Drift wrapped itself so thickly around the nurse that the Diver couldn't see her. The shifting colours shone so bright he couldn't look at her anyway. He left her there and went down the street.

He walked until he found himself at the intersection where he had last seen his son alive. He stopped by the ATM, which was still dropping its strange currency onto the ground. There didn't seem to be any more of it now than there had been before. Maybe a wind came along every now and then and moved it. Or maybe something else happened.

The Drift seemed to be more active here, too. It swirled around the cars left in the street and on the sidewalk. It moved in a circular motion, like a whirlpool. As if more of it was flowing into the intersection every second. It spun around an open spot in the middle of the street. The place where the homeless man had sat down so long ago.

The Diver stood there for a moment, looking at all the abandoned cars. He wondered what had happened to the people that had once been in them. Then he went out into the street, to the empty spot the Drift had left for him. The Drift swirled closer and faster now, a blur of colours. The Diver sat on the ground and opened his arms and let the Drift shroud him.

Beat
THE GEEKS

Otto notices the rash on his arm during an episode of *Beat the Geeks.* This is the season of the reality science genre. Actors infiltrate university classes and seduce the profs with essays secretly written by their rivals and teams of relationship therapists. The actors break up with the profs in lecture halls full of students by reading their email exchanges aloud, until the profs throw their laser pointers at them or run from the room. Other actors pretend to be grant administrators. They drop by labs to tell researchers they've won millions in funding. They say with a straight face that nothing is more important than the researchers finding out whether fruit flies can conceive of an afterlife. Hidden cameras record everything. Viewers vote on which actors did the best job. The winners get spots in real movies. Websites keep track of scientist suicides.

Otto sits on the couch with his tablet and watches an astrophysicist hold the hand of a woman in a black dress as they sit on a bench by the ocean. The astrophysicist tells the woman the latest theories all point to the universe being infinite. He says this means that anything imaginable is out there, as well as lots of things that aren't. He looks up at the sky and says somewhere the two of them are sitting on this same beach on another earth, having this same conversation. The woman is actually transgendered and used to be a man, but the astrophysicist doesn't know that. She looks over her shoulder, into the hidden camera mounted in the collar of a black Lab eating a dead seagull, and smiles. The astrophysicist keeps staring at the sky. He says there are an infinite number of them playing out this very scene throughout the universe right now, but Otto has already fallen asleep.

By the next morning, the rash has spread across Otto's body. He scratches at it on the way to the shower, tearing off flakes of skin that drift to the floor. After his shower, he checks his favourite porn sites on the tablet before getting dressed. There are more than a thousand updates since he checked last night. He gets ready to masturbate as he skims through the pictures and videos at the kitchen table, but there's nothing he hasn't seen before. He makes scrambled eggs and toast for breakfast.

After he washes the dishes and puts them away, he watches a show in which actors posing as lab assistants add chemicals to scientists' experiments to create humorous results, such as explosions that set the scientists on fire, or fumes that cause the scientists to hallucinate and call their department heads to tell them what they really think of their lab space. Otto keeps scratching his rash the whole time and wonders if it has something to do with his unemployment.

Otto has been out of a job for three months. He used to work in a lab himself, growing stem cells into human body parts to be used for transplants. Then his job was outsourced to a lab in Brazil. The manager who escorted Otto and his box of personal belongings out to the parking lot told him the new lab was run mainly by robots. "It's just skin," he told Otto. "It grows itself." The box of Otto's personal belongings still sits by the door, where he dropped it when he came in that day.

Otto decides the rash is probably from a lack of exercise. He puts on a layer of sunscreen and goes for a long walk, past rows of coffee shops full of other unemployed people and bus stops with homeless men sleeping on the benches.

When he comes back, he is sunburned despite the sunscreen. He closes all the blinds and has a cool shower, but it doesn't do anything to soothe the burning in his skin. He goes to bed and has nightmares about a world in which the sun never sets and is always at high noon. He scratches at himself in his sleep. He doesn't see the skin flakes fall to the floor and skitter away. He doesn't see them join together into a blob and creep under the bed.

The next day, after peeling off more chunks of burned, dead skin and dropping them on the floor, where the blob consumes them when he's not looking, Otto goes to a walk-in clinic. He asks the doctor for cream for his rash and sunburn. She writes him a prescription to make them both go away. She tells him she saw a show about a rise in solar flares. She says maybe this could be the cause of the rash and burn. She says the sun is going to collapse in on itself and suck them all into it. She says it's going to be the opposite of the Big Bang. She says then things are supposed to start all over again.

Otto doesn't know if that means the world will never end or it will never begin. He asks the doctor if she made the show up, if it's really just a placebo. The doctor adds a note to the prescription and says she's stocking up on drugs for when the end comes. She says she doesn't think it'll be long now. She says Otto should make sure to use all of the cream. Otto imagines what would happen next if this were a video on one of the porn sites he follows.

Otto goes to a nearby supermarket to get his prescription filled. The supermarket is identical to the one in his neighbourhood. The pharmacy inside is in the same place as the one in his neighbourhood. Even the pharmacists look the same. Otto browses the magazine aisle while he waits. All the same actors are on the covers. He doesn't even need to read the articles to know what they say.

When he goes home, the blob of skin has shaped itself into a small child, a toddler. It hides in the closet while Otto makes himself a sandwich. It eats little pieces of dandruff, forgotten hairs, a toenail, and grows larger.

Otto takes off his clothes and rubs the prescription cream all over his body. He doesn't want to get any on the couch, so he stands while he watches the latest episode of *Beat the Geeks*. Actors pretending to be government officials present scientists with fake meteorites holding fake alien fossils. The scientists hold each other and cry.

The winning actor is announced at the end of each *Beat the Geeks* episode. The actors thank their agents and talk about how the show was a great opportunity. Videos behind them show the faces of the scientists when the hosts break their disguises as cops or university janitors or homeless people on the street and tell them the truth, that everything is fake.

Otto never watched *Beat the Geeks* when he was still employed as a lab assistant. He was afraid he'd see himself on it one day. But now he can't get enough of it. He'd watch it every waking minute if he could.

When he goes to sleep that night, the creature creeps to the side of his bed and breathes in his breath.

When Otto gets up in the morning, he finds the creature sitting on the couch, going through his box of personal belongings from the lab. It's fully grown now, but not quite formed. Its skin looks melted, and hair juts out of its body in scattered clumps. But Otto can tell he's looking at himself. It's even wearing the pants and shirt he wore the day before.

Otto stares at the creature and it stares back at him. He yells at the creature to get out of his place. It yells the same thing back at him. He says he's calling the cops. It says the same thing back to him. He calls the cops. It goes back to looking through the box.

By the time the police arrive, the creature has grown to look like Otto even more. He can't tell the difference between them anymore, and neither can the cops, two female officers. One of them asks if Otto and the creature are twins. Otto says he doesn't know who or what this thing is, but he wants it gone. It says the same thing about him.

The cops ask for ID. Otto pulls out his wallet and shows them his driver's licence. The creature pulls out a wallet of its own and shows them its licence. Otto recognizes it as an old one he'd put in a box in the closet for safekeeping. The cops give Otto and the creature their business cards. They tell Otto he's going to have to work this out with himself and then they leave. Otto thinks about double dates.

He doesn't know what else to do, so he sits beside the creature on the couch. They look at each other for a while. Otto tells the creature he's not going anywhere. He doesn't have anywhere to go. It says the same thing back to him. He picks up his tablet and they watch the news and a shopping show and a basketball game and more shopping shows. They watch tornadoes destroy trailer parks on a weather show, and they watch sharks attack scuba divers on a travel show. Then they watch the same news shows and shopping shows again.

During all this Otto notices the creature scratching a rash on its arm. His own rash is gone. He wonders if it was the cream or the shower. He wonders if maybe he's the creature, and it's him. Then he wonders if he's on a new show. Perhaps the new trend is making fun of the unemployed. He looks around for cameras but can't see any. But that doesn't mean they're not there.

That night, it crawls into bed with him. It lies on its side, facing away from him, and sleeps. He thinks about rubbing the prescription cream into its skin. He thinks maybe this will make it go away. But he's afraid to touch it.

In the morning, it wakes him up by telling him about the dream it had. The world was empty except for it. It wandered around the city streets, doing whatever it wanted – eating food, taking clothes, driving cars. Never seeing another human being but its reflection in store windows. Otto had the same dream, but he doesn't say anything.

Otto watches the creature dress in one of his suits and put on his favourite tie. He watches it print off a resumé and leave. He stands at the window and watches it go down the street, then he goes back to bed. He looks at the cops' cards and tries to masturbate. He thinks about the cameras. He can't get it up. He goes back to sleep.

He wakes in the afternoon but doesn't get out of bed. He thinks maybe the creature is gone for good now, but it comes back in the evening. Its tie is loose around its neck, and its breath smells of alcohol. It sits on the couch and stares at nothing. "It's tough out there," it says after a while.

Otto heats them cans of soup for dinner. They don't speak as they eat. They go to bed together after dinner. Otto doesn't dream at all that night.

In the morning, the creature dresses in the same suit and puts on Otto's favourite tie again. It prints off more resumés. It goes out the door and down the street once more. Otto doesn't get out of bed. He lies there and doesn't think about anything.

When the creature comes home, it looks at all of Otto's porn sites. Otto closes his eyes. When he opens them again, the creature is sitting on the couch, but it's dressed in a different shirt and tie. Otto must have slept all night and the next day. The creature watches *Beat the Geeks*. Hidden cameras film cancer researchers watching a fake news show about a cure for cancer being found. The researchers cry. An actor comes into the room and says he's the head of human resources. He says the company won't be needing them anymore. The cancer researchers cry some more.

Otto sees the box of his personal belongings back by the door before he falls asleep.

When he wakes, it's night. He doesn't know how long he's been asleep this time, but he's sore all over and thirsty. He tries to sit up but he doesn't have the strength to move. There's enough light from *Beat the Geeks* in the other room that he can see the creature leaning over him, watching him. Its breath smells of alcohol. Its skin is sunburned, patches already peeling off.

It's a special episode of *Beat the Geeks*. The show secretly revisits the scientists it had tricked in the past to see what's happened to them. The astrophysicist sits on the bench by the ocean, alone, staring up at the sky. He talks to himself, but the microphones can't pick his words out of the wind. The alien researchers study new meteorites. They keep the fake ones with fake alien fossils on a shelf in their lab. The fruit-fly researchers say fruit flies can conceive of an afterlife, but that doesn't mean they believe in it. The researchers say they'll keep up their tests.

Otto waits for the host of whatever show he's in to step out of the closet or climb in through the window and point to all the hidden cameras.

He imagines a world somewhere out there in the universe where he is alone, with no double lying beside him.

He imagines a world where he's still working in the lab, growing body parts for other people.

The creature leans down toward Otto, and he closes his eyes. He feels its breath on his lips.

He imagines a world where anything is possible.

The FURIES

Maybe I was the one who made the Furies. Maybe we all made them. I'm not sure how it happened and I was there when they were born. But I wasn't the one who set them loose on the world. They did that all on their own.

I'll tell you the story as best I can, but I was on a lot of drugs back then. We all were. Designer drugs. Different from the ones I'm taking now. Who can say what they did to my memories? Do you really know what everything you've taken has done to your mind?

Some of you may be thinking I shouldn't tell anyone what I saw. What if they come for me next?

But that's exactly why I am telling you. Because I'm afraid. Not afraid that they'll come for me. I'm afraid that they won't come.

I guess I should say I'm sorry, even if it is too late.

Anyway. This is the way I remember it now.

* * *

THE WAY the Furies began was with another model shoot. It was a small job, a day's worth of work to profile a new line of Dior ties for women. The ties looked just like men's ties except for the patterns, which were some intern's idea of what women would want to wear: Medusa heads and bloodied mobs of women tearing people apart and Amazons and that sort of thing. The ties were just accessories but they were Dior, so that still meant an ad buy and marketing campaign, even if it was only at the back of magazines.

One of the agencies I sometimes worked with hired me to manage the campaign, and because I'd blown all my savings on a hazy, summer-long trip through Thailand and Cambodia, I signed on. I won't mention the name of the agency because no one there was to blame for what happened next.

There's not much you can do with ties in a photo shoot, so I knew I'd have to get creative. As soon as the agency texted me the contract, I went for a drive in my Tesla. I'd bought the car with money the same agency had paid me to do the Green Coffin campaign. You may as well live life while you can, right? I didn't have any destination in mind. I just drove to see what the night held.

The bigger agencies have location scouts and professional networkers for jobs like this, but all I had was me. That was partially why I took the drugs. Sometimes I felt like different people and I could see things from their perspective. It seemed to work out all right most times, so I didn't feel any need to change.

I'd started driving at night after my mother was killed in a car crash. She'd been coming home from her shift at the club, driving her Cavalier that cost more to fix than monthly payments on a new car would have. But who was going to loan her the money? She looked like a welfare junkie on paper, because her income was mostly cash. A guy who was getting blown by an escort he'd met on Tinder ran a stop sign and T-boned her. I hadn't even recognized the car in the tow yard afterward when I'd gone to pick up her things. It was just a crumpled mass of metal and broken glass stained with different fluids. It was something that shouldn't have existed at all. That was when I decided to get into the commercial photography business. I wanted to make the world look better than it really is.

The night drives were where I got most of my ideas. I'd once organized a Polo underwear shoot in an abandoned farmhouse I'd found on the side of a country road. Another time I set up an H&M shoot for their website in a decommissioned submarine turned party boat. I'd learned about the sub from a group of men on a bachelor party who were stopped in the middle of the street, trying to bring the would-be groom in the limo back from an OD. I'd even once done a Prada wedding dress shoot at the scene of a fifteen-car pileup that had killed three. The world is a constant disaster, and the only way to escape it is through the dreams we sell each other.

So I drove around at night, which wasn't that bad given my terrible insomnia in those days. Between the drugs and jet lag and parties, it was a wonder any of us slept at all. I don't sleep much these days, either, but for entirely different reasons.

The Furies shoot happened the way it did because I was following a fire truck with lights and sirens going when I heard the story about the bones on my phone's news stream. The Tesla's speakers made it sound like the voices of the newscasters were inside my head. Construction of the new Heritage Park Mall had been delayed because workers had uncovered the fossilized remains of some sort of dinosaur. The fire truck stopped in front of a burning church at the side of the road right after that, and the voices in my head fell silent as my phone's battery died. Maybe that should have been a sign to me, but signs only become clear afterward, when you look back at the ruin you made of your life.

I kept on driving, past the burning church and through the night to the mall. It was maybe half an hour down the road, if I recall correctly, which I may not. The mall was being built in some neglected farm fields outside the city, where there was nothing else in sight. Like it was a mall for ghosts, or people who no longer existed or didn't exist yet. I didn't recognize any of the plants growing in the fields around the mall. I didn't know if they were crops or wild, mutated growths of some sort.

Maybe half the mall had been completed and the parts that were done looked like any other mall in any other part of the country. The wings that weren't finished were just metal beams sticking out of the earth, like the skeleton of some massive creature beyond my understanding. The mall was lit up where it was done, but the lights were all off in the parking lot. There was a ring of lights blazing like small suns at the far end of the mall, though, like some sort of modern Stonehenge. I drove over to them, across a parking lot so empty it didn't even have lines yet.

The pavement ended twenty or thirty yards before the lights, fading away in muddy earth. I left the Tesla at the edge and walked the rest of the way. The ground sucked at my feet, like it was trying to pull me down, and I tried not to think about what it was doing to my Kenneth Cole shoes.

The lights ringed a great pit in the ground, but that was all I had time to see before glowing wisps of light came out of the mall's skeleton. The silvery wraiths transformed into two security guards wearing jackets with reflective stripes. Their jackets were stained with dirt, as if they'd fallen to the ground and hadn't bothered to clean up afterward. They were pointing handguns at me like they were cops or some other people who thought they were important.

"This is a secure site," the closer one said. "We could legally shoot you right now."

"I don't know how secure it is if I could drive right up here," I said. I didn't address the rest of his comment, because experience has taught me it's never a good idea to argue with people pointing guns at you.

"Is this some sort of test?" the other one asked. He spoke with a British accent. "Because we should have been warned there was going to be a test."

"How much to let me see the bones?" I asked.

They looked at me for several seconds, then glanced at each other. And I knew I had them. Security guards are never paid enough to actually care about security. They can always be bought.

"Are you a thief?" the first one asked.

"Why would I be here if I was a thief?" I asked. "The mall's not even done yet."

"He means an antiquities thief," the British one said. "We were warned people might try to steal the bones and sell them."

I didn't know why anyone would want to steal dinosaur bones, but who knew why any of us wanted what we did. I shook my head and slowly reached into my pocket to take out my wallet. They watched me but didn't say anything. They didn't lower their guns, either.

"I just want to look at the bones," I said and took out two hundreds. And they put away their guns and came over to take the bills out of my hand. I stepped to the edge of the pit and looked in without any more problems.

The pit was maybe fifteen or twenty feet deep. The bones jutted out of the ground at the bottom, only partially uncovered. If they were from a dinosaur, then it was a dinosaur unlike any I'd ever seen or imagined. The bones were great black shiny things that curved and twisted like tentacles frozen in mid-movement. I say shiny because they reflected the light like they were made of glass or chrome or some such material. Some of them reached for the stars overhead, while others wrapped around and through their fellows. Each of them was at least twice as tall as me and it looked like only the tips of them had been excavated so far.

"What on earth is it?" I asked, because it was all I could think to say.

"I think it's something from some other earth," the British one said. "I had a girlfriend who went to university once. She said there were all these ages to the earth where it was like a different planet. I think it's from some age that nobody even knew existed."

"I had a girlfriend who got crazy religion," the other one said. "She said dinosaurs were a trick by the Devil to get people to believe in evolution. So maybe the Devil left it here."

"Why would the Devil care if people believe in evolution or not?" the British one said. "Plenty of people who believe in God do the Devil's work."

"What if the Devil evolved like the rest of us?" the first one asked. "What did he evolve from?"

I looked around the edges of the pit. I saw an excavator and a dump truck parked in the shadows. I knew these bones wouldn't be here for long before they were removed and taken to some museum somewhere. Then this pit would just be another empty hole in the ground.

"How much for me to bring some friends back tomorrow night?" I asked.

The two security guards fell silent now, and I turned back to them. I could read the uncertainty in their eyes. I'd been in this situation enough times before. They were weighing the easy money against the possibility of being found out. They glanced at each other again, maybe gauging each other's level of comfort and complicity.

"That would be expensive," the British one said. "Because you're not just some casual passerby if you want to come back with friends."

"My friends are models," I said. And I could see in their eyes that was worth more than any money I had to offer them.

I went back to the Tesla and drove away before they could argue with me. I was in my bed by the time the sun rose, still wearing my muddy Kenneth Coles. For the first time in weeks I slept soundly. Who knows what I dreamed of?

* * *

I RETURNED TO the mall the next night in an old cargo van I'd bought years ago for shoots. I'd added a couple of bench seats and a card table in the back, all bolted to the floor. I normally left it in the parking lot of a Walmart near my condo, so I was really just moving it from one mall to another.

A couple of the models, Portland and Winter, sat in the back. The third model, Titania, sat in the passenger seat with her feet on the dash. Those weren't their real names, of course. Those were their model names.

No one is really named Titania or Portland or Winter. But no agency is going to hire a model named Emily or Madeleine or Sarah. They were still young models, at a point in their career where they couldn't say no to driving in an old cargo van to a pit in the middle of nowhere. They weren't household names yet. Not like they are now.

"One day, when we're famous, we will look back at this day and laugh," Titania said as we drove through the night. She wore a sundress and didn't try to hide the fact she had nothing on underneath.

"There aren't enough drugs in the world to make me laugh about this," Winter said from the back. She sat beside Portland, staring at the photographers on the bench seat across from them. Zimmer and his assistant, Lucky, who were too busy checking their gear to bother looking at the models.

"I've probably got something for that," I said and took one of the baggies out of my pockets. The one with the little purple pills.

"What are those?" Titania asked, eyeing them.

"Internet Trolls," I said. "I had them specially made for me by this chemist I know."

"We eat Internet trolls for breakfast," Titania said with a laugh but she took the bag and passed it around. I don't know who had the pills and who didn't. I just know there were a lot less of them when the bag came back to me.

"This night is like the bottom of the ocean," Titania said, gazing out the passenger window.

"You're a poet," I told her. "That sounds like something a poet would say, anyway."

"I saw this show about the ocean," she went on, like I hadn't spoken. "There are these creatures that have lights that hang in front of their mouths. The lights are to attract other fish to get eaten. The light is a trap. But the other fish go toward it anyway."

"They probably don't know it's a trap," I said. "I don't think any fish actually wants to get eaten."

"Maybe they're models," Zimmer said from the back. "They can't resist the spotlight."

"The fish know it is a trap," Titania said. "They know they will be eaten. But they go anyway. Because it is the only thing of light and beauty in their short, dark lives. They dream of the light and being eaten."

I must have blacked out for a bit while I was driving, because the next thing I remember is pulling into the empty mall parking lot. The security guards were waiting for us when we arrived, standing at the edge of the pit in between two light stands rather than hiding in the shadows. The dirt stains were gone from their jackets, as if they'd cleaned up for us. They didn't point their handguns at me this time, which I was relieved to see. This night could have gone in so many directions.

"Are these the help or are they props?" Titania asked as we all got out of the cargo van.

"I'm Morrison and this is Jesus," the one with the British accent said. I wasn't sure if those were their real names or more working names, like they were models of a different sort.

"Jesus?" Portland asked. "Like the Messiah?"

"I play lead guitar in a band," Jesus said, like that explained it all.

Zimmer and Lucky ignored the security guards and went over to the edge of the pit and stared at the bones.

"This is one seriously messed-up world," Lucky said.

"It's perfect," Zimmer said.

"Are those even bones?" Winter asked, staring down into the pit. She shivered and hugged herself, like it was cold. Maybe it was. I'd had trouble telling the temperature ever since I'd started with the Internet Trolls.

"What else would they be if they weren't bones?" I asked.

"It looks like nuclear waste or something," she said.

"There was a palaeontologist here today and she said they were bones," Morrison said. "She just didn't know what they were the bones of."

"I think I'm going to need more drugs," Titania said, going back into the cargo van to change. The other models looked at the pit a moment longer, then followed her without saying another word.

Jesus dragged a ladder out of the shadows and lowered it into the pit while the models changed into the Dior suits and ties the courier had delivered earlier in the day. The two guards watched the van like they hoped they could catch some glimpse of the models, but I'd covered the windows with aluminum foil the same night I'd bought it. Sometimes I locked myself in there in the day and tried to pretend I was someone, anyone else. I never could but maybe someday.

Zimmer and Lucky climbed down into the pit and set up their camera gear amid the bones. I looked back out across the empty mall parking lot, at the dark clouds that were beginning to drift across the moon, and tried not to shiver myself.

The models came out in their suits and they were transformed. They were no longer the young women who'd been doing drugs in an old cargo van. Now they were executives who radiated power and confidence. They were creatures who belonged to some other plane and who were only temporarily visiting. They were ethereal. A shudder ran through me from I don't know where.

The models went over to the ladder and Jesus practically slid down it to help them descend. Morrison put his hand on my shoulder, as if to steady himself, but didn't say anything. The models smiled a little, as if they knew their power.

But none of us knew what was to come.

The models didn't have to be told what to do. They draped themselves over the bones, lounging on them like they were some sort of modern furniture. They played with their ties suggestively. Winter put the tip of her tie, the Medusas, in her mouth. Titania mock hung herself with her tie of the Amazons. Portland palmed the end of her tie, the one with the mob of bloodied women, and blew a breath toward Zimmer, who was already shooting with his camera. As if she were blowing him a wish.

You can't teach someone how to be a model. All you can do is create a setting or a scene or whatever you want to call it and find a way to let them follow their instincts, to let their true selves out. All you need to do is give them a few cues and they will become what they always have been.

"You're goddesses of a lost world," I called to the models from the edge of the scene. They looked up to the heavens like they truly were fallen and didn't belong in this world. The lights from Zimmer's camera flashes turned their skin ghostly. Those strange bones shone with their warped reflections.

"You're man-eaters," I said, "and the whole world is afraid of you." And now the models pretended to be hunting something through the bones, their teeth bared as if they were ready to pounce. Zimmer shot his camera like a machine gun while Lucky moved the light panel around through the bones to illuminate the models. I could hear Zimmer's breathing through the rapid fire of the shutter.

"Give us that look," I said. "The one that says maybe one day you'll come for me." I stood behind Zimmer when I said it, and they looked right into the camera and through it. I felt another chill inside me, as if something I couldn't see had passed through my body.

Then it happened. Titania stepped behind Portland and grabbed her tie, pulling her back against one of the larger bones thrusting up out of the ground. Winter stepped in and took hold of Portland's hands, raising them above her head and pinning them to the bone. She leaned in and kissed Portland, hard. The two of them pressed back against the bone. And then the bone broke, snapping just behind Portland's head under the weight of their kiss. The top of the bone fell to the ground and black powder billowed out of both ends, in a cloud that engulfed the models.

"Are you fucking kidding me?" Winter said, coughing and gagging as Zimmer clicked away. The ethereal spirit she'd been seconds ago was gone now. She let go of Portland and staggered away, waving her hands to clear the cloud from her face. "This is worse than that garage shoot."

"I think I swallowed some," Titania said. She bent over and stuck her finger down her throat. She immediately started gagging, but she didn't throw up. I hadn't seen her eat anything all night, so I didn't think there was anything in her stomach to actually expel.

Portland just stood there, leaning against the broken bone. She kept her hands above her head, as if the broken part of the bone was still there.

"I feel even more high now," she said. "What was that stuff?"

"It looked like bone powder," Lucky said.

"Bones don't have powder," Zimmer said, still shooting the models.

"These aren't exactly normal bones," Lucky pointed out.

"They broke the bones," Morrison said, holding his head in his hands. "We are in so much trouble."

"Maybe we can glue it back together," Jesus said, looking down at the broken piece of bone lying on the ground. "Maybe no one will ever know."

"They have scientists whose job it is to know that sort of thing," Morrison said.

"I don't care, it was worth it," Jesus said. "You only live once."

Titania just kept on trying to make herself vomit.

"I really don't think you're going to get it out that way," I said.

"It makes me feel better," she said, in between gags. "It's stress relief."

"I am done for the night," Winter said. "I am done for fucking eternity." She tore off the tie and threw it to the ground. I felt the shoot slipping away. Then Winter tore off the suit and wiped the powder from her face with the jacket before throwing it to the ground, too. She stood naked amid the bones. The security guards stared at her. I stared at her. The other models stared at her. Zimmer kept shooting and Lucky kept angling the light panel to get the best light on her.

That was when the rain started.

There were no warning drops to let us know, no gentle mist to give us time to seek shelter. We were suddenly in a downpour that instantly drenched our clothes, those of us wearing clothes, anyway. Winter just turned her face to the sky and laughed.

We all went back up the ladder and piled into the back of the cargo van, joined by Morrison and Jesus this time. We pulled aside the aluminum foil and stared outside as the rain turned the ground into mud and raised steam from the lights. We were in darkness in the van except for the glow of Zimmer's camera screen as he scanned through the photos he'd taken so far.

"You're all going to be famous," he said. "If you don't kill yourselves first."

The models' faces appeared ghostlike around him as they looked at the pictures.

"Do we have enough?" I asked. "Because we should get out of here before the storm gets any worse."

The models looked away from the photos of themselves and stared at me.

"We shouldn't be driving in this van, let alone in this storm," Winter said. I couldn't see if she was still naked or not.

"What if we get stuck out there somewhere?" Portland asked. "I don't even know where out there is."

"We're stuck here," I said.

"But the mall is here," Titania said.

"It's not even built yet," I said.

"Actually, half of it is built and running," Morrison said from somewhere in the darkness. "The lights are on and there's a roof and everything."

"It's like a real mall only without all the people," Jesus said from somewhere else in the van. I was having trouble placing people's positions. "It's like a dream mall."

And that was how we found ourselves in the mall. We went back out into the storm, which was a biblical downpour now. I could barely make out the lights around the pit. Jesus and Morrison led us to a row of steel beams sticking out of the ground much like the bones in the pit and we followed them, trudging through the mud, until we reached a wall of plastic sheeting. The other side was lit up and I could see dim shapes and colours through the sheeting, but it was like looking through a frosty window.

Jesus pulled open a flap in the sheeting and we all went through to the other side. The security guards were right — it was like a real mall.

The ceiling was finished in here, protecting us from the rain. The tiles of the floor were so shiny and new they reflected the lights from the ceiling overhead. I could hear mall music playing faintly through hidden speakers. There were even stores in here. There was a coffee shop to our left and a frame and photo shop beside it. A lottery kiosk was in front of us, and a fountain behind it, with a geyser of water shooting a dozen feet up into the air. To our right was a sporting goods store and a bank. It looked like any other mall, except the signs over the stores were paper banners, and they had the names of businesses I'd never heard of.

The coffee shop was named Expresso, and the frame and photo shop, I Was Framed. The bank was called Bank of Nowhere while the sporting goods shop had a sign that said No Quarter. It was like that for every store as we wandered through the mall. They all looked real – the clothing stores had clothes on the shelves and mannequins in the windows, the jewelry stores had rings and bracelets and earrings in their displays, the bookstores had rows of books, and so on – but they were obviously fake stores.

"What is this place?" I asked. Already I was thinking about what kind of shoots I could set up in there.

"It's the proto-mall," Morrison said. "The mall they create before the real mall."

"Why would anyone want a fake mall?" I asked. "Aren't malls fake enough to begin with?"

"It's like an ad," Morrison said. "They use the proto-mall to sell the mall to the investors and the real stores. So everyone can see what it will look like when it actually opens."

"Like an ad campaign," I said. The security guards nodded, but no one else responded. I looked at the models and saw them staring at the fake stores with glazed eyes. Maybe they were stoned again. Maybe there had been something in that bone powder.

"Do they need the muzak for the proto-mall, though?" I asked. "It's really annoying."

"What muzak?" Morrison asked, and the others looked at me. I realized they couldn't hear it, so it must have been coming from the drugs. I just shook my head and didn't say anything else about that.

I saw now that Winter was wearing Jesus's jacket. I hadn't noticed him give it to her. Or maybe she had taken it. You never know what a model will do.

"I am so fucking hungry," Titania said.

"There's a food court, but none of the food is real," Morrison said. "It's all plastic displays."

"It doesn't matter, they'll just throw it up again, anyway," Zimmer said, and Titania gave him a look.

"I need a washroom," Portland said and Morrison pointed down a side hall. "I'll take you to the staff one," he said. "The mall ones are just props right now, too. We found that out the hard way during one of the tours with the retail scouts."

They went down the hallway and the rest of us continued deeper into the mall. I wasn't worried about Portland being alone with the security guard. I'd once seen her chase down a man who'd taken her picture during a shoot in a school playground. Sure, the man's kids had slowed him, but she would have caught up anyway. She was like some kind of superhero when she was high from the camera. She beat him so badly his kids had to help him to his feet. Then she ran back to the playground to continue the shoot. She was the type who could go far in this business if she didn't OD or marry someone.

The lights flickered a few times and we all looked up at the silver snowflakes suspended from strings far over our heads. There were other things up there, too: satellites and angels and little drones. The theme didn't make any sense to me but I decided it was time to keep things like that to myself.

"How long do you think it would take them to send help if we are trapped here?" Winter asked. "Would anyone even know? Are we even in cell range?" She looked at me as if this entire situation was my fault. Maybe it was in a way.

I took out my phone and looked at the signal, but there wasn't one. I put it back in my pocket and didn't look at Winter again.

"We can always call for help if we need to," Jesus said. "We've got a full communication centre in our office. But there's nothing we haven't been able to handle ourselves yet."

Winter looked back at him and wrapped his coat tighter around herself. "What if it just keeps raining?" she asked. "What if it's the end of days and the mall floods with water and we drown?"

"We'll dig drainage trenches with the excavator outside," Jesus said. "And if that doesn't work, there's a sporting goods store at the far end with kayaks and canoes. We'll keep you safe one way or another." He smiled at her and she smiled back.

"But who will keep you safe?" she asked and laughed, and he laughed along with her.

"We probably should figure out a plan in case this storm lasts and we do get stuck here," I said. There were enough clothes in the fake stores we could stay warm if the power went out, but we'd need to find something to eat. Even the models would get hungry eventually. Then there was the matter of the road. It was probably already flooded in places. I didn't know how long it would take to drain, and we still had to edit the photos and maybe even finish the shoot. I looked around the mall again.

"Maybe we should set up in here," I said. "It's a bit meta, but that could be all right again by the time the campaign starts."

"I don't like being in a mall without people," Winter said. When I looked at her, I saw that Jesus now had his arm over her shoulder. "It's like a ghost mall. Or maybe we're the ghosts."

"It's not completely empty," Jesus said. "I'm here."

"We should fuck," Winter said.

Jesus stared at her, even though that's probably what he had been thinking about all along. Zimmer and Lucky barely seemed to notice as they looked around at the mall, probably gauging the photo opportunities. Titania just rolled her eyes.

"Everywhere we go, she always wants to fuck," she said.

"It's the best stress relief there is," Winter said.

"I'm not arguing the point," Titania said.

"Come on," Winter said and led Jesus into a nearby store. Whiskey Wear, a men's fashion shop. He stared at her the whole time like he wasn't sure if she was real or not. Once they were in the store, she shrugged off his jacket and leapt upon him, wrapping her arms and legs around his body as she kissed him. They fell behind a display of pants and disappeared from sight.

The rest of us waited outside. We all knew it wouldn't be long. This sort of thing happened all the time on location shoots. When models were stressed or bored, they almost always turned to drugs or sex, and sometimes both. It could wreak havoc with a shooting schedule, but there wasn't much you could do about it. If the model stormed off because she was too stressed, you no longer had a shoot, after all.

It took even less time than I was expecting, though. Jesus suddenly screamed and came running out of the store. He was naked and still erect. His shoulders and chest were covered in blood. He held a hand up to his neck, where the blood seemed to be coming from.

"She fucking bit me!" he cried.

That didn't really surprise me because if anyone was the type of person to bite, it was a model. Hell, there were many men who would pay to be bitten by a model. I'm not saying I agree with it or even understand it. It's just that kind of world.

When Jesus staggered up to us and took his hand away from his neck to check the bleeding, though, I saw this wasn't any ordinary bite. A chunk of his neck was missing. I could see the raw, open meat before he slapped his hand back over his wound to cover it.

"What did you do to her?" I asked, starting toward the store. It must have been bad, whatever it was, to make her bite him so savagely. What if he'd done something to her face? I didn't even know if I had all the photos I needed yet.

"How about what she did to me?" He stumbled around behind Titania, putting her between him and the store. She stared at him as he checked his wound again. "Look at all this blood, man. I'm like stigmatic or something now."

I stopped moving toward the store as Winter came running out of it after Jesus. She was naked and covered in blood, too, although I didn't see any wounds on her body. So the blood must have been all his.

That wasn't the only thing that made me stop. There was also the fact that she picked up the clothing racks in her way and threw them to the side, as if she had superhuman strength. Or inhuman. They crashed into other racks or the walls, but she didn't seem to notice. She didn't take her eyes off Jesus. She held a broken aftershave bottle in her hand, the end all jagged shards of glass.

And her eyes were black now. Completely black. As if she'd put in some sort of strange contact lenses when they'd been in there fucking.

She was smiling as well, or maybe snarling. It was an expression somewhere in between the two.

"Somebody stop her," Jesus said. He tried to push Titania toward Winter, but Titania wouldn't go. Instead, she turned to face him and I saw her eyes were clouding over and turning black, too.

"What is wrong with all of you?" Jesus asked, backing away from her.

"We're man-eaters," Titania said with a grin that showed too many of her teeth.

"And the whole world is afraid of us," Winter said with a laugh as she came on.

I recognized the words. They were parroting what I'd said to them earlier.

Jesus fumbled for his gun, but Titania was on him before he remembered he was naked. She moved with surprising speed, grabbing him and throwing him to the ground. She went down with him, biting at his neck herself. A second later, Winter fell upon him, too, ramming the broken aftershave bottle into his side with a scream matched by his own. I watched, paralyzed, as blood sprayed all over the three of them.

"What are these crazy bitches on now?" Zimmer asked, bringing his camera up to shoot the scene.

But then Portland knocked him aside as she came out of nowhere, throwing herself through the group of us watching and down onto Jesus with the others. She took his penis in her mouth, and for a second I thought she was trying to give him a blow job during all the chaos. Then she ground her teeth together and Jesus let out an even worse scream. Portland tore her head away from him and took his penis with her. I could see it in her mouth, blood oozing from it. She snapped it down like a crocodile swallowing a big hunk of meat. Her eyes were as black as the others' and I understood then what was happening.

The black powder from the bones. It had done something to them. It had turned them into these crazed creatures.

I ran forward and kicked Portland in the face. She somersaulted backward off of Jesus and sprawled face down on the floor. I had to stop them from killing the security guard; I didn't think that would be covered by my insurance. I grabbed Winter by the hair and threw her to the side. She screeched, making a sound more like an animal than a person. She lashed out at me with the bottle and raked my side, and I felt the glass cut me through my jacket.

Jesus managed to push himself to his feet, even though Titania was still clinging to him and biting at his neck. She wrapped her arms and legs around him like he was giving her a piggyback ride. He managed a half-run, but for some reason he ran back into the store. Maybe he was blinded by all the blood in his face.

Portland and Winter leapt to their feet and chased after him, ignoring me and the others. They brought him down just inside the store, tackling him and crashing into a trio of mannequins modelling clothing. Jesus screamed again as he fell under their weight, and then the mannequins toppled over on them, hiding the scene from sight.

"This is crazier than usual," Zimmer said, checking his camera to make sure it hadn't been damaged when Portland had hit him.

"We should do something," Lucky said, staring at the shaking mannequins. "We should call security."

"He is security," I pointed out.

"I mean the other security guy," Lucky said.

But Morrison came up the hall toward us at just that moment. He was walking rather than running. He was also holding his head with one hand, which I didn't take to be a good sign.

"That model of yours hit me with a fire extinguisher and then she ran off," he said. "And I think she took my gun. Is this some sort of girls gone wild shoot?"

"We need to call the police and get out of here," I said. "Not necessarily in that order."

"We need some backup all right," Morrison said. "Where's Jesus?"

Jesus cried out again, but it was a sound like he was coming now. An ecstatic cry, not one of pain or fear. We all looked back at the store in time to see Titania rise from the pile of mannequins. She was drenched in blood and grinning. She held up both her hands and it took me several seconds to realize what she was holding. Jesus's head. For some reason Jesus was smiling. She brought his head to her face and kissed it, like he was a lover she hadn't seen in some time.

And I swear he kissed her back.

"I think we should probably take our chances with the storm now," I said.

We all ran back the way we'd come. I looked over my shoulder several times, but I didn't see the models chasing us. They must have been busy with Jesus. I tried my phone but still couldn't get a signal. We all tried our phones but none of us could get signals. Maybe it was the storm. Maybe it was something else.

"Are we all on drugs right now?" Lucky asked as we went.

"Maybe we need more drugs," I said.

"We need to get to the security office," Morrison said, pointing down the hallway where he'd led Portland earlier. "We can call the police on our comm gear."

"I think we may need the army," I said, but we followed him down the hall anyway. We passed a fire extinguisher lying on the floor, and I kicked it out of the way. It was surprisingly light and bounced off the wall and back into our path, nearly tripping me as I leapt over it.

"It's just another prop, so it's empty," Morrison said. "Otherwise she probably would have crushed my skull with it."

I looked around for his gun, but it didn't look like she'd dropped it anywhere in the hallway. So either she'd hidden it somewhere or she still had it.

Morrison led us past the washrooms and through a blank door at the end of the hall. We stopped there, because we were in the security office. But it wasn't what we had expected. There were screens all over the walls, and electronics gear on tables. Some of it was probably surveillance gear, and some was probably the communications gear Morrison had mentioned. It was hard to say for certain because someone had smashed everything in the room. The screens on the walls were all shattered and everything else had been hammered and beaten so heavily I couldn't even recognize what anything was. A tool box was open in one corner of the floor, hammers and screwdrivers and wrenches scattered around it.

"It doesn't look like we're calling anyone for help now," I said.

"We can call them, but I don't think they'll hear us," Morrison said, looking around. "She must have come in here after she knocked me out. But why would she do this?"

"Because they don't want us to escape," I said.

"But why not?" Lucky asked. "They must want out of here just the same as us."

"Because they're hunting us," I said.

Morrison stared at me but didn't say anything. I understood. He hadn't seen what the rest of us had.

"So what do we do now?" Zimmer asked me. I was in charge of the shoot, after all.

"Now we get in the van and drive until we get stuck," I said. "Hopefully they don't like getting wet and won't follow us into the rain. They're still models, after all."

We went back out into the mall but we stopped right away. We could see the models had come this way by the trail of blood that led past the hallway and out to the plastic curtains at the edge of the mall. A big long smear of blood, as if the models had dragged something past and outside.

"They went back to the pit," Zimmer said. "They're already at the van."

"Then we go the other way," I said. I headed back into the mall. "We find a place to hide until someone comes for us or the storm lets off enough that we can make a run for it."

We ran through the mall for a time, but we had to stop every few hundred feet so Zimmer and Lucky could rest. They were burdened down by Zimmer's cameras and their bags of gear. I considered telling them to leave it, but I knew their gear was worth a small fortune. I didn't want to have to pay for it if the insurance company walked away from this mess.

The trail of blood led into the men's wear store where the models had killed Jesus and disappeared in the mess of mannequins still on the floor. We went past it and kept going. For a moment, I thought maybe we were safe.

Then we heard the call for help as we went past a lingerie store a few stores down. It was called Lucky Lady, but as it turned out there was nothing lucky about it for us.

We stopped and looked at the store but saw no one. We looked at each other and I could see everyone else was wondering the same thing:

had we really heard someone call for help or had we just imagined it? What if we had been affected by the strange powder in the pit as well? Who knew what it could be doing to us, to our minds.

Then one of the change room doors at the back of the store swung open and we heard the same weak call for help again. So faint I couldn't even tell if it was a man or a woman.

"Is there anyone else in here?" I asked Morrison, but he just shrugged.

"There's not supposed to be anyone here," he said, looking around. "But people keep sneaking in. Could be some urban explorer kid, or maybe a bone hunter."

"Let's help if we can then," I said. "The more of us there are, the more of a chance we stand against the models."

We went into the store and walked slowly past the bins of panties and bras, and the mannequins on stands wearing more panties and bras and nighties and that sort of thing. We kept an eye on that open change room door the entire time. I came around a rack of flannel pajamas and saw the body lying there on the ground. It looked like a bloodied, misshapen man, curled up in the fetal position. I couldn't see his face because his arms were covering his head. But I could see the bloody ruin of his groin. It was Jesus.

But that was impossible, because I'd seen the models tear Jesus's head off.

"Help me," the man on the floor said again, but this close I could hear it wasn't a man's voice at all. It was a woman's voice.

"We need to get out of here," I whispered and backed away, even as Morrison stepped forward to look down at the body.

"Jesus?" he asked.

The man on the floor chuckled in that woman's voice and sat up. As soon as he dropped his arms away from his head, I saw that it was Jesus but it wasn't. It was Titania, wearing Jesus's skin like a suit. She was wrapped up in it, but it fell from her shoulders as she got to her feet.

She was wearing a red bra and panties, but they were mostly covered in blood and shreds of meat.

"Jesus isn't here anymore," she said with a smile, and I saw more bits of flesh caught in her teeth. "It's just us goddesses of a lost world." More of my words.

Then two of the mannequins threw themselves off their stands and onto Morrison, screaming. Because they weren't mannequins at all – they were Portland and Winter posing as mannequins. We hadn't noticed because we were too intent on the body. And now they carried Morrison down to the floor.

"Oh no!" he cried. "No no no no no!" And then Titania stuffed a pair of panties in his mouth and down his throat, choking him.

We didn't even try to save him. I don't feel bad about it. You wouldn't have tried, either. No one ever does. We ran back out into the mall and headed for the exit one more time. I knew now the models had tricked us and made the trail to force us deeper into the stores. Deeper into their hunting ground. Maybe they were trying to force us all the way to the food court, where they would finish us off.

Our only hope was to get back to the cargo van and then . . . and then I didn't know what.

We had to stop even more often as we ran now, as Zimmer and Lucky were obviously getting tired from carrying their gear all this time.

We paused by the lottery kiosk to catch our breath, and I looked back for any signs of pursuit. We couldn't see the models, but I heard Morrison cry out again.

"Yes!" He screamed this time. "Yes yes yes yes!" Whatever the models were doing to him, it sounded like he was enjoying it. But I knew that couldn't be the case, not after what I'd seen. And I knew I didn't want to find out the truth first-hand.

"You have to drop everything," I said to Zimmer and Lucky. "We can't keep stopping. We have to get out of here."

"I'm not going to leave my cameras just lying around a mall," Zimmer said. "Especially a fake mall."

"If we don't leave it, we're going to be the ones lying around the mall," I said. "In pieces."

"All right," Zimmer sighed and turned to Lucky. "Give me the tripod, at least. It's my favourite tripod."

Lucky opened one of the shoulder bags he was carrying and took out a tripod. He handed it to Zimmer, who took it and then smashed Lucky in the leg with it.

Lucky cried out and fell to the ground, grabbing at his knee. Zimmer stepped over him and pulled the camera bags free of his grasp. Lucky reached up for him, but Zimmer stepped away before he could grab hold. Zimmer shouldered the bags and looked at me as he started to walk toward the plastic curtain at the end of the mall.

"That should buy us the extra time we need now," he said.

I looked down at Lucky, who was writhing on the ground in pain. He clutched at his injured knee with one hand and reached up to me with the other. "Don't leave me here," he said. "Not like this."

Another one of those strange cries echoed through the mall again, this time louder. The models were coming. The lights flickered again, this time going out for a couple of seconds before they came back on.

"I'm sorry," I said to Lucky and I followed Zimmer, because I knew I couldn't save him.

"I hope they get you next!" Lucky screamed after me. "I hope they get all of you next!"

I went out into the storm. The rain was coming down even harder now, which I hadn't believed possible. The lights around the pit were just a dim glow I could barely make out. I couldn't see the cargo van at all, until the headlights suddenly came on in the darkness. Zimmer was trying to escape. He was going to leave me like we had left Lucky and the others.

I struggled through the mud to get to him before he could drive away. I slipped and fell, got to my feet and then slipped and fell again. The rain battered me and made a sound like something hissing all around.

Zimmer wasn't having any more luck. I was close enough to see the cargo van rocking back and forth, its wheels spinning in the mud. It wasn't going anywhere. Which meant we weren't going anywhere.

I stopped in front of the van and stood there lit up by the headlights. Zimmer stared out through the windshield at me and took his foot off the gas. The van sat there, idling, while we stared at each other.

"I have an idea!" I shouted at Zimmer. His expression didn't change, so I wasn't sure if he'd heard me or not.

I looked over my shoulder at the mall and saw the lights flicker and die once more. This time they didn't come on again. But the lights around the pit stayed on. I knew they would draw the models as they looked for us. I was counting on it, in fact.

I went around to the passenger side of the van and tried the door. It was locked. Zimmer and I looked at each other some more through the window, and then he unlocked the door. I opened it but didn't get in.

"Give me one of your cameras," I said.

"But you're not a photographer." His eyes strayed to the floor between the seats and I saw the camera bag lying there. I grabbed it and started to pull it toward me. He reached down and pulled it back. For a few seconds we yanked it one way and then the other in a tug-of-war.

"You don't know what those cameras are worth," he said.

"Whatever it is, our lives are worth more," I said. "Now give me the bag or I'll kill the entire shoot and you'll never get your fee."

He finally let go and I pulled the bag to me and opened it. I took out one of the cameras inside and slung it around my neck as I went over to the pit. I worked my way around its edges until I found a couple of tool boxes and canvas bags on the ground. One of the bags held safety vests, the other a rolled-up tarp. I unrolled the tarp and dropped one end into the pit. I put the tool box on the other end to anchor it. I looked back in the direction of the mall but I still couldn't see anything. All this might have been quicker with Zimmer to help me, but I knew he wasn't going to get out of the van as long as the models were running free.

I went around to the ladder as fast as I could and climbed down into the pit. I splashed through puddles over to the loose end of the tarp and lifted it over the bones, pulling it back toward the ladder. I climbed out of the pit again with the tarp in my hand and pulled the ladder back up after me. I laid it over the end of the tarp so it was anchored on this side now, too. The tarp stretched across the pit like a walkway. Or a runway.

I ran back around to the opposite side, slipping in the mud and nearly falling into the pit. But I recovered my footing and put the camera on top of the tool box. I programmed it to take a photo with flash every two seconds. I returned to the van as the camera flashed behind me.

"You are destroying a good camera for what?" Zimmer asked, staring out into the storm as I climbed back inside the van and shut the door after me. I still didn't lock it. I knew the door wouldn't keep the models out if they saw us there. And if my plan worked, I was going to have to move fast.

"Just wait," I said.

We didn't have to wait long. We sat inside the van in silence for maybe two minutes, watching the empty landscape outside light up every few seconds from the camera's flash. It was like some sort of Giger scene.

Then there was another flash and the models were there, a few feet in front of the van. They moved in a pack and thankfully they were turned away from us and toward the camera. Their naked bodies were slick with blood despite the rain, and there were chunks gouged out of each of them, on their necks, legs and torsos. I didn't know if they'd done it to themselves or if one of the other men had managed to do some damage before the models had killed them. Because it was obvious the others were all dead. The models had things braided in their hair that I almost didn't recognize: fingers, pieces of bloody bone, scraps of flesh.

I wanted to turn my face away so I didn't have to look upon them, but I managed to keep watching, to make sure my trap worked.

The models moved to the edge of the pit, staring at the camera on the other side. If they went around the edge of the pit, we were lost. But I was gambling they'd be as drawn to the runway I had created as they had been to the camera. I was hoping the constant flashes of the camera would blind them enough that they wouldn't look too closely at the runway and see it for what it really was.

My bet paid off, as the models suddenly threw themselves onto the runway at the camera. They were so quick they made it halfway across before the tarp collapsed beneath their weight, and they fell screaming into the pit.

"What have you done?" Zimmer whispered. I didn't reply because I was already out of the van and heading over to the pit as quick as I could without falling down again. The end of the tarp that I had weighed down with the ladder had come free and fallen into the pit. But the other end was still stuck under the tool box. The models could pull themselves up out of the pit if they noticed.

I looked over the edge and saw them down there amid the bones. They reached up for me with hands that looked more like claws now and screamed their rage. The camera kept flashing.

They seemed to realize what I was doing at the last second. They lunged for the tarp as I reached the tool box. I kicked it into their faces, and they pulled the tarp down themselves. Now there was no way out.

That didn't stop them from trying. Portland and Titania clawed at the side of the pit directly beneath me, trying to dig their hands in enough to get firm holds so they could climb up. Instead they just tore out handfuls of mud, and more of the pit's walls showered down upon them. Winter tried to pull herself up one of those tall bones, maybe to throw herself off it in an attempt to reach me once she was high enough, but it snapped under her weight and she fell down to the earth. The camera that I'd put on top of the tool box lay at their feet now but continued to flash away.

I saw one of the ties from the photo shoot lying nearby, the one of the bloody women tearing apart a body. I knew I'd never be able to wear a tie again if I got out of there alive.

I went over to the excavator that was parked nearby. Thankfully, the keys were still in the ignition. I started it up and then I stared at the controls for several seconds. I'd once driven a front-end loader around an obstacle course in Vegas, and the gearshift and other levers and buttons looked to be more or less in the same places. I raised the arm up and down and made scooping motions in the air for a couple of minutes, until I was comfortable with operating the excavator. Then I drove it back to the edge of the pit. I was relieved to see the models still inside, snarling and clawing at the air.

I looked around until I saw a mound of mud nearby that was higher than the surrounding earth. I figured that was the dirt that had filled the pit in the first place. I dropped the scoop into the mound and lifted up a great mass of mud. I swung the scoop around, over the pit, and dropped the wet earth down onto the models.

It knocked them to the ground and half-buried them amid the bones. They screamed at me some more as they struggled to free themselves, but I was already swinging around for more dirt by the time they got back to their feet. I wasn't sure if burying them alive would kill the models or not. But I figured it would at least stop them from killing us.

After I dropped the second load of earth on them and knocked them down again, Zimmer suddenly appeared out of the rain. He climbed up on the side of the excavator and banged on the window of the cab.

"Keep the scoop over the pit for a minute," he yelled over the sounds of the excavator's engine. "This is going to be the photo shoot of the year. Maybe even the decade." Then he climbed up onto the arm of the excavator, straddling it, and pulled himself along its length, to the scoop that now hung empty over the pit.

The models saw him up there and leapt into the air and climbed the bones, trying to reach him. But Zimmer was too far away. He placed his feet on the scoop for support and leaned back against the excavator arm to steady himself. Then he pulled a camera out from inside his jacket, where he had been protecting it, and brought it to his eye. That was what had got him out of the van. He wanted the shot.

I was tempted to keep scooping the dirt down onto the models, to let Zimmer fall down into the pit and to hell with him. But I wasn't that far gone yet.

The models beat me to it, anyway.

Winter suddenly pointed at Zimmer, and I saw the gun in her hand. Morrison's gun. I don't know where she'd been hiding it, but she was aiming it at Zimmer now.

He saw it, too. He turned and screamed something I couldn't hear. I started to bring the scoop back, but too late.

Winter fired the gun and Zimmer jerked and slumped down on the scoop. For a moment, I thought he was going to fall in, but he managed to hang on. He even brought the camera back to his face for another shot.

And Titania leapt up from one of the highest bones, holding the tie with the Amazon pattern in her hands. She snapped it up and caught the long lens of Zimmer's camera with it. She pulled herself up the tie in an instant.

Maybe Zimmer could have saved himself if he had dropped the camera. But he hesitated. I saw it on his face: he was thinking about the photos he'd taken. If he dropped the camera into the pit, they would be lost. But if he didn't drop it, he would be lost.

He finally let go of the camera, but it was too late. Titania was high enough now that she was able to catch onto his leg as she fell back down with the camera. She bit into his thigh through his pants, and Zimmer screamed and looked back at me.

There was nothing I could do. If I swung him back toward the edges of the pit, I would be bringing Titania closer to freedom. All I could do was move the scoop up and down, trying to shake them loose.

Then the other two models leapt off their own bones and caught onto

Titania's legs. They clawed their way up her, until they reached Zimmer. And then I looked away as the screaming really started.

I didn't bother trying to run because I knew there was nowhere to run. I couldn't get away from the models. I sat there in the cab of the excavator and closed my eyes and waited for them to come for me.

"God!" Zimmer cried out. *"God!"*

The screaming stopped after a time and then there was silence except for the sounds of the rain hitting the excavator's roof. This went on for a minute or so before I opened my eyes again.

The models were pressed up against the windows of the cab, watching me. Titania was on the windshield, Winter on the left window and Portland on the right. They each wore different pieces of Zimmer's clothing. Titania wore his shredded shirt, and Winter his jacket. Portland wore his belt tied around her neck. They smiled at me and I could see the blood and shreds of meat and clothing in their teeth. I waited for them to open the door and pull me out or maybe swarm in and tear me apart. But instead they just gave me a look that I recognized, even though it took me a few seconds. It was the same look they'd given the camera when we had been shooting earlier, like they were seeing right through me to everyone else in the world.

"Maybe one day we'll come for you," Titania said, parroting my words.

Then they all dropped to the ground as one and ran through the night, back into the mall.

I waited for them to come back but they didn't. Eventually the rain washed away the last of the smears of blood they had left on the windows, and I got out of the excavator. The lights of the mall came on again as soon as I set foot on the ground. I sat down at the edge of the pit and stared at what was left of Zimmer decorating the bones until the rain stopped and the sun lit up the sky like it was going to set the world on fire.

That was where the day shift security guards found me when they arrived to relieve Morrison and Jesus, and followed the blood trail outside.

They called the police, who called the SWAT team and ambulances and firefighters when they arrived and saw the bodies. They put handcuffs on me and shoved me into the back seat of the cruiser they pulled around to the edge of the parking lot, and I didn't struggle.

"You need to bury the mall," I told them. "It's the only way to be sure."

But they didn't understand, not even after they watched the mall's security videos and saw what the models did. They brought me into an office in the mall, still handcuffed, and I tried not to scream at the stores and all their mannequins. The models could be anywhere. They sat me down at a table with a laptop on it and played the videos for me. I closed my eyes so I didn't have to see what they did to Jesus and Morrison and Lucky. But one of the SWAT guys held my eyes open when the video showed the models running back into the mall again after they'd killed Zimmer but spared me. They left a trail of bloody footprints behind them on the floor. They looked up at the camera and smiled. They ran through the fountain and out of the frame. The video cut to the next camera, but the models didn't appear.

"Where are they?" the man holding my eyes open asked. A half-dozen other cops stood in a circle, looking back and forth between the laptop, the door and me. They kept their guns in their hands the whole time.

"I don't even know what they are," I said. "So how can I know where they are?"

They took me in to the police station after that, where they searched me and found my drugs. I told them they should probably get rid of the pills because I didn't know what role they had played in all this, but the booking officer just put them in an evidence bag. They took me into an interrogation room and questioned me some more. I told them everything, although I admitted the drugs may have altered my perception of things. They asked me where I had found the models and why I had hired them, but I didn't really have an answer they liked.

"It's just business," I said.

They had to let me go after a time, even though I asked to stay in their jail cell. They said as far as they could tell, I hadn't actually done anything wrong. I wasn't sure about that, but I was too tired to argue with them.

I went home and tried to sleep but my insomnia was back. I lay there in the bed and saw the models in the pit whenever I closed my eyes. I heard the cries of the other men, the cries that sounded like they were welcoming whatever it was the models did to them. I wondered what they had been thinking about when they died. What they had been experiencing. After a few hours of that, I got up and scanned the news feeds on my tablet.

I read the stories about the Mall Massacre, as it was already being called. I stared at the still photos of the models that had been blown up from the security video. The Furies, everyone was calling them. They looked into the camera and smiled their bloody smiles. That look gave me a chill again.

That was days ago. I still haven't slept. I don't know what's real anymore, what actually happened and what I just dreamed up afterward.

The models are still out there. They are still on the hunt. We all know this because of the other killings. The two protesters outside the abortion clinic the night after the Mall Massacre. Dragged into a van much like mine and carried away by the models, their remains found in a Dumpster several blocks away. The window dresser who was pulled out of a Holt Renfrew window the next morning and torn apart by the models, who were dressed as homeless people. They ran into an alley afterward and disappeared again. But they're still out there. I know we'll see them again.

In the meantime, I drive through the night. I don't think I'll ever do another photo shoot again. But I can't stop looking for the models.

Last night, I drove back out to the mall. The whole thing was behind police tape, and I couldn't even get into the parking lot. I pulled the Tesla over onto the shoulder of the road and looked at the lights around the pit in the distance, at the ghostlike figures climbing in and out. Investigators in hazmat suits. Maybe they'll find some clue to the models and maybe they won't. Whatever they find, it's too late for me.

I closed my eyes as I sat there, wondering why the models hadn't killed me. I heard Zimmer's last words again. "God! *God!*" I thought again about the story Titania had told me about the fish that swam toward the light, even though they knew it was going to be the end of them. I thought maybe she had been trying to tell me something even back then, but I didn't know what.

I wish I knew how to find the light in all this darkness.

We Are a Rupture
THAT CANNOT
BE CONTAINED

At first it was just oil that leaked from the ruptured pipe at the bottom of the ocean, so we didn't work that hard to stop it. We had all lived through oil leaks before, after all. We tried to plug it with waste, with boatloads of debris scooped out of one of the great floating garbage patches in the ocean. We thought maybe we could recycle the problem away. But the pressure just forced the garbage back out, an underwater geyser of everything we'd discarded and forgotten. So we settled for skimming the oil off the ocean surface. We shipped it to the same refineries we would have anyway, and pumped it into our cars, only now with a few more dead turtles and pelicans in the mix.

But then other things came out of the pipe. The ghosts of all those who had died at sea. They got caught in the containment booms and nets, and their cries drove the whales and dolphins up onto the beaches. That's when we knew we had to do something. Our tourism industries were in trouble. No one wanted to walk on sandy beaches covered in rotting blubber. So we turned to desperate measures. We dropped gravestones into the pipe to contain the dead, and then poured in concrete after the gravestones. We threw some bibles in from all the religions for good measure. We said goodbye to our fortunes and stopped the oil, the oil that would have saved our economy, the oil that would have saved the world as we knew it then.

But it was too late. Other things seeped through the layers of concrete and gravestones and bibles and petroleum-eating bacteria. Like ghosts but worse. Our forgotten memories. The time we stripped naked for each other at summer camp. The time we looked away when the boy across the street was getting mugged. The time we drove across that dog on the country lane and saw the puppies moving in its stomach and kept going because there was no one else around to witness it. Until now. Now they poured out of that ruptured well and bobbed there at the ocean surface for everyone to see. And we thought it couldn't get worse than that.

And then it got worse than that. Then the fantasies came bubbling out. The secret things we thought about each other. The secret things we imagined doing to each other. The secret things we imagined being done to us. And we looked at each other with shock and awe, wondering how we could have thought the things we thought. So we lit the ocean on fire to burn it all away. But that just turned all our fantasies into ash that rained down on us for weeks afterward, reminding us every day of everything that was wrong with us.

And then the same thing happened at other wells. Pipes ruptured and our nightmares spilled out. A spectral Lenin wandered the frozen steppes, hawking Pepsi to every living soul he encountered. Our future ghosts dug up the graves of our parents and had sex with their corpses. Our houses and office towers caught fire and burned without consuming anything, without going out. The smoke cast a shadow over our lands, a shadow that never lifted.

And so we were faced with a choice. We could live with it. We could live with ourselves – our true selves – flooding the planet. Or we could end it. We could destroy every oil facility and pipeline on the planet with nukes and whatever else we had. We could end ourselves.

And we thought this. This. This is what happened to the dinosaurs.

The Calling
OF CTHULHU

I tell my clients everyone goes through three emotional stages after losing a job: denial, rage and acceptance. I tell them they won't be able to find a new calling until they move on to the third stage. I tell them world destroyer, god of war, gateway to the apocalypse and earth devourer are no longer acceptable callings.

Most of my clients went through the denial stage centuries ago, when people lost faith in them and the other gods. The rage stage? Well, you could blame a lot of the bloodshed of the last few hundred years on that. My clients may have lost most of their powers along with their followers, but they still know how to work people behind the scenes. Things have been quieter lately, though, thanks largely to the agency's placement rate. Eighty percent, if you don't count the Great Old Ones. We try not to count them because they throw the numbers off.

Cthulhu was a perfect example of that. He skipped denial entirely and went straight to rage, and he showed no signs of moving on.

A *National Geographic* sub woke him when it was looking for shipwrecks and lost planes in the Bermuda Triangle but found his sunken city instead. All those aircraft and ships that went missing in the region over the years? That was Cthulhu sleepwalking. He would have destroyed the *National Geographic* sub, too, if not for the giant squid that had happened

145

by at the same time, drawn by all the commotion. He was in a much better mood after he'd had something to eat.

I didn't see any signs of trouble in our first meeting. Cthulhu sat hunched over on the reinforced bench in my office, an airplane hangar converted by Thor and his company – because some of my clients, like Cthulhu, need the space. He didn't do much but ooze slime on the floor and glower at the photos of Percy on my stone desk while I filled out the forms about his next of kin (Shub-Niggurath, but if it wasn't available, any of the Mi-Go race would do), employment history (architect of nightmares) and hours of availability (one eternity is as good as another). I offered him a chocolate from the bowl on my desk but he just slapped his tentacles together and said he was trying to cut down.

He did get a little testy when I asked him what kind of work he was interested in. He said he'd like to turn all of humanity inside out and chain us up in his sunken palace so the kraken could feast on our entrails. But he quieted down when I told him we'd already found work for the kraken in the *Twenty Thousand Leagues Under the Sea* attraction in Tokyo Disney. Then I told him about the three stages and sent him to a job laying telecommunication wires for Google along the ocean floor. I figured that was the end of it, but the sisters whispered disagreement in my head. I should have listened to them.

I didn't have time to think about Cthulhu for a while after that, because one of my other placements, Prometheus, was causing problems.

Prometheus worked in the new Mount Sinai Hospital (also built by Thor and his construction company). I'd found him a job as an organ donor. Specifically, as a liver donor. A team of doctors took out his liver for a transplant every day. It was so routine they didn't even put him under for it. They just cut it out of him while he lay in bed watching movies. A new one was usually growing back by the time they stitched him up.

The head of Mount Sinai had once told me medical experts figured one in two liver recipients in the country had Prometheus's liver in them.

And a Harvard economics prof had emailed me to say Prometheus's livers were good for the economy. Liquor sales were up nearly twenty percent since his livers hit the market. It was called the Prometheus Effect. There was even a brand of tequila named after him.

But right before I'd met with Cthulhu I had received an email from head office in Atlantis saying Prometheus was refusing to provide any more livers. I met the hospital's CEO in her office. Her desk was very modern, all metal and glass. There were no pictures on it, but there was a bowl of sugar cubes. She kept glancing at the door that led to the private balcony off her office while she talked to me.

"Prometheus is on strike," she told me. "He won't give us any more livers unless we give him a cut of the profits from our transplants."

"How big a cut?" I asked.

She shook her head. "It doesn't matter. He signed a contract, and the contract doesn't say anything about cuts. If we were to give him a deal, then everyone would want one." She took a sugar cube from the bowl and studied it. "The head surgeon just wants us to grab security, put him under and go back to slicing. I thought I'd give you a chance to talk to him first."

"I'll take care of it," I said.

She got up and opened the door to the balcony. A winged horse stepped into view and she fed it the sugar cube. The sisters hissed at it, but I cleared my throat to cover the noise.

"We're looking at expanding the Prometheus program," the CEO said. "We want to move into other organs. Eyeballs, lungs, maybe even heart transplants. We need him to agree to that, too."

"He'll definitely want a cut of those," I said.

"One of your hair clips is loose," she said, kissing the winged horse on its nose.

I saw myself out. I found a washroom and refastened the clip. I hummed a song about blood and vengeance to the sisters until they settled down. Then I went to visit Prometheus in his private room.

He was lying in bed, watching old Wile E. Coyote cartoons. He wore a hospital gown but I could see the bandages on his side through a gap in the fabric. "And I thought I had it bad," he told me, still watching the cartoon.

"Where did you get this idea for a strike?" I asked him. There were a couple of chairs in the room but I didn't sit down. I wanted to be free for action in case he tried anything.

He switched from the cartoons to a news show about labour troubles at a shipyard in India. I'd already received the memo about it. The shipyard specialized in breaking apart old tankers into scrap metal. But it had been shut down by a general strike, led by Shiva, the god who used to have four arms until he'd lost one of them in an on-site accident.

Shiva was speaking into the camera now. "Our demands are simple: full medical and eighty percent dental." Behind him, undestroyed ships clogged the shipyard and surrounding bay. "The theists of the world must unite," he added. I was glad he wasn't my placement.

"You signed a contract," I said to Prometheus.

"I can still feel all those livers I've given away," Prometheus said. "Every drink everyone takes. That should be worth a cut."

"What are you talking about?" I asked.

"When someone with one of my livers has a drink, I get a little bit of their buzz. I'm drunk all the time. I think it's some sort of quantum effect."

"What do you know about quantum anything?"

"I saw a show about it on the oracle box," he said, nodding at the television. "These people know things that even the gods never learned."

"That's because the gods were too busy destroying everything to bother understanding how it worked," I said. "Anyway, we're here to talk about you, not the gods."

"They've had their time," Prometheus said, nodding in agreement.

"Maybe they can give you a drug for the liver thing. You don't need more money. What would you do with it, anyway? They take care of everything for you here."

Prometheus switched the show to some sitcom. He muted it but kept watching. "Everyone lives in nicer places than me. Even the people who aren't real."

I looked around the hospital room. It was a private room, but it was still just a hospital room.

"You want your own place," I said.

"They can operate on me in it – I don't care. But I want furniture and a bigger oracle box and all that." He nodded at the sitcom. "Everything everyone else has."

"They want more of your organs," I told him. "They want your eyes and your heart and whatever else they can take."

"Not a chance," he said. "You have no idea how much all this hurts."

"You let them take a few of those from time to time, and I can get you your place."

He thought it over. "And a cut."

I opened the drawer of his bedside table and looked inside. It was full of magazines, candies, bloody scalpels, cellphones – you name it. Prometheus had always been a klepto. I took a bag of potato chips and went over to the window.

"What are you doing?" he asked me.

I opened the window and dumped the chips on the ledge. I only had to wait a few seconds before a crow landed on the ledge and started pecking at the chips.

Prometheus shrieked and pulled the covers over his head. The sound and movement startled the crow, which flew off with a chip, but Prometheus didn't see it go.

"Close the window!" he cried. Crows were his weak spot.

"No cut," I said. "Do we have a deal?"

"All right," Prometheus said from under the covers, then added, "but I want all the windows sealed."

I went down to the parking lot and called the CEO on my phone rather than go back to the office. I didn't want to see that winged horse again.

"A place of his own?" she said. "Why didn't he just ask us?"

"His kind aren't used to asking," I said.

"I've got my hands full with just him," she said. "I can't imagine what it's like working with entire pantheons."

"Some days are better than others."

My day didn't get any better. I got home just in time for the latest episode of *Legendary Date*. I let my hair down, then settled on the couch with a glass of wine and watched as a six-hundred-year-old vampire named Artalia went on a date with an accountant named Erin to a restaurant. It didn't start off well.

"You're looking at the waitresses more than me," Erin complained, folding her arms across her chest.

"I'm just hungry," Artalia protested. He looked at her and licked his lips. I was hoping he'd spring across the table for her throat, and maybe she'd stab him with the steak knife. You know, a real date. But that was all I got to watch because, just then, Mercury knocked on the door. "We have a crisis," he called without waiting for me to answer.

It had to be serious, indeed, for head office to send Mercury out at night. His overtime was a killer. I sighed and put my hair back up and turned off *Legendary Date*, which prompted a chorus of complaints in my head.

"Oh, you already know how it's going to end," I told the sisters. "They're going to go back to her place and she won't invite him in, so he'll go stalk some neighbourhood cat instead. Nobody gets any real action on these shows."

I let Mercury in and he looked at the photos lining the front hall while I changed in the bedroom.

"It's Cthulhu," he said, but I had already figured that much. "On the way to his undersea cable job he sank a convoy of cargo ships carrying Hyundais to Brazil. Hyundai is going to sue."

"Aren't they insured?" I asked.

"The insurance company is invoking some clause about acts of gods," he said.

I came out of the bedroom dressed in my work suit and the sisters all bound up. Mercury still didn't look at me.

"Is this picture of Perseus with the sword from the old days?" he asked, nodding at one of the photos. "Those rocks look like your old hideout."

"Let's keep our work and home lives separate," I said.

"I'm just wondering how you got a photo of back then," he said. "Did the oracle take that?"

"Let's go to the office so I can get to work," I said.

Mercury whisked me back to the office in his arms, which was much less comfortable than a limo or helicopter but much faster. He had the good grace to pretend not to notice the sisters trying to squirm free to snap at him.

It was a long night of phone calls, including one with Google's head of HR. "Not a good fit," she said. "We're cancelling the contract. You understand." And I did.

When Mercury brought Cthulhu back to see me just before dawn, I didn't speak. I stared at him from behind my desk. I wanted to see what he had to say for himself. Mercury muttered something about going for a coffee and disappeared. Cthulhu waved his tentacles at me for a moment, then said, "The silent treatment won't work on me. I've spent eons in the deepest silence imaginable, so far down that your screams would take a thousand years to reach the surface."

"Couldn't you hear whale songs down there?" I asked. "I read somewhere that they reach every part of the oceans."

Cthulhu sighed. I gagged at the stench, but he didn't seem to notice. "They need to sing about something else besides fish," he said.

I sighed myself. "I thought we had the perfect match for your skill set," I said. "What happened?"

"It was my eldritch powers. I couldn't help but hear every call on those undersea cables. Read every email. Every attachment." He slapped his tentacles over his eyes and the oozing holes on the side of his head that may have been his ears. "It drove me madder."

Well, I couldn't argue with that. I scanned my file of recent job postings. "How do you feel about working in cold water?"

"I did destroy the world once with an ice age," he said. "That was a long time ago, back before I killed the dinosaurs, but I think I could do it again. And I'm good with tidal waves. And whirlpools." He flapped a different tentacle each time he spoke, as if ticking off positive traits about himself. That was a good sign, but it was clear he still had a long way to go.

"Those all very impressive skills," I told him, "but there are more efficient ways to destroy the world now. The mortals can manage it all on their own with bombs and carbon emissions."

Cthulhu dropped his tentacles to the floor and sighed once more, so I steered the session back to the positive. Once I could breathe again.

"You're on the right track," I told him. "The Canadian government needs a new icebreaker to patrol the north."

Cthulhu lifted a tentacle in my direction. "An icebreaker?"

"An ice destroyer," I said, trying to encourage him.

Cthulhu lifted another tentacle. "To destroy the north," he said.

Small steps, I reminded myself.

He took the bowl of chocolates from my desk with another tentacle and dumped the whole thing into his mouth, glass and all.

"Do they still have those little white whales up there?" he asked. "The tasty ones?"

Mercury came back with coffee for him and me, and I had him take Cthulhu to the new work site in the frozen north. Mercury was only gone for a few minutes before he came back.

"Better keep yourself on call," he said. He glanced at the puddle of slime Cthulhu had left behind on the bench and floor. "I don't think you've seen the last of him, and head office is watching this case closely."

He disappeared once again, and the sisters hissed at him. I longed to set them free but what kind of example would that send to my clients?

Instead, I went online for an update on the Shiva situation. The strike was spreading. Shipbreaking yards all across the continent had closed. Shiva was talking to a reporter about the possibility of workers starting communes.

"Imagine if we were all shipbuilders instead of destroyers," he said.

Thor wasn't going to like that competition.

I spent the rest of the afternoon making routine placements: a couple of Valkyries as pilots with Virgin Airlines, some satyrs as tree planters. Things went so smoothly I left work early and hurried home to try to watch *Legendary Date* again. In this episode a ghost named Huntley took a librarian named Ashley to a sports bar. It didn't start off any better than the other date. Huntley levitated a couple of beers from a nearby table over to theirs, and the owners, a pair of men wearing baseball caps, came over to reclaim them.

"Bring it," Huntley said, punching the nearest one. For a moment, I got excited at the prospect of violence and the sisters lashed about, hissing with delight on my head. But then Huntley dematerialized and the men with baseball caps were left trying to grab on to air.

Ashley sighed into the camera and said, "Every man I date is the same."

That was when Mercury knocked again.

"I hate to say I told you so," he said through the door.

"This had better be good," I groaned, putting up my hair.

"You have no idea," he said.

I finished my wine in one gulp and turned off the television, ignoring the sisters' pleas to finish watching the episode. I knew how it would end and it wouldn't be in blood and fire. I opened the door for Mercury and went into the bedroom to change.

"How is Perseus anyway?" he asked, studying the photos in the hall again.

"I wouldn't know."

"He hasn't been to see you in all this time?"

"Not everyone needs my help," I said. But that wasn't true. All the gods and demigods and immortals eventually came to my office for help. I'd never told anyone that was the reason I'd taken the job in the first place. For the day that Percy finally showed up and I could look upon him in the flesh once more.

"Let's just get back to the office," I said.

It turned out Cthulhu had taken a wrong turn somewhere in the Canadian north and wound up off the coast of Alaska instead, where he had attacked a cruise ship called the *Ice Maiden*. He spent several hours tearing the ship apart and using parts of it to smash the nearby glacier the passengers had been photographing. At least he'd let all the passengers and crew abandon ship first. I supposed that was some sort of progress.

While I waited for Mercury to bring Cthulhu back into the office, I made a call to Neptune.

"How's the deep-sea salvage business working out for you?" I asked him.

"It's picking up with global warming," he said. It was hard to understand him because he was speaking underwater, but I'd had a lot of practise with the gods of the depths. They were often the hardest to place, so it took a little more one on one. "The strange storms are sinking more ships. And the rising water levels are claiming more villages. Soon the whole world will be one giant ocean again."

"Well, until that day comes, you're going to need to keep working," I said. "And I'm assuming you've already got the *Ice Maiden* contract?"

"Poseidon tried to underbid me but everyone knows I do the quality work," Neptune said.

"I'll be sending some help your way," I said and hung up as Mercury brought Cthulhu back into the office.

"What were you thinking?" I asked Cthulhu as Mercury went off for coffee again.

"I'm an ice destroyer," Cthulhu said. He explored my desk with a tentacle, but I'd put the chocolates in a drawer before his visit. I slapped the tentacle away from the photos of Percy. "I destroyed the ice vessel. And the glacier. I multi-tasked." His body shook and slime oozed from his maw onto the floor. I took this to be laughter.

"We're lucky no one was killed," I said.

"They're lucky," Cthulhu said. "They mistook me for a giant squid when I first surfaced. In the Old Days, I would have used their skin as sushi wraps for such an insult."

"You had sushi in the Old Days?"

"We invented sushi. Although what we ate was still alive. Fresher that way."

I kept my thoughts about the resemblance between Cthulhu and squid to myself. Instead, I said, "Well, you've got one chance left. As it turns out, Neptune won the contract for raising the *Ice Maiden*. As a favour to me, he's agreed to take you on as his apprentice. You'll be cleaning up your own mess this time." I'd work out the details with Neptune later. He still owed me one for the whole *Flying Dutchman* incident.

Cthulhu crossed his legs and inspected his talons. He slurped a rotting fish off one of them. "Neptune is half my age."

"He knows the oceans better than anyone else." Other than Poseidon, of course, but I kept that to myself. I didn't want to get involved in that rivalry.

"I've been in those oceans since before they were even oceans."

"What were the oceans if not oceans?" I asked.

"You don't want to know," Cthulhu said. "Your little mind would melt into goo that even I wouldn't want to taste."

"Look, this is an excellent opportunity for you. There's more work for Neptune than even he can handle. He's going to need help and I can't think of anyone more qualified for deep-sea salvage than you." Other than Poseidon. But I liked the idea of sending Cthulhu back under the ocean for good.

Mercury returned with a tiny espresso mug and a saucer, so I figured he'd gone all the way to Italy. I let him finish the espresso before I had him take Cthulhu back to the sunken *Ice Maiden*. Then I went to the hospital again to check on Prometheus.

They'd moved him into a private suite. It had four rooms: a living room, bedroom, bathroom and kitchen. All new furniture. Sealed windows. He was sitting on a leather sofa in the living room when I arrived, but the big-screen monitor was turned off. He was just staring into space. Staring with one eye. The other was covered by an eye patch.

"How are the new transplants working out?" I asked.

Prometheus just nodded and smiled. I wondered if he was sedated.

I looked at the blank television. I'd never seen it turned off before. "Is it broken?" I asked. "Do we need to get you a new one?"

Prometheus kept on smiling. "Remember when I said I could still feel everything from the livers they put in other people?" He pointed at his eye. "I can still see from the eyes they've put in new people. I can see everything they're seeing. Everything. It's a little blurry, but it's better than the movies."

I didn't know what he was talking about until one of the sisters whispered an explanation in my ear. "Ah," I said.

"Tell them they can take whatever organs they want," Prometheus said. "I don't even want a cut anymore. I've got all the payment I need."

I went downstairs and called the CEO from the parking lot. I didn't tell her everything Prometheus had told me. I just said he was happy with the new arrangement.

"The program is working better than we thought," she said. "It's going so smoothly I'm going to get a Prometheus eye for my husband for Christmas. He's got bad glaucoma."

I disconnected without saying anything at all.

I went back to the office to finish up the Prometheus paperwork and a few other files. It was a quiet day until a few minutes before quitting time, when I heard a gurgling from my coffee cup. I looked into it and saw Neptune's face floating in the mug.

"I thought I told you not to do that anymore," I said.

The coffee swirled around until it formed a miniature Neptune. He climbed out of the mug and began to pace my desk, leaving wet footprints behind. "We need to talk," he said.

I moved all the loose papers out of his path. "Let me guess, Cthulhu isn't working out."

"He's more interested in playing with the ship than salvaging it," Neptune said. "He raises the lifeboats to the surface and then sinks them again. He makes squid noises the whole time we work. And he keeps leaving to chase boats the media have chartered. He's like a little boy in a bathtub."

I moved the final report on Prometheus out of Neptune's path and then paused. I had an idea.

"I can't work with Cthulhu," Neptune said.

"No, you can't," I said. "I've got the perfect job for him." I shooed him back into the mug and then I made some calls.

I placed Cthulhu with the shipbreaking yards closed down by Shiva's strikes. The strikers had all left now – they'd turned some of the old tankers into floating gardens and sailed off to sea with Shiva in a happy commune – so the owners were eager for a replacement.

And what a replacement Cthulhu has turned out to be. I watched him that first day through a livestream. I got the idea from Prometheus. Now anyone in the world can watch Cthulhu work.

The camera showed nothing but a rusting battleship adrift in the harbour when I logged on. But it didn't take long for Cthulhu to rise up underneath it and roll it over onto its side. Water sprayed everywhere. Cthulhu roared at the battleship and smashed his tentacles down upon it, rupturing its hull. He tore off pieces of the bridge and threw them onto the shore, where salvage crews waited in fortified bunkers made by Thor. He ripped cables from the deck, then tore open the deck itself and smashed his fists down into the ship's depths. He lifted handfuls of bunk beds and dining tables to the sky and roared again, his tentacles flailing.

Definitely third stage.

I shut down the computer, turned off the lights and went home. I poured myself a glass of wine and let down my hair, then curled up on the couch to finally enjoy *Legendary Date*.

In this episode a succubus named Glynda and an investment banker named Dylan went on a date to an amusement park. They ate cotton candy and played ring toss, and Glynda won Dylan a pink hippo. They took it on the roller coaster with them, and they screamed together and held hands in the loop.

Dylan drove Glynda back to her lair and they stood in front of the cave for a moment, talking about the good time they'd had. The sun was setting and the sky was as bloody as the night Percy had come for me. The sisters and I held our breath and waited.

"Yog-sothoth!" Glynda said.

Only it wasn't Glynda, it was Mercury, hammering at my door again. "We have a crisis," he added.

"The door's open," I called. He came in and the sisters rose up out of my head and hissed at him in unison.

"The ancient one has dematerialized –" Mercury said, but that was all he got out before he turned to stone. At least the sisters had been restrained and hit him with only a minor enchantment – he'd just be stone for a few minutes.

Enough time to watch the end of *Legendary Date*.

Glynda stepped back into her cave with a smile and disappeared into the darkness. Dylan hesitated a moment, looked at the camera, then followed her into her lair. He slipped a knife out of his pocket because you never know with succubi.

The sisters hissed with pleasure and I settled back into the couch to watch the end of the date.

One day.

One day there would be a knock on the door and it wouldn't be Mercury.

One day Percy would come for me again.

We Are
ALL GHOSTS

This is the way the world ends.

Not with a bang, but with the silence of the grave.

I don't bother testing the walls of the tomb you've buried me in. I know there's no way out. After all, you built it to contain not only me, but what's inside me. I cannot escape. We cannot escape.

But I must tell you, I'm not the villain you think I am. Not any more than I was the hero you once thought I was.

I'm just a man. A man with a curse you don't understand. Not yet. But you will comprehend it someday. Not that it will do you any good.

I know what the pipes leading into the tomb are for. I would have done the same thing if I were you. But it won't work any better this time than it did for the inhabitants of the Frozen City.

Instead of looking for a way out after I drop into your trap, this tomb that is no bigger than a jail cell, I kneel by the coffin on the floor and rest my hands on it. Providence's coffin. I suppose I should thank you for that, even though it's empty inside. There's nothing left of her.

Nothing but the memories.

* * *

B Y NOW you've probably figured out the stories I told you in the mission debriefings were lies. Maybe you knew it even then, in the interrogation rooms after you flew me back home. How could you not suspect there was something different about me when I was the only one who returned from the Frozen City? When I said I had no memory of what happened to the others, no memory of what happened on the mission at all before waking up on the icy floor of that sunken tomb in that forgotten city? When I said I didn't feel any different than before?

The truth is I remember everything.

I remember the afternoon when I returned from teaching my Intro to Archaeology class to find Smyth sitting in my office, even though my office door was still locked. He said he worked for the government, although not any branch I'd ever heard of because it didn't have a name. He pulled out a phone and showed me the satellite shot of a dark mass buried in ice. I remember the question he asked.

"What does this look like to you?"

I studied the image. A Rorschach blot.

"Bones," I said.

He put the phone away and stood. He looked at the door like he'd already forgotten me.

"The bones of a city," I said. Because why else would he seek out an archaeologist with a picture like that? He thought the ruins of a civilization were buried down there.

Close. It was the ruin of civilization. But we didn't know any of that back then.

Smyth looked at me again, but his expression didn't change.

"You're going to assemble a team," he told me. "No one who knows anyone else on it beforehand. No one who will talk. No one who can't leave their life behind the minute I call. If word of this gets out, I'll never call. And you'll never have your chance to explore this city."

And then he left me there, wondering why he'd chosen me. I wasn't anyone special. I'd done a few digs in Peru and written a few papers on the religious customs of a tribe that had sacrificed themselves to extinction centuries ago. I was a nobody in my field.

I understand now that's why he came for me.

I was expendable.

We were all expendable.

* * *

A SCREAM FROM the pipes breaks the silence. You've opened something. The security gates or airlocks or whatever it is you've put in place to keep me in this tomb. Or rather, to keep what's inside me in this tomb.

I wish you luck.

I open the coffin and look down at the empty space where Providence should be. I think of the last time I saw her.

The time I killed her and doomed us all.

* * *

I CHOSE PROVIDENCE to be on the team even though Smyth wanted only people I didn't know. How could I not invite her, the star student of the department thanks to her work on Aztec transformation rituals as passed down through oral histories? She single-handedly made us rethink everything we knew about their religious sacrifices.

And, of course, we were in love.

I know it's a cliché. The aging professor and the star graduate student. Maybe Providence was young and naive. Maybe she was just using me to get ahead. Maybe she would have left me after she graduated and secured a job somewhere. But maybe she wouldn't have.

I'll never know.

We had dinner with wine and candles and I told her what Smyth told me. Then we made love with more wine and candles. That was the last time we even kissed.

Providence said we had to pretend we didn't know each other. She said we had to treat each other like the Aztecs treated their sacrifices. So we sat in different parts of the military cargo plane that flew us to Antarctica when Smyth called. We shook hands with everyone else on the team I'd assembled – all strangers to me, I swear, and all nobodies I'd found through their scholarly articles. Providence and I introduced ourselves to each other on the plane like we'd never met before. She was so good at not knowing me that I wondered if she'd been practising it.

When we reached Antarctica, we all ate together in the cafeteria of the base camp that had been built over the Frozen City and talked about what we'd find when the robots finished digging the hole down through the ice. Some of us thought perhaps another Easter Island, monuments dedicated to a race that had wiped itself out. A couple of us wondered aloud if it was perhaps the lost city of Atlantis. Even though we were all academics, none of us were willing to make disparaging remarks about that. We were all gathered there in Antarctica, after all.

Providence was the only one to voice what we were all secretly thinking. That maybe it was something older than we'd ever dreamed of finding. Something more ancient than Easter Island and even the idea of Atlantis. The city of a forgotten race. That put an end to our speculation, and we spent the rest of our wait in silence.

We held our breath in the control room as we watched the first camera feeds of the Frozen City's empty streets, of the strange melted buildings lit up by the robots' lights.

We huddled in groups and tried to make sense of the glyphs inscribed on every surface, of the undulating pathways paved with some glittering substance we couldn't identify, of the abstract sculptures that looked as if they'd been carved from bone.

We looked for signs of life, for bodies or skeletons, but saw nothing. Whoever or whatever had lived in the city was gone.

I split us into groups for the initial exploration and I teamed up with Providence. Smyth just nodded when I handed him the paperwork outlining the survey plans. He assigned each group a military escort.

Men in black uniforms with every weapon I could imagine – assault rifles, handguns, grenades, knives – but no insignia on their uniforms. For all the good they did.

And down we went in the elevator shaft the robots had carved out of the ice, into the Frozen City.

I know you've seen the recordings we made with the hand-helds. But the films don't capture what it was really like. The stillness in the air. The silence except for our steps, and the drips of the ice melting from the buildings under the heat of the lights we set up. The way the twisting shapes of the buildings made you dizzy if you looked at them too long. The shadows that fell where they weren't supposed to fall.

I shouldn't have lied. I don't mean in those debriefings, when I said I didn't know what happened. I mean I shouldn't have lied about not knowing Providence. Then Smyth wouldn't have let us come. Then Providence would still be alive, and I wouldn't be what I am now.

Then maybe the world wouldn't be ending.

But I did lie, and here we are, buried together.

* * *

THERE'S A moment of silence after the metal sounds. Then the pipes start to shake and rattle in place. I know what's coming down them.

Like that'll stop the ghosts.

I feel them stirring inside me now, restless to get out. The periods between them waking are growing shorter. Soon they won't sleep at all.

Soon they will be free.

The water erupts from the pipes and pours into the room. Within seconds, it's up to my ankles. There's nowhere for it to escape. It'll rise until it reaches the ceiling.

And then you'll turn the temperature down and freeze me, won't you? You'll turn the water to ice.

You'll freeze me like the ghosts had been frozen all those ages.

* * *

THE THING I didn't tell you in the debriefings was I was the one who woke the ghosts.

Providence and I found a tomb half-melted out of the ice. A stone building with a stone door. It was like the ancient crypts you see in cemeteries, once you looked past it not having any right angles or even straight edges. It was like something fluid that had been fixed in place by the ice. Or maybe just our lights.

The soldiers forced open the door with a crowbar and scanned the inside with their guns, then nodded at us. So that tells you how much good they were.

The tomb was empty except for the sarcophagus. Which resembled any sarcophagus I'd ever seen as much as the tomb resembled a human tomb. It was a rough oval shape, but there were stone outcroppings here and there in what seemed like random directions. As if it housed filaments, or maybe tentacles. Or who knew what?

Except, of course, we all know what it housed now, thanks to the things that haunt our city. The things that live in the shadows. The things that spread the shadows.

Providence and I decided it was a sarcophagus because that's what we were looking for as archaeologists. And we were right. So we opened it like we'd opened so many similar resting places before.

No.

I opened it.

I took the soldiers' crowbar and levered it into a crack in the sarcophagus and popped the lid. It made a sound like the screaming of the pipes when you released the water.

And the screaming went on as the ghosts came out.

How can I explain them to you?

Imagine the things that live in the darkest depths of the oceans, the things you can only glimpse in nightmares. Now put them in a partially thawed tomb in a city buried under the Antarctic ice. And try to imagine the way they felt waking after being trapped there for thousands of years.

Maybe I was spared because I was the one who freed them. Maybe because they needed a host. I have no idea. But I wish they hadn't spared me.

Yes, I know what happened. They took the others. They took Providence and the soldiers. They went out into the Frozen City and took everyone. Nothing but screams escaped the shadows.

And they hid them in me.

Who knows why. Maybe the ghosts are feeding on them while resting in me, growing stronger.

Maybe the ghosts turned Providence and the others into more ghosts.

Maybe the ghosts saw how much I loved Providence.

Maybe the ghosts saw how I would do anything to free her.

* * *

I GET INTO the coffin to stay dry a few minutes longer. I stare up at the blank stone ceiling overhead. The water splashes around the edges of the coffin.

I know you're trying to do the right thing.

Just like I tried to do the right thing when I came back from the Frozen City.

They sealed the tunnel with ice when I climbed back out of it, alone. They left the robots down there and watched the live feeds, but nothing else happened. The ghosts were gone. They were in me now.

They put me on a plane back home. The plane had arrived filled with soldiers and left with me and no one else. Smyth and the others who had stayed in the base while we descended into the city flew out on a different plane. I was dangerous cargo now.

I spent a month in quarantine. They studied me with X-rays and MRI scans and radiation meters and all sorts of things I didn't understand. They didn't know what they were looking for. So of course they didn't find it.

More men named Smyth interviewed me in a conference room with metal walls deep under the city. They asked the same questions over and over and recorded the answers on multiple recorders. They wanted to know what had happened to everyone who had disappeared. They wanted to know what had happened to Providence and the soldiers who had been with us.

I told them I didn't remember anything.

I told them I didn't remember anything because I didn't want them to know what I had done to Providence.

I told them I didn't remember anything because I still didn't understand what had happened.

So I said nothing, and they let me go back to my job. The men named Smyth said they'd be in touch.

I didn't have any teaching duties, as I was officially on sabbatical now. I'd been expecting to be part of the exploration team of the Frozen City for months, if not years. I had nothing to do. I sat in the quiet of my office and tried to make sense of things.

Instead, I heard the voices.

At first I thought it was students playing some new instrument outside. They were always experimenting. One year it would be Japanese drums, the next it would be Mongolian battle horns.

But the more I listened, the more I realized it wasn't music. It was voices. It sounded like chanting, but chanting underwater. It took me days of listening to realize the chanting was coming from inside me. It followed me around, in my office, in my home, in the grocery store, fading in and out. No one else showed any signs of hearing it, and I worried I had caught some sort of illness from the Frozen City.

I couldn't sleep. The voices drove me into the night. I roamed the streets in my car, wondering what they were trying to tell me. Until I came across the men assaulting the woman.

And that's how I became a hero.

I saw them dragging her off the street and into the dark parking lot behind a church. Three of them. I jumped out of the car and ran at them without a second thought, because I saw her face.

Providence.

I screamed at them to free her. Only it wasn't a scream that came out. It was a ghost.

The same chanting voice I'd been hearing for days rose up inside me. "Fhtagn ssw'nafh!" I cried. Or, more accurately, I burbled. For now I sounded like I was talking underwater. That may have had something to do with the ghost exiting my mouth.

Even now, after so many of the ghosts have escaped into the world, I still find them hard to describe. This one was like a cross between a jellyfish and the remains of a man. It flopped onto the ground and shook for a moment, and we all stared at it. Me, the other men, the woman who I realized now wasn't Providence at all. I'd never seen her before in my life.

"Wgahst'nar phl'unk!" I said. I suddenly felt so empty I fell to my knees.

And the ghost rose up and threw itself at them. The men screamed as it dragged them into the shadows behind the church. And then the screams turned into other sounds I still don't know how to describe. But I don't have to. You've heard them at night while you cower in your bedrooms.

The woman screamed, too, but it left her alone. She ran off into the night, and the sounds in the shadows ceased. And then it was just me and the silence again.

Only I wasn't alone. I could feel the ghost in the shadows. Watching me. Waiting. For what, I didn't know at the time. All I thought was that it was over. That whatever had crept into me in the Frozen City had left me now. That it wasn't my problem anymore.

I threw myself back into my car and drove home as fast as I could. I locked myself in my bedroom and kept all the lights on. For the first time in days, I slept.

I woke to a story in the newspaper about what had happened. The woman who wasn't Providence had gone to the police. She said three

men she didn't know had grabbed her on the street when she was walking home after her shift at the bar. She said they'd been drinking in the
bar all night. They were trying to drag her into an empty parking lot for
God knows what when another man had shown up. She said he yelled
at them and something came out of his mouth, something that took the
other men into the shadows. She said she thought he was some sort of
thing, because she saw tentacles waving from his face, and his hair was
floating, like he was in the water. The police cautioned women about
walking alone at night and taking drugs.

I went in the bathroom and looked at myself in the mirror, but I
didn't see any tentacles. My hair stayed matted to my head.

I got in the shower to wash away the memories of the night before.
And the voices started inside me again.

* * *

YOU KNOW the rest, of course. That woman was just the beginning.
There were many more after her. Too many to just pass off as drug
hallucinations or mental illness. You didn't know what was going on.
Neither did I.

All I knew was the voices grew inside me with their strange chanting,
night after night – "Urbl'phhar mypr'ttsh urbl'phhar" – until I couldn't
stand it any longer and went out into the dark to escape them.

And every night they drove me to Providence.

Providence being pulled into a van by two men in the parking lot of
a grocery store, until I jumped out of my car and yelled at them. And a
thing like a squid with crab legs slipped from my mouth and ran at them,
wrapping both up in its tentacles and dragging them screaming into the
van. It slammed the doors shut behind it and the woman who wasn't
Providence screamed even louder than the men and got into her own
car and drove away, leaving the groceries lying on the ground around a
trail of water and slime that led from me to the van.

Providence being beaten by a man in a house as I drove past. I stopped and got out of the car and yelled at him and a thing like an eel made of a thousand other eels flew through the glass without breaking it, and the lights inside went out and the cries began.

Providence being held hostage in a liquor store robbery. The man inside wore a stocking over his head as he held a gun to her cheek. The police turned to look at me as I hit the brakes on my car and jumped out, screaming. A scream that travelled through the air like a manta ray made of writhing shadows, a darkness that engulfed the man and took him into the back room, where he disappeared forever, just like all the others, as I got back in the car and drove away, leaving the woman who wasn't Providence shaking with terror in my wake, the cops standing there not knowing what to do at all.

After that, I started wearing a mask I bought in a gift shop. It was really just a white strip that covered my eyes. But it was enough for the media.

Ghost, they called me. The first real superhero.

* * *

THE WATER is at the edge of the coffin now, so I close the lid. That won't stop it from getting in, of course. But after decades of digging up the dead, I know there's a custom to these things.

I hope you've inscribed the proper warnings on the outside of this tomb. I'd add my own if I could. But, as we all know now, the warnings only work if the people who dig up the tomb can read them.

And who knows what strange creatures will find us?

"Pthhh'gatt mlew'hag," I say, the words escaping me. The ghosts sense something happening. They sense another entombment. They want to get out.

And I can't stop them.

I've never been able to stop them.

And the truth is I've never really wanted to stop them.

* * *

I ROAMED THE night, fighting crime. Releasing the ghosts within me to take the criminals into the shadows. To make more shadows in the corners of the city.

Like any hero, I even had a secret sanctuary. In the days, I visited Providence's grave. Sometimes I brought her flowers. I sat on the grassy plot for hours at a time, listening to the music inside me. I felt most comfortable there when it rained.

There had been a small funeral service for Providence after I returned from Antarctica. I signed off on the termination paperwork. Cause of death was listed as disappearance while on a freelance dig. Not connected to the university at all, so the department wasn't liable. Everyone came out to the service. I was the only one who wept. Which is probably how someone put things together and started the rumours that brought Smyth back to me.

Yes, I had the secret sanctuary, the tragic past, the mask. All the trappings of a superhero. I wasn't really fighting crime, though. I wasn't really a superhero.

I was just looking for a way to free Providence.

I knew that the women I kept seeing as Providence weren't her. I knew it was just a trick of the ghosts to anger me, to make me release them. I figured the only way they could know about Providence and me was if they had her in there with them, trapped in me somehow.

And I thought if I let enough of the ghosts out, maybe she could slip out, too. Maybe they'd free her, or maybe she could find a way to escape. Maybe we could be together again.

So I started looking for crimes where maybe none existed.

I drove down to the hooker stroll. I put on my mask and stood near a couple of sex workers on a corner. They looked at me but I shook my head, so they went back to waving at the passing cars. Every now and then one would slow, but it always sped up again when the driver saw me.

I only had to wait a few minutes before a man got out of another car parked down the street and walked up to me. He told me to stop harassing his women. I told him I was just keeping an eye out for criminals. He told me to move along before there was a real crime. I told him I was here for the real crime. He lifted his shirt to show me a gun tucked into his pants. I opened my mouth and screamed ghosts. Two of them came out. One took him into an alley, the other went after the women. I didn't care. They were criminals, too, in their own way.

Neither of the ghosts were Providence.

I stopped at a random bar. I put my wallet on the counter and pulled money out of it to pay for drinks. It was stuffed with twenties; I'd gone to the bank first. I made sure everyone could see my money. I got drunk and then I left. I heard men following me.

I staggered into an alley and fumbled my mask on. When I turned to face them, they had knives in their hands. They dropped them at the sight of my mask and ran. They didn't even make it to the street before the ghosts pulled them deeper into the alley.

The ghosts weren't Providence.

Sometimes I didn't even need a crime to release the ghosts. I was stopped at a red light when I was rear-ended by a taxi driver. He got out of his car saying something about the brakes. I got out of mine screaming, and the ghosts took him and slithered down a manhole with him. The ghosts weren't Providence.

The people in the back seat of the taxi filmed the whole thing and sold the film to the media. Luckily, I still had my mask on from when I'd gone after some street-corner drug dealers. But things changed after that.

The next morning I woke up to a new headline: Superhero? Or supervillain? A photo of me with something unrecognizable emerging from my mouth. Something long and sinewy, and wet and serrated.

My eyes were completely black. It was the first time I'd seen myself releasing a ghost.

I didn't recognize the man in the photo.

* * *

THE WATER seeps into the coffin now. Streams of it coming in through the cracks. My whole body shakes as I struggle to contain the ghosts. I can hear more metal sounds as you do whatever it is you're doing with the pipes.

Releasing the chemicals that will turn the water to ice?

Releasing poison?

Releasing something you've come up with to make the ghosts sleep?

None of it will matter. The ghosts always wake in the end. The ghosts always escape.

* * *

YOU KNEW it was me when the city started to change, didn't you? When the buildings began to cast dark shadows that didn't move no matter the position of the sun.

When the buildings began to twist upon themselves in impossible shapes.

When the symbols started to appear in the sidewalks and on the walls.

When the voices began to chant in the night, from the alleys and the sewers and the abandoned buildings.

When people started to go missing in record numbers.

That's when Smyth came to visit me in my office. I was sitting there, listening to the songs inside me, when he walked in without knocking even though the door was locked. He looked at the glyphs I'd marked on the walls with a knife and my blood, and then he sat down in the chair where students had once sat.

Where Providence had once sat.

"You need to tell me what's going on," he said.

"Ssshhllaat'in verden'tik," I said.

"Tell me what happened in the Frozen City."

"Ia ia ia ia."

He looked at my desk. At the photo of Providence surrounded by a ring of teeth and bits of bone and fingernails and other things. "You lied to us, and you're the only one who came back."

I wanted to tell him I wasn't sure I had come back. I wanted to tell him that even if I had, I thought I wasn't the only one.

"Fffhtg'pp," I said instead, the voices welling up inside me.

"We're going to have to do something about this," he said.

"Myllrhet'et," I laughed.

After he left, I went down the hall to look at myself in the restroom mirror. My eyes were black, and my skin was writhing, flesh-coloured worms. The head of the department came in to the restroom but stopped when he saw me.

"Ghost," he said. "You're the Ghost."

So I unleashed the ghosts on him.

After all, whether I was a superhero or a supervillain, I had to protect my secret identity.

And then I went out into the melting city in search of Providence.

* * *

YOU KNOW how this story ends.

I stalked the streets of the city. I turned day into night, and night into nightmare. The mayor declared a state of emergency and people fled, but no one came to help. No one would come while I was loose.

The government revealed the secret of the Frozen City and you exchanged your theories about what had happened.

I was a host for some horrible disease that I'd brought back from the Frozen City. Scientists said I should be called Vector, or maybe Carrier, not Ghost.

I was a superweapon, released from a lab of the Frozen City, or maybe even developed by our own government using technology from the Frozen City.

I was an inhabitant of the Frozen City who had switched places with the real me. I'd escaped into the world to wreak havoc and set the stage for an invasion of the rest of my kind.

None of these things were true.

After Smyth's visit, I knew what was true.

I was still me, the same me who'd gone to the Frozen City with Providence. But I was turning into something else. I was turning into a real ghost, the kind I carried around inside me.

I wondered about them. I wondered if maybe they, too, had once been people like me. I wondered if they'd been changed by the Frozen City.

I wondered if Providence was a ghost like the others now.

And I wondered if I no longer carried her inside me at all, if I'd already released her into the world but hadn't realized it.

I kept visiting her empty grave every day. Maybe I was waiting for a sign. Maybe I was waiting for you to finally do something. Which you did when Providence's grave opened beneath my feet and I fell through the trap door you had built and into this waiting tomb, and then the ceiling slammed shut again.

But by then it was too late, wasn't it?

* * *

THE WATER rises up around me in the coffin now, lapping at my face.

I wonder how many other Frozen Cities are out there, buried in the ice.

The ghosts inside me cry out. They want to escape their tomb. They want to escape me.

I wonder who will find me in the future. Who will break open my grave and release me?

Now the water is at my mouth. The ghosts scream.

Providence, I am so sorry.

I open my mouth and the ghosts rush out of me in a flood that cannot be stopped.

The Deity Salesmen
ALWAYS RING TWICE

The smell of smoke from a distant fire was in the air when the deity salesmen rang the doorbell.

Albee answered the door the first time. He wasn't sure why he bothered to leave his miniatures in the garage and walk all the way to the front door, but he did anyway. The only people who ever rang the doorbell were salesmen. Usually they were trying to sell lawn-care treatments or window cleaning or even new roofs. Like Albee would be around long enough at his age to enjoy a new roof.

When Albee and Church had first moved into the neighbourhood, the bell had rang almost every day with kids coming to the door to sell them cookies or chocolate bars or just to ask for their recycling for bottle drives. The kids had stopped ringing the bell after the accident. Now it was just the salesmen.

This was the first time they'd had deity salesmen come to the door, though. Albee knew about them, of course. He'd seen them sitting at bus stops and, one time, wandering around the abandoned Avalon housing development a half-dozen blocks over. Albee sometimes drove through there at night, when he was supposed to be at the grocery store. He liked to park and look at the half-built neighbourhood, where some of the homes were actually complete but empty. He'd try to imagine all the different lives he could have lived. Church was in some of them but not others.

The one night, he'd seen the deity salesmen coming down the street toward him when he was stopped in front of a lot that held only the wooden frame of a house. Someone had left naked store mannequins inside the unfinished home, with red plastic cups crushed in their hands, as if they were holding a party. The deity salesmen wore their black pants and black glasses and white shirts, with ties and shoes the same colour as the cups the mannequins held. They walked the deity between them, holding its hands like it was a small child. It was the size of a child, but that was where the resemblance stopped. The deity had been all horns and wings, and Albee had started the car and driven away from there before he got a closer look at it.

The travelling deity salesmen who came to Albee's door this afternoon could have been the same ones he'd seen in the Avalon development, but he wasn't sure. They all looked the same to him in their uniforms. The deity was different, though. This one was small and hunched over, as if it were curled around some deep pain inside itself. It was as black as – night? No, something even blacker than night, whatever that could be. It had tiny wings that looked stuck to its back, as if they'd never been used for flight, and pointed ears and a snout. It looked a little like a bat, if a bat were made of stone darker than night. At least it was more or less humanoid, Albee thought. He'd seen others that weren't and figured they had to be tough sells.

"Do you have a deity in your life?" the salesman on the left asked, skipping any sort of greeting and going straight to the sales pitch. "Because if you don't, we'd like to talk to you."

"I've got a deity," Albee said, because he'd seen a video once where a man with tattoos of an elephant creature wielding flaming swords had said you could get rid of deity salesmen by telling them you already had a deity. The man had been standing in a Starbucks for some reason, and people kept looking at him and the camera. The man said most deities didn't really get along and tended to fight if they found themselves in the same house. It was like politics, the man said, or pets. Albee didn't know if what the man said was true or not, and the Starbucks setting didn't help make up his mind. But he figured he could trust him because someone who was willing to tattoo elephant creatures on himself was obviously someone of great conviction.

"Lying is a sin to many deities," the salesman on the right said. He looked at Albee through his glasses as if he could see straight into his soul, if Albee had such a thing.

"Maybe you can leave me a card and I'll call you later," Albee said. He wanted to close the door and get back to his miniatures. He wanted the deity salesmen to move along before Church came to the door and talked to them. There was no telling what she might do these days.

"We're talking about a deity here," the first salesman said.

"This is a once-in-a-lifetime opportunity," the other salesman said.

The deity didn't say anything. It just stood there, hunched over, staring up at Albee with those black eyes.

"I'll think about it," Albee said and closed the door in their faces.

He made sure to lock the door and then he went back to the garage. The miniatures were the same as he'd left them. They were always the same as he'd left them.

They covered a sheet of plywood he'd set up on sawhorses in the centre of the garage. Model houses the same as the street outside. Even the trees and sidewalks and cars were the same. Albee had gone to a 3-D-printing service and had them print off models from an online street view. He'd spent the last few years painting the houses to look like the houses outside. He'd put little squares of fake grass around the houses to resemble the green lawns of his neighbours. He'd bought fake plastic trees and placed them in yards. He'd bought little plastic figurines of people that he'd dressed in outfits he'd ordered online to look like his neighbours. Whenever anything changed in his neighbourhood, he changed the miniatures to match. When the Wyatts next door had painted their house red, he'd taken a picture of the side of their house and matched the same shade of red for his model. When the Tannens up the street had split up, he'd taken the Rich Tannen miniature out of the house and put it back in his tool box of miniatures. He kept the Tannen children miniatures in a zip-lock bag in the tool box and he put them back in the house every second week. The only thing that wasn't true to life was the Wyatts' tree, which in the tabletop neighbourhood didn't shed leaves that blew all over everyone else's yards. Albee didn't really know how he'd replicate that and didn't want to think about it, because it was enough work just raking up those leaves every day. They never seemed to stop.

Albee looked down at his neighbourhood, at his own house. The figurine of Church was in the backyard, working in the garden where she spent most of her days. He was in the garage, where he spent most of his days. His figurine looked down at a sheet of balsa wood painted to look like the table he looked down at now. The figurine of the boy, their son, was in his bedroom, where he hadn't been since the accident. All was as it was supposed to be.

Except for the travelling deity salesmen. Their figures stood in front of the door of the model house where Albee and Church lived. The little figure of the deity stood between them. Albee stared down at the miniatures. He had never seen these figures before. He didn't move or look away, even as the doorbell rang again and again for several minutes before finally stopping.

Albee went to the tool box on one of the shelves in the garage. The real tool box, not the one he kept the spare miniatures in. He took out a pair of barbecue tongs he'd put in there for some reason he could no longer remember. Maybe he'd foreseen this day. He went back to the miniature neighbourhood and picked up the salesman on the left with the tongs. He took it over to the recycling bin in the corner of the garage and dropped it in. Then he went back and did the same thing with the salesman on the right. When he went back for the deity miniature, it was gone. He stared down at the front doorstep of the miniature home for a moment, but it was like the deity had never been there. He looked around the little house, peering into the bushes and even under the car in the front driveway to see if he had knocked it aside somewhere. But he couldn't see any sign of it. He looked on the garage floor under the neighbourhood, but there was only a couple of fallen screws and some paint stains. He kept looking all over the neighbourhood for the missing deity, until Church called him into the house for dinner.

When he went into the kitchen, he found the deity, the real deity, sitting at the table with Church. It was perched on the back of one of the chairs, like some sort of bird. He stopped and stared at it and it stared back at him with those black eyes.

"I heated up some soup," Church said. "The roasted tomato. And I made grilled cheese sandwiches." She was already sitting at the table. There was a streak of dirt across her brow, just under where the grey started. Like an accent. She looked out the window, at the street, as if what was out there was somehow more interesting than what was in their kitchen.

"What is that thing doing in here?" Albee asked. He looked around for an open window, thinking maybe it had flown into the house and didn't know how to get back out.

"A couple of nice young men came to the door," Church said. "They said it was a deity of love. Imagine that." She looked at the deity and smiled. The deity looked at her and then back at Albee. It didn't smile.

"I already told them no," Albee said. "We don't need a deity."

"What's the harm in a deity?" Church asked.

"Tell that to the Middle East."

"This isn't the Middle East yet."

"What sort of love?"

"What do you mean?" Church looked at him.

"What sort of love is it a deity of?"

"I don't know," she said. "But we could use any sort of love at all now, don't you think?"

Albee went to the front door again and looked up and down the street. He didn't see the deity salesmen anywhere. They were gone, but the smell of smoke was still in the air. And the lawn was covered in leaves from the Wyatts' tree again. Those strange leaves that curled up on themselves and turned red almost the instant they fell from the tree. Not for the first time, he wished the tree would fall like its leaves. Preferably on the Wyatts' side of the fence.

Albee thought about getting in his car and looking for the salesmen but he knew he'd never find them. They probably had a car hidden around the corner. They were probably driving back to their deity warehouse right now, laughing at Albee and Church.

"They said they'd come back tomorrow to see how we liked our deity," Church said from the kitchen. "They said we could return it if its love didn't work for us."

"How much did it cost?" Albee asked, still scanning the street. He thought he saw the blinds move in the front window of the house across from them. There was no car in the driveway, but the Wellingtons were retired and Linda Wellington often stayed home while Richard golfed. Albee suspected Richard golfed because Linda stayed home, but that was none of his business.

"That's the best part," Church said. "It didn't cost anything. It was free."

Albee stared at the Wellingtons' house for a moment longer. If Linda Wellington had seen Church take the deity, the whole neighbourhood would know soon. Linda had once worked in PR and she still thought it was her job to get the message out, whatever message might find its way to this sleepy street.

Albee thought about leaving the door open to see if the deity would leave on its own, but who knew what else might wander in? He closed the door and locked it, then went back to the kitchen.

"No good will come out of this," he said as he sat down at the table, across from the deity.

"What good ever comes out of anything?" Church asked.

They ate in silence, Albee and the deity looking at each other and Church looking out the window. Albee didn't really like roasted tomato soup, but he couldn't be bothered to complain. He thought Church needed something to do. Both of them had needed something to do since the accident and the leave from work and then early retirement that had followed.

After a time, the window began to rattle. Albee looked outside and saw a stream of those red leaves from the Wyatts' tree whip past, carried by the wind. The clouds were dark now and churning in the sky. Not moving, just churning.

"Was it supposed to rain today?" he asked.

"Is anything ever supposed to happen?" Church asked.

There was a loud bang, like someone had shot at them from the next room. Albee actually ducked in his chair, thinking maybe it was a random shooter, before his mind registered the rolling vibration of the thunder passing through their house.

"That was lightning," Church said, rather unnecessarily, Albee thought.

"I think it hit our house," Albee said. He shook his head at the deity. "I told you no good would come of that thing." The deity just shifted a bit on the chair, adjusting the grip of its claws. It kept on watching him. Albee saw its claws were gouging the wood frame of the chair, but he decided not to say anything about that. The table and chairs had been Church's choice and he'd never cared that much for them, anyway.

When Albee went back out to the front step, he saw that the lightning hadn't hit their house. Instead, it had hit the Wyatts' tree. The lightning had blown the tree apart, and it had fallen into the Wyatts' roof, caving in a section of it. A jagged shred of trunk still poked up over the fence, like a knife pointing at the sky.

Albee stared at the fallen tree and his neighbours' house, then looked up. The dark clouds had stopped churning and were drifting apart. Patches of sun shone through here and there. He didn't see any sign of rain. When he looked back down at the street, the pavement was dry.

The Wyatts came out of their house, then, to look at the damage. Albee waved at them, the reflexive greeting of neighbours. They waved back and then stared up at the tree stuck in their house.

"Everyone's all right then?" Albee called over to them, and they both nodded in response. They folded their arms at the same time, in that way couples have of mirroring each other, and shook their heads at the tree together.

Albee turned to go back into the house before they could ask any questions. He didn't feel right about this. Just a short while ago he'd been thinking about their tree falling over and now it had. He didn't know if it had anything to do with the deity or not, but he didn't want to answer any questions in case they'd seen the deity. It was this sort of thing that led to higher fences and anonymous complaints to the city about people parking in the street.

He bumped into Church, who was standing right behind him, also staring at the tree.

"Will you look at that," she said. She looked up at the sky. "What do you suppose caused it?"

Albee went past her without answering. He looked for the deity in the kitchen, but it was gone.

"Where is it?" he asked.

"Where is what?" Church said from outside, still staring next door.

Albee gazed around the kitchen but didn't see the deity anywhere. Maybe it had disappeared just like the miniature deity had vanished. He shook his head and sighed, then went to the cupboard that held the Scotch. He poured himself a glass and went back into the garage. That was where he found the deity.

It was perched on top of one of the storage units, looking down at the model neighbourhood. He didn't know how it had got up there, let alone opened the door to the garage. Maybe it had flown, but its wings still looked stuck to its back. Maybe it had climbed up there. He stopped thinking about that when he looked at the neighbourhood.

It looked mostly the same as when he'd left it. The difference was the Wyatts' tree. It was stuck in the roof of the Wyatts' house now. The roof was caved in, revealing the hollow space inside the Wyatts' house. Albee had never bothered to fill in the interiors of the model houses, mainly because he didn't know what most of them looked like inside. The remains of the model tree were scorched, as if it had been hit by lightning as well.

Albee stared at the model tree and house, then up at the deity. It stared down at him without blinking. He thought it stared down at him without blinking, anyway. He couldn't really see its face in the shadows.

"Shoo," he said, but the deity didn't move. He thought about opening the garage door so it could leave, but he was afraid the Wyatts might see it. He settled for taking his Scotch and leaving the garage. He locked the door behind himself. He wondered which had happened first, the real tree falling or the model tree falling.

The city sent out a crew within the hour to chop the tree into small pieces. They loaded the pieces into a long truck and covered the Wyatts' roof in a blue tarp. Albee watched the whole thing from the window of the guest bedroom upstairs. When the city workers drove away, Albee dropped onto the bed without taking his clothes off. He'd had several more Scotches by this point. Before he fell asleep, he heard Church come up the stairs and pass by the bedroom. She paused at the door to the boy's room, as she did every night. She had once suggested they take everything out of the room and put it into storage.

"We could paint it," she had said. "Make it a guest room."

"Who would visit us?" Albee had asked.

It was that same day that he had gone out and bought everything for his model neighbourhood. He didn't know why. He'd sometimes played miniatures with the boy. Dwarves and orcs and that sort of thing. He told himself his models were different, although he wasn't sure exactly what they meant.

Sometimes Church lay down on the boy's bed when Albee wasn't around, when he was out parked in the abandoned Avalon neighbourhood, dreaming of other lives. He knew she did so because he could see the outline of her body on the boy's sheets when he returned home. She never asked him where he was, so he didn't say anything about that.

When he thought about the boy, he wanted to weep. He closed his eyes as he lay there on the bed, to hold the tears in. He tried to imagine what the boy would have looked like now, but he couldn't even remember what he had looked like back then.

Church moved on, to the bedroom they had once shared on the other side of the boy's room. Albee fell asleep wishing he could see the boy one more time. He dreamed of the neighbourhood in flames. He was standing in the street, looking at the burning houses. He had a sense of something terrible coming down the street behind him, but he couldn't bear to turn around and face it. Maybe the dream was because of the smell of smoke in the air. Maybe it was something else.

He woke in the morning to the smell of coffee. When he went down to the kitchen, he found Church had already poured him a cup and made a breakfast of scrambled eggs and toast. She was standing in the middle of the kitchen with her own coffee, staring at the deity perched on top of the fridge. Albee looked at the deity himself as he reheated his meal in the microwave. He didn't know if Church had let it out of the garage or if it had got out on its own. He wasn't sure he wanted to know.

"I think I'll take it out into the yard," she said. "It looks like it could use some sun."

"It's a deity, not a plant," Albee said.

"Everything needs the sun."

"I don't want the neighbours to see it."

"Maybe they all have deities, too," Church said. "Maybe they're hiding their deities away. Maybe I'll bring our deity out and that will be all they need to bring their deities out. Maybe we'll have a block full of deities."

Albee went to the front door and grabbed the keys from the dish there without taking his breakfast out of the microwave.

"Where are you going?" Church asked.

"I'm going to find those deity salesmen."

"But we haven't even finished our trial period yet."

"Do you really think that's how it works?" Albee asked, walking out the door.

"Everything has a trial period," Church called after him. "I thought you of all people would understand that."

Albee drove down the street and around the corner. He kept on driving, until he found himself in the abandoned Avalon neighbourhood. He parked in front of a lot that held just a billboard of a home. The picture on the billboard was faded from the weather and peeling, but Albee could still make out the shape of the house, the ghostlike forms of the children playing on the lawn while a man barbecued and a woman gazed at the sky and laughed. He looked around but didn't see a home like that anywhere. He didn't see any travelling deity salesmen, either. He put the car back into drive and kept going.

He went through all the surrounding neighbourhoods but he couldn't find the deity salesmen. He'd known they wouldn't come back. Albee and Church were stuck with the deity. He didn't want it even if it was free. There was always a cost with deities. He was starting to understand that now.

He stopped at a red light by the grocery store. There were no other cars and no pedestrians waiting to cross. It was just a random red light. He sat there and looked out the window while he waited. A plane flew through the sky overhead, trailing a banner behind it.

Problem Deity Hotline, it said, followed by a phone number. Albee took it as a sign, because what else could it be? He memorized the number and then drove on when the light turned green.

He returned home around noon. The plane was gone from the sky now, likely because the churning clouds were back. They blocked out the sun and looked like they were about to fall on the neighbourhood. That wasn't the only thing. All the trees on the street had died. Piles of leaves sat on the ground around them, the wind of Albee's car stirring them up as he passed. He was so busy staring at them he almost missed his house as he approached. He looked down at the last second, just in time to see the boy run out into the street toward him.

Albee swerved to avoid hitting the boy, even as a part of his mind screamed at him that the boy wasn't there, that the boy couldn't be there. The other part of his mind watched with shocked resignation as the car bounced up over the sidewalk on the opposite side of the street, the impact knocking his hands free of the steering wheel. The car drove into the front of the Wellingtons' house, smashing through the front windows and into the living room before jerking to a sudden stop that set off the airbags. That's the way Albee remembered it, anyway. Because one second he was driving along the street, looking at the strange clouds and the dead trees, and the next second he was staring through the windshield at Linda Wellington, who was cowering on her couch, screaming and hitting the front of his car with a pair of binoculars she held in one hand.

"You'll scratch the paint!" he cried at her, before he realized the absurdity of what he was saying. He got out of the car and stumbled back through the wreckage of the window, toward his house. He looked around the street but he didn't see the boy, because how could he see the boy? The boy was gone and he wasn't coming back. He hadn't been there in the street. Albee had dreamed him.

Almost against his will, Albee looked up at the boy's window in their house and saw the shape pressed up against the glass there. It wasn't the boy. It was the deity.

"That's enough!" he screamed at the deity. "You'll scratch the paint!"

Church opened the front door just before he reached it. She shook her fist in his face.

"This is what you do?" she yelled at him. "This is what you do when you're in the garage?"

It took him several seconds to see she held the miniature of the boy in her hand.

"It's the deity," he said to her. "The deity is pretending to be the boy."

She stared down at the miniature in her hand instead of answering. Albee pushed past her and went into the house. He took the stairs two at a time and went up to the boy's room. But the deity wasn't there. It was just the boy's empty room like usual. Albee saw Church's shape on the boy's bed.

He went back downstairs and into the garage. The deity wasn't there, either, but the figure of the deity was back. It was in the boy's room in the model house. The boy's room that no longer held the boy.

Albee went back to the front door. Church was still standing there, looking at their car in the living room of the Wellingtons' house. Linda Wellington had stopped hitting the car with her binoculars and had disappeared now. The deity sat on the roof of the car, amid the broken glass and wood that had fallen on the vehicle. It looked back at them with eyes as black and expressionless as ever.

"I don't understand," Church said. "You drive this street every day."

"It was the boy," Albee said.

Church looked down at the miniature in her hand. Albee didn't tell her about the night before, about how he had wished he could see the boy one more time. Instead, he reached into his pocket and took out his phone. He called the number he had memorized for the problem deity hotline. It rang twice and then someone answered.

"What's the nature of your deity?" a woman's voice asked.

"The boy," Albee said again because he didn't know what else to say.

"Don't worry, we get a lot of this kind of call," the woman said. "Can you give me your address or the last known address of the deity's manifestation?"

"Avalon," Albee said.

"Avalon?" The woman asked.

"The housing development," Albee said. "The boy."

Now Church turned to look at him. The deity just kept on staring at him.

"We'll find it," the woman said. "We'll send someone around in the morning." And then she was gone.

Albee put his phone away and looked up and down the street. The neighbours that were home had come out of their houses now and were looking at their dead trees and the clouds churning overhead and Albee's car in the Wellingtons' house and at the deity perched on the roof of the car.

"Who were you talking to?" Church asked.

But Albee didn't answer. He just went inside and straight up to bed. He pulled the covers over his head without undressing and he stared into the white light of the sheets as he listened to the sirens and voices of the firemen and paramedics and Church talking to the police outside. He waited for morning.

The dawn came with an orange glow through the sheet. Only it wasn't dawn. When he got up and went to the window, the sky was still dark. The orange glow was on the horizon. Flames leapt up into the sky several blocks over. Albee knew what was burning. The Avalon neighbourhood.

He looked in the boy's bedroom and saw Church sleeping in the boy's bed. He went downstairs without waking her.

He didn't see the deity in the kitchen or the living room, but he heard a sound in the garage for a moment, before the sirens started up in the distance and drowned it out.

It sounded like someone was crying. Like a boy's sobbing.

Albee went and stood by the door of the garage for a moment. Now he could hear it better. Yes, it was definitely sobbing. It may have been the boy again. He didn't want to open the door to find out, but he couldn't help himself.

When he opened the door and stepped into the garage, he found the model neighbourhood on fire. The houses at the end of the street, where Albee took the turn to drive to Avalon, were burning.

The boy wasn't there but the deity was. The deity was the one sobbing. It stood in the middle of the model street, looking at the burning houses. Its body shook with its sobs, and now it let out a keening sound. It looked at Albee and he was shocked to see black tears filling its eyes and rolling down its misshapen cheeks. It looked down at the neighbourhood and another pair of model homes burst into flames. The fire was coming down the street toward their house.

And now Albee could hear screams outside. The screams of his neighbours.

"What have you done?" he whispered to the deity.

He hit the button on the wall that opened the garage door and stepped out into his driveway. The sky was a mix of orange and charcoal now, as the glow from the fires mixed with the smoke in the air. He turned and saw what was coming down the street toward them.

A flaming angel.

It was twenty or thirty feet tall – Albee couldn't tell for certain, on account of it being made entirely of flame. It had great burning wings that swept the air, reaching out to the trees and houses it passed and lighting them afire. The entire street was ablaze behind it. Even the pavement burned where it had stepped. Albee could barely look at its face, it burned so bright, but he thought he saw an expression of rage twisting there in the flames.

His neighbours were fleeing their blazing homes behind the angel, screaming as they ran out into the night and saw what had caused the fires. Some of them ran back into their homes, for who knew what. Maybe just to hide. Others got into their cars and drove away, weaving through the flaming footprints of the angel. Still others just stood in the street and stared.

Albee knew why the angel was here. The people from the problem deity hotline had sent it. It was here for their deity.

He turned and looked for the deity in the garage, but it was in the driveway with him now. It stood beside him and reached up to him with one clawed hand. Just like the boy had done when he was little and learning to walk. Albee couldn't help but take its hand. It felt rough and cold in his, like he was holding hands with a statue.

The angel roared when it saw the deity, and the sound shook the neighbourhood like thunder. Car alarms went off, joining the wail of smoke detectors. The angel's fires flared up and it expanded, doubling in size. The street was as bright as day.

The angel came at them in a rush. It flowed more than ran across the distance between them. The houses and trees on both sides of it burst into flame. Albee stumbled back into the garage but the deity stepped forward to meet the angel. It pulled its hand from Albee's and hopped down into the street. It was still sobbing and keening as it went. When it reached the street, it turned to look back at Albee with those black eyes. Then the angel loomed over the deity and its wings swept forward, encircling the deity and engulfing it. The flames of the angel flared so bright that Albee had to look away. He hit the wall several times until he found the button that closed the garage door, but it didn't work. Albee realized the garage door was burning. He looked down at the model neighbourhood now and saw all the houses burning. Including theirs.

He saw the figure of the boy catch fire in his room. He didn't know when Church had put him back there but she must have done it at some point. He leaped forward to save him, but the boy melted almost instantly. He disappeared into the flames before Albee could reach him.

Albee looked out into the street and saw the angel turn and go back the way it had come. The pavement burned in a pool in front of their house. The tree in the Wellingtons' yard burned. The Wellingtons' house burned. Albee's car, which was still embedded in the Wellingtons' living room, burned. There was no sign of the deity. The angel had taken it.

The smoke alarms went off inside the house and Albee snapped his gaze back to the model. The boy's room was burning now. The boy's room where Church had been sleeping.

"Church!" Albee cried and ran back into the house. There was smoke everywhere. He met Church as she was coming down the stairs, a wreath of smoke trailing after her.

"The boy's on fire!" she screamed at him. "The boy's on fire!" Her hands were red and blistering already from where flames had burned them.

He rushed past her up the stairs, to the boy's room. He knew the house was lost, but maybe they could save something from the boy's room. The bed the boy had slept on, or maybe some of his clothes. The photos on the walls. Something, anything.

But the room was entirely ablaze. He couldn't even get close to it because the walls of the hallway were burning. Great wings of flame leapt out the door of the boy's bedroom, and Albee knew in an instant that everything was lost.

Church screamed behind him, a high, keening noise that wasn't unlike the sound the deity had made. Albee turned and caught her hand in his. Together they stumbled down the stairs, through the smoke and flames, their screams merging with the screams of the smoke alarms.

They emerged into what seemed to be the end of the world. Both sides of the street were just walls of flames now, as the houses and trees and yards burned. The angel had disappeared with the deity, gone back to wherever it had come from. The sky was full of churning smoke from all the fires. There were sirens and alarms in the distance, but he didn't see any fire trucks or police cars on their street.

Their neighbours were fleeing their homes, running for the ends of the street in either direction. But Albee and Church didn't try to escape. Instead, they looked back at their house and watched the fire consume it.

They fell into each other's arms and hung on as the world burned around them, because it was all they had.

You Shall Know Us
BY OUR VENGEANCE

Noir had just finished killing Van Gogh in his bedroom when the angel spoke to him for the first time.

"That was messy," it said.

It had been a very messy kill, in fact, on account of Noir using a knife on Van Gogh, who hadn't even been able to get out of his bed. Noir could have used a gun and done the job with one shot. He could have been distant and merciful instead of close-up and cruel. But the Choir had told him to use a knife.

"Make it hurt for a long time," the Choir had said when they'd called him earlier that night to give him the job. "This contract is all about sending a message."

So Noir had gone to Van Gogh's building, which was the tallest residential tower in the city. There were taller commercial towers, but the office towers were always taller. He'd taken the elevator up to Van Gogh's condo. It wasn't the penthouse, but it was close enough there wouldn't be a difference to the average person on the street. Noir had unlocked the lobby door and elevator using a pass he'd bought from another freelancer like himself who specialized in such things. He tried not to look at the mirrored parts of the elevator's interior. Whenever he caught a glimpse of his own reflection lately, he saw the face of one of his previous victims instead. He took that as a sign it was probably time to get out of this line of work. But he had a few more jobs to do first. Like Van Gogh.

Noir had simply walked out of the elevator and into Van Gogh's condo like he belonged there. The walls were mostly windows, but where they weren't Van Gogh had hung photos of city scenes: car accidents, faceless people running from someone or something, the windows of other people's apartments, that sort of thing. The furniture was all red. Noir knew exactly what kind of person Van Gogh was before he went into the bedroom.

Noir had surprised Van Gogh in the middle of fucking a sex doll. It was a cheap inflatable doll made of plastic, even though Van Gogh was clearly the type of person who could have afforded a more lifelike model. Its limbs were duct-taped to the bed frame and Van Gogh was pumping away when Noir walked into the room. Van Gogh looked over his shoulder at Noir but didn't stop fucking the doll. Van Gogh had a tattoo of bat wings on his shoulder blades, or maybe they were devil wings. Noir wasn't entirely sure and didn't care.

"I didn't order anyone from the agency tonight," Van Gogh said.

"I'm from a different agency," Noir said and took the knife out of his jacket pocket.

"Ah, damn it, not a blade," Van Gogh said. He rolled off the sex doll and reached for the bedside drawer, but Noir beat him to it, kicking it shut with one foot and trapping Van Gogh's hand inside. He didn't listen to anything Van Gogh screamed after that.

He lay down on the bed when he was done, between the sex doll and what was left of Van Gogh. That was when the angel spoke to him.

"That was messy," the sex doll said in a voice that sounded like a woman who'd inhaled a bunch of helium.

Noir reacted instinctively, rolling over and ramming the knife into the sex doll's throat. There was a bang like a balloon popping and air hissed out of the doll. That didn't stop her from turning her deflating head to look at Noir.

"Oh, come on, what am I going to do to you?" she said. "I'm a sex doll. I'm still taped to the bed, for Christ's sake."

Noir stood back up and looked around the room. He didn't know what was going on. He'd been caught so off guard he'd left the knife in the doll's throat. He wondered if maybe someone was watching the room through a spy camera and using the sex doll's voice equipment to speak to him. But he didn't know why someone would do that.

"Take me home with you, Henrik," the sex doll said. "Do that and maybe I'll save your soul."

Noir stared at the doll. "How do you know my name?" he asked. For Henrik was his true name. Noir was the name he had given himself when he'd started in this line of work. It was a way of distancing himself from what he did for a living. Henrik wasn't the sort of person who could kill other people. But someone named Noir? A man named Noir could kill someone slowly with a knife and not lose any sleep over it. That's what he'd thought, anyway.

Noir gave each of his victims code names for the same reasons. He named them all after artists. Van Gogh. O'Keefe. Caravaggio. Blake. And so on. It made what he did somehow more acceptable. Like the killings were works of art, something beautiful. You did what you had to in order to get the job done.

Noir had never told anyone about the code names he used for victims or the name he used for himself. The Choir never even addressed him by name when they called. He was just a series of numbers: a phone number, a bank account number, a number of victims. Eleven so far.

"Twelve successful hits and you quit," the sex doll said, as if reading his mind. Because that was his plan. Twelve hits and then retire with the small fortune he'd saved. Twelve hits and it would be time to kill Noir and become someone else. Maybe even Henrik again.

But nowhere in his plans had he ever accounted for a talking sex doll that knew his real name.

Noir walked around the bed, examining the sex doll from different angles. It looked like a sex doll and nothing more, except for the fact that it turned its head to follow him around the room.

"Who are you?" he asked. "And why are you talking to me?"

"Isn't it obvious?" the sex doll said. "I'm an angel."

"No, that wasn't immediately obvious." Noir stopped on the other side of the bed.

"You'd prefer a burning bush?"

"I'm not really a religious man, so all of this is probably wasted on me."

"Nobody is religious until it's too late," the sex doll said. "Now, could you remove your knife from my throat and seal the wound with a piece of duct tape? Once all the air leaves this body, so do I. But my job here is not done yet."

"You're nothing but air?" Noir asked.

"It's an angel thing," the sex doll said. "It would take the rest of your life to explain and you probably still wouldn't understand."

Noir thought it over but didn't see that he had anything to lose if he did what the sex doll asked. So he tore a piece of duct tape from one of the doll's wrists, then slid his knife out of the doll and quickly taped over the hole. The sex doll was a little softer now, but still usable, if that had been his inclination.

"Now untie me and let's get out of here before someone else shows up," the sex doll said.

"Who else would show up here?" Noir asked. Not for the first time, he had the sudden worry that he would arrive at a contract to discover he was the contract. That's why in his plans he was twelve and out. He'd never even met the Choir, so how could he trust them?

"I don't think either of us would want to find out," the sex doll said.

Noir still didn't know what was happening, but he decided to go along with things for the moment, mainly because he didn't know what else to do. If he left the sex doll in Van Gogh's place, he was potentially leaving a witness behind. So he cut the tape binding the doll to the bed frame and freed it. The sex doll tried to sit up but couldn't quite manage. It raised itself a little, like it was doing a sit-up, then fell back down.

"I don't have the strength to move this body about," the sex doll said. "You'll have to carry me."

"What kind of angel are you that you can't even move?"

"I'm an angel that manifested in a blow-up doll. We don't have a lot of say in these matters."

"I kind of expected angels to be more impressive." He lifted the sex doll up by an arm, keeping it clear of the mess on the bed.

"We move in mysterious ways and all that," the sex doll said. "Now scrub the scene and let's get out of here."

Noir took the sex doll into the main room and propped it on a chair near the elevator. He opened the backpack he'd left on the floor there and took out a spray bottle. He went back to the bedroom and sprayed it all over the remains of Van Gogh and the bedsheets. The chemicals in the bottle started breaking everything down immediately and dissolving any signs of Noir he may have left behind. He wiped down all the surfaces with a cloth. Finally, he used the same spray bottle on the floor, walking backward across the condo to clean away any traces of his footprints.

"I would have just burned the whole place," the sex doll said.

"Draws too much attention, even if it is simpler," Noir said.

"Simple has nothing to do with it. It's about sending a message. Angels are all about sending messages."

"Were you the one that hired me then?" Noir asked.

"Angels do not work in the cheap currency of the mortal world," the sex doll said.

"Yet here you are in a blow-up doll."

"Even the angels must be punished for our sins."

Noir carried the sex doll into the elevator and they went down into the lobby, then walked out to the car, which was still where he had left it in the street. Noir didn't worry about the cameras. The same man he had paid for the pass also took care of that. There was an economy for everything.

Noir drove for a while in silence, wondering if he had imagined the whole thing with the sex doll. Maybe it was like the faces he saw. Maybe he had PTSD. He had killed eleven people now, after all. That was bound to do something to your mind.

"Are we there yet?" the sex doll asked from the back seat, where he had laid it to keep it out of sight.

"I thought angels were supposed to be all-seeing or all-knowing or something," Noir said.

"You're thinking of God," the sex doll said. "And Santa Claus."

Neither one of them said anything else for the rest of the trip home.

Noir lived in a shipping container in the parking lot of an abandoned Home Depot. The parking lot was full of shipping containers like his. Some of the other residents had set up patios on the roofs of their shipping containers, or surrounded them with artificial grass and little white plastic fences, but Noir hadn't done any of that. He didn't even have a mat in front of the door cut in the side of the container. It wasn't really a place he thought of as home.

He parked in front and went inside, taking the sex doll with him. He locked the door behind them. It was a basic model container, so there were no windows. No one could see inside. He put the sex doll on the floor by his gun case, then changed his mind and moved it over to the little Ikea table against one wall, placing it on one of the chairs. He didn't want it near his guns.

"Is this where you live?" the sex doll asked, looking around slowly. "Or is this just where you take people to kill them?"

"I don't need anything special," Noir said.

"Clearly."

"You know what I've done but you don't know where I live?" Noir asked.

"Your life doesn't matter enough to pay that much attention to it," the sex doll said. "No human's life matters that much."

"I'm not planning on staying long anyway."

"Your lives are pretty short. I don't know how you can stand it."

"I meant I didn't plan on staying long here," Noir said.

"That's probably not a bad idea, given your line of work."

As strange as it was to be having a conversation with a talking sex doll, Noir found it even stranger to be talking to a partially deflated sex doll. He went over to his bag and took out the lighter he always kept in there in case he needed to burn the crime scene or the target. He went back to the doll and tore off the tape covering the hole in its neck.

"What are you doing?" it cried. "I haven't even passed judgment yet." It batted at him with its balloon arms.

Noir pinched the hole shut, then flicked the lighter on and held the flame against the plastic.

"Son of a bitch, that hurts!" the sex doll cried. "Are you some sort of sadist as well as a killer?"

"I thought you said you were an angel," Noir said. He kept burning the plastic, until it melted together and sealed the hole.

"I am at the mercy of the body I am trapped within. You see how you fare when you're the one burning."

Noir dropped the lighter to the table and held the plastic together a moment longer, to make sure it wouldn't come apart.

"Motherfucker," the sex doll said. "Don't do that again."

Noir released the doll and the seal he'd made held. He blew on his fingers, which he just now realized he'd burned.

"Such a strange vessel," the sex doll said. "I wish I could have done that little trick with some of my other incarnations. It would have made my time spent on the earthly realm a little less unpleasant."

Noir searched the doll until he found the nozzle to reinflate it, which was on the back of its neck.

"Let's not make this weird," the sex doll said.

"I think it's a little late for that," Noir said between breaths into its neck. "So just how long do you plan on staying anyway?"

"I have as much time as there is breath in this body. Once the last breath leaves, I am freed from this prison."

"So you're just like the rest of us then." Noir sealed the nozzle again and pushed it back into the doll. It started laughing and he thought maybe he'd tickled it somehow. Then he saw it was looking directly at the family photo on his Ikea bookshelf.

"Oh my God," it said. "Is that all you want?"

He turned the chair so it faced the wall, and thankfully the sex doll didn't keep looking over its shoulder at the photo. It just stared at the wall instead and shook its head.

"You humans never cease to amaze me. Some of you dream up such miracles as nuclear bombs and black holes, but most of you never fantasize about anything more than reproducing. Look at me. I am a wonder of the modern world, a complex mix of chemicals and electronics and theories of psychology. I am a prime symbol of capitalism, of the marvels of the supply chain and economics. And all most of you can think about it is sticking your cock in me and moving it about until some primal trigger goes off. You yearn for the heavens but you're too busy fucking your lives away to figure out how to reach them."

Noir went over to the photo and laid it face down, so the sex doll could no longer see the picture of him and the woman and the children. He went to the sink and began to wash the knife.

"What's this philosophy lesson going to cost me?" he asked. "Or is it a gift from those heavens I can't reach?"

"Nothing in this world is ever free," the sex doll said. "Not even a simple thing like murder, as you well know."

Noir laid the knife down in the dish rack and turned to look at the sex doll again.

"How do I know you're real and I'm not just imagining you?" he asked.

"You shall know us by our vengeance," the sex doll said.

"That sounds like kind of a rehearsed line. Like it's what you say to everyone."

"Do you have a history of imagining sex dolls possessed by angels? Because if so, then yes, you may be crazy."

"I'm pretty sure you're the first. What I meant is how do I know you're a real angel?" Noir wasn't a religious person given his occupation, but he figured if he was going to believe he was having a conversation with a talking sex doll, then he should probably consider the possibility it was telling the truth when it said it was an angel.

"Well, I know your real name, which no one else knows," the sex doll said.

"It wouldn't take an angel to figure that out," Noir said.

"And then there's the fact that I know you're about to get a call for your next contract, and I know who it will be."

Noir took his phone from his pocket. As soon as he held it in his hand, it began to vibrate with an incoming call. The Choir.

"Hallelujah," the sex doll said.

Noir looked at the sex doll and then back at the phone. He hit the talk button.

"I terminated the contract," he said into the phone.

"We expected no less," the Choir said. It really was a choir of voices, men and women, dozens of them all speaking in unison. Maybe it was a group of people, maybe it was one person using some sort of voice app to disguise his or her identity. Noir had never known the truth. It didn't matter. To Noir, the voices were just the Choir.

"We have a new contract for you," the Choir said. "Marked urgent."

"I'm not sure I'm ready for another contract," Noir said, looking at the sex doll. "I may have some issues."

"The employer is only in town for a short time," the Choir said. "The contract needs to be fulfilled before the employer leaves."

"What's the contract?" Noir asked. Because maybe it was time to finish the twelfth job and get the hell out. He walked over to the gun case to check his inventory, even though he knew it off by heart. Old habits.

"Priest named Roman at the Blessed Virgin Mary Church," the Choir said. "Basic contract, no special requests."

"I'm en route," Noir said and disconnected. He slid the phone back in his pocket and selected a Glock from the case. He didn't bother grabbing any extra clips. It was a priest – how much trouble could he be? He turned around to find the sex doll had turned in its chair and was looking at him.

"Let's get going before Roman closes the Blessed Mary and turns in for the night," the sex doll said.

No, Noir decided. Not the sex doll. The angel. If it knew what the Choir had said, if it knew his name, that was enough for him to believe.

"Are you here for me?" he asked. After all he'd done, he probably deserved worse than an angel.

The angel laughed. "I don't care about you," it said. "I'm here for the priest."

* * *

NOIR PUT the angel in the front seat of the car when they drove to the church. He didn't feel comfortable having it sitting behind him now that he thought it was actually an angel. He kept his gun in his lap, even though he didn't know if it would do any good.

"What you said earlier about saving my soul, did you mean it?" he asked as they travelled the deserted streets.

"I said maybe," the angel said. "Maybe I'd save your soul."

"You're not really offering me much incentive to help you," Noir said.

"Look, saving souls isn't really what I do," the angel said. "That's the job of other angels. But I can put in a good word if it means that much to you."

Noir shook his head but the angel didn't seem to notice. Or maybe it just pretended not to notice. He glanced in the rear-view mirror to see if anyone was following them and then looked away when he caught sight of his reflection.

"What about Heaven?" he said.

"What about it?" the angel asked.

"What's it like? Is it anything like the stories?"

"I don't know. I've never been there."

"But you're an angel."

"That's like saying you should have been to Gotham City because you call yourself Noir," the angel said. "Have you ever been to Gotham City?"

"How do I know you're an angel and not a devil?"

The angel turned its head to look at the darkened buildings they passed.

"There's not much of a difference, to be honest."

Noir dropped his right hand to the gun and drove one-handed the rest of the way.

"What did Roman do?" he asked. He didn't normally care why his contracts had become contracts. But he didn't normally have an angel along for the ride.

"He has sinned," the angel said. "Why else would I be here?"

"Maybe to save someone?"

"That would be a miracle."

"We've all sinned," Noir said. "Some of us worse than others."

"I know," the angel said, turning to look at him and then back at the empty street. "I've seen it. But you will all be judged in time."

Noir didn't ask any more questions as he drove. He tried to imagine what sort of sins a priest would commit to earn a visitation from an angel. The things he thought up made him lower the window for air.

He parked on the street a half block away from the church. He could have parked directly in front of the church because there were no other cars there, but he didn't want to stand out in anyone's memory.

"Don't go anywhere," he told the angel. "This won't take long." He hoped no one came along and saw the angel sitting there in the car. He didn't want someone to steal it.

"I'm coming with you," the angel said. It pawed at the door handle with its plastic hand for a few seconds before sighing. "Damn this body. This is like a cosmic joke."

"I don't really want to roam the streets with a talking sex doll," Noir said.

"That is nothing compared to what will roam the streets one day," the angel said.

So Noir went around to the passenger side and pulled out the angel. But when he closed the door, the angel's hand somehow managed to get caught in it.

"Fuck fuck fuck fuck fuck fuck fuck," the angel said.

Noir opened the door again and freed the angel's hand. It turned its head to stare at him like he had done it on purpose.

"Sorry about that," he said.

"Are you really?" the angel asked.

Noir tucked the angel under his arm and walked to the church as fast as he could. He didn't see anyone watching but that didn't mean they weren't. He went up the steps of the church and opened the front door, grabbing the handle through the sleeve of his shirt so as not to leave fingerprints. He took the angel through the lobby and into the area with the pews. He didn't know what it was called and he didn't want to ask the angel for fear of being judged. The lights were on inside, but only at half level. Candles burned on a table against the back wall. There was no one else in sight. It must have been near closing time, if churches closed. He wasn't really sure about that.

"All right, where's the contract?" Noir asked.

"All good things come to those who wait," the angel said. "And many things that are not so good, as well."

Noir sat in a pew halfway up the aisle. He propped the angel beside him. They both looked at the empty cross hanging on the wall behind the altar.

"It's nice that we're alone," Noir said.

"It's almost like divine intervention," the angel said.

Noir took a hymn book out of the shelf on the pew in front of him. He flipped through the pages but he didn't recognize any of the hymns.

"Is he ever coming back?" Noir asked.

"Who?" the angel asked, and Noir nodded at the cross.

"Oh, him," the angel said. "Would you come back here if you didn't have to?"

They sat in silence for a while longer. Noir could hear the sounds of someone moving around in a back room. He made sure the safety was off on the Glock. He thought about saying a prayer but then realized he didn't know any.

"What's your name?" he asked the angel to pass the time.

"Amber," the angel said.

"That seems like a strange name for an angel," Noir said.

"It was the name on my package. One mortal name is as good as any other."

"Amber the angel." It didn't sound quite right.

"Amber the angel of death," the angel said, which Noir thought sounded a little better but not much.

That was when the priest came out of a door in the back corner of the church. He was dressed in a black robe, like he was presiding over a trial. He walked over to the table with the candles and blew them out before he noticed Noir and the angel sitting in the pew.

"Good evening!" he called with a little wave.

"It most certainly is," the angel said. Noir could only think of it as the angel, not as Amber. "For the moment of judgment is upon us."

The priest squinted at them, as if he were trying to make them out in the half-light. He walked down the steps and came along the aisle toward them, stopping a few pews away when he could clearly see Noir was sitting with a sex doll. "This is inappropriate," he said.

"You're a fine one to talk with all that you have done," the angel said.

The priest looked back and forth between the angel and Noir. "Are you some sort of ventriloquist?" he asked. So Noir figured priests weren't any better than him when it came to seeing angels.

"No, that is definitely not what I am," Noir said. Although he had once killed a man who had a puppet hanging on the back of his bedroom door.

"He is just as fallen as you, though," the angel said.

"If you're looking for sanctuary for the night, we don't do that here," the priest said. "I'd suggest the mission over by the park."

"We are not here for sanctuary," the angel said. "We are here for punishment."

Noir shrugged because he didn't really know why they were here. Well, he knew why he was here. Which was all that mattered in the end.

"Punishment," the priest said, staring at the angel. He picked up a hymn book from a nearby pew and blew imaginary dust from the cover.

"You have worn garments of cloth made of two kinds of material," the angel said. "Polyester cotton blends more times than it is fit to mention in a house of worship."

The priest stared at the angel. Noir turned to stare at the angel.

"You want him dead because of the clothes he wears?" he asked.

"This is about sin," the angel said. "And no sin is greater than those committed by a representative of God."

"We all wear blends," Noir said. "This is the twenty-first century."

"I admit we've fallen behind in our judgments," the angel said. "We're trying to catch up. We'll get to you all in time."

That was when the priest ran. He lunged past them, heading for the front doors. Noir raised his gun and shot the priest. Only the priest threw the hymn book at him as he ran past and Noir shot it instead. The book exploded into a storm of pages as Noir hit it with three bullets. He spun in the pew to shoot the priest in the back, but stopped when the angel started screaming beside him.

"I have to see it!" the angel said. "Or it does not matter. Bring me to him so I can see it."

So Noir grabbed the angel and ran after the priest, who was already through the doors and outside the church. By the time Noir made it down the steps, the priest was halfway up the street. His arms and legs flailed to the sides as he ran, as if he were some sort of mad scarecrow come to life.

"Surely even a mortal like you could manage to shoot him from here," the angel said.

The angel was right: it was an easy shot. But Noir didn't want to shoot the priest outside. It would be too noisy and it would draw witnesses. Witnesses who couldn't help but notice the man hanging on to a sex doll. He wasn't sure why the priest wasn't calling for help, but that was working in Noir's favour for the moment.

Noir followed the priest up the street, tucking the angel under his arm as he ran. He closed the distance between them quickly even though he was saving some energy for when he caught the priest. But then the priest glanced back at Noir and swerved to the left. He went through the entrance of a cemetery, pushing open the gate with his shoulder and not bothering to close it behind him.

"How fitting," the angel said. "Strike him down now among the dead he has betrayed."

But when Noir followed the priest into the cemetery he saw that it wouldn't be that easy. Roman ran through leaning, moss-covered grave markers toward a tent in the middle of the cemetery. Candlelight flickered from inside the tent. The priest was going for help.

"You have my blessing to kill whoever is inside that tent along with the priest," the angel said.

"I've never killed someone outside of a contract before," Noir said.

"What's one more murder in the dark stain that is your soul?" the angel asked.

The priest paused outside the tent and looked back at them again. Then he opened the tent and fell inside. Noir caught a glimpse of a woman in there, sitting on an air mattress with a candle beside her. She looked up from the book she was reading, and then she disappeared as the priest zipped the tent shut.

"Shoot them through the tent," the angel said. "She is just as deserving of judgment for sheltering him."

"I'm not going to kill some innocent woman," Noir said.

"That is why you could never be an angel," the angel said.

"I imagine there are a lot of reasons I could never be an angel." He put the angel down on the ground outside the tent and opened the zipper. He pushed open the flap and looked inside the tent.

And the woman sitting on the air mattress shot him.

Noir barely had time to register the small handgun she held in a two-handed grip and the flash from the muzzle before a line of fire suddenly flared along his left side and the crack of the shot snapped in his ears.

Noir shot at her reflexively several times as he fell back among the graves. She spun to the side and cried out, so he knew he'd hit her. Then the flap dropped shut again.

Noir lunged into the tent without taking the time to check his wound. He wasn't sure if the woman was dead or not and he didn't want to give her time to recover or the priest time to grab the gun. He knew he was hurt bad because of how slow he moved, and the fact he couldn't help but cry out as he crashed into the tent. He'd have to figure out how bad later.

The woman was lying half off the air mattress, curled up in the fetal position. The candle had fallen onto its side up against the back wall of the tent but it still burned. The gun was on the air mattress, and the priest was reaching for it on his knees but he froze when Noir came through the opening.

Noir waved him away from the gun even though he could have shot him and terminated the contract right there. But the angel had said it wanted to watch. So he kept his gun trained on the priest and reached back out into the graveyard. He felt around until he touched the angel, then he grabbed it and pulled it inside the tent. The priest remained on his knees and stared at him the whole time.

"Who's she?" Noir asked, nodding at the woman. He thought maybe she was a homeless woman who camped out in the cemetery, but if so she was well armed for a homeless person.

"She's a prostitute I've been trying to save," the priest said. "She has no part in whatever this is."

"A whore just like Mary," the angel said. "We should have just burned the entire world when we had the chance."

"Oh, fuck you," the woman said without looking at them. "Fuck all of you in your tight asses."

Now Noir took a second to glance down at his side. He was hoping to find a torn strip in his jacket, or some other sign the bullet had only grazed him. But there was a dark, wet hole instead, which told him the bullet had gone straight in. His jacket was soaked with blood. He needed to get to his doctor soon.

"I beg you for your forgiveness," the priest said to him. "I didn't know that what I had done was still a sin."

"Tell the angel, not me," Noir said. "I'm just the executioner."

The priest stared at the angel like he still didn't believe it was real. Noir knew the feeling. The woman looked over her shoulder at them and somehow managed to laugh at the sight of the angel.

"It's always about fucking with you lot, isn't it?" she said.

"Shut your damned mouth, whore," the angel said. "Or you will be next on my list of judgment."

"Just when you think you've seen every kink," the woman sighed but put her head back down.

"All right," the priest said, turning to the angel. "I, ah, I beg you for your forgiveness."

"Not like that," the angel said. "You must treat my earthly body in the manner which it deserves."

"I, ah, I," the priest said.

"Lie me down and spread my legs," the angel said to Noir.

"I'm not really comfortable with this," Noir said.

"And you think I am?" the angel said. "The sooner we do it, the sooner it's over with."

So Noir laid the angel on its back in the tent, which was beginning to feel crowded. He placed its legs around the priest, who was looking pale now.

"Confess your sins," the angel said to the priest.

"I have, uh, worn garments . . ." the priest said and then his voice trailed off.

"Whisper them into my pussy," the angel said.

The priest looked at Noir, who could only shrug. He wouldn't have done it himself, because he figured the priest was a dead man either way. He just wanted to get this done so he could call his doctor and see if he was going to live or die himself. He was feeling light-headed, and he wasn't sure if it was from the adrenalin or the blood loss.

"Oh, like you've never done that before," the woman said without moving from the fetal position.

The priest glanced at her and then bent down and placed his face in the angel's lap. He laid his hands on the angel's legs for support. He began to mutter words that Noir couldn't hear.

"That's it," the angel said. "Just like that."

Noir looked away because he didn't want to watch this. So he missed the priest grabbing the fallen gun and jamming it into the angel's pussy. He only realized what was happening when the priest pulled the trigger and a blast of escaping air from the angel hit him.

Noir brought his gun up and shot the priest in the forehead. He pulled the trigger twice, but the gun only fired once before the slide locked back.

He was out of bullets. There was still a spray of blood as a hole appeared in the priest's head. He slumped back down into the angel's pussy again, even as the angel continued to deflate.

The woman suddenly rolled to the side and through the tent wall, like a ghost. For several seconds, Noir thought she was another strange creature like the angel. Then he saw the ragged cut in the fabric of the tent near the floor. She'd sliced an opening in the wall of the tent. Maybe while she'd been lying there, maybe sometime before. He figured it wouldn't be a bad escape hatch for a prostitute to have.

"Help, for the love of God, help!" she cried in the night. "They killed our father!"

Noir couldn't even shoot her to shut her up because he was out of bullets. He should have brought more magazines along with him, but he hadn't been expecting this. Who could have known a priest would be so much trouble?

"Our time here is nearly at an end," the angel said as it continued to deflate. "Thank God."

The woman kept on screaming outside but her voice was growing fainter now. Noir went back through the flap and looked around. He saw people converging on the tent from all directions. Men and women with long hair and wearing layers of clothes. He could tell from a glance they were homeless people. They'd probably been sleeping in different parts of the cemetery, maybe even in tents of their own. They closed in on him with knives and bottles and wrenches in their hands. He spun in a quick circle and counted them.

There were eleven of them. The same number of contracts he'd terminated.

Twelve contracts if you counted the dead priest inside the tent.

And now he saw their faces. They were all the victims he'd killed before. There was O'Keefe staggering through the graves holding the wrench, with Caravaggio clutching a broken wine bottle close behind. Rembrandt came around the side of the tent with a screwdriver in his hand. Frida came out of the darkness behind the others with a small blowtorch in her hands. And so on. Noir wasn't sure what he was imagining and what was real. He suspected it no longer mattered.

He went back inside the tent and looked for the woman's gun, but it was gone. She must have taken it with her when she ran. The priest still lay there, face down in the angel's crotch. The angel was as gaunt as a concentration camp survivor now. The back wall of the tent was burning, ignited by the fallen candle.

"Let the rest of the air out of me before I catch fire," the angel said. "I don't want to burn to death. That hurts like hell."

Noir remembered its earlier words that it was trapped in this body until the last breath left it. He didn't move.

"So that's how it's going to be," the angel said. "All right, I will personally deliver your soul to where it belongs. How many can truthfully say they were led to judgment by an angel?"

Noir considered asking the angel if it meant to deliver him to Heaven or Hell. He doubted it was Heaven, given what he'd done in his life, but maybe he still had a chance because he'd helped the angel. Then he remembered the angel had said it had never seen Heaven.

"What are you thinking about?" the angel cried as the flames began to lick at its feet. "Deliver me, for fuck's sake!"

Noir was thinking that it didn't matter. He didn't want anything more to do with angels, not after tonight.

He dropped the empty gun on the ground. He'd always told himself that when he finished his twelfth contract he would kill off the Noir character. He just never thought it would happen like this. He closed his eyes and thought of the photo in his home. He turned to leave the tent.

"You can't be serious," the angel said, as if it were reading his mind again. "You can't choose that mob of fallen mortals over me. They'll tear you apart." And then it cried out as the flames caught hold on its legs and the plastic began to bubble and melt.

"I think I'll take the fallen mortals over dead angels," Noir said. He left the angel screaming in the burning tent and went out into the night with his arms spread wide, to meet whatever fate awaited him at the hands of his fellow men.

The Last Love
OF THE
INFINITY AGE

I come back to life when the sleeper nuke Doc Apocalypse hid in the subway system goes off and destroys the city. Except I'm not really dead before that. I'm stuck in the Frozen Zone of the city with a few thousand other popsicles who got caught in the crossfire back when the Union of Soviet Super Comrades brought the Cold War home to us.

One minute I was standing there in the flower shop, a bouquet of flowers in my hand for Penny. The woman who had just sold me the flowers told me with a smile to have a nice day. Then there was the sudden white light as the Comrades' flash freeze hit. And for the next twenty years I was a block of ice in the flower shop, a bouquet of flowers for Penny frozen in my hand.

Then there's another flash of light, this one from Doc Apocalypse's nuke, and the ice melts away and I'm shaking uncontrollably as I stand there in the ruins of the flower shop. I'm ankle deep in water. The roof of the shop has collapsed. The woman who sold me the flowers is scattered around the room in frozen chunks. She doesn't know how lucky she is.

The flowers have shattered in my hand and are just ice shards melting away in the water now. I leave them and crawl out through a narrow passageway left amid the fallen beams and ceiling tiles. I follow the light and sound of car alarms.

Outside, the city is melting. Waterfalls pour down the sides of buildings that are still standing. Other buildings have crumpled into themselves under the weight of the ice, or parts of them have broken off from the nuke's shock wave and fallen into the street. The entire side of an office tower down the street has come off completely, crushing all the cars and pedestrians frozen underneath it. People still sit in the offices inside, some of them blocks of dripping ice at their desks and conference tables. Others have been freed from their prisons like me and are stumbling around the skating rinks of their floors.

I watch a man in a suit and tie break his way out of a frozen cubicle a few levels up. He steps forward, into the air, because the rest of the office has fallen away. I don't bother yelling a warning to him. He never listens. He can't hear me, or maybe he doesn't want to hear me. He falls, screaming out of sight behind the jumble of rubble in the street. He hits something metal on the other side and the screaming stops. No heroes come to save him. They're too busy trying to save us all.

Trinity flies overhead just then, ripping a white line through the burning sky. His suit is torn and scorched from the nuke, but he doesn't waver. Nothing can hurt Trinity. The people he loves, though, they're a different story.

Cries go up across the city at the sight of him. He doesn't look down at us. It's a day like any other.

I don't waste time watching him disappear into the clouds still mushrooming up from ground zero. I run down the street, out of the Frozen Zone.

The first time I thawed, I thought maybe the USSC had won the Cold War. Before I was frozen, it was always cities in some other country being turned into snow globes. Never here. When I stumbled out into the ruins of my city that first time, I thought they had detonated the nuke to finish us off. And when I saw Trinity fly across the sky, I thought he had come to save us.

Now I know better, of course. And I wish our fate was something as simple as being oppressed by a bunch of communist supers. You never know how bad things can get until things get that bad.

I hit the border of the Frozen Zone, where the ice and water turns into the buckled asphalt of the street outside, torn up by the nuke. The first few times I'd come this way, I'd stumbled and fallen, wasting precious seconds. I've done it enough times now that I don't even notice the change in terrain.

The air is a swirling fog of dust and shards of paper. Most of the buildings have collapsed, but a few stand here and there, skeletal grave markers looming over the remains of the city. Fires burn everywhere and no one comes to put them out. They're all trying to catch up to Trinity.

Everyone but me. I'm just trying to get home to Penny.

There are people on the streets with me. Ashen from the dust cloud, like ghosts. I don't bother talking to any of them. I've learned all I can from them already, in the other times I've thawed. They are the ones who told me I haven't woken up into the Cold War. It's been over for nearly a decade, ever since Trinity found the USSC's secret space station and warped it back in time, flying one of the strange aerial patterns only he understands around it until it winked out of existence. We found its remains later, when a water probe deep inside the moon drilled into the station. Trinity had sent it back to a time when the moon had occupied the same point in space. The USSC were just dust now.

The people on the street are the ones who explained to me that I've woken up in the Infinity Age, a time when everyone has a superpower. Well, almost everyone. All those who got a shot of the super serum as children. There are still a few old-timers like me around, whose only power is a lack of power.

I run past them all, and they wave a greeting. They don't bother trying to talk to me anymore. They understand I'm in a race against time.

Cars and buses are scattered around the streets, some on their sides or flipped over, others crushed by pieces of metal debris I can't even recognize. There are a few that are still right side up, still seemingly in working order, but I ignore them. I know from past experience that they're useless, their electronics knocked out by the nuke.

I run even though I'm out of breath. I'm not in good condition after being frozen for twenty years. And I still feel a little frosty. But I have to run. I have such little time.

I met a woman once, one of those ghosts, who was going through all the cars looking for a working phone. She said she just wanted to message her lover in Paris. He was too far away to ever reach again, she said, but if she could only see his face, or even read his words, all this would be bearable. I don't know that she's right, but I don't know that she's wrong, either.

And she told me that some people had chosen to be frozen in their homes when the Cold War came home, to wait for their partners trapped in the Frozen Zone. I don't know what Penny chose to do. Maybe she's in our house now, frozen in a cryogenic chamber in our bedroom, waiting for me. I have to get home to find out what happened to her.

I've never seen that woman again. I wonder if she ever found a phone that worked.

I reach the parking garage in record time. Trinity makes his second pass overhead as I hurry down the ramp, trying to keep those extra few seconds. He rips the sky open in a line that intersects with the other one. He's too far away to see his face. I wonder, as I always do, what he thinks when he looks down at us.

The top floors of the garage have collapsed and are a jumble of wreckage, but the entrance and exit are still relatively clear of debris. It took me several thaws to find this place. There are only a few hubcaps and a single side mirror that catches my reflection. I ignore what I see there. I pick up the mirror and go down to the lower levels, passing the cars I know I can't use. I find the one that still works two floors down. I use the side mirror to shatter the driver's side window and then toss it aside. The car's alarm goes off. I get in the car and hit the start button. I don't bother with the seat belt. I take the levels of the parking garage as fast as I can and drive out into the ruined street above. I want to make as much ground as I can before Cyborg stops me.

I smash through the debris on the street and knock the dead cars out of the way. I ignore the airbag that goes off and punches me in the face. I get maybe a block more than any other time before Cyborg leaps from the remains of a building that's been torn in two and lands on the street in front of me. His feet dig up more asphalt at the impact.

"Stop and produce identification for the vehicle emitting the alarm," he says.

Cyborg was one of the first supers, back before I was frozen. A self-made hero, not serum-made. He'd once been part man, part machine. Now he is part machine, part corpse. The metal parts of him are rusty where they're fused with his flesh, but most of that flesh is gone. He's half metal, half bone rattling around inside the metal. A skull is all that's left of his head, the implants from the power suit holding it in place atop the lifeless but still operating body. A metal chip dangling from his spine by some wires talks for the dead hero.

"Produce identification or I will be forced to make a citizen's arrest," he says.

I stop the car and get out. Trinity crosses the sky overhead once more, adding a new line. The light that shines forth cuts through the smoke and haze, but not in any way anyone wants to see.

Cyborg ignores the real danger above us. I guess to his programs, Trinity is no threat. "The car alarm indicates a crime in progress," he says. He lifts an arm with a gun mounted on it. The gun is the kind you normally see mounted on attack helicopters. But the end of it is splintered away, like something has exploded in the barrel. "Are you a criminal?" he asks, those empty eye sockets staring at nothing at all.

The hero is dead, but his cyborg circuitry survives. It's attempting to follow its logic routines as best it can. There's no reasoning with it. I've tried too many times.

"I left my ID in my office," I say. "I'll just go get it."

And I run past Cyborg and continue down the street. He keeps the gun pointed at the car, which continues to sound its alarm. In the air above me, a scattering of men and women, some in colourful suits, others sporting wings, chase after Trinity. Too late. Always too late.

I climb over a scorched refrigerator that's fallen into the street from somewhere, then dodge around a burning office chair. I jump over a tricycle with melted wheels, kick aside a mess of photo frames all fused together. I remember shopping with Penny in a department store for things for the house. My heart pounds in my chest so hard I think I may have a heart attack. Not for the first time, I wish I had joined the lineups for the super serum shots all those years ago.

But we weren't sure what it would do back then. The researchers who developed it said it was just a shot to help our bodies fight the new generation of superbugs that threatened to wipe us out. It was supposed to accelerate our defences, to help them adapt and evolve quicker than the bugs evolved. But even the scientists admitted they didn't know what the side effects would be. I don't think anyone could have predicted the mutations it caused in youth when they hit puberty, mutations that we came to call superpowers.

Maybe if I'd been injected with the super serum, too, I wouldn't be staggering with exhaustion as I run home. Maybe I wouldn't be worrying about dropping dead in the street from a heart attack. Maybe I'd be leaping what was left of the buildings in a single bound. But it's too late for all that now.

The next time Trinity crosses the sky, the air around him explodes with blasts of all different sizes and colours as heroes and villains alike open fire on him with their weapons and powers. Trinity just absorbs them as usual. He's the most powerful hero of all, the recipient of a secret government variation of the super serum. After he evolved, he destroyed the lab and the scientists and the formula itself for fear it would fall into the hands of a villain. If he'd only known he would become the greatest villain the world had ever known, maybe he would have destroyed himself as well. Maybe.

I hit the intersection a few seconds before the bus. I pause and use the time to catch my breath as it drives up the street toward me. The Human Cannon and Pulsar are on the roof, blazing away at Trinity overhead. The other heroes watch from their seats inside, unable to do anything from this distance.

The bus doesn't slow but I've learned to grab on to the side and pull myself in the open passenger door. Rally is behind the wheel as always, and he nods at me.

"You're early," he says, steering the bus around a couple of crashed taxis without losing any speed.

"I've been working on my route," I gasp.

It doesn't save me any time to reach the intersection a few seconds early, because I have to wait for the bus anyway. But hopefully the little bit of rest will give me more energy when I need it later.

The inside of the bus is full of the heroes who can't fly or hover, who can't leap into the air, who can't join the fight against Trinity. Not unless someone can get a lucky shot in somewhere and bring him down for a few seconds. Then this batch and all the other buses and trucks and cars full of heroes and villains chasing Trinity across the city can pile on. Maybe they can stop him from rising up into the air again through the force of sheer numbers. Maybe they can finally stop him from ending the world again.

I sit in the front seat closest to the door, beside Siren, as always. She smiles at me, as always, and says, "Maybe this time."

I nod at her but don't say anything, just like usual. I work on breathing as deeply as I can. I'm trying to supercharge all my cells with oxygen.

Siren was the one who'd first explained to me that Doc Apocalypse had set off the nuke to try to kill Trinity, not wreck the city. Back before all this started, Doc Apocalypse had sworn to destroy all the major supers before one of them destroyed the world. Everyone had thought him a typical mad genius, but now we all saw he'd been right about the future. For all the good it did us.

The nuke hadn't killed Trinity. It had done something far worse, Siren explained to me on one of our many bus rides. It had killed tens of thousands of people, among them Trinity's secret lover. Secret because a hero like Trinity couldn't reveal too many details of his personal life. It would make everyone he knew a target for villains. But there were rumours. Siren said she'd heard it was Electron Girl. The Leprechaun, who sat in a different spot in the bus each time, said he had it on good authority it was Shiva, but he wouldn't tell us what that authority was. Legion swore one of his ghosts had seen Trinity kissing the Manhattan Effect up in the sky one night.

It didn't matter. Doc Apocalypse had killed her with his bomb, whoever she was, and Trinity was going to bring her back to life. He always brought her back to life. And he always ended our lives in the process.

We drive for a few minutes in silence, except for the artillery sounds the Human Cannon makes and the sizzling in the air from Pulsar's blasts. And Rally's humming to himself as he steers around wreckage in the street. I've lost count of how many times I've done this with them, and I've never once seen him brake for anything in the road.

The next time I look at Siren, she's turned into Penny. She smiles at me, and I can't help but smile back, even though I know she's not really there. She takes my hand and puts it on her belly, and I feel the baby kick against my palm. So strong.

"Thank you," I say. Penny just nods and puts her hand on the back of my head. We rest our foreheads against each other for a moment.

Then there's the bang of displaced air as Masterminds teleports in overhead in the *Quantum Sailer*, just behind Trinity. Masterminds is getting closer and quicker each time. Maybe someday he'll figure out how to get here from his secret dimension before Trinity rises into the sky and starts his pattern, perhaps even before Doc Apocalypse sets off the nuke that's condemned us all. And maybe he can stop this all from happening.

But not this time.

Masterminds' clones all open fire at once with the guns mounted on the *Sailer*. Purple beams lance out and strike Trinity, shells burst all around him with green flashes, a net that seems to be the opposite of colour hurtles through the air and wraps itself around him. The net is a new one. Masterminds is always experimenting.

And Trinity shrugs them all off. As he always does. He continues to fly along, ripping the sky open behind him and letting more of that white light through. He stares straight ahead, like he can't see any of us. Or won't.

Rally shakes his head and eases off the gas a little. "Checkered flag time," he tells me.

Penny gives my hand a squeeze and then lets me go, and now she's Siren again. "You'll make it one of these times," she says. "Maybe even this one."

I can see in their eyes that they all hope I can find Penny. Their loved ones are too far away for them to reach. The only way they have to see them again is to stop Trinity. But I have a chance at seeing Penny again, even as the war rages on. Maybe this will be the time.

The Masterminds clone flying the *Quantum Sailer* turns it in the air and accelerates after Trinity. The other clones all begin shouting instructions through loudspeakers.

"All flying heroes set up a screen between the Frozen Zone and 32nd Street," one of them says, fluid leaking from the helmet protecting his massive brain. Teleportation is hard on the Masterminds. "Those of you with projectile or plasma powers, concentrate them into a force wall. The others form a human wall behind them. Swarm him like a bee and try to bring him down to ground level. In Trinity Museum Park if you can."

"Flying villains form a high-altitude blanket between Trinity Museum Park and the point of our last teleportation," another of the Masterminds says, sparks flying from his helmet. "Force him down with everything you have. Ground-based units spread out throughout the same area. Grab him and hang on."

They're not orders for this time. It's too late. We've already lost again. We can't stop Trinity. They're orders for the next time. Trinity can hear them, of course, but there's nothing anyone can do about that.

Then Masterminds crashes the *Sailer* into Trinity, and there's a purple flare from the new force field, but it doesn't matter. The *Sailer* spins down into a residential neighbourhood a few blocks away. Trinity weaves in the air a little, shaking his head, and then continues ripping the sky open.

Rally slams the button that opens the door and takes his foot off the gas completely. This bus full of heroes isn't going to make a difference in the fight now.

"Don't stop," he says to me, and the others shout encouragement as I jump out the door and hit the street rolling. I know they want to come with me as I race back into the past, back to my wife and home in the suburbs and an era where there were no supers like Trinity. But it's too late for all of that now. It's too late for them.

I've done this so many times I know how to roll perfectly and come up running. I cross the street as the bus continues on past me. The Human Cannon and Pulsar keep on firing at Trinity, even though there's no point now. I guess that's what makes them heroes.

The sky is on fire from everyone trying to stop Trinity. It's actually burning in places. The flames suck away the oxygen, and I have to take deeper and deeper breaths as I run, but it seems like I'm filling my lungs with nothing at all.

I sprint down a couple of alleys that I've learned shave off a few seconds from my travel time, and I emerge in a neighbourhood of houses. The doors hang open, the windows are shattered. No one has lived in these places for a long time. I don't know what's happened here while I've been frozen, and I've never taken the time to learn. Not when I'm this close.

Trinity rips overhead in a different direction as I turn at the next corner. A howling sound I've never been able to identify follows in his wake. I think sometimes that it's the sound of his grief, but I don't know.

Then there's the *Quantum Sailer* lying wrecked in the ruins of a couple more houses, flickering in and out of existence. Some of the Masterminds's clones lie in the street, their helmets shattered from the impact. Purple fluid is everywhere.

One of the gunners is still hanging off his gun, waiting. He sees me coming and fires the gun at the burned-out minivan in my path. The minivan vanishes with a whoosh of air sucking into the space where it had been. I run through the area without breaking stride. The clone waves at me and then slumps behind the gun.

I don't stop to talk to him. I've already done that. He's the one who explained to me that Trinity can't do everything. Trinity can't raise the dead. Trinity can't stop time. But he can turn it back. So every time Doc Apocalypse sets off the nuke that kills his love, Trinity rips open the heavens and resets the clock, taking us all back to the months before the nuke. Back to the time when his love was still alive. None of us knows what he does with his lover. Does he reveal what's going to happen? Do they look for a way to escape? Or do they just live each day like it's their last?

Then the nuke goes off, and Trinity throws himself up into the sky to rewind it all again. To rewind us again.

We're all trapped in his dream.

I can't blame him, really. I understand. I hope to hell all the heroes and villains manage to stop him someday. But I understand.

I turn again at the next intersection, where four cars have somehow managed to crash into each other, and there it is. My home. The house I shared with Penny before I was entombed in the Frozen Zone. I run across the neighbours' lawns to get to it, jumping over the little fences and decorative hedges. A house is burning now because of the debris that's fallen from the sky. Smoke alarms are going off inside all the other houses, and people stagger out of their homes. Neighbours I don't recognize. More ghosts. They point up and scream as Trinity passes overhead one final time.

I hit our lawn and cross it in a couple of steps. I have no air left in my lungs at all now. I won't be able to speak if I find Penny inside. But I still might be able to hold her. It's been my best time yet. I've never made it past the burning house before.

I touch the door handle with my fingertips –

– and then there's a flash of white light, and the whole world screams.

There's a Crack
IN EVERYTHING

The dream of the angel didn't go at all like it was supposed to happen.

Lucien found himself in a tower in the dream. He knew from the view of the city spread out beneath him and the river that wound through it that he was in the Relic in London. He could see Trafalgar Square in the distance and Parliament. So that part of the dream had all gone according to plan. But for some reason the buildings were in ruins and the Thames was burning. The city was wreathed in smoke. That was definitely not part of the plan.

Neither was the angel that came across the bloody sky toward him. Its wings were great arcs of flame and it left a trail of smoke and ash in the air behind it. Lucien wasn't supposed to see the angel in the dream. Lucien was supposed to be the angel. He was supposed to shine with golden light, not flames. He was supposed to see the world from the angel's perspective, to look down upon the city from the Relic like he was looking down from Heaven.

That was the dream he had paid the sorcerer for, with an extra fee for targeting the wealthy demographic around the world. The dream was supposed to be an ad for the Relic towers being built in cities around the world: London, New York, Vancouver, Hong Kong, Moscow, Paris. The tallest towers in the world, and the largest architectural project in

229

human history. The first towers to have religious relics embedded in their walls or showcased in their lobbies – fragments of the Shroud of Turin, splinters of the cross that had borne the weight of Christ, cups that the saints had drunk from, that sort of thing. The relics that made people feel closer to the angels that had now come back. The relics that made the angels feel like heavenly angels again, despite everything they had done since they returned. The dream was supposed to bring people hope once more. The dream was not supposed to be a nightmare.

In this dream Relic, Lucien stood in the skeleton of an office. The entire floor was empty – there were no cubicles or desks or chairs or any other signs of life. There was just the emptiness framed by the metal and glass of the building's walls and ceiling and floor. It was more like the idea of an office than an actual office. The dream had gone wrong even here. Lucien had paid for it to tap into the dreamers' minds and show the workspace or homes they had always fantasized about. Lucien was certain he had never fantasized about finding himself alone in an empty room in the sky, with an angry angel bearing down on him. To top things off, Lucien was naked for some reason. He knew if he was visiting a Relic for real, he would likely wear one of his Hugo Boss suits, or maybe Dior business casual. He didn't even sleep naked.

Still the angel came across the sky. And now the windows rattled and the floor shook as it drew near. Somewhere, a phone sounded, its ring tone a klaxon alarm. Lucien knew who it was and didn't want to answer. He didn't want to wake up. Even though he knew the dream was bad, he knew that things would get worse when he woke.

But there was no stopping the angel. It came on, directly at Lucien. Flames raged in its eyes and it screamed at him, a sound that was like the sky ripping open. Lucien knew there was nowhere to run or hide, but he tried to shield himself anyway. He threw up his hands and turned away as the angel smashed through the windows before him in an explosion of fire and glass. A wave of heat surged over and through him, and now

Lucien screamed as his skin instantly bubbled and blistered. The hot wind flowed down his throat, and he choked like he was drowning on it.

The floor collapsed beneath Lucien before the angel could reach him, and he fell. He fell from the idea of an office into a real office, complete with Herman Miller desks and chairs and cubicle dividers and all the other props that gave meaning to people who worked in offices. He landed on a marble boardroom table with an impact that knocked the burning wind out of him and filled his vision with stars, but which didn't really hurt him. This was a dream, after all. He lay there, stunned for a moment, spread out like some sort of sacrificial victim on the table. He looked up and saw the angel hovering in the air overhead, where he'd stood seconds ago. It reached down for him with blazing hands. Was it trying to save him? Or was it trying to finish the job it had started? Lucien wasn't sure. Again, this wasn't the dream he'd ordered from the sorcerer.

Then this floor of the tower gave way, too, and Lucien was falling once more, in a shower of chairs and desks and filing cabinets and computer monitors and too many other things to register. This time he fell into a dark void underneath the office. It was as empty as the sky the angel had travelled across to destroy the tower. Lucien had the sudden feeling of weightlessness he had only known in dreams. He opened his mouth to cry out, but he couldn't breathe because the wind of his falling was too strong.

Lucien fell toward a light beneath him, a golden glow where everything disappeared. He thought maybe it was a fire of some sort caused by the building collapse, but there was no heat. Just a brightness that grew more and more intense, like he was falling into an Instagram photo of the sun. Just as the light turned his skin golden, he woke in the darkness of his bedroom, thrashing under the Tom Ford duvet.

He could still hear the klaxon alarm of the phone from the dream, and it took him several seconds to realize it wasn't just a fading memory but came from his iPhone on the bedside table.

He rolled over and saw the caller ID. Babel. His contact name for the client. Lucien sighed and hit the answer button.

"Did you have the same dream?" the client asked without waiting for Lucien to even say hello. He never waited for Lucien to say hello.

"I'm not sure," Lucien said. "Are we awake now or are we still dreaming?"

"That was a fucking nightmare," the client said. "That was the sort of dream that kids have when they hit puberty."

"I'll talk to the sorcerer. I'll see what we can do."

"Fix this now or your career will be a nightmare that you'll wish you could wake from," the client said.

Lucien exited the phone app and stared at the ceiling for a moment. He couldn't see any cracks up there in the concrete and ductwork. It was a solid building that had once been a factory before it had been converted into condos. He turned on the iPhone's flashlight and shone it up there, anyway, just to make sure the ceiling wasn't about to collapse.

Then he opened his Facebook and Twitter feeds and checked for comments. There was nothing new beyond the usual spam updates about products people had supposedly bought and places they were apparently enjoying. But he saw his follower numbers dropping as he looked at the screen. People knew what had happened. Either they'd had the same dream or they'd heard about it. His network was ghosting on him.

"I know, I know, you told me so," Lucien said to Kia. She didn't have to say anything from under the sheets for him to know she was awake, too. They'd been together long enough that he just knew things like that now.

"That was definitely one of the stranger dreams I've had," she said. Her words were slightly slurred, so she must have still been a little drunk. They'd celebrated the launch of the ad campaign before they'd gone to bed by drinking several bottles of designer vodka one of his other clients had gifted him months earlier. The bottles had all been natural flavours that Lucien suspected didn't even exist in real life: starberry and etherflower and such. The night had ended with Kia tying him to the bed with his Alexander McQueen ties and riding him until he came so hard in her that he randomly thought of the space shuttle *Challenger* blowing up. It may have been premature to celebrate before the dream had gone out into the world, but in all his years as a brand consultant none of his campaigns had ever failed or even gone wrong.

Until now.

"You need to get the sorcerer to make this right," Kia said.

That was when Lucien noticed the flicker of light coming in through the open door of the bedroom. Orpheus must have been awake and reading or playing a game in his room. Lucien hoped he hadn't had the same dream. The dream was supposed to have been targeted to adults in certain income and geographical ranges only, but who knew what else had gone wrong?

Lucien checked the time on the iPhone: *3:12 a.m.* floated over the image of Orpheus. His son was standing amid the rubble of a bombed-out neighbourhood and laughing at a costumed Mickey Mouse holding a knife to the throat of a man in an orange jumpsuit kneeling in the ruins. They'd been in Banksy's Hyperland when Lucien had taken the photo – a surprise visit after Orpheus had said the other kids in his class were talking about it. Lucien had ordered the tickets the same night Orpheus had mentioned it, before another father could beat him to it.

Lucien sat up in the bed and put his feet over the edge. It was a California king, raised so high he had to drop slightly off the bed to touch the floor. The floor didn't feel like it was going to collapse under his weight, so he stood and went down the hall to Orpheus's room. The light continued to flicker through Orpheus's open doorway, as if it were moving. It wasn't the overhead light or bedside lamp then. Had Orpheus taken the Navy SEAL flashlight from the tool kit? Whatever he was using, he didn't seem concerned by the sounds of Lucien's approach.

Lucien reached the doorway to Orpheus's room and looked inside. He stopped at what he saw there. The angel from his dream was perched on the end of Orpheus's bed, like a crow on a tree branch, staring down at Orpheus. Its flaming wings were folded behind it, but the golden light that Lucien had fallen toward shone from cracks in its skin. It turned its head to look at Lucien, but all Lucien could see was more light spilling from its eyes.

Lucien cried out and threw himself at the angel, trying to knock it away from Orpheus's bed. He knew even as he did so that it was an act of pure instinct, that he couldn't possibly stand a chance against an angel. He'd seen the videos of what they'd done in Berlin and Jerusalem.

But the angel didn't try to fight him. Instead, it slipped backward, toward the window. Or rather, it seemed to fall backward across the room, throwing out its arms and legs as it went but keeping its wings tucked behind itself. It kept looking at Lucien even as it slid through the closed window without breaking the glass.

Lucien stumbled forward and fell onto the bed now that there was no angel to hit. He reached out for it, maybe to grab onto it, maybe to push it away. He wasn't sure what he meant to do. But the angel was disappearing into the night outside, falling across the sky, away from the condo and dwindling to just another light in the city skyline. For a few seconds, it drifted in front of the dark shape of the Relic under construction in the distance, a faint star barely visible in the void of the unlit building. Then it faded away, as if it had never been there.

Lucien twisted around on the bed to see what the angel had done to Orpheus. His son was sitting up now, staring at Lucien in confusion. He wore plain Old Navy pajamas but they didn't hide the cracks of light that ran along his body. The light shone from him nearly as brightly as it had the angel.

Orpheus noticed the light radiating from his body a few seconds after Lucien did. He stared down at himself as Kia burst into the room.

"What did you do?" she cried as she took in Orpheus's condition, as if Lucien were somehow to blame. Maybe he was, he thought in that instant.

It was the same angel from the dream he had ordered from the sorcerer, after all. Maybe it had somehow escaped the dream.

"What's wrong with me?" Orpheus looked down at himself and then at Lucien and Kia. "What's wrong with me?" he asked again.

"The light," Lucien whispered, because a whisper was all he could manage. "You have the light."

Kia put both hands over her mouth. "Tell me this is a dream," she said. "Oh please, tell me this is still the dream."

* * *

THEY TOOK Orpheus to emergency right away. They dressed in business casual, taking care not to wear anything with logos. They wanted the doctors and nurses to take them seriously but they didn't want them to feel challenged. Lucien told Kia about the angel as they put on their clothes, but she just looked at him and didn't say anything, so he wasn't sure if she believed him. He wasn't sure if he believed it. Maybe he hadn't been fully awake and he'd dreamed it.

They didn't touch Orpheus because they weren't sure if the light was infectious or not. The glowing lines of it in the boy looked the same as the ones in the angel. Maybe it spread by contact. Maybe some other way. Lucien didn't want to find out.

Kia told Orpheus to put something on over his pajamas and he got a Nike athletic hoodie from his closet. As Lucien watched his son put it on, he realized that brand was forever ruined for him now.

"Maybe it's not the light," Kia said as they drove to the hospital. They took the Range Rover rather than the BMW because they didn't know what else they'd be facing this night. "Maybe it's something else."

"It's not a cough or a fever or swelling," Lucien said. He scanned the sky for the angel, but all he saw were the lights of drones flitting about in the darkness. "It's not one of those things where the signs can mean anything at all. The only other thing that would make you glow like that is a leaking nuclear reactor."

"Maybe it's just temporary then," Kia said. "Like when those kids get cancer."

Lucien didn't say anything to that. He didn't know much about the light, other than what he'd read online. He knew it was connected to the angels and almost always fatal. He was aware some people argued about whether the angels were punishing or saving the children, but he'd never given it much thought until now.

"Do I have cancer?" Orpheus asked from the back seat. "Am I going to explode?"

"You don't have cancer," Kia said, turning to look at him as if he'd done something wrong. "Cancer only happens to other people."

Lucien called the sorcerer on the drive to the hospital. The sorcerer answered after one ring.

"Well, that didn't go as expected," the sorcerer said.

"That wasn't a dream, it was a nightmare," Lucien said. "I don't recall ordering a nightmare."

"I did warn you when you bought the dream that the results can be unpredictable," the sorcerer said. "It's right there in the contract."

"Maybe you should have a specific list of all the possible things that can go wrong in the contract," Lucien said. "Like those side effects they put in drug ads."

"We're dealing with angels," the sorcerer said. "There's already a list of that stuff. It's called the Bible."

Lucien slowed but didn't stop for the red lights. There was no one else on the road. He knew the cameras were fining him for running the lights as he did so, but he didn't care. He'd work it out later. If there was a later.

"It came into my home," Lucien said. "It attacked my son."

"The dream wasn't targeted at youths," the sorcerer said. "It shouldn't have done that."

"The angel," Lucien said. "The actual angel came into my son's room and gave him the light."

"That's a new one," the sorcerer said.

"Is he talking about me?" Orpheus asked from the back seat.

"I don't even know," Kia said. "I just don't know." She looked back out the window, at all the closed stores and empty streets. "It's like some sort of apocalypse."

"Meet me at the church," the sorcerer said. "We'll figure this out."

"This had better not cost extra," Lucien said. He disconnected as the lights of a police car flashed behind them.

"Keep driving," Kia said. "Just get us to the hospital."

"If we don't stop we'll be going to the hospital in a body bag," Lucien said.

"Do we have the gun?" Kia asked. She opened the glove compartment and looked inside.

"It's in the BMW," Lucien said. He'd put it there the last time he'd gone to meet the sorcerer.

"Why don't we have a gun for each vehicle?" Kia cried out at him.

"Because I never imagined this night," Lucien said, pulling over and into an empty parking spot on the side of the road.

"Guns are for the worldly and the weak," Orpheus said. "The holy spirits are the shells that puncture the void."

"What the hell are they teaching them in school now?" Lucien sighed.

He watched the cops get out of the car and walk up behind them. A man and a woman. The woman was taller than the man, which Lucien thought strange. He couldn't ever remember seeing a woman cop taller than a man before. This night just kept getting odder and odder.

The woman went up the passenger side and the man came along the driver's side. When they drew even with the rear seat, they both stopped and stared at Orpheus. Lucien thought about getting his wallet out to speed things along. Maybe they wanted his driver's licence, maybe they could be bought off. But he didn't want to move, for fear of them thinking he was going for the gun that he'd left in the other car.

"The only authority we recognize is the authority of nothing," Orpheus said.

"Orpheus, Jesus," Lucien said.

The cops backed away from the car then. It was like the scene was rewinding, as they went back to their car and got in. They just sat there, looking through the windshield at the Range Rover.

"Are we free to go?" Kia asked.

"I have no idea," Lucien said. He wondered if he could rewind the entire night like that.

He put the car into gear and eased away from the curb. He kept watching the cops to see what they did next. He was ready to brake and pull over again, but they just kept sitting there. The lights on the cruiser turned off.

"We are ethereal," Orpheus said.

"So it seems," Lucien said as they drove away.

"I don't even know what that means," Kia said. "And I don't want to know."

They pulled into the hospital parking lot a few minutes later and Lucien repressed a shudder at the sight of the building. He hadn't been back here since Orpheus was born. It was one of those places that made him feel uncomfortable. The architectural style was from the 1970s, and the whole place looked more like a prison than what he thought a hospital should resemble. But the newer, more modern hospitals were a longer drive, so here they were.

The light shone through Orpheus's clothes just as brightly inside the ER as it did out in the night. When they checked in at the nurses' station, some of the men and women sitting nearby left their seats and went to the far ends of the room. They kept an eye on Orpheus from their new seats as they checked their phones. Lucien didn't know what he would do if any of them took a photo, but he knew he would do something.

He didn't have to find out, though, as the nurse took them straight into a private examination room. The walls were covered in poster illustrations of the human body and all its mysterious parts. Orpheus closed his eyes at the sight of them and climbed up on the exam table with them still closed. Lucien felt like doing the same thing because the posters looked like they were from the 1970s, too.

The nurse put on a robe and gloves and a face mask before she took Orpheus's temperature. She used a thermometer to scan Orpheus's forehead from several inches away. She didn't touch him once during her examination. Lucien felt like he was in an episode of *Star Trek* or something.

"Should we be wearing those, too?" Kia asked.

"They probably don't even do any good," the nurse said. She took a plastic baggie from a drawer. It looked like a sandwich baggie but she dropped the thermometer into it and sealed it. "We just don't know yet. But I figure why take the chance? I'd like to live long enough to have kids of my own."

"I thought only children got the light," Lucien said.

"So far," the nurse said. "But who knows what angels think? The light is as mysterious as all the other miracles."

"I'd hardly call this a miracle," Kia said.

"Well it's sure not natural," the nurse said.

"Will someone please tell me what's wrong with me?" Orpheus asked, opening his eyes again and looking around the room as if noticing where he was for the first time.

"There's nothing wrong with you," Kia said. She reached out a hand like she was going to touch his head but stopped short. "We're the ones there's something wrong with." That didn't make any sense at all to Lucien, but most of this situation didn't make any sense to him. He wondered if there had been something in the vodka they had drunk earlier in the evening.

"You're going to see Jesus," the nurse said, hugging herself. "Because why else would the angels be here? You're too young to be held to blame for anything, so they must be here to deliver their blessing upon you."

"I think that's enough," Lucien said. Now he really wanted a mask and gloves. He had a theory he'd never shared with anyone that religion was something viral you could catch if surrounded by infected people too long. Who knew the state of his immune system at the moment?

The nurse was already stepping out of the room, though, leaving them alone with their son. He stared at them until Lucien felt uncomfortable and looked away, because he didn't know what to say or do. He took out his phone and looked at the photos of Orpheus. Orpheus on the rope tower in the school playground. Orpheus reading something on the tablet while lying on the couch. Orpheus striking a karate pose in the kitchen while he helped Kia make cookies. Lucien looked for any sign of light in the photos, but all he saw was Orpheus healthy and happy. Just another boy who still had his whole life waiting to be lived.

Kia stood by his side and looked down at the photos as well. She ran her fingers over Orpheus's face on the screen and then stared at him sitting there on the hospital bed, the light running like glowing scars across his face.

The phone rang then. It was the client. Babel. Kia stepped away as Lucien answered.

"People are cancelling their orders in Relics all around the world," Babel said. "I had a dream of building them, and now your damned dream is going to make them all fall down."

"I'm already fixing it," Lucien said.

"And how exactly are you going to do that?" Babel asked. "This is like a 9/11 that doesn't stop."

"I'm meeting with an expert right now," Lucien said and disconnected as a doctor walked into the room.

The doctor stopped just inside the doorway. He put his hands on his hips as he studied Orpheus without looking at Lucien or Kia. His scrubs were wrinkled and there were dark stains on one leg. It looked as if he hadn't shaved in days and brushed his hair in even longer. He looked exactly like Lucien thought a doctor should look, which gave him some small sense of relief. Like this was all a normal medical emergency that could maybe be treated.

"He's got the light," Lucien said, as if it weren't obvious. But he felt he had to say something.

"How do you know that?" the doctor asked, as Orpheus continued to glow through his clothes.

"What's the light?" Orpheus asked.

"That's a good question," the doctor said. "If I knew the answer to that, I wouldn't be working the night shift."

"The angels know," Lucien said. "It was one of them that gave it to him."

"We can't even say for sure if the angels know," the doctor said, looking at Lucien for the first time. "It could be an infection they don't understand, too. If one of them would ever talk to us, maybe we'd have a better idea. But I don't think that's going to happen anytime soon."

"Am I going to explode?" Orpheus asked. "Am I a suicide bomber?"

"They're just some cracks," the doctor said. "There's a crack in everything. That's how the light gets through."

"Is this really the time to be making jokes?" Lucien asked.

"I can't think of a better time to make jokes," the doctor said. "But all right, tell me when the angel visited."

"A few hours ago," Lucien said. "It was from a dream . . ." He trailed off because he wasn't entirely sure how to finish that sentence.

"It was the angel from the dream everyone just had?" The doctor raised his eyebrows. "You see all kinds of things in this job."

"It's my fault," Lucien said, looking at Orpheus. He shouldn't have hired the sorcerer. But who could have predicted this?

"A lot of parents blame themselves," the doctor said, nodding at him. "But as far as we can tell, the only ones to blame are the angels." He looked back at Orpheus. "Are you seeing or hearing anything unusual?" he asked.

"How about the fact that he's glowing brighter than Chernobyl's core?" Lucien said. "How about that for something unusual?"

The doctor steepled his hands in front of him, like he was thinking about praying. "Every one of the children infected by the light so far has had some unique presentation. One of them started speaking Latin. Another chimed like a bell all day long. It's part of the process."

"Process," Lucien said. He felt dizzy. He put his hand against the wall to steady himself. His fingers covered an illustration of someone's brain. "You make it sound like it's something normal."

"Maybe it is," the doctor said, spreading his hands wide now. "We just don't know yet. It's too new."

"He's been saying strange things," Kia said.

"Strange like what?" the doctor asked.

"I see Heaven," Orpheus said, and they all turned their attention to him again.

"Strange like that," Kia said.

"Heaven," Lucien said.

"What the nurse and people like her think is Heaven," Orpheus said. "That's what I see. When I'm dreaming. Or just thinking."

"Just when you think you've heard it all," the doctor said. "So what does Heaven look like?"

Orpheus closed his eyes again and frowned. He thought about it for a few seconds before answering. "It's like if you took all the photos on your phone and put them all together."

"So Heaven's, what, the people you know and love?" the doctor asked.

"It's just what is," Orpheus said. "It's everything that is."

"Oh my God," Kia said to the doctor. "You have to do something."

"There's nothing we can give him for seeing Heaven," the doctor said.

"Am I going to die?" Orpheus asked and they all looked at him again.

"I'm just going to talk to your parents outside for a minute," the doctor said and went back out into the hall.

"Where are you going?" Orpheus cried as Lucien and Kia followed the doctor. "Don't leave me here!" He looked around at the medical illustrations as if they were zombies waiting to come to life.

"We love you," Kia said. "Just stay here. Please stay."

"Shouldn't you be examining him or something?" Lucien asked as they went out into the hall and closed the door to the room behind them.

"You're right, he's got the light," the doctor said. "I've seen it enough times before that I don't need to examine him."

"So what do we do?" Kia asked.

"You try to make him comfortable before the end," the doctor said. "Because we don't have any way of stopping it."

The doctor stretched his arms above his head, and Lucien wondered if he was doing some sort of yoga exercise. This close, he could smell the other man's sweat. He could also see the script of a tattoo on his stomach, peeking out from under his scrubs. The bottom of some word that Lucien couldn't make out. What was it? he wondered. A name? A motto?

"There must be some experimental treatment somewhere," Lucien said. "Something we have to pay for ourselves."

"Or maybe some clinic in another country," Kia said. "Even one of those countries that aren't tourist countries."

"There aren't any treatments because we don't know what it is," the doctor said. He dropped his arms back to his sides and didn't move now. He looked defeated. Or maybe uninterested. Lucien wasn't sure which. "It's like trying to treat a nightmare."

The lights flickered overhead and Lucien looked up at them, but the doctor didn't seem to notice.

"But he sees Heaven," Kia said. "It must be different. That must be a sign or something."

"They all see or experience something," the doctor said, shrugging. "It's part of the process."

"If you say process one more time, I'm going to open up a crack in you," Lucien said.

The doctor nodded like he'd heard that before. "We can't stop it," he said. "You need to prepare yourself for what's going to happen. The light is going to spread until it covers every part of him. Then he's going to disappear."

"What do you mean, disappear?" Kia asked.

The lights flickered again, longer this time. The doctor still didn't seem to notice.

"I mean vanish like he never existed," the doctor said. "The other stuff, the speaking in tongues and hearing voices and seeing Heaven and whatever else, that gets worse as the light spreads. It's like they're in some sort of other world at the end."

"How long do we still have him for?" Lucien asked.

The doctor looked at the door to the exam room. "About twenty-four hours usually, once the physical symptoms start to present themselves."

"Twenty-four hours," Kia said. "Twenty-four hours ago, I had a normal boy and a normal life. You're telling me twenty-four hours from now I won't have either."

"Maybe less," the doctor said. "But probably not any more."

Lucien felt dizzy again and leaned against the wall. It was cool on his back. He wondered what viruses were crawling onto him from its surface at that second.

"It's like a terminal cancer," the doctor said, "but kinder in its own way. It's fast and painless."

"That's some bedside manner you have," Lucien said.

The doctor nodded like he understood. "If you want, I can give you some false hope," he said. "That way the whole thing will really catch you by surprise."

"There are alternative therapies," Kia said. "I know there are. I read about one on Facebook."

The doctor stepped aside as a nurse pushed an empty bed past. He stared at the bed and didn't say anything. For the first time, Lucien wondered what it was like to be a doctor, to be someone who could save lives and yet be utterly powerless like this.

"Just tell us what we need to do," Kia said.

"You're talking about the kid who didn't die," the doctor said, watching the nurse take the bed around the corner. "Or at least she hasn't died yet."

Lucien looked up and down the hallway until he saw a sanitizer dispenser on the wall. He went over to it and cleaned his hands. He thought about covering Orpheus's entire body in sanitizer.

"There is a cure," Kia said. "I know there is."

"That case is being studied," the doctor said. He kept staring after the nurse and the bed that were no longer there. "But we can't recommend that sort of treatment."

"I thought that whole thing with the girl was a hoax," Lucien said. "One of those fake crowdfunding things."

"It probably is," the doctor said. He finally looked back at them. "But even if it isn't, we can't save a life that way. That's not what we do here."

"Who does do that then?" Kia asked.

The doctor didn't say anything. Kia stepped closer to him.

"What if it was your kid?" she asked.

"You think I'd ever have kids after what I've seen?" the doctor asked. He cupped his hands and blew on them, as if he were cold.

"Just give us a name," Lucien said. He didn't see any other choices and, as the doctor had pointed out, they didn't have much time. "Something. Anything."

The doctor looked around before answering, as if he were afraid someone might hear them.

"A sorcerer," he said. "You want a sorcerer."

"A sorcerer," Lucien said.

"A sorcerer is why we're standing here, talking to you," Kia said.

"If you really want to save your son, then you should be talking to him, not me," the doctor said. "Because there's nothing I can do."

He turned and walked down the hall, to see other patients or take some drugs in a washroom or have sex with a nurse in an empty room or do whatever it was doctors do once they're done with you. "The thing you have to remember is that we all die in the end, no matter what," he called over his shoulder. "It's how we live that matters."

Lucien and Kia went back into the examination room. Orpheus was drifting in the air now, a few feet above the ground. He was also halfway through the wall, as if he were turning into some sort of ghost before their eyes.

"No no no no no!" Kia cried and grabbed onto Orpheus's visible hand. She pulled him back out of the wall and down to the ground. He stood there, looking around as if he hadn't just been floating away from them.

"We're going to find you a treat somewhere, okay?" Kia said. "There must be a coffee shop somewhere in this place."

"I don't need a treat," Orpheus said. "There aren't any treats in Heaven. Or any coffee shops."

Kia looked at Lucien. "You need to do something," she said. "Now."

"Okay," Lucien said. "It's all going to be okay." Although he thought it really wasn't going to be okay.

"What's a sorcerer?" Orpheus asked.

* * *

THEY MET the sorcerer in a cemetery, outside a boarded-up church. The church had been abandoned even before the angels came back. It was probably going to be turned into condos at some point. But for now it was just an empty church. It was the same place where Lucien had met the sorcerer the first time, when he'd hired him to create the dream.

The sorcerer was waiting for them when they parked the car in the lot. There were no other vehicles. He stood in the middle of the cemetery, drinking a Starbucks as he watched the sun rise. He wore the same black suit as before and Lucien still couldn't identify the brand. He looked like he could have been a businessman on his way to work, except he was standing in an overgrown cemetery. He stared straight into the sun without squinting or blinking.

"Maybe we need a priest instead," Kia said as they sat there for a minute.

"The priests are what got us into this trouble in the first place," Lucien said.

He left Orpheus and Kia in the car. Orpheus had started to drift away again during the drive to the church, sliding up through the roof. Kia had pulled him back down. She seemed to be the only thing that kept him tethered to this world. Lucien was afraid to touch his son, for fear that he might not be able to.

He looked at the church as he walked over to meet the sorcerer. There were sheets of wood covering the windows, and someone had spray-painted graffiti over the doors, which Lucien assumed were locked. *Go Home.* There were some holes in the sides of the spire, and the cross at the top of it was bent to the side. He could see light flickering through the holes, and he knew there was an angel inside the church.

"Maybe there was some confusion when we spoke the first time," Lucien said to the sorcerer. "I wanted a dream that showed an angel's perspective from the Relics. I wanted people to see what it would be like to live in the highest and holiest buildings on Earth. I didn't want the apocalypse."

The sorcerer nodded like he understood. "Maybe the apocalypse is the angel's perspective," he said.

"It was supposed to be an ad," Lucien said.

"It was an ad using an angel. Even I don't understand them, and I get my powers from them."

Lucien didn't know much about sorcerers but he knew they had received their special abilities when the angels had fallen from the

Heavens and down to earth all those years ago, after the events of Berlin. Some people had said the world deserved the angels in those first few days after Berlin, but no one said that now.

"There's a bit of uncertainty built into the process," the sorcerer added. "We're still in the early days here."

"Please don't say *process*," Lucien said.

"We can try again, but I can't guarantee the results will be any different."

"What about my son? Can you save my son at least?"

The sorcerer looked up at the church spire and the light emanating from it. "It was the actual angel from the dream?" he asked.

"The very same," Lucien said. "Did I make it up? Did I bring it into the world somehow?"

The sorcerer shrugged. "I modelled it on an angel I've been studying," he said. "Because that's how these things work. Maybe there was some sort of connection there." He sipped his Starbucks. "I wonder if anyone else was visited by it."

"Just tell me how to save him," Lucien said. If the sorcerer's powers were linked to the angels, maybe he could create miracles.

"I imagine you took him to the hospital and the doctors told you there was no hope."

"Is this the part where I say there's always hope?" Lucien looked back across the cemetery at the car. The flashes of light from within it were just as strong as the light coming from the church.

"There is hope. Of a sort," the sorcerer said. "Not the kind the doctors can accept, however. But you have to look at things differently from them. They see the light as an illness, a condition. They look for a cure, but it's the wrong way of looking."

"Are you telling me you know what the light is when no one else does?" Lucien asked.

"Of course not," the sorcerer said, still looking at the spire. "Not even the sorcerers know what the light is. Just because the coming of the angels somehow gave us powers doesn't mean we understand them any more than you do. For all we know, the angels don't even know what the light is."

"Jesus, why am I even here?" Lucien sighed. He looked around at the grave markers. He noticed the dates on them for the first time. 1863–1865. 1862–1869. 1812–1818. They were all the graves of children. They were standing in some sort of children's cemetery.

"The light comes from the angels, so some find it helpful to use the framework of the divine," the sorcerer said. "Think of it this way. We live in a fallen world and your child is in the process of leaving it. Call it what you will. Purgatory. Hell. The mortal. The light is freeing him. Some see it as salvation, not an illness."

Lucien kept staring at the grave markers. He wondered what these children had died of. If they had been freed, where were they now?

"But there is a way of stopping the light," the sorcerer went on. "I have seen it work in the past. I know children who are still among us because of the actions their parents took. For better or worse."

"Who do we have to kill?" Lucien asked, forcing a smile.

"Another child may work," the sorcerer said, looking at him again.

Now Lucien stared at the church. He shook his head, but only a little.

"The light is taking your son," the sorcerer said. "The only way he can be pulled back is by an act of darkness that is the equivalent. A blood sacrifice. That's why the doctors don't talk about it. They can't trade one life for another. It's in their code. But parents have different codes."

"What's the code of a sorcerer?" Lucien asked. "What's the code of fucking up the biggest ad campaign in history? What's the code of telling me to go and murder someone else's kid?" He found himself pointing at one of the grave markers at his feet, as if the child that lay in the ground there had been murdered in such a fashion.

"Maybe you haven't noticed, but we live in a world without codes now," the sorcerer said.

"I can't," Lucien said, turning away from the church. "How would I even . . . ?"

"I can tell you what's worked in the past, but I can't be an accomplice," the sorcerer said. "There are laws that apply even to me. I've told you the truth, but what you do with it is up to you."

"And what about the dream?" Lucien asked.

"I just told you how to save your child," the sorcerer said. "Let's call it even."

Both of them looked back up at the spire as an angel appeared in one of the holes in the side of the tower. It was the same angel that had been in Orpheus's room. Lucien really wished he had the gun in the Range Rover. He didn't know if bullets would affect the angel or not, but he wanted to find out.

The angel looked down at him as if it knew what he was thinking. Then it took wing, dropping out of the church and soaring over the cemetery. It crossed over them but didn't look down again. It gazed off into the distance, at who knew what.

"If that's not a sign, then I don't know what is," the sorcerer said, but Lucien was already running for the parking lot.

Kia was watching the angel as she hung on to Orpheus. "What did the sorcerer say?" she asked Lucien as he got back in the car.

"He said we have to sacrifice another kid to keep Orpheus here," Lucien said.

"Is that all?" Kia asked.

* * *

THEY FOLLOWED the angel. Lucien ran red lights and stop signs again to keep up with it, and veered into the oncoming lane to pass slower cars. People honked and yelled at them, but he didn't pay them any attention. No cops pulled them over this time. The angel hung in the air overhead a few times as they drove, as if waiting for them to catch up, but it never looked back at them.

"What are we going to do when we catch up to it?" Kia asked. She was holding Orpheus all the time now, as he bobbed about in the back like a balloon filled with helium. He'd floated right through his seat belt.

Lucien didn't have an answer for her. He didn't know what he would do. He didn't know why the angel was leading them the way it was, but he figured the sorcerer was right, that it was giving them a sign of something. He'd figure out later exactly what it meant.

"We don't have much time," Kia pointed out, pulling Orpheus back down out of the roof again.

Lucien looked at Orpheus in the rear-view mirror. The lines of light had spread even more across his son's body, and now Lucien could barely stand to look at him he was so bright.

"The angel is my grandfather and you know what that can do to a country but the church will always remain temporal and shiny no matter what the waves wash away from the soul," Orpheus said as he bumped against the ceiling.

"Oh God," Kia said.

"God can't help us," Lucien said. "God is the problem here."

"Maybe it was the vitamins I took when I was pregnant," Kia said. "Maybe it's your sperm. Do you think your sperm are too old?"

Lucien only slowed his chase of the angel when he saw where it was leading them. It drifted in a circle over Orpheus's school. As they approached and Lucien let the car drop down to the speed limit, he saw the playground on the other side of the fence topped with razor wire was full of children. It was the recess break. The angel stared down at the children and they screamed and reached up to it or ran and hid under the playground equipment.

"What is it doing?" Kia asked. "Is it going to infect the rest of them?"

Lucien knew it wasn't going to spread the light to the other children. That's not why the angel had led them here. He looked at the playground full of children and thought of the cemetery.

The gate to the parking lot opened for them and they drove in and stopped beside the playground, still looking up at the angel circling overhead. It had drifted higher in the sky and looked no bigger than a hawk or some other bird. Many of the children had already lost interest and had returned to chasing each other or going down the slides. Some of those who still paid attention threw sawdust up in the air or punched the sky as if they thought they could strike the angel.

"We could just grab one and go," Kia said. "Nobody would probably even notice."

"The other children might notice," Lucien pointed out. Although when he looked around the playground he saw the children weren't paying any attention to them at all.

"And what would they say?" Kia asked. "Some grown-ups took a child. It happens every day. They probably couldn't even describe us properly."

"The school has cameras," Lucien said. It was one of the things they paid for, after all.

"What difference does it make if they identify us later?" Kia asked. "Once we've saved Orpheus."

Lucien looked back up at the angel. Is that why it had led them here? Was this some sort of test to see what they were willing to do to save their son? If it was, he didn't know the correct answer.

And then it was too late anyway as Miss Edge, Orpheus's teacher, came out of the playground toward them. Lucien got out of the car and walked to meet her before she could see Orpheus in the back seat.

Lucien was convinced that Miss Edge wasn't her real name, that she'd changed it to sound more authoritative and forceful. He had a number of theories about her real name, but none of those mattered right now.

"It's quite something, isn't it?" she asked, looking at him even as she pointed up at the sky. "We've had firefighters and police officers visit us before and once even the mayor. But we've never had an angel."

Lucien felt like asking her if they'd ever had a sorcerer visit the school but kept the question to himself.

"What do you suppose it wants?" he said instead.

"Oh, who knows what the angels ever want." Miss Edge said. "One stood on the roof of my cousin's house for a full week and never said a word why. All their plants died and their cat ran away and never came back. When it finally left, their entire neighbourhood lost power for a day and the utility company couldn't figure out what caused it." She smiled at Lucien. "We missed Orpheus today. Is he sick?"

"He's just feeling a little . . ." Lucien trailed off. He wanted her to supply the illness she wanted to imagine. Then he wouldn't have to answer any more questions.

But Miss Edge looked past him then. Lucien knew without turning around that her gaze had been drawn by the light in the car. Maybe Orpheus had even drifted through the roof again before Kia could pull him back down.

"Oh no," she said. The way she said it made Lucien think she really meant it.

"It's not –" Lucien stopped. "It's curable. I know how to cure it."

"I'm so sorry," Miss Edge said, even as she took a step away from him.

Lucien remembered the first meeting they'd had with Miss Edge in her classroom, when Orpheus had started at the school. They sat on the little children's chairs around a tiny table. Lucien felt like a giant. He worried the chair might collapse under his weight. They looked at the crayon drawings on the walls. Houses with families outside and dogs and cats and bright yellow suns. Lucien remembered a drawing of an angel among them, but he didn't know now if it had really been there or if his mind was just making things up after the fact.

"You should have reported this," Miss Edge said. "When did it happen?"

"We don't even know what's happening," Lucien said. "So how can we say when it happened?" He stopped, then added, "We don't want the other kids to make fun of him." It seemed like the sort of thing he should say.

"The other children love Orpheus," Miss Edge said, but in such a quick way that Lucien suspected it was a standard response to a parent's concern. "But obviously he can't come to class anymore."

Lucien remembered there had been construction paper and crayons on the table during that first meeting with Miss Edge. He'd picked up one of the crayons, a black one, and held it in his hand. He didn't know when he'd last held a crayon before that. He couldn't remember if he'd ever taught Orpheus how to colour properly. He wondered if he was somehow to blame for the light.

"It's not contagious," Lucien said. "Or we'd have it, too. It's the angel." The angel itself was drifting away from the school, as if losing interest in them now that it was clear Lucien and Kia weren't going to do anything.

"It's school board policy," Miss Edge said. "He can't come back until he has a doctor's note."

"A doctor's note."

"Saying he's cured."

Lucien kept his gaze on the angel. He wondered where it was going now.

"We have to do something," he said.

"I can make up a lesson plan," Miss Edge said.

"A lesson plan won't save him."

"I'm sorry," Miss Edge said, then added, "I'm a mother, too."

That last bit surprised Lucien. He'd never thought of her as a mother. He glanced at her hand but didn't see a ring. Another sign he'd got wrong. Maybe he'd been getting them wrong all along and just hadn't realized it.

He turned and went back to the Range Rover. He didn't know what would happen if the angel disappeared on them. He had a feeling that it was the only link to saving Orpheus.

"I'll pray for you," Miss Edge said. "I'm not really a believer anymore, but I'll pray for you."

"It's prayer that got us all in this mess in the first place," Lucien said.

"The effort of the ascent matches only the infinity of the wait to those who have accomplished the inevitable," Orpheus said as Lucien got back in the car. He was glowing so brightly now that it left spots in Lucien's vision when he looked away.

"Hush," Kia said. "Just hush."

Lucien started the Range Rover and began to drive after the angel even though he still couldn't see properly.

"Where are we going now?" Kia asked.

"Wherever the angel takes us," Lucien said. He looked up at the sky but he couldn't see the angel now. It had become another one of the black spots.

The spots didn't fade like normal spots in his vision did. He could barely see as he drove toward the exit of the school parking lot. He thought he was all right to drive, as no one else was coming in or out of the parking lot. Then one of the spots turned into a girl running out from between some parked cars and across the lot, right in front of them.

Lucien drove into her before he could stop. The Range Rover shook with a stronger impact than he had imagined possible. He had a glimpse of the girl flying away from them, like the angel had flown through Orpheus's window. Then the airbag hit him in the face and an explosion of light turned everything white.

It was Orpheus's voice that brought him back.

"The time is never the time, the end is never the end, the world is never the world," Orpheus said from the back seat.

Lucien shook his head and suddenly his vision was clear. He saw the crack in the windshield where the airbag must have hit it. The world divided in two. The deflated airbag hung from the steering wheel and lay on his lap. He looked over at Kia and saw her staring in front of the Range Rover even as she continued to hang on to Orpheus. He followed her gaze to the girl lying there, crumpled on the ground.

"The things you see are never unseen even before they are seen by the unseen," Orpheus said. The edges of Lucien's vision strobed with light although he didn't know if it was from Orpheus or the after-effects of the accident. He didn't want to look back to find out.

He got out and went to the girl lying in the parking lot. Her arms and legs were bent at angles he knew they shouldn't have been. Her clothes were so torn from the impact that Lucien couldn't even see a logo or guess the brand. She was five, maybe six years old. She looked like a scene from some sort of activist video.

Kia stumbled to his side and fell to her knees as she looked at the girl. She was still hanging on to Orpheus's hand. He floated upside down above her like a balloon. "It was an accident," she said.

"Yes," Lucien said, although he wasn't certain of that. He wasn't sure if he'd been blinded by the spots in his vision or if he was just making that up after the fact. He thought it was entirely possible he'd seen her and kept driving anyway. He didn't know what to believe.

"Does it still count if it was an accident?" Kia asked, and Lucien knew she was talking about what the sorcerer had told him.

But they both saw the girl was still breathing from the pink bubbles that formed on her lips.

Lucien looked around and saw the children in the playground gathering by the fence and staring at them. Miss Edge was standing in the middle of the parking lot screaming into her phone. They didn't have much time. He looked up and didn't see the angel in the sky anywhere. Just Orpheus drifting back and forth above them.

"Oh God oh God oh God," Kia said. She smoothed the girl's hair and then put her hand over the girl's face. Over her nose and mouth.

"Mommy," the girl said through Kia's hand.

"I can't," Kia said, moving her hand to stroke the girl's cheek. "Oh my God, I can't, I'm so sorry, I can't." She began to weep now.

Lucien slipped his hand around the girl's throat. Her skin was hot to the touch. He knew all he had to do was squeeze. No one would ever see it but him and Kia. Miss Edge and the children would just think he was trying to help. Her crushed throat would just look like more damage from the accident. Because he knew he could say it was an accident. The girl had run out from between the cars, after all. He knew that even if she didn't die, she was badly hurt. Her spine was probably damaged, and maybe her brain. Who knew what kind of life lay ahead of her? The best-case scenario for her now was likely to become a poster child for some charity. But he could still save Orpheus.

He felt the girl's pulse flutter against his fingers, and he knew in that moment he couldn't do it. He remembered the first ultrasound where they'd been able to hear Orpheus's heartbeat. He thought about the girl's parents listening to their own ultrasound heartbeat. He thought about them somewhere out there in the world, perhaps preparing at this very moment to come and pick up the girl from school later. They would ask her how her day had been, what she'd learned, who she'd played with. They'd go to bed thinking about what kind of person she'd be in later life. Perhaps they'd think of grandchildren and maybe even great-grandchildren.

He felt the girl's heartbeat again and pulled his hand away. He looked up at the sky but the angel was long gone. It was like it had never been there at all.

The police arrived a minute later. It was the same pair of cops that had stopped them earlier. The man pulled them away from the girl and made them sit on the ground behind the Range Rover. The woman kneeled by the girl's side and said words to her that Lucien couldn't hear.

"If she dies, the light is going to be the least of your problems," the male cop said to Lucien.

"Don't you even want to take our statements?" Lucien asked.

"I don't need your statement to know what happened here," the cop said.

Lucien understood in that moment the cop knew all about what the sorcerer had told them, and what they'd been thinking when they had come here.

"It was an accident," he said.

"That's what they always say," the cop said.

The paramedics arrived a few minutes after that, followed by the firefighters and more cops. There were vehicles with flashing lights and sirens everywhere. The men and women in uniforms all clustered around the girl but they kept glancing at Lucien and Kia sitting on the ground, and Orpheus floating above them, his mother his only tether to the earth. The paramedics called in a helicopter and it came with a sound like it was tearing the sky open. It landed in an empty part of the parking lot, and the wind from it blew Orpheus about so much that Kia almost lost her grip on him. She cried out and hung on with two hands now. The paramedics wheeled the girl to the helicopter on a stretcher. They loaded her inside and the helicopter took off again, rising up into the sky and flying away in the same direction the angel had disappeared.

After it was gone, the firefighters and paramedics and cops all left, too. The ones that had been first on the scene were the last to go. The woman cop got back in their car while the man looked at Lucien and Kia.

"I can't tell if you're at risk of more accidents," he said.

"We just want to go home and hold our boy," Kia said.

"Where were you when the angel broke into our house and infected our son?" Lucien asked. "What are you going to do about the angels?"

The cop looked at him a moment longer without saying anything. Then he went to join his partner. They sat in the car and looked at their computer but didn't look at Lucien and Kia again.

Lucien got to his feet and looked over at the school but the playground was empty now, the children and the teachers all gone. He and Kia got back in the Range Rover. Orpheus shone so brightly now they couldn't even look at him. Lucien could barely make out Kia in the seat beside him.

"We are all right," Orpheus said. "We will all be all right in the end, until we are no more."

"What do we do now?" Kia asked, her words little more than a whisper.

"Now we kill the angel," Lucien said.

* * *

LUCIEN WENT back to the church as the sun was setting. The sky was flat and strangely empty of aircraft. Lucien couldn't even see the lights of a drone anywhere. He wondered if there had been another terror attack somewhere, and then he realized he didn't care.

He'd left Orpheus and Kia at home. The boy shone too brightly to even look upon now, and his speech was incoherent. Kia's hands had kept slipping through his arms, and she'd had to repeatedly grab on to him to keep him from floating away.

"If you can't kill it, don't bother coming back," she'd said. "Because I'm going with Orpheus wherever he's going."

Lucien brought the gun with him this time. It sat beside him on the seat like another passenger. A Glock handgun made of composite plastic. The perfect gun for a white-collar professional like himself. It was stylish without being aggressive and it still got the job done, at least in the shooting ranges and simulations, which were the only places he'd used it. Lucien thought the Glock should be in a design museum or art gallery somewhere if it wasn't already. Like the iPhone and the cubicle, it was the sort of product that changed generations. It was the gun of the future that everyone was living in now.

The parking lot in the cemetery was still empty when he arrived, the church still boarded up and abandoned. But he saw the flashes of light from inside the spire again, so he knew the angel was back. He suspected it was probably waiting for him, but that didn't change his plans.

He called the sorcerer from inside the Range Rover. The sorcerer answered after just one ring, as if he were expecting the call.

"You want another dream," the sorcerer said, as if he knew why Lucien was calling.

"Can you take something from real life and make it into a dream?" Lucien asked.

"I can do anything with a dream," the sorcerer said. "But I feel I should once again point out the potential problems if an angel is involved."

"I want you to take what happens next and turn it into a dream," Lucien said. "I want the world to see what happens to the angel. I want everyone to see there won't be an apocalypse."

He disconnected before the sorcerer could say anything else and got out of the Range Rover. He flipped the safety off the Glock as he crossed the cemetery. He tried to keep his breathing deep and even, like the instructors had taught him in the shooting exercises he'd often done on corporate retreats. But the exercises had involved rampaging co-workers and terror attacks, not angels waiting for him in forgotten churches.

He wasn't surprised to find the front doors of the church locked when he reached the entrance. He didn't bother trying to kick them open because he knew they would be reinforced on the inside. Every teenager and homeless person in the city had probably tried to break in here at one time or another.

He went around the side of the church and checked the windows until he found a loose corner in one of the pieces of wood covering the glass. He wrenched at it with his hands and pulled it open more, cracking the wood and then bending the broken piece back on itself. Now he could see a corner of the stained glass: a man with golden skin on his knees as he looked up at something Lucien couldn't see. Lucien smashed the glass out with the Glock and then pulled himself through the opening he'd made.

It was so dark inside it was as if light didn't even exist. He took out his iPhone and turned on the flashlight, then looked around for a moment. He was surprised to see the inside of the church still looked like the inside of a church. There were pews in orderly rows, with hymn books scattered on the benches. An empty cross hung on the wall behind the altar. There were no people but there were definitely signs of them. Clothes were scattered about the pews, covering most of them.

No, not scattered, Lucien realized. They were placed there in an orderly fashion. Pants and skirts resting on the seats, shirts and blouses draped over the backs of the pews. Shoes on the floor. The clothing was both adult and children's. It was as if someone had come in here and laid out all the clothes to create the idea of a congregation. Or as if the people in the clothes had all vanished into thin air at the same time during a service.

Lucien stared at the scene for a moment, then found the door that led to the rear area of the church. He went through and stepped into a scene of destruction. The ceiling was partially collapsed and the ground littered with debris. A stairway hung in the air in front of him, reaching up into the darkness. The bottom few steps were broken off and lay in fragments on the ground. Lucien looked up into the void overhead and saw the stairs circling their way up the inside of the spire. A light flickered somewhere near the top, and Lucien could hear whispers even though he couldn't make out the words.

He pulled himself up onto the broken stairs and climbed higher into the spire. He used the phone to light the stairs as he ascended. He didn't want to step into any gaps and fall back to the earth, not when he was this close to the angel.

The whispers became clearer as he went. He began to make out individual words.

". . . redemption . . . purify . . . legion . . . sacrament . . ."

The words were all in different voices, as if there were many angels up there speaking. Lucien tightened his grip on the Glock and kept climbing.

The angel was waiting for him on a landing partway up. It was a secret library of sorts. Three of the walls were covered in shelves that bore ancient-looking tomes: the sort of leather-bound books that you'd see as props in movies or rich people's homes. The fourth wall was mostly missing, a ragged hole that opened into the night.

The angel stood there glowing with light, but not as brightly as Orpheus now was. It fell silent when Lucien appeared and it studied him as he stepped onto the landing and pointed the Glock at it. Its wings drifted behind it, the flames curling about the edges of the books but not igniting them.

"Whatever you did to my son, I want you to stop it now," Lucien said, and he was surprised at how calm he sounded.

"The seraphim are beyond the reckoning of the fallen world is always falling and we cannot save the unsaved who will not be saved who are kingdom come," the angel said, each word in a different voice. So at least there was only one angel, Lucien thought. Unless there was more than one in the same body. He only had so many bullets, though, so he didn't want to think about that.

"I don't know if you're speaking gibberish or angel or if you're just insane," Lucien said. "I want you to take the light back from Orpheus. If you don't . . ." He dropped the iPhone to the ground and wrapped his free hand around the wrist of his shooting hand while he assumed the firing stance he had practised in the simulations. He doubted he'd sway the angel with his words, but he didn't want to just shoot it in case his bullets did nothing at all. The Glock was the one piece of leverage he might have.

The angel didn't move but its wings drifted forward, curling around Lucien on either side.

"The now is the only when and there are no other times that can be saved so rejoice that you have known this when for it no longer is and can never be again," the angel said, but this time it spoke all of its words in Orpheus's voice.

Lucien didn't know what that meant. Perhaps the angel was toying with him. Perhaps it meant Orpheus was gone and the angel had somehow claimed him. Perhaps all the voices it spoke in were victims of the light. Perhaps it was trying to appeal to his emotions, hoping he wouldn't shoot it if it spoke with his son's voice. There were more *perhaps* than he could think of in that moment, and none of them meant anything.

The iPhone rang with Kia's ring tone, but Lucien didn't even glance down at it. He kept his eyes on the angel. Its wings drifted closer to him, until he could feel the heat of the flames on his skin. No, not heat. Something else entirely. More like a pulling on his skin, as if his body were being sucked toward the wings.

The iPhone stopped ringing and now the angel spoke again. Only this time it spoke with Kia's voice. "Oh my God, Lucien, I can't hang on to him anymore! He's nothing but light now! I can't even see him anymore!"

Lucien pulled the trigger of the Glock, once, twice, three times. The landing flashed with even more light and the crack of the Glock firing in the confined quarters was louder than thunder. It was like the world itself was breaking apart.

Lucien stared at the three holes that had suddenly opened up in the angel's chest. Golden beams shot out of them like flashlights. The walls smoked and blackened where the beams touched them.

The angel and Lucien looked at each other for a moment, and now the angel was silent. Lucien couldn't pull the trigger again. He couldn't even move. He was paralyzed, but he didn't know if it was shock or fear or something else that kept him frozen.

"Oh my God is dead," the angel said, in a voice Lucien hadn't heard yet. It sounded like wind chimes and angry wasps at the same time.

Then the angel's wings flared and vanished, like candles blown out by a sudden wind. The angel leaned forward and fell. It hit the landing and crashed through it, falling into the darkness beneath them. Debris from the shattered landing rained down after it.

Lucien managed to step back onto the stairs before the landing gave way beneath him. He stared down after the angel. It bounced off the walls as it fell, and the spire of the church shook all around him. When it hit the ground below, the spire shook harder, as if a shock wave had just passed through it. The golden light flared up, so bright that Lucien had to squint.

The spire continued to shake around Lucien so hard he put a hand against the wall to steady himself, but it was no good. The wall cracked under his fingers, lines shooting out in all directions like lightning bolts. Then shards of wood began to fall down upon and past him from above, and he knew the spire was collapsing. He heard the iPhone ring again and he realized it was somehow in his hand once more. He had picked it up without realizing as the tower came apart.

It was Kia again. "He's floating away!" she screamed. "He's floating up into the sky and I can't hold him down!"

Lucien looked out through the hole in the spire and saw the lights of the city out there, the world that kept on existing even though it was coming apart in here. He saw the skeleton of the Relic looming above it all, reaching up to the heavens. He looked for Orpheus but couldn't see him among all the other bright lights.

He'd failed his son, his family. He hadn't protected Orpheus and the boy had become infected with the light. Because of the dream Lucien had wanted. He hadn't killed the girl to save his son. He'd thought maybe killing the angel would be enough, but it wasn't.

"Are you there?" Kia cried. "Where are you?"

Lucien knew there was only one thing he could do. He looked down into the light of the fallen angel below him. And then he stepped into the abyss and fell down after it, into the collapsing ruin of the church.

"He's coming back!" Kia cried. "He's falling back down to me."

Lucien could almost sense Kia opening her arms wide to catch their son. He closed his eyes but he could still see the light through his eyelids. As he fell toward it, he wondered if he was still dreaming and what would happen when he woke.

The Only
INNOCENT SOUL
IN HELL

I've seen every kind of sinner you can imagine in Hell. Murderers and mass murderers. Blasphemers and heretics. Identity thieves and spammers. And many more you can't imagine. I'm the first demon you'll meet when you arrive here, but trust me, I won't be the last. My name is Molox, and I'm the Infernal Gatekeeper to Hell, the Endless Keeper of the Books of Sin, the Unholy Judge of the Damned.

Well, those used to be my titles. These days, I'm known as the Processing Clerk, Department of Admissions and Exits. I feel the new title lacks the menacing weight of the older ones, but the lower-downs say we have to keep up with the mortal world in order to stay relevant.

I used to think the new title didn't make any sense. Department of Exits? No one exits Hell. Not since the Orpheus Incident, anyway, and we cracked down on security after that.

But then Alistair Black fell into Hell.

He didn't look like anyone special when the angel dropped out of the clouds overhead and threw him into the Pit of Endless . . . sorry, the waiting room. The thousands of damned who still had to be processed lifted their arms to the angel and cried out for salvation, but angels never save anyone. It went back up into the clouds, and the damned returned to milling about, looking for someplace to rest. The floor is too hot to sit on for long and we have only thirteen chairs in the waiting room, twelve of them with broken legs. The one good chair is there so people keep their sense of hope that things may get better for them. That makes it all so much worse when it never gets better. Welcome to Hell.

Alistair would have disappeared into the crowd, but my imp Malachi scampered over and dragged him to my desk, snapping at any of the other sinners who got too close. I should have known something was up then. Malachi has a knack for getting into trouble. It's what imps were spawned to do, after all.

Alistair looked like the opposite of trouble, though. He was the sort of person who'd blend in with any crowd. Average build, average haircut, average face. He had no defining characteristics, nothing that made him stand out. He wore what he had on at his death: a suit and tie that made me think lawyer. We get a lot of lawyers in Hell, so I'm pretty good at spotting them. He even held a phone in his hand. He looked almost hollow in his perfect humanness.

But while Alistair didn't look different than anyone else, he acted in a way I hadn't seen a sinner behave since the German wars ended and all those Nazis showed up in the waiting room acting like they owned the place. Some of the demons took notes from that lot. As for Alistair, he just shook his head like he was irritated by being here. Like he was above Hell.

I knew before he said anything that he was going to deny all his sins. Everyone does. But you don't catch the angel express to Hell unless you belong here. Unless deep down you know you should be here.

But the thing about Alistair Black was he was telling the truth, in his own way.

"There's been a mistake," he said as Malachi dragged him forward with a demented cackle. "Call another angel to take me out of here."

I finished my lunch before answering him: a Big Mac I'd taken from the last sinner I'd processed, an investment banker who'd died at his desk of a heart attack while eating the hamburger and was still clutching it when the angel dropped him off. Free food from sinners was one of the perks of my job.

Most people start to sweat and shake when they stand before me, if not scream in terror or pass out. The investment banker actually had another heart attack. I took that as a compliment. I spend hours between shifts polishing my scales and sharpening my claws and arranging my spines. It's nice to know the effort is appreciated.

But Alistair didn't do any of those things. He didn't even lose his colour like most sinners do when they avert their gaze from me and finally notice my desk. It's made of damned souls who have been stripped of their flesh and fused together, still alive. It's a real mood setter.

Alistair didn't care. He just glanced at the desk and then looked around the waiting room like he was bored.

Granted, the place didn't look as momentous as it had in the old days, when it was burning pits and rampaging skeletons and such. Now it's all industrial carpeting and inspirational posters on the walls and music piped in from the malls in your realm. There are some human torments that even demons can't improve upon. Although sometimes, on special occasions like Easter, we like to drag what's left of John Lennon to the main office and have him sing "Imagine" over Hell's PA.

I've learned not to complain about the changes. The last thing I complained about was the backlog of new admissions when all those Nazis showed up, and they sent me Baal as an assistant. His talent for looking into sinners' souls to find their most hidden fears makes him well suited for the suffering side of our business, but not so good at processing. He'd get so excited when dealing with new arrivals he'd start torturing them on the spot instead of sending them off to their proper level. Which made it really hard to process the other damned in the waiting room, who tried to flee in terror when they saw what Baal was doing to the people around them. No one was happier than me when Baal disappeared one shift in an explosion of smoke and flames, the result of an ill-advised summoning by a mortal. Well, maybe the damned were happier. But that wasn't going to last. Besides, one day Baal would be back. As long as he wasn't assigned to my department again . . .

As Alistair gazed around the waiting room, I realized I'd read his expression wrong. He didn't look bored so much as he looked jaded. Like the sinners who sometimes hide out in the crowd here for centuries, trying to avoid getting processed. As if they've beaten the system. Like a few hundred years makes a difference. Everyone comes to my desk eventually, if only to put an end to the waiting.

But Alistair shouldn't have been that used to Hell yet, considering he'd just arrived. Something wasn't right.

I belched a bit of fire as I pondered the situation.

Alistair looked back at me and frowned. "Didn't you hear me?" he said. "I don't belong in Hell."

"I'll be the judge of that," I said, which was true. My particular talent is to see where sinners belong in Hell. In fact, I'm the only demon with that particular talent. Most of the others were spawned for torment and suffering, but I was spawned for processing. So be it. Someone has to think about where in Hell you belong – we can't just have you wandering around looking for the torment you like best. Hell isn't a mall, although we do have several floors that are malls. And offices. We're also working on an airport level, where the flights are cancelled for all eternity.

But looking at Alistair, I wasn't sure where he belonged. He was so perfectly blank.

Malachi grabbed the phone out of Alistair's hand and nibbled on it. Alistair gave him a look but didn't say anything. Just as well for him. Sometimes Malachi was much more, well, impish. Like when he swapped sinners' eyes with his own.

"There's never been a processing error before," I said, although I will admit that's a hard thing to prove.

Alistair shrugged at me. "Possess me and look at my life. The evidence will speak for itself. You'll see I haven't done anything worthy of damnation."

I leaned back in my chair, which caused several of the souls trapped in it to whimper a little as my spines sank into them. A suitable fate for all those Nazis. I studied Alistair some more and still saw nothing. But I knew there was more to him than met the eye. He shouldn't have known about my power to possess sinners. He shouldn't have known anything about the admissions process yet.

I shrugged back at Alistair, which made the chair scream. There was only one way to find out what was going on here.

I left my body and possessed Alistair. That's when the problems started, and not just because I hate being in mortals. I immediately missed the comforting weight of my scales and talons, and the warm glow of the fire that burned in my stomach. And having only one heart – well, it doesn't bear talking about. It's almost as repugnant as having a soul. But the real problem was that Alistair was telling the truth. There were hardly any sins in him at all.

Before you start to panic and take a bath in holy water, don't worry, demons can't just possess whoever they want in your world. First, we have to be invited to your sordid realm through a summoning, like when Baal disappeared; and then you have to mess up the binding circles enough that we can manifest ourselves and grab you. So you're safe. Unless, of course, you've done something wrong and find yourself in Hell, where we can possess you freely and at will. There. Feel better now?

Every demon possesses mortals differently, but here's how it works with me. When I possess you, I can relive your whole life if I want. But I'm drawn to those moments where you sinned. So as soon as I entered Alistair I went where his soul took me.

I was a young Alistair in a garage. The door was closed, the only light a bare bulb overhead. A puppy in a metal cage at my feet. A can of gasoline in my hands. I poured the gasoline through the bars of the cage, onto the dog, which whimpered and then began to bark and bite at its wet fur. I didn't care. The people who owned the dog were in Mexico on holiday. The neighbour looking after the dog was shopping. No one would hear. I dropped the can and took out a lighter. I couldn't help but smile as I introduced the puppy to its own Hell.

Now I was an older Alistair, a student in law school. So I'd been right about that part. I was standing over my professor, an old man who always wore a cardigan, and who was now tied to the table at the front of his classroom. I wore judge's robes, and I held a large law book over my head. A tome, really. The professor's mouth was stuffed full of pages from another book, so he couldn't make a noise no matter how much he tried.

"The real question," I said, "is this a crime of passion or premeditation?" And then I brought the law book down onto his head over and over.

And now I was Alistair in my late twenties. I sat in a church, alone in all the pews. Another tome on my lap, but the cover suggested it wasn't the sort of thing you normally find in a holy place. Human skin. I smiled at the Jesus hanging on the wall. "I know how to beat you," I said.

There were other moments, of course – no one has a clean soul, not even those who get into Heaven – but nothing more serious than those. And they weren't necessarily enough to warrant eternal torment and suffering. Heaven is full of murderers, after all. And, strangely, there was nothing after Alistair's twenties. Like he hadn't sinned once after that day in the church, even though his earlier sins suggested he was on the fast track to being a sociopath and serial killer. He looked to be in his late thirties now, but no one went a decade without sinning. Not even the angels.

I settled back into my body and stared at Alistair. "What are you doing here?" I asked, and Malachi capered around him in a circle, crooning to himself as he swallowed the last bits of the phone.

"Like I said, there's been a mistake," Alistair said, ignoring Malachi. He looked at the clouds again, and this time he smiled. "Get me my ride out of here."

I scratched my back with my tail while I considered the situation. More than eight trillion served and we hadn't had a wrong admission yet. Still, just like the virgin birth, there's a first time for everything.

I shrugged and waved down the next angel that threw a sinner into the crowd. It swooped in and hovered above us, blowing Malachi and the damned away with the wind from its wings. Alistair and I had to hang on to my desk to stay where we were. The angels were always showing off like that.

"What is it you desire of one of the host of God?" the angel asked, its voice like wind chimes full of hornets. See what I mean?

"I'd like you to do your job," I said. "This one doesn't belong here."

The angel looked at Alistair and its eyes flashed gold. "He is a sinner. He belongs to Hell now."

Alistair shook his head. "There's no evidence to support that," he said. Lawyers.

"List me his sins," I said.

"The murder of dozens," the angel said. "Rape. Bestiality. Incest. Blasphemy. Suicide. The chronicle is as long as the list of demons in Hell. And as sordid."

"He hasn't done many of those things," I told the angel. "I see only one murder. And really, who doesn't want to kill their professor?"

The angel shone with indignation. There's no telling them they've done something wrong.

"You see?" Alistair said. "A mistake."

"I have seen his sins through the eyes of God," the angel said and now his own eyes turned black. "God does not make mistakes."

I thought about pointing out if that were the case there'd be no need for Hell, but I just waved him off before all the damned stampeded over here to plead for his mercy and crushed us underfoot. "Never mind, I'll take care of it myself," I said. I could see I wasn't going to get any help from him. Typical.

The angel disappeared into the clouds again with a single sweep of its wings, knocking Alistair and me and all the sinners to the ground. The trapped souls of my desk screamed after it. When we picked ourselves up again, Alistair frowned at me.

"You should have made him take me out of here," he said.

"Take you where?" I asked.

Malachi scampered back out of the crowd and shook his fists at Alistair. We both ignored him.

"To Heaven," Alistair said.

"Heaven?" I asked. "What makes you think you deserve to be in Heaven?"

"Well, I don't deserve to be here," he said. "And I'm dead, so where else am I going to go?"

You sinners have such limited imaginations sometimes.

"You know, I have a feeling something is not quite right about this," I said.

Malachi screeched in agreement. Or maybe disagreement. Who knew with imps?

"You can't hold me if I don't belong here," Alistair said. "That's kidnapping."

"So call the police," I said. "We have lots of them in Hell."

Alistair opened his mouth and then closed it again. He looked around, but it wasn't a random look. It was almost as if he were searching for someone he knew. I wasn't sure what to make of that but filed it away.

"Tell me about your death," I said.

He stared at me for several seconds before answering. "What do you mean?"

"I mean, how did you die?" I was puzzled about that. The angel had said suicide, but I hadn't seen it in his sins. A big one like that should have drawn me to it before the other transgressions I'd witnessed. But there was no sign of it in his soul.

"You heard the angel," he said. "I killed myself."

"But how?" I asked. Patiently, because I have all eternity.

Alistair frowned at me. "What difference does it make?"

"Tell me or I'll let the imp loose on you," I said, and Malachi bit off one of his own fingers in excitement. That's all right. They usually grow back, although not always in the same places.

"You can't do that," Alistair said.

"You're a sinner in Hell. I can do what I want."

Alistair looked at Malachi chewing his finger for a moment and then shook his head. "I don't remember," he said.

"You don't remember how you died?" Interesting. Generally, the only sinners who don't remember their deaths are those who die in car accidents or bombings or something fast like that. I'd never before had a suicide who couldn't remember the way they'd chosen to die. Most didn't want to remember it – everyone regrets leaping off a bridge the second they're airborne – but they did actually recall the details. I wondered if the angel had been mistaken, if Alistair's death had been something other than a suicide. "You didn't die that long ago," I pointed out. Not unless the angels had a worse backlog than Hell.

Alistair folded his arms across his chest. "I want to talk to another demon," he said.

I've learned when people make that particular demand the time for polite conversation, such as it is in Hell, is over. So I possessed Alistair again, only this time I didn't look for his sins. I looked for his death.

I can go anywhere I want in your life. I can relive any moment, not only the sins. It's just the sins that usually interest me. The rest of your existence – well, I'm sure it's as dreadfully boring to you as it is to me. So I went straight to the end of Alistair's life. And I found the suicide, even though it didn't draw me at all, which was strange enough. Even stranger was my possession. Instead of being inside of Alistair, occupying his body and mind, I stood behind him. We were in the bathroom. Alistair stood looking at himself in the mirror. I was insubstantial, like the ghosts we use to carry messages between the realms. Malachi was perched on one of my wings, inspecting his own spectral limbs with fascination.

This had never happened to me before. I wasn't even aware it could happen. But, as you'll find out, Hell is full of surprises. I thought for a moment that it was some sort of glitch, that I'd manifested in Alistair's life before the possession had entirely finished. But when I tried to step in to him, I couldn't. Something was blocking me. It's like there was no room in there for me. I looked at Alistair closer, trying to figure out what was going on.

He was wearing the same suit and tie he was wearing in the waiting room. He was holding the same phone to his ear.

"I'm never coming in to work again," he told whoever was on the other end. "I was thinking about one last shift, just so I could cut open your entrails and run them around the office like computer cables. But I think you'll suffer more if I just let you keep living your pathetic life." He hung up without listening for an answer.

Well. This was intriguing.

Malachi didn't seem to think so, though. He jumped down from my shoulder and hopped off into one of the other rooms, gibbering away to himself. I kept watching Alistair, who didn't seem aware of our presence.

"I loathe you so very, very much," he told his reflection. "I've had fun, but I just can't stand you anymore." He picked up a kitchen knife from the counter and began to cut his face with it.

This wasn't like any suicide I'd experienced before. Usually there was weeping and depression and pain and such. Sure, sometimes there was self-loathing, but I'd never seen it to this extent before. In fact, I realized as I watched Alistair cut himself, it went beyond self-loathing. He carved the skin off his face and sawed his nose off. He sliced off his ears. He hacked off pieces of his tongue. Soon we were standing in a pool of blood. I wish I'd been more substantial so I could have enjoyed its warmth.

When Alistair was done with his face, he moved on to the rest of his body. He left the eyes alone though. He wanted to watch what he was doing to himself. I fast-forwarded through the moment because, as entertaining as it was, it wasn't helping me to understand what Alistair was hiding. Because there was no doubt he was hiding something. How could he claim to not remember this way of suicide? And if he actually didn't remember it, well, then what was really wrong with him?

He staggered out of the bathroom, dragging his now useless and shorter right leg after him, and I followed. Judging by the amount of blood he'd lost and was still losing, he didn't have long left in this mortal world before he went off to wherever he was destined to go. Which should be Hell, judging from this memory, only it was a memory that Alistair didn't seem to be aware he even had. If I were new to the job, I might think maybe he had a split personality or something like that, but I'd processed enough people with that condition – usually management types, for whatever that's worth – to realize it had no bearing on things. But this was something completely different. This was like watching someone who wasn't Alistair at all.

He went from the bathroom to a bedroom. There were a couple of skeletons in the bed, with room enough for a person in between them. Very cozy.

Malachi squealed from the living room, so I went out to see what had him so excited. The place had been savaged. The walls were streaked with blood, some fresh, some old. The furniture had been shredded with a knife, maybe the same one Alistair had used on himself. The floor was covered in shards of broken and bloody glass. A bonfire was raging in the fireplace, which was piled high with burning books. Presumably from the now empty bookshelves lying in pieces about the room. Malachi stood in the fire, trying to pick up the books, but he was too insubstantial to manage it. He shrieked in rage and jumped up and down in the flames.

Just then Alistair stumbled out of the bedroom and fell into one of the chairs.

"This is how you imagined it would end, isn't it?" he said. He gouged out one of his eyes and threw it into the fire. Malachi opened his mouth to catch it, but it just sailed through him. Malachi sighed.

"It's a shame I can't do to you all those other things you fear so much," Alistair went on. "But you have to make do with what you've got at hand, I guess." He took the knife and rammed it through his other eye, into his brain. "I'll see you in Hell!" he cried as he convulsed several times. Then he was still.

Ah. Now I understood.

I went over to the fire to make sure. I looked at the books Malachi had been trying to pick up. Malachi tried in vain to grab the eyeball, which was sizzling away. The top book was the tome bound in human skin I'd seen in the church. *The Necronomicon.* Everything you ever needed to know about summoning demons but were too afraid to ask.

"Baal," I said, turning back to Alistair's body. "What are you doing in there?"

For a moment nothing happened and I almost thought I'd been mistaken. Then Alistair chuckled and sat up. He looked at me, one eye sightless, the other with the knife still in it.

"How'd you know it was me?" he asked, and now his voice was like the buzzing of flies. Malachi spat at him and he spat back. Mutual dislike or friendly greeting? Who knew?

You're probably wondering how I was able to talk to Baal in Alistair's memory. It's a demon thing. Once we've been in your mind, we never really leave. So Baal, or at least part of him, was still alive in Alistair's mind, even though Alistair himself was dead and in Hell now. And Baal – well, who knew where Baal was these days? It didn't matter. All that mattered was that he had once possessed Alistair.

"Was it the book?" he asked. "I knew I should have gotten rid of it sooner. But it comes in handy for certain things."

"The book just confirmed it," I said. "But what gave you away was the comment about knowing the things Alistair was afraid of. That's your talent."

The fact that Baal had possessed Alistair also explained why I was displaced from Alistair's body in this memory. I couldn't occupy it because there was already another demon occupying it.

Baal pulled out the knife and Alistair's eye came with it. He didn't seem to notice. "Yeah, I guess that was a bit of a giveaway. But I didn't know you'd be here watching me."

"Alistair's in Hell," I said. "It's my job to look at his life."

"So the angels took him for his sins anyway," Baal said, and then the buzzing in his voice turned almost wistful. "But he won't be staying in Hell, will he?"

"No," I said. "He wasn't the sinner. You were."

Baal shrugged and tossed the knife into the wall, where it buried itself up to the eyeball. Malachi eyed the eye and licked his fangs. "I am what Hell made me," Baal said. "Unlike this sad excuse of a sinner, I don't try to deny or change that."

"You know I have to report this," I said.

"He summoned me," Baal protested, looking at me with those sightless sockets. "I'm innocent. I was just doing my job, torturing the damned while you were wasting time with your precious paperwork, when all of a sudden I find myself in the mortal world in a binding circle. And here's this flesh puppet pointing out the gap in the circle, saying, 'Oops, I guess I made a mistake. Now you can possess me and do all sorts of terrible things to people in this world.' Who could resist that?" He took Alistair's phone out of his pocket and waved it at me. "It's all in here. He kept videos of everything."

"The paperwork is important," I protested. "How are we supposed to keep track of –"

"He's worse than some of us," Baal interrupted. "We would have had good times together in Hell."

"You may still get your chance," I said.

Baal studied me. "What do you mean?"

"I mean I think Alistair is done with Hell, but maybe Hell isn't done with him just yet."

"You have a plan?" Baal asked, and now his voice was the sound of saws in flesh.

"Maybe I don't have to report you after all," I said. "If you don't say anything about this, then I won't tell the lower-downs."

Baal chuckled again. "I'll see you in Hell, my brother."

"I'll see you in Hell," I agreed, and then I left Alistair's life and went back to my own.

Now Alistair was in front of me again, his eyes and ears and nose and skin all intact once more. I wanted to reach out and pull him closer with my talons. I wanted to flay him and eat his disgusting organs. I wanted to rip out his eyes and turn them to face him so he could see what I was doing. I wanted to . . . well, you get the idea. Instead, I forced myself to remain calm. I did have to admire him a little. It was a good plan, and he almost got away with it.

"It turns out you're right," I said. "You don't belong here."

He looked at me for a moment, and then he smiled. It was the same smile as when he tortured that dog.

"I told you there was a mistake," he said.

Malachi leapt for his eyes, but I knocked him away with my tail. He wasn't allowed to torture Alistair. Not yet.

"There was no mistake," I said. "The angel was right to bring you here. You did all those things it said. Only it wasn't you, was it?"

His smile only faltered a little. He was a cocky one. He would have made a good demon. He still might someday.

"I was possessed," he said, without missing a beat. "Nothing I did was my fault. It wasn't even me doing it. It was Baal."

"No, it wasn't you doing it," I said. "But you enjoyed it as much as if you were doing it, didn't you? After all, you were still along for the ride, so to speak."

"I know the laws," he said. "Both human and infernal. Technically, I never committed a crime worthy of Hell."

"No, Baal did," I said. "You made sure he'd do all the things you secretly wanted to do when you left that mistake in the summoning circle."

"He took me over," Alistair said. "He made me do things against my will. You can't be held accountable for the things you do under duress like that."

"You didn't do anything against your will." I put my feet up on my desk and studied my talons. It was probably time for another sharpening. But first I had to get rid of this processing backlog. "I mean, of all the demons you could choose to summon, why Baal? Why not Azaziz, who can make gold out of dirt and teach you the secrets of transmutation? Why not Gwynesh, who can take the form of any succubus you desire and satisfy your every craven – and no doubt unimaginative – sexual desire? Why not me, who can tell you the secrets to staying out of Hell?"

Now Alistair didn't say anything at all, just eyed Malachi, who glowered at him and chewed on the end of his tail.

"You chose Baal because he can see your secret fears," I said. "Which means he can also see your secret desires. You let Baal possess you – you made Baal possess you – so he would do those things and you'd have the memories. But none of the sin would be yours. You could live a life worthy of the deepest floor of Hell, but you'd get to escape Hell."

Alistair couldn't help himself. He laughed. "And I did it, didn't I?"

"You did," I agreed. I smiled with him.

"I beat Heaven and Hell," he said. He looked up at the clouds overhead, which were threatening to rain down lightning now. "I won. Where's my ride out of here?"

"You might have beaten Heaven," I said, "but you certainly haven't beaten Hell. You've only delayed your damnation."

"You said it yourself," he said, looking back at me. "I didn't do those things. It doesn't matter if I enjoyed them or not. I didn't do them. The facts of the case are what they are."

"You didn't do them," I said. "But you will."

Now his smile faded and he showed his teeth. "What do you mean?"

I kept on smiling. "You can leave. We have to let you leave. You're not worthy of Hell. Not yet, anyway." I waved over the next angel that fell through the clouds, and the damned cried out at the sight of it. "But you're certainly not worthy of Heaven, either."

"Where are you sending me then?" Alistair asked, for the first time looking anything other than confident.

"You're one of the lucky ones," I said. "You're being given a rare gift that most mortals don't get. A second shot at life. You're going to be born again. Same soul, new body."

"You can't do this to me," Alistair screamed as the angel descended toward us. "I haven't done anything."

"Not yet," I said. "But you will. You can't help but be true to your nature."

The angel landed and sent everyone flying again, except for me. I hung on to my desk and explained things as clearly as I could so that even an angel could understand it. By the time I was done, Malachi had dragged Alistair back out of the crowd.

"I'll just do it again!" Alistair screamed. "I'll do it for the rest of eternity! I'll summon another demon and keep killing and torturing and sinning and there won't be anything you'll be able to do about it!"

"Eternity is a long time," I said. "You'll slip up eventually. And we'll be here waiting. Hell waits forever."

"Take me to Heaven!" Alistair screamed at the angel, and the other sinners in the waiting room screamed the same thing and surged toward us.

"Heaven is only for the pure," the angel said, its voice like the wind. "You are of the flesh and the sin. It is to the flesh and sin that I will return you."

And then they were gone, and the sinners all fell back to the ground weeping. Alistair's last words were lost in the howl of the angel's ascent back up into the storm and to the mortal world. I had no doubt I'd see Alistair again, though. In fact, I was looking forward to that meeting. And I had some ideas for a new floor of Hell we could create just for him.

I was so lost in the daydream of Alistair's future suffering that it took me a moment to notice Malachi screeching at the latest sinner to arrive. For some reason the angel that dropped off the sinner was coming over to my desk, followed by what seemed like all the damned in the waiting room again, begging him for salvation. Then I realized there was no sinner and it was the angel itself that Malachi was screeching at.

"What do you want?" I asked the angel.

"There's been a mistake," the angel said, its voice thunder that dropped the sinners in the waiting room to their knees. "I don't belong here."

Yes, it was definitely one of those shifts.

A Murder
IN HELL

People die in Hell all the time, but I'd never seen a dead demon before. Not until now.

I stared down at the body of Zqqerrty'fll sprawled lifelessly on the office floor near the water cooler. There wasn't a mark on his scales, but the fire in his eyes had gone out, leaving nothing but black, empty holes. The first murder in Hell, and I didn't have a clue what had happened.

I thought it was the first murder anyway, but I couldn't say for sure. I'm not an archivist demon. My name is Molox, and I'm more of a special investigative demon. I'd be a cop if there were such things as law and order in Hell. But there's not. There's only fear and punishment.

Killing the damned doesn't count as murder, of course, because they're sinners and they get what they deserve. Besides, the damned don't stay dead in Hell. Sure, they die horrible, violent deaths when we load them onto Flight 666, the plane that crashes for all eternity into the Lake of Fire, or when we lock them in the Zombie Mall overnight for the rest of time, or when we force them into the Elevator of Doom, or when we . . . well, you get the idea. But after they die, they always wake up back in whatever level of Hell they started in. And we do it all over again. Getting killed in Hell is just your damnation. But coming back to life

283

and finding yourself still in Hell, with no chance of ever escaping – that's your real punishment.

But no one had ever murdered a demon before. In fact, I had thought we couldn't be killed. But here I was in Infernal Office 272B, looking down at Zqqerrty'fll's body, as my imp, Malachi, capered around the scene, gurgling with delight. Or maybe despair. It's hard to tell with imps. Besides, I wasn't really paying attention to him on account of the demon looming at my side. Beelzebub. One of the lower-downs that really put the fear and punishment into Hell – so much so that even other demons like myself got nervous in his presence.

"Well, what manner of madness do you think happened here?" he asked. He slapped his face tentacles together to make the words, and splattered me with black ooze. I didn't dare edge away from him, though. And I didn't answer his question because I didn't know the answer. I had no idea what had happened here.

The truth is that I'm not really good at my job. I was spawned to be a processing clerk in the Department of Admissions and Exits, not a special investigative demon. But I kept encountering strange cases and solving them, like the innocent sinner who the angels dropped into the waiting room of Hell, to say nothing of the angel who sought asylum in Hell. It was all part of being on the front lines of the admissions process, but the lower-downs were so impressed that they decided Hell needed a special investigative demon. And so I was reassigned from my comfortable desk of living bone in the Department of Admissions and Exits to roam around Hell, solving problems that didn't fall under anyone else's job category.

For instance: we'd heard rumours that people in the mortal realm were receiving phone calls from their damned relatives and friends in Hell. It took me a while to figure out that all the screaming in Hell sometimes created a sort of signal that the newer, more sensitive phones on the market could pick up. It was all very complicated and involved frequencies and spectrums and other things that a couple of engineers explained to me at Malachi's urging. The imp could be very persuasive. The solution to the problem was simple: we made the sinners scream a different way. You can't ever accuse Hell of being stuck in the old ways, as delightful as they were.

Mostly though, my job consisted of tracking down demons who'd wandered away from their job to get a snack or find a warm, fiery place to nap. It was a hard problem to get a handle on, as most of the damned didn't exactly rush to report their torturers missing. Although some did. That's Hell for you.

When Beelzebub opened the hellmouth into the abattoir where I'd been on my lunch break and pulled me through into Office 272B, I thought it was just another missing demon case. That was before I saw the body now before me on the floor. The body I couldn't explain.

I looked around the office. The damned condemned to the desks here barely looked away from their computers. They kept on typing, and none of them raised a hand to take the blame for Zqqerrty'fll's death. I wouldn't have either. I looked back at the body.

It had to be murder, because demons don't die of natural causes. But there was no blood, no chunks of meat torn from an attacker in his claws. All he held was paperwork. His shirt was still tucked into his dress pants, his tie still perfectly knotted. For some reason the pattern on the tie matched the pattern in the worn carpet: golden cherubs playing harps on a brown background. Something R & D must have dreamed up to further torment the damned. Sometimes the devil is in the details.

I sighed and scratched my head with my tail. "This is all really a bit beyond me," I said.

I didn't point out to Beelzebub that I didn't really have any talent for this kind of work because I hadn't been spawned for it. Demons don't have any choice in our particular talents. One eon we're just mindless lava, happily bubbling away, and the next we're being bound into our forms by the spawning demons. And they didn't understand the process any better than us. They just spoke the ritual words of binding that had been in their minds when they'd been spawned, without even knowing what they meant. Hell works in mysterious ways and all that.

Beelzebub apparently didn't want to hear my confession of ignorance, because he wrapped one of those face tentacles around my neck and lifted me up to stare into his maw. The remains of some meal or another still twitched in there, and I looked away before I recognized it. The damned sank lower in their chairs. I caught sight of Malachi scampering away to hide in a cubicle, the papers from Zqqerrty'fll's talons clutched in his little claws. Not for the first time, I wished I'd been spawned as something simple like an imp.

"Hell needs a special investigative demon," Beelzebub said, his spittle burning my skin. "Hell does not need a failed special investigative demon."

"But I'm sure I can figure it out," I said. "It may take me a few minutes, though."

"Say my name three times when you have found the murderer," Beelzebub said, dropping me and glowering at the damned huddled behind their computers. "But do not punish them yourself. Save that for me."

I almost felt sorry for the damned. Almost.

Beelzebub left us then, tearing open a hellmouth in the wall to a level of Hell I didn't even dare gaze upon. Thankfully, he pulled it shut again after stepping through. I didn't need all the things on the other side looking over my shoulder as I worked.

I sighed again as I looked at the damned in their cubicles.

"I don't suppose anyone is going to own up to this?" I asked, but they all kept their heads down. I would have done the same thing.

I studied the damned. There were only a witch's dozen of them. A manageable list of suspects. I could have gone back to the Department of Admissions and Exits for some information on them, but the only clerk there, Baal, had gone missing again. Well, not exactly missing. We knew where he was. He'd disguised himself as a sinner and was hiding out in the vast crowd in the waiting room. He'd left behind a note in the form of another sinner crucified to the wall with shards of bone ripped from the sinner's own rib cage. The sinner wailed that Baal wasn't coming back until we found him some help filling out the Books of Blood. Baal was tired of inscribing all the names of the damned in the Books by himself, and he was even more tired of chasing down sinners to carve new pages for the Books out of their flesh.

But there was a spawning freeze on, so there would be no help for Baal. The crucified sinner suggested we invest in a computer system, and I told him that was a good idea and he should bring it up with Beelzebub. He stopped wailing after that.

So here I was, a dead demon at my feet and an office full of damned I didn't know anything about. Some eons it doesn't pay to get out of the lava pits.

At first glance, the damned in Infernal Office 272B didn't seem different from any of the other damned in Hell. They had the thousand-year stare. They stank like mortals tended to stink after ages of not being able to bathe or put on deodorant and perfume. They wore the same clothes they'd died in, which was the only way I could tell them apart.

Most of them typed idly at their keyboards now that Beelzebub was gone. They couldn't help but keep working – that was the nature of their damnation – but they obviously didn't see any point in trying hard to finish whatever it was they were doing.

Three of them, however, worked at a frantic pace, typing as if their lives depended on it. A man whose hair was impossibly well groomed, and whose tie was perfectly knotted. I decided to call him Pride. The other man wore a golf shirt stained with blood from stab wounds. He didn't look like the type to get into knife fights, so I figured him for the fatality of an affair. I named him Adultery. Then there was the woman who wore a ripped business suit with a corset showing underneath and rope burns around her neck. Lust.

They were my suspects because ... well, I didn't really have a good reason other than they kept working hard. But that was enough in Hell.

Malachi wandered back out of the cubicle. He was munching on the papers he'd taken from Zqqerrty'fll's talons. I snatched them away and shoved them into my shoulder spines for safekeeping in case they were evidence. Malachi shrieked at me, but he was always shrieking at someone. Maybe someday the spawning demons would provide me with a translation demon so I would know what Malachi was shrieking about.

I was so lost in glowering at him that I almost didn't notice when one of the damned spoke up. A fat man wearing a housecoat who barely fit in his cubicle. Gluttony. All the sins looked to be represented here in this office.

"He just collapsed," the man said. "Like he had a heart attack."

"Demons can't die of heart attacks," I said. I looked back down at Zqqerrty'fll. I didn't think we could, anyway. What would the odds be of all his hearts stopping at once?

"Maybe it was a stroke then," Gluttony said.

"Or an act of God," one of the others said, now that the silence had been broken. A woman in a hospital gown with an IV bag draped over her shoulder. Pestilence. She turned back to her computer when I looked at her, realizing her choice of words hadn't been well thought out.

"What was he doing when he collapsed?" I asked.

Gluttony shrugged, and his body rippled and shook. Malachi circled his cubicle, crooning at him.

"He was just reading the report," Gluttony said, his eyes flicking to the papers in my shoulder spines.

The report. The damnation of these sinners was they had to write a new report for Zqqerrty'fll each evening. The truly fiendish part of the damnation was they didn't know what kind of report he wanted. It could be anything. Cost-benefit analyses of adding a new speed to windshield wipers. The chemical makeups of the gases given off by Ikea furniture. A quarterly report of a fictional restaurant. They never had any idea. Only Zqqerrty'fll knew. And he never told anyone what he wanted until after the reports were written.

The ones who guessed the correct subject were rewarded at least. Zqqerrty'fll gave them a pass from having to work overtime for a shift. But every one of the damned who submitted the wrong report was forced to work overtime. Overtime in this office meant time was actually stretched so it made everything feel like it took longer to do. It doesn't sound that bad until you've lived a few centuries of it.

I knew the chance of coming up with the report that Zqqerrty'fll wanted in any given shift was about the same as finding an innocent sinner in Hell. Most of the damned didn't bother. They couldn't help but work on the reports – they were bound to their fate just as much as we demons are bound to our bodies -- but many of them simply typed random words into their computers or created random graphs and charts. This had resulted in a few interesting accidents, such as the time one of the sinners had written the sequel to *Hamlet* without even realizing it. Zqqerrty'fll had laughed about that one the last time I'd run into him at the lava pits. He'd tried to describe the sinner's expression when he'd realized what he had done and Zqqerrty'fll had ripped up the report and eaten it in front of him, but it was one of those things where you had to be there.

So why were Pride, Adultery and Lust working so hard to finish their reports, especially now that Zqqerrty'fll was dead? There was something going on. I just had to figure out what.

"I'll give a day off to the first damned who tells me what really happened to Zqqerrty'fll," I said.

It was unthinkable. None of the damned in Hell ever got a reprieve like that. What would be the point of Hell if you got to escape it? Also, I wasn't sure if I had the authority to authorize such a reward. But this was an extraordinary circumstance, so I felt justified in making such an offer. Besides, who would they complain to if I didn't honour the offer?

Equally unthinkable was the fact no one answered me. They all looked at each other but didn't say anything. No one knew what had happened to Zqqerrty'fll. No one except the murderer or murderers. Whoever had killed Zqqerrty'fll had managed to do so in a way that the others hadn't noticed.

I looked back at Zqqerrty'fll for clues. There was nothing unusual about his appearance, except for the fact he was dead. If there were no signs of struggle on or around Zqqerrty'fll, then how could he have died?

I clasped my claws behind my back and paced around the body. It was something the mortals did to help them think. Malachi did the same behind me, gibbering quietly to himself.

Could Zqqerrty'fll have been poisoned? The water cooler by him was empty, but that didn't mean anything. The water cooler was supposed to be empty. Another way to torture the damned. Perhaps it was something Zqqerrty'fll had eaten?

I went into the break room and looked around, but I saw only the usual things. A vending machine stocked with potato chips and chocolate bars. A fridge with nothing in it. A microwave with a cup of cold coffee on the tray. I dunked Malachi's face into it and made him drink some. He coughed and squealed but didn't die, so I figured it was just Zqqerrty'fll's forgotten coffee. The damned weren't allowed such treats as hot coffee, after all.

But then I went back into the office and caught Lust taking a sip of hot tea from her mug. She put it down hurriedly when she saw me, but not before I noticed the steam rising from the mug. The look on her face told me she knew she shouldn't be drinking a hot drink. Yes, something was definitely going on here.

I wondered if one of the damned had managed to smuggle in some sort of secret weapon from the mortal world. Maybe this was another new phone incident. I stomped over to the cubicles and tore out the desk drawers of the damned in search of a secret technology capable of killing a demon. But I didn't find anything other than staplers and rubber bands and Post-it Notes and the usual office supplies. Nothing that could have reduced Zqqerrty'fll to the pitiful shell of the demon he'd once been.

Malachi kicked over the garbage cans while I worked, emulating me. He threw crumpled balls of paper at the damned with screeches of rage or maybe glee. Then he stuck his head in an empty chip bag hidden near the bottom of one can and started licking the inside of it.

Wait. An empty chip bag? The damned shouldn't have been able to buy chips. The vending machines were supposed to be locked down with wards that kept them permanently out of order to anyone but demons. The same with the microwave. Temptations that could never be realized. But these office appliances obviously didn't have wards. Either that or the damned had found some way around them, which was impossible. Just as impossible as Zqqerrty'fll's death.

I went through the garbage in the office and found more empty chip bags in the cans belonging to Pride, Adultery and Lust. So my initial suspicions of them had turned out to be accurate. But I was no closer to solving the murder.

"Almost done," Pride said. For a moment I thought he was talking to me, but then Adultery and Lust nodded. I glanced at the clock on the wall to see how close they were to finishing their shift, but there was no clock on the wall. There was just a circular patch of paint a different colour where the clock had hung. Brown instead of the cubicle grey the walls now were. The custodial demons had cut a few corners the last time they'd painted. But I guess they had a lot of Hell to cover.

I looked around for another clock, but I couldn't see one anywhere in the office. Just more brown circles.

I scratched my head with my tail again as I pondered. So many clues, but I didn't know how to put them together . . .

And why would Pride announce he was almost done? Was there something special about his report? Was he writing a murder confession? I looked at his monitor but the words on it didn't make any sense. They were nonsense, gibberish in a made-up language, accompanied by a few strange shapes and doodles.

I went around the other cubicles, looking at all the monitors. Everyone's report was meaningless: Pestilence was writing some sort of diary about her life in Hell. A man in a T-shirt and ripped jeans I decided to call Sloth was just holding down the *A* key and watching the letter repeat itself. Gluttony was using his mouse to draw a picture of the office, complete with a stick man representation of me and a little stick man Malachi. The real Malachi screeched at the sight of his double and attacked the monitor.

Then I looked at Adultery's monitor. His report was written in the same strange language as Pride's, and repeated some of the odd shapes. He typed even harder as I looked over his shoulder. As did Lust. And her monitor showed the same thing. They were all working on the same report. And hurrying to finish . . .

Why would the three of them be working on the same report? I was so intent on the question I barely noticed Malachi drag Gluttony's monitor to the floor and start biting it.

I pulled the papers from my shoulder spines to see what sort of report Zqqerrty'fll had been reading when he'd dropped dead. But it wasn't a report. It was a memo summarizing all the things that had gone missing around the office.

The clocks on the walls.

The locks on the restroom doors.

The pentagrams and wards that were supposed to seal off the vending machines and microwave.

The office time sheets.

That was all I could make out because Malachi's saliva had melted the rest of the words. But that was all I needed. The missing items had one thing in common.

They were all related to binding and imprisonment in the office.

I slapped my head with my tail. Now I understood.

I looked at the damned again as Malachi threw himself upon Gluttony with a screech of delighted rage. Or maybe raging delight.

Gluttony screeched himself. But I didn't pay attention to him or Malachi. I was looking at Pride and Adultery and Lust.

"I know what you did," I said.

"Too late," Pride said with a grin and hit the enter key. Adultery and Lust did the same at their keyboards. They looked at me expectantly.

Malachi screeched again and fell off Gluttony. He shook like he was being electrified, which he normally enjoyed. But this time he gurgled a few times and then curled up on the worn carpet, as still as Zqqerrty'fl.

I sighed, and the smiles faded from the faces of Pride and Adultery and Lust.

"That didn't exactly work out like you'd planned, did it?" I said.

They just turned paler shades of pale than the damned usually are in Hell. They knew they were in deep trouble. The deepest levels of Hell kind of trouble.

I looked at their monitors again. The words and symbols were glowing now, pulsing with power.

"We can make a deal," Pride said.

"After you killed my imp?" I said and shook my head. "Beelzebub Beelzebub Beelzebub."

The hellmouth opened in the wall again and Beelzebub crawled through from a place best not described. Screams rent the air and the damned put their hands to their ears. I guess they couldn't appreciate the disturbing harmony.

Beelzebub snapped his face tentacles together and black liquid sprayed the room, splattering me and the damned. I chose not to say anything about it, but Lust began to silently pray. A little late for that.

"You have solved Zqqerrty'fl's murder," Beelzebub said. It was a statement, not a question.

"Yes and no," I said, then quickly explained before he could choke me again. "Technically, I don't think Zqqerrty'fl was murdered."

Beelzebub looked down at Zqqerrty'fl's body. "I see no signs of life."

I pointed at the damned in what I hoped was a dramatic fashion. "A million monkeys typing on a million typewriters for a million years will eventually produce the works of William Shakespeare," I said. The way Pride and Adultery and Lust sagged lower in their seats told me I was right.

"What does that Shakespeare seraphim have to do with this?" Beelzebub asked. "Did he murder Zqqerrty'fll?"

I tried not to sigh out loud. "No, the damned did," I said. "Or rather, they figured out how to unbind him."

"It was an accident!" Lust shrieked, which just told me it wasn't.

Beelzebub turned to her and rubbed his tentacles together. She passed out, falling face-first onto her desk. That wouldn't help her, either. Hell would still be here when she woke up.

I lifted up Pride's monitor so Beelzebub could see it. "Type enough meaningless gibberish for an eternity and eventually you'll stumble across something that has meaning," I said. "Like an unbinding ritual."

I looked down at Pride. "My guess is you stumbled across a simple spell first. Something that broke the wards around the microwave and vending machine. Something that made the clocks disappear. Am I right?"

Pride looked around as if searching for a place to hide. But this was Hell.

"That's right," Adultery said. "It was his idea."

"I was helping you and this is how you thank me?" Pride said, glaring at him.

"You only told us because you couldn't manage the unbinding on your own," Adultery said, shaking his head. He turned to Beelzebub. "I'll tell you everything in return for leniency." He knew better than to ask for immunity.

"We were going to find a way to escape!" Pride said, then slapped a hand over his mouth, as he realized he'd said too much.

"There is no escape from Hell," Beelzebub said.

"There's never been a murder in Hell, either," I said, nodding at Zqqerrty'fll.

Beelzebub stomped over to Pride's cubicle to inspect his monitor more closely. He glanced down at Malachi as he went.

"What happened to the imp?" he asked.

"The latest ritual of unbinding," I said. "I think they intended to use it against whoever replaced Zqqerrty'fll. To buy themselves some time while they figured out their next spell. They probably thought it was going to take me out, but I guess the ritual saw Malachi as the more immediate threat."

"Next spell?" Beelzebub asked.

"The one that will teleport them out of Hell or make them invisible or summon an angel or whatever it will do. The one that will unbind them from Hell."

The looks on the faces of Pride and Adultery told me I was right.

Beelzebub wrapped a tentacle around Pride's face and lifted him from his chair. "Where did you send Zqqerrty'fll?"

"I don't have a clue," Pride cried around a mouthful of oozing black sucker. "All we did was unbind him. One minute he was here, the next he wasn't."

Beelzebub looked at me. "Well, special investigative demon, how shall we punish such a transgression?"

I could see his problem. Unbinding a demon with a random ritual wasn't exactly a common sin with a clear punishment. But I had an answer. I was starting to get the hang of this special investigator business.

"Baal needs help in Admissions and Exits," I said.

Beelzebub just stared at me with all those eyes.

"There's a backlog," I said. "He can't record the names of the newly damned fast enough in the Books of Blood."

Then Beelzebub started to shake. It took me a moment to realize it was laughter. Either that or he was about to explode. Maybe it was both.

"I didn't know the situation was so dire," he said, and I knew he'd caught on.

"Oh, it's dire all right." I smiled at Pride and Adultery.

"I will, of course, authorize overtime," Beelzebub said.

"I think they'll need to work around the clock until we're caught up," I said.

Pride and Adultery cried out in horror as they suddenly understood. Even Lust moaned a little.

The punishment was to be more paperwork, but now they would have no freedom to write whatever they wanted, no freedom to come up with new rituals. Instead, they'd have to record the names of all the damned in Hell, every new arrival, while time moved even slower for them. They'd spend the rest of eternity filing paperwork.

Beelzebub ripped open another hellmouth in the wall, to the waiting room at the entrance to Hell. He tossed Pride and Adultery and Lust through. Then he looked at the other damned. "How do we ensure these ones don't come up with another ritual?"

"That's exactly what we want them to do," I said. I turned to the damned. "From now on, your reports are to be about one thing only. How to spawn a demon that cannot be unbound."

They groaned but started typing. They couldn't do anything else. They probably wouldn't figure it out. It would have happened already if it were possible. But maybe they would. Then we'd come up with something else for them. There's always a new torment in Hell.

"Perhaps we should transfer you to R & D," Beelzebub said.

"I'm still learning how to do this job," I said.

I went through the hellmouth and Beelzebub closed it from the other side. There was a larger crowd of damned than usual in the waiting room. Among them were a number of people missing arms and legs. The sort of thing you see in war victims, but this group were all wearing tuxedos and formal dresses. They were telling others in the waiting room how they'd been watching a production of *Faust* when the actor playing the demon had suddenly leapt into the audience and began tearing them apart. Like a real demon.

I'd solved another mystery: where Zqqerrty'fll had gone. But I decided not to tell Beelzebub, in case he thought I was the best demon to bring Zqqerrty'fll back to Hell.

I watched as Pride and Adultery dragged Lust into the crowd, in search of a way out. But this was Hell. There was no way out. I let them be for the moment. The anticipation of their new damnation was a torment in its own right. And I hadn't even told them the best part yet: they'd be donating the flesh for the new Books of Blood. Baal was going to like having assistants. Now I just had to find him in this crowd to tell him the good news.

Before I could start looking, Malachi scampered out of the crowd, chewing on something that looked like a finger. I didn't bother reprimanding him. He'd earned a treat.

I hadn't really expected him to stay dead. It was impossible to truly kill an imp. Hell knew I'd tried. They always came back, though. This looked like the same Malachi anyway. But who really knew with imps? He climbed up my scales and settled in among my shoulder spikes, where he crooned happily, or maybe sadly.

I sighed and stepped into the crowd, to begin my search for the demon hiding among all the sinners.

We Continue to Pray
FOR SOMETHING TO END OUR PRAYERS

We expected the world to end in fire, or maybe flood. An asteroid from the heavens, perhaps, or a drowning ocean from the melted ice caps. We expected a plague to arrive on every flight that descended into our cities, for our own bodies to rise up against us. We expected something apocalyptic. Something we deserved. We watched the skies and the seas. We watched each other. And we waited.

The first sign we had was when all the people died in that church in Nashville. They went in for morning service in their best clothes and didn't come back out. Those of us who didn't love God as much as they did arrived later to pick them up and found everyone inside dead. The bodies were all still sitting in the pews, still holding hymn books, collection plates, cellphones. And, despite what some of us later said, they weren't all pointing at the Jesus hanging on the wall.

At first we assumed it was a mad gunman or a suicide cult, because it had all the signs of a mad gunman or a suicide cult. Except there weren't any wounds on their bodies, no traces of poison or chemicals in their systems. The autopsies revealed there wasn't anything wrong with them other than their hearts had all stopped beating at once. We searched for a reason but there was no reason.

So, as we usually did in those days, we talked of miracles and divine, secret plans. We argued on news shows and comment threads about whether this was the rapture or a freak event, a statistical anomaly. We wanted to know why they were special. We wanted to prove they weren't.

And then the same thing happened in other churches. Detroit. Little Rock. Houston. That airport church in Toronto. The body count hit the hundreds. We stopped arguing about the existence of God and instead wondered why he was massacring his followers.

And we couldn't get enough of it. More people went to church for the first time than we could remember in our lives. We watched videos online of people fighting to get into services until the servers crashed, or we were the ones elbowing and kicking others aside to get through those doors before they closed. We prayed – some of us openly, some of us privately – but we all prayed. We prayed we would be next. This was the kind of time we lived in. This was when we thought there was still someone to hear our prayers.

And then it spread outside the churches.

An entire aisle full of shoppers in a Toledo Walmart dropped to the floor in unison, like they were one of those flash mobs. We found the pilots of an Air Canada flight dead in their seats after the plane landed in Vancouver. A squad of firefighters went into an office tower in New York to investigate a gas leak and collapsed in a pile on the cafeteria floor. There was no gas leak.

We didn't know why they weren't all taken at once, why instead they died over the course of the summer. Some of us who were experts on the subject – and we didn't know we had experts until then – went on the news shows to say God was waiting for us to confess our sins before he took us. Or waiting for us to finish our good deeds on earth. Or waiting for us to finally accept Christ into our hearts. Others said Heaven was likely a bureaucracy, a government office for souls, and it took a while to process everyone. So we accepted Christ into our hearts even if we didn't believe in him, and we confessed our sins in the sanctuaries of our bathrooms, and we smiled at each other in the motor vehicle licensing branches and tried not to get upset about the waiting.

But then it spread to those of us who weren't Christian. Buddhist monks dropped in the streets in Thailand. An entire parade ground of soldiers fell dead in China in mid-salute. That's when we worried it was some new disease, a new bird flu. We put on the surgical face masks again, although some of us had never taken them off. Then a hundred men in a mosque in Iran bent to the floor in prayer and didn't get up again. We ran photos of them in the Iranian state media; row after row of them slumped with their heads to the floor. Forever frozen in prayer. We said it was a Jewish chemical attack. We ran the same photos in the Israeli media. We said it was proof the Iranians were experimenting with chemical weapons. This was back when we still had governments.

But there was nothing wrong with these people who had died, either. Our autopsies on the monks showed no signs of bird flu, or any other flu, although many of the monks had undetected cancers related to air pollution. We released medical reports that showed the men in the mosque died just like the others, of failed hearts. We argued about secret weapons and poisons, about state assassinations, until that night when every single person in Jerusalem dropped dead.

We wondered if our gods were fighting and prayed for them to stop or prayed for them to hurry up and end it all. We prayed to each other's gods, just in case. Those of us who were still atheist held street celebrations in cities around the world on the same day. We called it Judgment Day. We said the gods were finally taking their own and leaving the world a better place. At last, peace on earth, we said. But when all the atheists dancing around the Burning Man effigy on that Seattle street dropped dead, even the ones dressed like Jesus, we went home and didn't celebrate anymore.

We grew desperate in our search for a cause, for something to explain it all. We speculated it was a new disease. An AIDS of the new century we hadn't discovered yet. A new Ebola. We argued about vectors and viral memes. We seized the bodies of the dead, sometimes with legal papers, sometimes with soldiers, and cut open their brains. We couldn't find anything different in them. Their dead brains were the same as the rest of ours. There was nothing in them.

We were dying and we didn't know what was killing us. We occupied the abandoned auto factories in Detroit. We cried out that maybe if someone brought the jobs back the dying would stop. We rioted in Paris and burned the Louvre. We shouted in the streets that it was the end of history. We staged coups in Africa and fought border skirmishes in South America. But none of us truly believed some government was responsible for what was happening. Our generals and presidents appeared in the media and apologized for not being able to attack anyone. We launched missiles into space in random directions, anyway, in case it was an alien attack. But we ran out of missiles.

A ferry drifted into a harbour in the Philippines with everyone aboard dead.

Passenger jets flew past their destinations and no one responded to our attempts at communication. The pilots of the fighters we scrambled reported no signs of life inside the planes before they went down into the clouds and crashed into the ocean.

Our research bases in Antarctica stopped sending us messages. We didn't dispatch anyone to investigate. We'd find out what happened to them later. If there was a later.

We kept on praying, even though we'd lost faith in our gods. We prayed to the forgotten gods: Anubis and Shiva and Zeus. We prayed to Gaia, to the earth itself. We prayed to the made-up gods: Cthulhu and the thetans. We prayed to Stephen Hawking and all the dead astronauts.

And then the statisticians and mathematicians among us produced the models that confirmed that whatever was happening was random. We didn't want to believe the first reports, from the group in Moscow, especially after they turned up dead themselves in their respective apartments. But our autopsies showed there was nothing mysterious about their deaths. They'd been poisoned with radioactive isotopes placed in their tea by some of us who belonged to a security force that was the latest in a long line of security forces. None of us were particularly upset about the killings. We didn't want to hear the message these dead men had been trying to tell us. We didn't want all the other deaths to be random. We didn't want them to be meaningless.

But then the special team assembled by Stanford and Cambridge said the same thing as the Russians did, and Google revealed its Black Lab had come to an identical conclusion. We looked at the patterns and they all said there was no pattern.

And that was the worst thing of all. Worse than when we first started dying. Worse than when day and night around the world turned into twilight and remained that way, when we realized time had frozen in place. As if the universe's operating system had crashed. Worse than when we realized we didn't need to eat or drink or sleep anymore, which meant we didn't need to worry about buying food, about securing shelter, about any of the things we had always done to make meaning of our lives. Worse than when we realized no one was dying now, even when we beat and stabbed and shot each other and ourselves, and we realized no one was ever going to die again. This was the way it was going to be from now on, and there would never be an escape.

It was just random. Nothing we've done has mattered. Some of us were taken but we remain. And now everything is over. We rest in our ruins and wait for a rescue that will never happen. All we can do is relive the past and what might have been. Perhaps we deserve better, or perhaps we deserve worse. But we deserve something.

We continue to pray. We turn our gaze to the empty sky. We pray for something to happen. We hide in the empty buildings. We pray for anything to happen. We call out to each other, a chorus of voices around the world. We pray for the dying to start again. We dig our own graves and wait. We pray for someone to hear our prayers. We would weep, but we have no tears left.

We expected the world to end.

NOTES

"Beat the Geeks" was originally published in *Tesseracts Eleven*.

"Déjà Yu Makes the Pain Go Away" was originally published in *Taddle Creek*.

"The Last Love of the Infinity Age" was originally published in *Abyss & Apex*.

"We Are All Ghosts" was originally published in *Innsmouth Magazine*.

"The Only Innocent Soul in Hell" was originally published in *On Spec*.

"We Are a Rupture That Cannot Be Contained" was originally published in *SubTerrain*.

"We Continue to Pray for Something to End Our Prayers" was originally published in *SubTerrain*.

ART CREDITS

Details from a selection of pulp magazine and sci-fi novel covers have been chosen to complement the stories throughout this collection, as well as assembled as a collage for the front cover. On the following pages, the full artwork and publication information for these works is presented. All illustration credit was sourced from the The Internet Speculative Fiction Database (www.isfdb.org), with the exception of the credit for *Operation Interstallar*, which was sourced from Project Gutenberg (www.gutenberg.org).

Cover collage; page 304: **Earle K. Bergey**, *Thrilling Wonder Stories*, August 1951.

Cover collage; page 306: **Earle K. Bergey**, *Startling Stories*, July 1950.

Cover collage; page 298: **Harold V. Brown**, *Startling Stories*, July 1939.

Page 6: **James B. Settles**, *Fantastic Adventures*, July 1949.

Page 8: **Allen Anderson**, *Planet Stories*, May 1952.

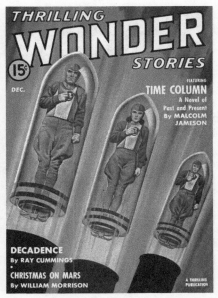

Page 22: **Bob Hilbreth**, *Amazing Stories*, December 1946.

Page 76: **Earle K. Bergey**, *Thrilling Wonder Stories*, December 1941.

Page 100: **Arnold Kohn**, *Amazing Stories*, May 1950.

Page 108: **Earle K. Bergey**, *Captain Future: Man of Tomorrow*, March 1944.

Page 142: **Malcolm Smith**, *Operation Interstellar*, 1950.

Page 176: **Robert Gibson Jones**, *Fantastic Adventures*, November 1952.